A Melody for James

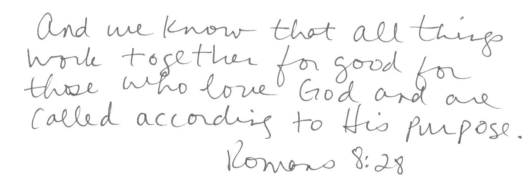

To Kimberly:

And we know that all things
work together for good for
those who love God and are
called according to His purpose.
Romans 8:28

Hallee Bridgeman

TABLE OF CONTENTS

Contents

♫ ♫ ♫ ♫

THIS BOOK IS LOVINGLY DEDICATED TO...

My mom, Kay:

Fourteen years ago, I woke up from a dream in the middle of the night on New Year's night, turned on my computer, and just started typing. Ultimately, I wrote *A Melody for James*. It was my first book, and, I wrote it entirely in secret. Every morning, from the hours of 4 to 6 AM, I wrote, getting this story out as quickly as I could but telling absolutely no one I was doing it.

Halfway through writing it, I printed out my progress and mailed it to my mom with a simple note. "I'm writing a book. Let me know what you think of it."

For a week, half a novel sat on my mom's counter because she was afraid to read it — afraid it would be bad and then she'd have to pretend she enjoyed it. Finally, she could ignore it no longer. She sat down to read and couldn't stop because she became so engrossed in the story. She got to the end of what I'd sent her, picked up the phone, and called me at work.

"This is your mother," she said by way of preamble. "I want you to quit your job, go home, and finish that book!"

So, here it is, Mama. The finished book, 14 years later. I hope you enjoy it as much the second time as you did the first.

♪ ♪ ♪ ♪

ANGELA Montgomery nearly missed it. She had lost herself in memories of her recent birthday celebration marking the passing of her 30th year on earth. Her husband, James, her junior by 2 short years, had gone all out. Being "much" younger, he had decorated the entire house with black balloons and held a surprise "wake" for the passing of her late youth. Daydreaming and lost in feelings of love and adoration for her beloved groom, Angela nearly failed to recognize the moment when it happened.

When her consciousness shifted from her reverie back to the present, for several breaths she simply stared at the smart board in front of her and ran through the calculations again. Then she tried to ignore the little shivers of nervous excitement that danced up her spine.

"Heeyyyyy ..." Donald Andrews clicked a few keys on the laptop in front of him, magnifying the image on the smart board screen so that it covered the entire wall. "Did we just ..."

Angela rose, her legs feeling uncharacteristically stiff, and walked forward while staring at the screen. "You know what, I'm cautiously going to say yes. Yes, we did."

Alvin Berry let out a loud, "Whoop!" He removed the ever present knit cap from the top of his head and tossed it into the air. The group collectively looked at each other and grinned. Years of work, and the breakthrough sat right there on that smart board, staring back at them.

"We should celebrate," Lorie Frazier announced. She pulled her glasses from her nose and casually tossed them onto the stack of papers in front of her. "We need to celebrate, then we need to call a press conference. But only after we get to the patent office."

Angela looked back at the screen. "We have to be sure."

"We're sure," Alvin said. "Look at that beauty. It is so simple yet so elegant."

"Call James," Lorie said. "Tell him to make us a reservation in the most ridiculously expensive restaurant Atlanta has to offer. Tell him we're going to celebrate."

Despite her naturally conservative nature, Angela started to let the feeling of giddy excitement take over. She laughed and hugged Don as she pulled her cell phone from her pocket.

Her husband would probably jump up and down or do a little dance of celebration. She felt like she might just as easily be making a call to announce that she was expecting their first child instead of the conclusion of this long project.

For five years, she and this amazing team of engineers had worked to perfect this revolutionary data storage solution. For five years, usually working six days a week, usually not less than twelve hours a day, they'd toiled in this basement lab in her inherited home. While she'd hoped and prayed for all that time, now that the reality of what they'd accomplished actually shone back at her from that beautiful smart screen, she realized she hadn't ever really been certain they'd succeed.

But they had.

She got James' voice mail. "Darling," she purred, knowing he'd hear the smile in her voice. "We did it. We're done. I cannot wait to show you. Come home. Come see. We need to celebrate."

As soon as Angela hung up, she gave Lorie a hug and said, "I vote for cheesecake."

"Copious amounts," the nearsighted genius agreed. "Oh! With strawberries! And really good coffee."

Angela felt her heart skip when the red security light started flashing. Her eyebrows crowded together in confusion. Why was the intruder alarm going off now?

Angela had inherited the farmhouse at the age of 17 from her late uncle and lived there throughout her lengthy matriculation at Georgia Tech. For a brief time when this venture was just beginning, she and her brand new husband, James, as well as their business partner and his best friend, Kurt, had all lived there under the same roof.

During the initial months and years, Kurt and James had renovated the basement entirely; installing a T1, a two post rack of networking gear, a four post rack of high performance servers; and most importantly, a state of the art security system, designed and built by her brilliant husband himself. For the last five years, they had hardened the basement into a panic room with steel reinforced doors, magnetic locks, and pinhole security cameras. It took two-factor authentication to even get into the room.

When the magnitude of the fact that the security alarm was still sounding sunk in, Angela whirled around until her eyes met Don's. When she spoke, she hated the shrill edge of panic she detected in her voice. "Back it up to the Snap."

His fingers clicked on the keys with the speed of machine gun fire as he spoke. "There's no time. We didn't do an incremental yesterday because the waffle was running a defrag."

"Right. Execute a differential and encrypt it." She waited a few heartbeats while Don's fingers played out a staccato percussion on his laptop.

With confusion clouding his eyes, he looked up and announced, "Our hard line is down."

Alvin pressed a series of keys on his computer and several small screens appeared on the smart board, all showing different angles of her home. Men in masks moved through the empty house with military precision, high powered and very deadly looking carbine rifles tucked tightly into their shoulders at the ready. They stared around every corner through the sights on the short rifles.

Lorie gasped and said, "What is going on? Who are they?"

Fear and panic tried to take over. Her stomach turned into ice and Angela felt like her breathing wasn't productive, like she could never get a deep enough breath. Focus, she said to herself. You will have time to be scared when it's over.

"Can you remember how we got here since the last backup?" Angela asked Alvin, her hand pointing in his direction like a knife blade. If she'd ever met anyone whose memory rivaled her husband's, it was Alvin.

His voice sounded flat, emotionless. "Yes. Of course I can."

She watched a crouched figure outside the entrance to the lab tape two liter plastic bottles filled with water to the hinges of the security door. The security that James and Kurt had installed was tight, state of the art even, and the door was sealed. But no seal in 100 miles would withstand the blast of a shaped charge pushing water ahead of a supersonic shock wave. It would slice through the steel door faster than the world's most powerful cutting torch.

Whomever these people were, they had known the defenses they would have to overcome. They were prepared. They had planned. They had obviously even rehearsed as was apparent in their staged and perfectly timed precision movements. And the most dangerous thing Angela and her team had for protection once that door came down were a few custom computer viruses.

She'd known the risks. The long term applications of the soon to be patented technology could not even be calculated. The reason they worked out of her home instead of in some downtown lab was for the secrecy of the project.

They'd taken additional precautions which Angela belatedly realized she had characterized as "paranoid." A commercial exothermic incendiary device much like a military grade thermite grenade perched atop each server array that would, when detonated, melt their way through the machines at over 4 thousand degrees Fahrenheit, effectively destroying everything in a completely unrecoverable fashion. They would burn 3 times hotter than molten lava and the crew would have to be careful not to look at them since the radiant energy was bright enough to blind them without a welding visor.

"Then destroy it. Destroy it all."

Lorie's finger hovered over a steel pin. "You're sure?"

The explosion above them shook the room. Alvin rushed to the inner door and made sure the panic room door remained bolted on all four corners. Angela closed the lid on her laptop and slid it into the 2 inch air gap between network switches. Then she draped her hand on Lorie's shoulder and whispered, "Do it."

She closed her eyes and started to pray as the room around her grew suddenly very hot and smoke started billowing up to the ceiling. "Heavenly Father, if I live through this, let me remain in Your will. But if I come home to you, Lord, please watch over my husband. Let him feel your comforting love and let him find the destiny you have in mind for him."

Smoke alarms went off and the lights flickered. Then she felt herself being picked up and thrown aside, riding on the wave of a perfectly timed blast. As she flew backward from the shock of the multiple explosions blowing open her steel door she prayed even harder — she prayed for courage, for protection, for strength.

As she landed and fell against the tower of computer drives, she watched the thermite spill and splatter like lava, setting the entire area on fire. Her last thought was of pain as a spray of burning powder fell on her chest.

♫ ♫ ♫ ♫

JAMES Montgomery stared at the blackened shell of what used to be his house. As the sun rose in the Georgia sky, he watched the last big fire department engine drive away. He felt empty, cold. He reached inside himself and tried to find anything — anger, grief — anything. He found only emptiness. Idly, he wondered why he didn't feel the least bit tired since he had last slept fifty hours earlier.

He watched as the coroner's office carried yet another body out of the black shell. So far, he counted six. Due to the heat of the fire, the bodies themselves were unrecognizable, but he'd identified his wife's wedding ring. What remained of her was charred beyond recognition, her body curled up into a tight fetal position.

Pugilism, the coroner had called it. Apparently, muscle and tendon burn at different rates making burned human bodies curl up and crouch like professional boxers. It was the kind of trivia that interested medical examiners offered when attempting to make polite small talk with the next of kin while standing over the earthly remains of the most important person in his world.

How? Where had they gone wrong? What part of the hyper-diligent security measures didn't get followed? Was this an insider thing?

"Mr. Montgomery, if it's okay I'd like to ask you a couple of questions," said the police officer who'd introduced himself hours before as Detective Roberts. James looked over at him with dry burning eyes. The detective had a lean athletic body, sandy blond hair, and laugh lines. He'd arrived with an older detective who sat back and let Roberts take the lead, obviously training him.

"It's fine," James answered, his throat burning. His voice sounded ragged, weak. He didn't like it. He didn't know if he would ever get the smell of smoke out of his nose or the other smell from his memory.

"That was a really impressive room you had in your basement. The security looks like it was amazing."

James raised an eyebrow. "That isn't a question."

Roberts nodded. "Why don't you just explain to me why you thought you might need a room like that in your basement, and maybe why you felt the need to keep thermite grenades handy."

"My wife —" his voice hitched and he cleared his throat and swallowed. "My wife," he began again, "was an information security engineer. She and her team were developing a technology for data warehousing that would, in a conservative estimate, be worth about a hundred billion dollars the first year."

Roberts paused in writing in his notebook. "I beg your pardon?"

"Most of this work was a secret. We retrofitted our basement because we felt like it was the most inconspicuous, secure location. Our intent was security by obscurity." James put his hands in his pockets and balled his fists. "Obviously, that was folly." He felt his phone and pulled it out. "I had a voice mail from her. They'd made a breakthrough." He accessed the message and played it on speaker for Roberts. His heart twisted painfully in his chest as he heard his wife's voice again.

"We had thermite grenades sitting on the stacks of hard drives so that if there was ever a security breach, they could just pull the pin and the data would be destroyed. We keep daily backups off site." He waved a hand weakly at the destroyed house. "It shouldn't have caused a fire to spread. The area was contained with two feet of cement on the ground and a ventilated chimney that had a battery backed up fan. I don't know how that happened."

The detective said, "Did you account for the idea that intruders might use high explosives?"

James shook his head. "That was a failure of our collective imagination."

"Any thoughts as to who did this? Any idea where we should start?"

James slipped his phone back into his pocket and ran a thumb over the keys. The late May wind picked up and blew his red tie over his shoulder. He took his glasses off and rubbed at his gritty eyes. "Detective Roberts, for a hundred billion dollars, I'd suspect your grandmother." He put his glasses back on his face and looked intently at the other man.

"There was a grad student applying for an internship. She let him walk through the lab, but didn't end up hiring him. I never met him. I'll have to see if the University can give you his name."

Roberts nodded and wrote in his book. "I appreciate that." He looked at the blackened home and then at James. "I'm sorry for your loss, sir." He pulled a business card out of his pocket. "Please let me know if you think of anything or if you learn of anything. Call anytime, day or night. Don't hesitate."

James took the card, read it, and immediately committed the information to memory. "Likewise, detective." He heard the squeal of tires and turned his head to see his best friend's car coming fast down his road. "There's Kurt Lawson, my partner. He may know more about the intern. He deals directly with HR stuff like that."

♪ ♪ ♪ ♪

RIKARD Šabalj stood on the banks of the Danube River. In the distance, he could see the walls of the Golubac Fortress of Serbia nestled into the cliff.

Fury burned hot in his chest. Plans had gone awry. He hadn't known about the thermite. If he'd known, they would have gained access to the room a different way. But, he knew that the second they filed the patent, all would be lost. The second he had audio confirmation of the breakthrough, he had no choice but to move and move fast.

The fire, the gunshots, the smell of the burning flesh — he lost control of the situation, lost two good men, and still didn't have the billions that had been promised to him.

The satellite phone next to him signaled an incoming call. He had no desire to answer it, but he did anyway. No one would call him a coward.

"Yeah," he said, knowing the caller would speak English.

"What happened?"

"Sometimes, plans don't work. I didn't have all of the information of their security."

"Police are at a loss. At least you covered your tracks well."

"I'm not concerned about the American police force. I'm just happy that my client doesn't know about my intent to betray them. They aren't happy with the failure, but at least I'm alive and not a rotting corpse staked to the side of the road to serve as an example." Needing to release some energy, Rikard picked up a stone and threw it as hard as he could over the cliff and toward the river. "Keep your ear to the ground. I won't return if there is any heat at all."

"I wouldn't want you to." After a long pause, the caller said, "We might have another way."

"Another way to what?"

"We have all of the preliminary research, thanks to your guy's hacking skills. We just need the capital to fund continuing the project. That's where you come in."

"Where am I supposed to come up with the capital to research a project worth billions?"

He could hear the smile in the replying voice. "You will acquire it."

♪ ♪ ♪ ♪

MELODY Mason stood in the shade next to the large pool house. All around her, Atlanta's *creme de le creme* mingled and networked. A few isolated teens took advantage of the cooling waters of the pool, but most of the adults remained dressed and coifed.

Melody brushed at her white sun dress, feeling a little out of sorts. Two weeks ago, she'd graduated from college, and for the last couple of weeks, she'd struggled desperately to find her purpose in life.

"Melly, there you are," Ginger Patterson said, wearing a vivid red dress and blue sun hat to protect her alabaster skin. Her blonde curls danced out from under the rim of the hat and her lipstick was as bright as the dress, if that were possible. "I'm so happy you were able to come to our little party."

A uniformed waiter approached carrying a tray that contained a bowl of cocktail shrimps arranged around a bed of ice. He offered some to Melody, who wrinkled her nose and shook her head.

"I have never missed a Patterson Memorial Day party in my life, to my memory," Melody said, lifting her heavy black hair off of her shoulders to catch a bit of the breeze. "It's like an official summer tradition."

"Where is your sister? I thought Morgan would be here by now."

"She's here. We came together. She's in the library with your Aunt Mildred, who is convinced that the room needs a decorating overhaul."

Ginger giggled and put her hand to her mouth. "Oh poor Morg. I should probably go rescue her."

A large man came toward them, wearing a patterned Hawaiian shirt that stretched over his large stomach. He was as tall as Melody's 5'10", but had such a commanding air about him that he always appeared much taller. He wore a cap with a Georgia Bulldog on it, and had a cigar clenched between his teeth. "Melody Mason, congratulations on your graduation. Dance and piano, eh? Plans yet?"

Melody smiled and held her hand out in greeting. "David, it's so good to see you. I expected you in New York for the ceremony."

As her late father's best friend and the guardian of her trust fund, David Patterson often acted as a surrogate father for Melody and her sister Morgan.

"I had plans to attend, but a very last minute issue cropped up." He removed the cigar and clenched it between his thumb and finger. "Never been a fan of that city. Anywhere you can't get grits for breakfast is not the place for me."

Ginger slipped her arm into her father's. "Daddy doesn't like to leave Georgia, do you Daddy?"

"Not even for a minute, my peach." He was jostled from behind and turned to see who had bumped into him. "Beg your pardon," he said to the young man.

"I'm so sorry, Mr. Patterson. I was trying to keep from getting splashed by the kid canon-balling into the pool." The man was incredibly handsome, with blond good looks and gray-green eyes. Melody looked him up and down. He wouldn't make a good dancer, no, but she thought he reminded her of a cowboy, with long lean legs, a small waist, and broad shoulders.

Ginger gasped and turned, rushing toward the kids in the pool. "Michael," she yelled, off to correct whatever kid would dare to splash some of the most important people in the southeastern United States.

David nodded. "No problem, son. Be more aware of your surroundings." He turned back to Melody. "Melly, come to dinner tomorrow. We need to see what your plans are now."

She smiled and broke her gaze off of the cute blond long enough to look at her guardian. "Sounds good," she said, not certain what she'd just agreed to.

The blond held out his hand and she placed her thin hand into his big, warm one. "Richard Johnson," he said with a smooth southern drawl.

"Melody Mason." She started to pull her hand away, but he resisted. She raised her eyebrow, and he smiled at her in a way that made her heart flip.

"It is a pleasure to meet you." He looked around. "If I told you that you were quite easily the most beautiful woman I've ever met, would you think that was some cheap line?"

Feeling her cheeks fuse with color, Melody nodded. "I likely would."

Richard sighed and brought her hand up to his lips. He brushed a kiss over the knuckles before releasing her hand. "Then I shall avoid saying it and just continue thinking it."

Melody laughed. "You're a charmer."

"When you're a poor intern among such established wealth, you have to use all your skills." He gallantly placed a hand over his heart. "May I offer you a drink?"

"That would be delightful, Mr. Johnson."

"Richard, please. I have a feeling we're going to get to know each other rather well. Now, your parents wouldn't be *those* Masons would they? I seem to recall ..."

Melody confirmed his suspicions. "Yes, I am quite sure you are thinking of my parents. And, yes, David is in charge of my trust."

"I read about that. I was a freshman in high school when it happened. Terrible thing, really."

Melody forced herself to smile and pretended that she didn't once more feel the stabbing loss of her parents after all these years. "How about that drink, Richard?"

He gestured for her to precede him toward the sparkling lemonade fountain. "I live to serve, ma'am, as every southern gentleman ought."

♪ ♪ ♪ ♪

"LADIES and gentlemen, this is your Captain speaking from the flight deck … Uuuuuuh …" The male voice blaring over the cabin speakers set Melody's teeth on edge.

"Just wanted to give you a quick update from the tower. We are cleared to land at Newark International but … Uuuuuuh … It looks like all flights departing Newark are delayed due to weather. Uuuuuuh … At this time, I'll ask everyone to return to your seats and fasten your seat belts. Ensure all tray tables are stowed and all seats are locked in the full upright position. We are second in line for landing … Uuuuuuh … Flight attendants secure cabin for arrival." The announcement ended with a very loud electronic click.

Melody pushed the button on her first class seat to raise it back up into the full upright position. She stacked her pillow and blanket in the empty seat beside her and then set all the of the remnants of her snack on the tray-table of the seat next to her. Within a few moments, the first class flight attendant collected everything and snapped the tray-table into place with a practiced movement.

"Can I get you anything else before we land, ma'am?" she asked. Melody shook her head but didn't say anything. Her thoughts had wandered to the reasons that the seat beside her remained empty.

The flight over the Atlantic to the romantic hideaway in England had been her very first international flight. This, the return trip to Atlanta, was her second. She had imagined that her first flight to another country would be spent alongside her husband. Now the very thought made her feel foolish and naive.

Just two weeks ago, she'd carried two cups of coffee and a little bag of bagels up the steps to Richard's apartment at nine on a beautiful autumn Atlanta morning. She had admired her wedding manicure as she pressed the doorbell, then had looked behind her as if someone might catch her breaking tradition in so shameless a fashion.

When he didn't immediately answer the bell, she'd raised her fist to knock. Finally, she'd heard movement through the door, and saw a curtain on the window next to the door move back a few inches.

She'd raised one of the coffee cups and smiled as Richard peered out at her through the window. She thought she'd seen movement behind him, as if someone else went through the room, but at the time was sure that she was seeing things. Now, looking back, she realized she'd seen exactly what she thought she'd seen.

The curtain had fallen and seconds later she'd heard the sliding sound of the chain lock. With a grin, she held up both cups of coffee as he opened the door.

"Happy wedding day," she'd said, just as happy and ignorant as a lark. "I know we aren't supposed to see each other today until I walk down the aisle, but I just couldn't stand not —" She'd started forward and stopped when she saw him shirtless, a sheet wrapped around his waist. A movement behind him had caught her eye as the door to his bedroom shut. Looking past him, she'd seen a pair of woman's high heels on the floor next to the bar that separated the living room from the kitchen. On the bar, an empty bottle of champagne sat next to two glasses. The red impression of lipstick could clearly be seen on one of the glasses, even from the doorway.

Cold fury had spread from her stomach to her chest. With a gasp, she'd looked at Richard's face. He'd looked — angry. How dare he look angry at *her*? "What is going on?"

"You aren't supposed to be here right now," he'd said in a clipped tone.

"Is that so?" she'd asked. "Well then, exactly who is supposed to be here? Who's here with you?"

Richard had relaxed his face and smiled with all of his charm, then stepped forward, forcing her back, and shut the door behind him. "No one is here. Don't be ridiculous. You better go, or we'll have bad luck. Isn't that how it goes?"

Melody remembered clenching her teeth so hard she feared that she would break one of them. "Yeah," she'd said with a dry throat. "Something like that."

Somehow, she'd managed to hold back from throwing the hot coffee in his face when he gripped her elbow and leaned forward to kiss her cheek. "That's a good girl," he'd said. "Off you go. I'll see you at four."

"Four. Right." As she walked away, she'd dropped the coffee cups and the bag of bagels in the garbage bin on his landing. Getting into her car, she'd started back home, but changed her mind. Instead, she had headed toward the airport.

She'd already packed her honeymoon bag. So, she parked in one of the many Atlanta Hartsfield International Airport's remote long term parking lots, popped the trunk of her little white Mercedes, and grabbed her suitcases and carryon bag.

When she arrived at the terminal from the shuttle, she'd gone straight to the ticket counter, butterflies leaping about in her stomach until she feared that she'd get sick. When it was her turn, she slid her passport toward the agent. "Hi. I have two tickets in my name — Melody Mason — leaving for London at midnight. Could I get on an earlier flight? And, maybe cancel the other ticket?"

The clerk's fingers had tip-tapped on the keys. She'd frowned at her screen. "There would be a charge."

Melody had smiled and just pulled out her onyx American Express. "Not a problem," she'd said. "I just want to make sure that second ticket is canceled."

"Is Mr. Johnson with you now?"

Melody had felt the burn of tears in her throat. "Why no. He's with some other woman in his apartment on our wedding day." Despite Melody's desire to hold tears at bay, her eyes had flooded. "Please," she'd whispered.

A look of sympathy had crossed the face of the clerk. "You know, it just so happens we have a special discount today. Let me see about waiving that fee." She'd worked quickly, her fingers clackity-clacking on her keyboard in a sing-song rhythm. "There."

She'd paused only long enough to grin, her eyes sparkling. Then clackity-clack, clickity-click until she'd said, "Looks like I have a flight leaving in an hour?"

"Perfect," Melody had said, scrubbing at her tear stained face.

A barrage of clackity-click-click-clacks followed then, in the space of a few heartbeats, the clerk had handed her a new boarding pass. "Thank you."

She had looked at her hand holding the boarding pass for her First Class flight. Her eyes could not move from the 2-karat ring on her left finger. "Are we all set?"

She'd had to buy it, because Richard had no money. That didn't matter to her in the slightest. They would soon be married — would become one in Christ. What did it matter whose name had originally been on the bank account?

"All set, ma'am. Have a safe flight."

Foolish girl, she'd thought to herself. Without hesitation, she'd slipped the ring off and set it in front of the clerk. "Here," she'd said, "go buy a new car or something."

The clerk had gasped and looked at Melody. "Ma'am, I cannot —"

She'd slipped her purse onto her shoulder. "Then throw it away. I don't care." She had turned her back on the clerk and the ring.

From her first class seat returning to the United States, as she looked out the window and watched the lights of Newark, New Jersey, grow closer and felt the shudder of the plane as it fought an east-coast storm, she wondered what she was supposed to do now that the honeymoon was over. She wondered if her ring was waiting for her in Atlanta.

♫ ♫ ♫ ♫

FOR the last several weeks, James Montgomery had worked and worked, stopping only to sleep and barely to eat. Being forced to sit in an airport terminal in Newark while trying to get back to Atlanta from London as a November northeaster raged outside might possibly be considered a good thing. He felt only mild irritation at the weather induced airport delay. After all, he'd needed a break. A forced stop. A forced rest. He stretched his long legs out in front of him, closed his eyes, and leaned his head back.

He momentarily looked at his laptop bag sitting at his feet and felt weary. Likely, he should open it and get some work done. Strangely, he didn't want to — not at all. The last e-mail he'd seen from his business partner, Kurt Lawson, encouraged him to take a few days off before returning to work. Kurt had run all the interference with the U. S. Government to ensure that the company remained in full compliance with all export laws. James didn't envy him that task.

While Kurt had worked like a mad man back home, James had spent the last week in London securing the partnership deal for a security monitoring equipment contract with an intelligence agency in England and still kept up with all the developments and progress of his Albany research and development, or R&D team, back in the States. That translated to twenty-hour days while suffering from serious jet lag. But, the timing was critical and he'd had no choice.

Now that he had wrapped up the deal and tied London up with a pretty bow, he had a little bit of breathing room. This contract would last for four years. It would take intense effort and a serious work schedule to meet all of their service level agreements, but he knew his company would not only meet, but would exceed the expectations of the British government. He knew it was only due to the development of the system that he'd secured the contract in the first place, and all of the glory for that belonged to his wife, Angela.

The thought of his late wife still brought a sharp twist of pain. In his near exhaustion, the back of his throat burned while he forced back the sting of unmanly tears. Why was the pain still so sharp six months later? When would that finally go away? Did he even really want it to go away?

Did the fact that he still felt this pain mean that he still had her beside him? If he let it go was he letting her go forever?

Two weeks after her death, he had been in a meeting with Kurt and one of the development teams. In the middle of the meeting he had said, "We need to run this by Angie," before he realized that he could never run anything by Angela again. Not ever. Not for the rest of his life.

Kurt had dismissed the team and pulled him into a bear hug until he cried like a baby in his best friend's arms. It was the first time he had cried in over 10 years and it took him completely by surprise.

More than once in the last six months, he had very seriously contemplated drowning his sorrows in a bottle. Angela would never approve, of course. Instead of toasting with champagne she preferred to celebrate with cheesecake. That sobering thought brought him back to honoring his late wife while he grieved her loss.

Angela's faith would have led her to encourage him to seek God instead of oblivion even though he didn't know how to do that. How does one seek an omnipotent being? He had no idea how one did that every day. Not like she did. Still, he had tried it. He had prayed and, in quiet moments, he had even pulled out the Gideon's Bible from the bedside table in his hotel room and read it late into the night or into the early morning hours.

Nothing seemed to help. Everyone treated him with such deference, and such copious amounts of dignity. "Don't mind him. His wife was murdered. You probably saw it on the news." It made him so angry; their sympathy, their condolences, their pretended understanding of what he was going through.

He'd tried working it away to no avail. He didn't know what else would solve his grief problem. He went to the hotel gym nearly every night and ran until his sides ached and his heart raced and his entire body hurt and it didn't help.

He occasionally thought about ripping his clothes and covering his head with ashes and screaming himself hoarse but always thought that notion through to its logical conclusion. It concluded with him never having enough ashes or screams to assuage the pain he felt. So he skipped it and got back to work.

One night while reading scripture, he came across a passage that read, "The truth will set you free." He set the Bible back in the drawer and slept like a baby having arrived at a new plan.

James remembered that the gates above the Auschwitz death camp just outside of Krakow in Poland read, *"Arbiter Mache Frei,"* which means, "Work will set you free." James ignored the greater truth and set about working. He worked so he didn't have to think about how much it hurt not to have his wife to go home to at night. He didn't have to think about how many times he listened to her final voice mail. He didn't have to think about how he would never see her again in this life. He worked and worked and worked.

Now, for the first time since that horrible night, he had no desire to work. Exhaustion made him not even want to think about it. His thoughts, instead, kept going to thoughts of his late wife and the truth of his life as it must now take place without her beside him. Even now, he still felt utterly unprepared to cope with it and he had no default distractions left to him. He let his mind wander anywhere but there or work.

Instead of opening his laptop and staring at the screen, for the dozenth time in the last half hour, his eyes wandered over to the woman sitting across from him. He remembered her from the terminal in London, but had not seen her on the flight. She looked to be in her early twenties with long curly black hair and a pretty face.

She sat sideways in the little airport chair, her back to the arm. She had her legs pulled up to her chest with her arms around her knees. James thought she must be very flexible to be able to sit like that in the little airport chair. In the hour since he'd sat down, she hadn't moved. She just stared straight ahead, across the terminal, out the window into the blackness of the stormy New Jersey night.

Her jet black hair fell in large curls around her face. As traditionally beautiful as she looked, that wasn't what caught James' attention. Instead, it was the sadness that seemed to emanate off of her in waves. There was more sadness than anger but there was something else, too. Betrayal? Loss?

Did they have something in common? Could he help her to soothe her sadness, ease whatever made her so unhappy? In a very unexpected turn to his thoughts, he imagined what she must look like when she smiled. How beautiful must that smile be?

Irritated at his thoughts, thoughts that followed so closely on the heels of his remembering times with Angela, he frowned and looked back at his laptop bag. Maybe he should start working instead of staring at some young raven haired beauty. Instead, he eyed her again, startled when he caught her looking back at him for the first time.

He noticed how vividly blue her eyes were. They made his mind trip over itself and for a moment, he couldn't think about anything but those sad blue eyes. Then his mental system rebooted and he felt the air return to his lungs.

"Can I help you?" she asked.

James cleared his throat. "Sorry for staring."

The woman raised an eyebrow. She obviously didn't expect his directness. "Is there something on my chin or something?"

He smiled. When was the last time he'd smiled? "No." Deciding to follow her lead and to stay blunt he said, "You just look incredibly sad and I know something about that."

"You know something about why I'm sad?" Her eyebrows lowered, her expression turned to a look of suspicion.

James shook his head, his lips pursing a bit. "I know about sadness."

He heard her sharply in-drawn breath. As she straightened in her chair, she pushed her hair off of her shoulders. "I would hardly think my feelings are any of your business."

The sound of her voice — cultured, smooth, southern — flowed like warm honey from her lips and surrounded him. He wanted to keep her talking. "Of course not. We're perfect strangers. But, at two in the morning, after that tumultuous landing in this storm, and every flight in this terminal delayed, you caught my attention and I just started wondering what could make someone so beautiful look so sad."

Honestly, he didn't know why he said that. It surprised him as much as it surprised her. Her blue eyes widened. Then they narrowed and icy accusation filled them. She pointedly looked at the ring on his left hand before meeting his eyes again. "And what would your wife think about your curiosity, I wonder?"

James felt the blow as if it had been physical. The pain that tore through him before was a splinter, a hangnail, compared to the crushing weight of torturous agony that rose up at her words. His stomach churned and, nauseated, he tasted bile in the back of his throat. He habitually ran his thumb over his wedding ring.

"She probably would have said we could pray ..." Then it occurred to him that he didn't owe this young lady an explanation. He didn't need to explain to her why after so long he couldn't yet bear to remove that band of gold. He felt a hard lump growing in his throat and he cleared it loudly and said, "You know what? Never mind. Please pardon my intrusion."

He reached for his computer bag and stood in one fluid movement. He stepped over stretched legs and then around someone sleeping against a duffle bag as he made his escape.

Distance. Distance away from the sad, angry blue eyed woman. Distance away from the memories that flooded his mind while he stayed trapped in this airport.

He stepped into the crowded bar at the end of the terminal. As he walked in, he spied a couple rising from a small round table. Moving quickly through the crowd, he grabbed the chair the man had just vacated, securing the table for himself before someone else could. He did not even want to suffer the temptation of sitting directly at the bar right now.

He lay his palms flat on the table and stared at the backs of his hands. His wedding ring gleamed in the fluorescent light. He had large hands, strong hands. But they hadn't been strong enough to protect his wife. His wife who gave her life for the future of his company. Of their company.

Grief choked him. Raw, fresh. Six months later, and the ache still twisted painfully. His heart ached. His stomach hurt. He wanted to find a hole and die, too. Maybe ripping his clothes and rubbing his head with ashes and wailing remained available as an option.

♫ ♫ ♫ ♫

MELODY felt the anger at the man immediately dissipate at the fallen look on his face. Before he even stood, she realized, instinctively, that there was no wife. At least, not anymore. The raw pain that flooded his eyes made her heart ache for him.

His long legs covered the ground in the terminal quickly, and Melody barely hesitated before scooping up her carryon bag and rushing after him.

If nothing else, she owed him an apology.

She saw him sit down at the little table in the bar, but when he didn't order a drink, she elbowed her way through the crowd and ordered two coffees. Armed with a cup in each hand she approached his table. Approaching strangers was entirely out of character for her, but she smiled and stepped forward as if she did it three times a day. She couldn't help but remember the last time she carried coffee in a cardboard cup to a man.

He sat perfectly still, as still as stone, staring at his hands that gripped the top of the table. When she set the coffee cup in front of him, he visibly jumped.

Melody lowered herself into the chair across from him. His angry glare did little to dissuade her. She took a sip of the hot brew and set the cup gently on the table. "I'm on my honeymoon," she said. "Well, returning from it."

The man raised an eyebrow, brown rimmed glasses bringing out the brown flecks in his hazel eyes. He had dark hair just long enough to show some curl. He wore a light blue dress shirt, unbuttoned at the collar. She could see the end of his red tie hanging out of his jacket pocket. The fabric of the shirt stretched across his broad chest. After working with the dancers at Julliard, Melody could recognize the build of someone who worked out with dedication.

"Honeymoon?" He looked at her bare left hand as pointedly as she had looked at his wedding ring moments earlier. "Alone?"

Melody no longer felt the sting of shame or tears at the thought. She had intended this trip to be a time of renewal. Of decision making. She had spent fourteen days in a hotel in London crying, praying, planning, deciding.

"Well, you know, there wasn't room for three." She waved a hand dismissingly. "Me, him, his lover."

A look of understanding gradually relaxed the anger. "I see." He took the coffee and raised it. "It's clearly no reflection on you. Though Though I just met you and don't know him, I already know that the man is obviously a fool. One hopes you exercise better taste in suitors next time around."

Melody giggled. "One certainly hopes." She liked the way he spoke, his diction and his careful enunciation. Stepping further out of her character and way out of her comfort zone, she reached forward and touched the ring finger of his left hand. She felt his muscles tense as if he were going to pull back, and felt them relax again. "What happened to your wife?"

He closed his eyes and took a deep breath. Melody started to pull her hand away, but he moved quickly and turned his hand around, so that their palms touched. Her skin tingled at the contact. He opened his eyes and cleared his throat. "Her name was Angela. And as crazy as it sounds every single time I say it out loud, she was murdered."

Melody might have expected almost anything but that. With a gasp, she leaned forward and took his hand with both of hers. "That's … awful."

Something inside him clicked and James found words pouring out of his mouth. "I keep expecting to wake up from this nightmare. Every night, when I go to bed, I want to wake up next to her." His eyes widened at his candor and he shook his head as he pulled his hand away. "I'm sorry. I must be more exhausted than I realized."

He started to stand, but Melody quickly spoke. "Please don't go."

He stopped halfway out of the chair and slowly lowered himself again. "I'm not sure —"

"You don't need to apologize. And we don't need to talk about it if you don't want to. It's just, for the last two weeks, the only people I've spoken to are the room service waiters at the hotel. I'd love to just talk. We can talk about anything you want."

His smile was a bit forced. "Anything?"

"Sure." She took another sip of coffee. "Where are you headed?"

"Home," he said. He cleared his throat. "Atlanta."

"Fancy that. I'm from Atlanta, too."

"Born and raised?"

"Yes, sir. Five generations worth of my family hail from Atlanta."

He leaned back in his chair and grinned a grin that made her heart skip a little beat. "A real Georgia peach."

Melody felt her cheeks burn a little. "What do you do?"

"I own my own business."

"What kind of business?"

"Mainly, I bury my head in circuit boards and technical manuals."

"Sounds exciting." She smiled a flirty smile. "I mean, who doesn't love a good technical manual?"

Picking up his coffee cup, he saluted her with it. "What about you?"

"Me?" She ran her tongue over her teeth. "I'm an heiress."

"An heiress?" His eyes skimmed over her. "Sounds complicated. Are you any good at it?"

"Not particularly."

He shook his head and laughed. "Seriously. What do you do?"

With a shrug, she propped her chin on her hands. "I have a degree from Julliard. I compose, some. And sing, some. And dance, a lot."

"A singing heiress alone on her honeymoon."

"That's me." She felt lighter. She kind of liked this game. It almost removed them from the real world.

"And now that the honeymoon is over?"

With a sigh she said, "That's the question, isn't it? I've considered going back to school."

"You could top Julliard?"

Melody laughed. "Right? I was thinking something along the lines of seminary."

He raised an eyebrow. "Now that is surprising. You don't strike me as a fire and brimstone kind of girl."

"No?" With a shrug, she sat back. "I really mean becoming a worship leader. Writing my own stuff."

"I see."

She narrowed her eyes. "What does that mean?"

He held up his hands. "Nothing negative. I don't know a lot about it."

"A lot about what?"

"Seminary. Worship. Church. Everything I know about religion I learned from my wife. Angela attended pretty regularly and I had just started going when —"

He broke off and she thought maybe they needed to steer the conversation away from his wife again. "Did you ever worship? Didn't your parents ever take you to church?"

"My parents," he said, sitting back and hooking his foot on his knee, "died when I was five. I remember them a little but I grew up in a home with eleven other boys. We didn't do church although some local churches brought us Christmas presents once a year. I usually scored some new socks or underwear."

Melody nodded. "I see." How different could their lives possibly be, even growing up in the same city? Her childhood consisted of private schools and *débutante* balls. He spent his youth in an orphanage where he desperately hoped for socks under the tree on Christmas morning. "That sounds really sad. I'm sorry."

He raised his coffee cup in a mock toast. "I told you I knew something about sadness."

Melody bumped her cup against his and they sipped. Then she said, "But look where life has led you. All the way to, well, New Jersey anyway."

With a shrug he took another sip of coffee. "Life always ends in death." He pulled a phone out of his pocket. "At least, that's been my experience." He glanced at the screen on his phone. "The airline just texted me to give me updated flight information."

Melody consulted her phone. "Me too."

He looked at his watch. "Looks like we'll be getting out of here in the next hour."

Melody raised her cup to him. "Praise the Lord," she said.

♫ ♫ ♫ ♫

A light touch on her shoulder startled Melody awake. It took a moment for her to regain her bearings. "Please put your seat up, ma'am. We're approaching Atlanta." The flight attendant moved to the next sleeping passenger in the first class cabin as Melody sat up and slipped her feet back into her shoes. She lifted the shade on her window and squinted against the bright dawn.

She turned her head and looked around behind her again, her eyes carefully scanning the full cabin. Every seat, save the one next to her that should have been her husband's, was taken. The curtain separating first class from business class remained closed. She'd hoped to catch a glimpse of her coffee companion. Maybe she'd spot him when she collected her luggage.

She looked out the window and watched Atlanta approach. She saw the sprawling estates on the outside of town and pinpointed a few owned by friends. The closer they got to the city, the smaller and smaller the yards got until she saw perfect picturesque neighborhoods that looked like little dollhouse towns. Outside of the airport, she saw the already heavy traffic on the knots of interstate systems working through one of the most heavily traveled cities in the United States. Already she didn't look forward to the commute home in the morning rush hour traffic.

Once the jet landed and they arrived at the gate, she grabbed her tote from under the seat in front of her and stood, relieved to be home. As Melody entered the terminal, she strode past the red jacket clad greeter and scanned the boards until she found the one that directed her to the appropriate baggage claim area.

After a brief stop in the ladies' room and freshening up by brushing her teeth and running a comb through her hair, she continued to baggage claim, hoping to catch a glimpse of her handsome stranger. Something about him made her hope she got the chance. She wanted to get to know him better.

As she waited for her luggage, Melody looked all around but never saw the man from the Newark layover. Disappointment weighed heavily on her heart. She should have waited for him on the plane. He would have had to pass her to disembark, and she could have walked with him. They could have at least traded names, if not phone numbers. But, that cup of coffee she'd shared with him before the flight had made the trip to the ladies' room an essential first stop. Now she'd missed him.

A few minutes later, after securing all of her luggage together, she headed to the exit to catch the shuttle to her car. The bright Georgia sunlight covered her in welcoming warmth after hiding in a soggy London hotel room for so long. She filled her lungs with warm Georgia air. As she slipped on her sunglasses and turned, her heart fell straight into her stomach and panic gripped her throat.

Richard stood outside the baggage claim door, clearly waiting for her. When he saw her, he stuffed his phone back into his pocket and clenched his fists as he stepped forward. "There you are. I've been waiting here for hours."

"The flight was delayed," she whispered. Then it occurred to her that she didn't owe Richard any kind of explanation. She cleared her throat and raised her chin defiantly. "What are you doing here? What do you want, Richard?"

♫ ♫ ♫ ♫

JAMES loitered near the taxi stand wondering what he thought he was doing. If the singing heiress was so interested in him, she would have waited for him to get off of the plane. Instead, by the time he entered the terminal, she had vanished clean out of sight.

He should have taken that as a hint that she just wasn't interested. But for some reason, he wasn't willing to believe it no matter how many times he told himself.

When she finally came through the doors, he straightened to intercept her. If nothing else, he wanted to learn her name. Maybe, when the pain of Angela's death didn't feel so fresh, he'd look her up. Maybe they could get to know each other better. Maybe they could just be friends. Maybe a genuine new friend would do him some very real good.

He watched her freeze as she slipped on her sunglasses. Even behind the dark frames, he could see the blood drain from her face. She put a quivering hand to her stomach. All of his senses came fully alert and James tried to spy out whatever had her so shaken.

He followed the direction of her gaze and spotted a man walking toward her — a very, very angry looking man. James deduced that this man was the fool of a fiancé who had been left at the alter over entertaining a mistress on his wedding day.

Acting on impulse, James found himself crossing the taxi lane and walking toward the couple. He hadn't heard the conversation but he could see the threatening body language and he didn't like it. He didn't like it at all. He stepped forward to stand close beside the singing heiress. As casually as he could manage, he slipped an arm around her waist. "There you are, darling." He made sure to speak loud enough for the fool to overhear.

♪ ♪ ♪ ♪

Melody tensed up when she felt the warm go around her waist. Her eyes shot up as she recognized the stranger from Newark. She removed her sunglasses and looked back at Richard. The expressions on Richard's face baffled her. She first saw utter shock, then pure hatred, then finally — and most surprising of all — fear bordering on panic.

Richard nodded at the man but his eyes remained locked on Melody's face. "What are you doing with *him*?"

Melody felt her layover friend's strong arm supporting her and found a sudden sense of courage. She slipped her sunglasses back on and grabbed the handle of her suitcase. "None of your business. And … I have nothing more to say to you." Smiling up at her knight in shining armor she said, "Shall we go, darling?"

"Of course." He gestured toward a taxi. "Your chariot awaits."

As she put her purse over her shoulder, Richard grabbed her arm and gave her a shake. "I'm not letting you go anywhere with him. You're coming with me and we're going to talk." He tried to pull her away.

"Let go of my arm, Richard. You lost the right to touch me or talk to me weeks ago."

"You have some serious explaining to do." Richard tightened his grip, forcing a gasp out her.

The handsome stranger stepped closer to the slightly smaller man and spoke very quietly to prevent any of the travelers around them from overhearing. "If you enjoy the use of that hand, and I'm guessing you do, I suggest you release the lady."

Richard sized him up and apparently concluded that he meant what he said. He let go of Melody's arm. To Melody he said, "What's this clown been telling you? Whatever he said, you know it's a lie. You can be sure of that."

"The only liar here is you," Melody said, somewhat surprised at how calm her voice sounded.

Her new friend turned and guided her to the waiting cab, placing his body between her and Richard. As James held the door open for Melody, Richard spoke up again.

"This isn't over," he called out.

The man paused and looked back. "No, I suspect not."

♫ ♫ ♫ ♫

MELODY felt the shaking increase until her whole body quaked. Adrenaline. Fear. Terror. Why was she suddenly terrified of Richard, the man with whom she'd intended to spend the rest of her life on earth? But, on an instinctive level, she now felt terrified of him.

She didn't object when the man from the airport got into the cab with her. And when he put his arm across the back of the seat, she scooted closer to him. She rubbed her arm where Richard had gripped her, knowing without a doubt she'd have finger and thumb sized bruises there tomorrow.

A shudder went through her so strongly that her teeth rattled. When his arm went all the way around her, she snuggled closer to him, needing to feel his warmth, wanting to feel safe.

"Thank you," she murmured.

"It was nothing," he assured quietly.

The cab driver looked at them in his rear view mirror. "Where to, folks?"

Melody spoke up. "Stop at the first place you see that serves waffles." She looked up at her handsome rescuer. "I'm starving."

He smiled down at her. "Great idea. But you know it won't be a minute until we stumble upon such an establishment here in Atlanta."

"I've been craving cheese grits for a week," Melody confessed. "No one told me they eat beans for breakfast in England. Who eats beans? For breakfast, I mean?"

James laughed. "I hope you at least tried some of the puddings."

Melody studied him, trying to determine if he was being serious or if he really had a perfectly deadpan sense of humor. "Well, when I found out what was in them, I thought I would rather die than put it in my mouth."

James laughed again. When was the last time he had laughed? "Now you're just being mean."

She could see her reflection in his glasses. "You never told me your name."

He grinned. "Neither did you."

She smiled back at his grinning face, enjoying his teasing tone. "You first."

"How about just first names and we can guess last names," he teased.

She grinned at his challenge. "Okay. You still go first."

He chuckled then lifted a hand and brushed a strand of hair off her cheek. "James. My first name is James."

Her smile grew, feeling the whisper of a touch of his fingers against her skin long after his hand was gone. "Well, you are an international traveler recently returned from England. And you are obviously very smart and a bit of a hero type the way you rescued me back at the airport. I'd have to say your last name is ... Bond."

Now he laughed in earnest. "Bond? James Bond? You couldn't get more original than that?"

She batted her eyelashes just as innocently as she possibly could and uttered with a syrupy southern drawl, "I take it you've been accused of being a spy before, Mr. Bond."

James couldn't hide his lingering smile. "And you, my singing heiress? Your first name please?"

"Well, Mr. Bond, my first name is Melody."

"Melody. Now, I have to say, that is a perfectly appropriate name for a singing heiress recently from Julliard."

Melody nodded. "I didn't get much mileage out of it. They actually expected me to sing and stuff."

James held out his right hand and she placed her fingertips in his palm. He very intentionally kept his grip gentle, tender. "It's really nice to formally meet you, Melody," he said, grinning a heart-stopping grin. Still holding her hand he said, "And of course, your full name is Melody ..." And in the most unexpected turn of events she could have imagined, his next words came out in a deep Scottish brogue, "Moneypenny."

It took a heartbeat or two to sink in, then she laughed until she thought she might hurt her insides.

They shared breakfast and talked. They had more coffee, and talked. They called for a cab that took them back to the off property long term parking lot and collected Melody's car and they talked the entire ride.

She battled the traffic into downtown Atlanta and took James to his hotel and they talked about absolutely nothing serious. They talked about how Atlanta had changed so drastically during the course of their lifetimes and speculated about future changes. They ate lunch together in the restaurant of the lobby of the hotel and talked some more.

All the while they laughed and teased and flirted. They talked about Angela and the dreams he once had for his marriage. They discussed the hopes and dreams he had for his company. They addressed the subject of music and Melody's favorite composers. They debated about Atlanta and college and football and London. They talked about how James had lived in the hotel for six months, and didn't want to move forward or move on.

Until now.

Late afternoon, James walked Melody to her car in the garage of the hotel. She leaned against the driver's door and looked up at him. "I don't want this day to end, James," she confessed.

"There are more days," he promised. He picked up a strand of her hair and twisted it loosely around his fingers. "Will you have dinner with me tomorrow?"

Jet lag made her head swim. "What day is tomorrow?"

James smiled. "Tuesday."

"Tuesday is weekly dinner with my sister." She ran a finger over the edge of his jacket. "Wednesday is church. You can come with?"

He shook his head, "Dinner." He insisted.

"Thursday then?"

He nodded. "I like Thursday dinners." James leaned forward to kiss her forehead. Melody closed her eyes and savored the feel of his lips on her skin. "Tell me your number."

"Let me get something to write it down with."

He tapped his temple. "I'll remember it."

"Seriously?"

He nodded. She recited her number and he released her hair. "I'll call you and see where we can meet Thursday," he said.

He reached behind her and opened her car door.

Melody couldn't stop grinning. "I'm looking forward to it."

As she shut the car door, he tapped the top of her car before stepping aside and letting her drive away.

She drove as quickly as she could. A song bubbled out of her and she needed to be at her piano, sheet music and blank staff paper in front of her. She had to write it down — the beautiful notes, the joy. She darted around the traffic as efficiently as she could and took every shortcut and back road she knew.

Thirty minutes later, she pulled up in to her driveway. Just as she turned the key to her car off, her phone announced an incoming text. Her stomach gave an excited little nervous flip.

Just wanted you to have my number. James

She took a moment to scold herself for selfishness. How selfish she felt for wallowing in her misery over being jilted by her former fiancé. James was a real man in every possible way she could imagine and James knew about actual misery. How terrible for her to whine and complain about poor little Melly whose fiancé was two-timing her when James would never see his wife again in this world.

She read his text again. With a grin, she started writing back as she got out of her car.

Did I thank you for being my knight in shining armor at the airport?

She felt the silly smile on her face and her fingers paused, wondering what else she should type. She briefly contemplated whether God put them together on that stormy night in Newark so they could help each other heal. If that were the case, she decided that any public or private humiliation she suffered at the hands of a two-timing man would be well worth it if meeting James was the intended outcome.

She felt grateful to God for many, many things now. She was especially grateful that she wasn't Richard's wife and had the freedom to go to dinner with James this Thursday night. She should write Richard a real thank you card and send a box of chocolates for his mystery girlfriend.

Thoughts about what dinner might involve filled her mind as she was lifted off the ground and her body slammed hard into her car door — so hard that the door shut and dented. Pain spread from her hip all the way through her chest and sucked the breath right out of her. Then, very strong hands grabbed her from behind and slammed her up against the door again. She heard her car window crack.

Before she could scream, a fist plowed into the side of her face catching her ear and jawbone, making her go limp, causing her to slump down, nearly unconscious, a loud high pitched whine in her ears and stars swimming before her eyes as the cement of her driveway slammed into her knees. She'd never felt pain like this in her life. It totally consumed and immobilized her.

Her attacker allowed her to fall to the ground then carefully kicked her twice. With a sickening sense of helplessness, she heard a sound like crunching celery as she felt her ribs snap under his well placed kicks. She felt the pain ripping her apart. Somehow through the daze, she found the strength to start screaming, and began to claw the ground, trying to get away.

"Don't you *ever* flaunt a lover in my face again, or else you won't even live long enough to suffer." Richard sneered as he kicked her one more time, this time low in the stomach. She felt the air rush out of her lungs and gaped and gasped for breath. When she finally inhaled, she screamed and sobbed and tried to roll away, but the pain was too great. "That's for all of the trouble you've caused me."

Melody's phone lay by her head. She clawed at the ground, trying to grab it, but Richard stomped on her hand with his thick boot heel. Her fingers spasmed beneath his heel like impaled worms struggling on fish hooks. "Who are you going to call? Who do you think can save you?"

"Richard!" She gasped. Her tongue tasted the coppery blood filling her mouth.

"Oh, does that hurt? Does it hurt? You leave me at the alter and you expect, what exactly?"

Melody sobbed.

"Aw. So sad. Maybe your new boyfriend can make you feel better." He ground his heel into her hand and she felt her entire body roll to the left as he used all his weight to crush the radial nerve. "You know something? I should just beat you to death."

He lifted his foot and she rolled into a ball. Then his heel crushed her phone and he ground it into the pavement before reaching down and picking up the shattered device. "Won't be needing this anymore."

She gasped as he lifted her head by her hair. She started to scream but he plowed his closed fist into the other side of her head. The force of the punch was so great and sudden that her face bounced off the aluminum tire rim of her car and her head struck the pavement again. She lay abruptly and perfectly still.

Eyes closed, struggling to breathe, Melody heard the leisurely click of

Richard's boots on the driveway as he marched away, heard him slam into his car, heard the squeal of tires. All the while she lay there, the world around her fading into black, then gray, in a daze of pain, disoriented, feeling no warmth on her skin from the dusky sky. Minutes later, she heard a neighbor's surprised cry as total blackness finally overtook her.

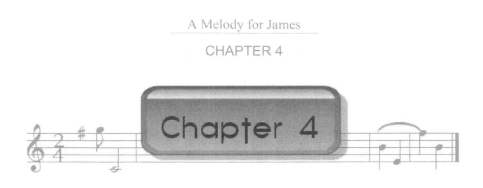

AROMATIC smoke billowed out and flew away into the Georgia breeze as Morgan Hamilton lifted the lid on the grill and stepped back. She placed two thick T-bones next to the foil wrapped vegetables on the grill rack.

"How do you like your steak?" she asked her dinner date.

Kurt Lawson took a sip of his iced tea and smiled. "Cooked well on the outside and a nice even medium in the middle," he said. "And thank you again. This is great." He gestured at the goldfish pond.

Morgan set her fork on top of the clean platter and rubbed her palms on the sides of her khaki skirt. She so wanted to impress Kurt. He'd come to church a few times, always alone, always right as the services started. From her perch in the choir loft, she always saw him come in and sit in the same spot, then leave immediately after. Yesterday morning, she'd paid extra special attention to her outfit, picking a blue dress that matched her eyes, curling her auburn hair so that it looked like she'd spent the day at the beach. Then she skipped choir and waited for him in the narthex.

Growing up within the social climate of high-end Atlanta society, Morgan had never been shy. When he'd come through those doors at 10:44 that morning, she intercepted him and introduced herself. She'd told him how she'd seen him from the choir loft and had wanted to ask him to dinner.

He'd seemed surprised, then almost pleased. They sat together for service and he'd invited her to lunch after, but she declined. Instead, she wanted to cook him dinner and have him say it was the best meal he'd had in a long while. She wanted him to walk through her home and admire her decorating style so that she could talk about her interior design business. Something about him... So, she'd invited him to her home the next night for dinner.

Morgan felt absolutely certain she had created a scandal among the other altos in the church choir. She didn't care a bit.

"We have a few minutes. Do you want to see?" A wave of her hand invited him to step down off of the deck and onto the river stone walkway. She had personally set every single rock on the path.

"You have this like a haven," he said. "It even feels cooler."

"The water, the plants, the shade; it is cooler. I love it." They reached the center of the yard and the stocked pond.

"Your dad built this neighborhood?"

Wistful, she thought of her father. "He built hundreds of neighborhoods and had a hand in a good portion of the downtown area. You know how it seems like every street in Atlanta is named either Peachtree or Mason? Well, he's that Mason. He had a vision for the city and the genius to see it come true." She pushed sunglasses on top of her head and sat on the little stone bench under the shade of the magnolia tree. "What about your father?"

Kurt shrugged and put his hands in his pockets. "I don't remember my father. I was literally dropped off on the doorstep of a boys' home when I was four. I don't have any real memories of anything before that. Nothing I can count on, anyway. I remember a swing set that looked like a pirate ship and I remember a bathroom that smelled really bad but I don't remember anything about my parents."

Morgan gasped and reached out, touching his forearm with her hand. "I'm sorry."

He just shrugged. "No big deal. I was just a kid. I'm thankful for the home. I didn't have the transient life of foster kids, and my best friend and I relied on each other there. That kind of bond doesn't come from a normal life."

"What's his name?"

"James. We're close to the same age, so we roomed together from the first night there. We shared classes in school, a dorm room in college, and now our names are together on our business. He's my big brother."

With a smile, Morgan stood and gestured back to the deck. She needed to check on her steaks. "What is your business?"

"Electronics. James is a genius with it. I do the PR work and the admin stuff and handle the legalities. He holes himself up in his lab and invents things, plays with circuit boards, and pops out whenever I need him to have a presence at a meeting. I have to remind him to eat and sleep sometimes."

"My late husband once dabbled in electronics," she said, wondering at the *faux pas* of mentioning a late husband on a first date.

He looked as surprised as he probably should have. "Oh?"

"Not too seriously. He'd been interested in them, so he invested in a few companies that focused on electronics. But he really just worked the stock market more than anything. Just like his dad expected of him." Morgan still felt a considerable amount of bitterness toward her once father-in-law for the amount of pressure the man had put on her late husband, but she tried to push it back.

"How did he die?"

Morgan cleared her throat. Pain, shame, and anger warred within her, each emotion struggling to win the dominant spot. "Over the course of a month, he lost everything we had in a snowballing series of bad investments. All that was left was this house and my business, the two things I owned free and clear without him. He hanged himself in his office bathroom on a Tuesday morning when London stopped trading."

"I'm so sorry, Morgan," Kurt said. He stopped at the base of the deck steps and put his hand over hers on the railing. Standing on the first step, she turned and realized she stood at eye level with him. He had gray-green eyes in a happy, tanned face. Everything about him — his smile, his relaxed manner — put her at ease and made her feel like she'd known him her whole life.

She smiled and turned her hand so that their palms touched. "Thank you. It's been a couple of years, but it still is sometimes hard to think about." She shrugged. "A girl likes to think her love is enough. But that isn't always the way it is." Needing to lighten the air around them, she turned back around. "Let's check those steaks."

As they climbed the steps onto the deck, Morgan heard sirens. She heard them from her downtown office all the time, but rarely in her safe little gated well-to-do community. As she listened, police cars raced past her house and turned on the next street over. From her vantage point on the deck, she watched and listened. Seconds later, an ambulance followed.

When it stopped in front of the house whose property catty-cornered her acreage, her stomach started turning in nervous little flips. With fumbling hands, she turned the dials on the grill to the 'OFF' position, cutting off the flame and turning off the gas.

"We have to go," she whispered.

Kurt was by her side immediately, a warm hand enveloping her elbow. "What's wrong?"

Morgan pointed at the distant lights of the emergency vehicles in front of the house adjacent to hers. "That's my sister's place."

Kurt looked over at the ambulance. Morgan watched him double check the gas dials then pull his keys out of his pocket. "I'll drive."

♫ ♫ ♫ ♫

MELODY lay unconscious on the hospital bed. One side of her face looked so bruised and battered that Morgan had a hard time recognizing her. She walked over and sat in the chair next to the bed and picked up Melody's unbandaged hand. It was so limp. Morgan fought back a sob. Melody never even got bad colds.

"I should have picked her up from the airport," she whispered as guilt tore through her. "Her car was there, but I should have picked her up."

"You didn't do this," Kurt said as he laid a hand on her shoulder.

Tears fell from Morgan's eyes. "Some first date, huh?"

His hand gently compressed the muscles in her tense shoulder, communicating comfort and understanding. They remained still in that silent tableau for perhaps a few minutes, neither wanting to change the moment, perhaps hoping that their silent concentration would hasten Melody's return to consciousness.

A few minutes later, two men walked through the door. Kurt glanced up at them and recognized the tall one with the sandy hair as Detective Roberts. With a bit of a sick feeling, he remembered Roberts as one of the lead detectives on the team that had investigated Angela Montgomery's death. It looked like his partner had finally retired. The man accompanying him today looked much younger, with dark hair and dark eyes and stood stiffly, as if at attention.

Roberts' eyes skimmed over Kurt, recognition dawning, but he did not speak to him. "Mrs. Hamilton," he began quietly but insistently as Morgan looked up, "My name is Detective Jeremy Roberts. Jerry. This is my partner, Detective John Suarez. We need to ask you a few questions about your sister."

"I don't know how much help I can be to you, Detective. I don't know what happened to her, or who could have done this to her. I'm afraid we all have to wait for her."

Suarez sat down across from Morgan and stared at her until she met his eyes again. He said in a very soft voice, "No one should get away with doing this, Mrs. Hamilton. No one. I take this kind of thing very personally. So while you don't think you can be of any assistance, I would consider it a personal favor if you could find it in your heart to humor me and let me do my job so we can catch this guy."

He kept his eyes locked on hers and she searched his face. He wasn't just reciting a script. He meant it. The sight of Melody in this condition angered this man, this policeman, on a personal level. She knew that he would not let this go. His sincerity moved her out of her very confining stress and worry. "Okay."

Suarez didn't smile. He just nodded. "Do you know if your sister has received any threats recently?"

"No."

"Have you seen any suspicious cars, people, or activity in your neighborhood recently? Anything at all out of place or out of the ordinary? Delivery vans delivering when no one's home? Lights on at odd hours? Dogs barking at odd times of day or night? Anything like that?"

"Not really. We live in a gated community. A family moved in about three houses down from her a few weeks ago, but other than that there's been nothing out of the ordinary."

He nodded again. "Do you know if your sister has any enemies, anyone who would want to hurt her?"

"Her ex-fiancé. Two weeks ago, she left him at the alter when she caught him cheating on her. His name is Richard Johnson. But I can't imagine him doing this to her."

"We'll need to talk to him anyway." Detective Roberts said. "How do we reach him?"

"I don't have his number. But my friend Ginger should be able to get it. Melody met Richard at a party at her dad's house."

"What's Ginger's full name?" asked Suarez.

Morgan felt Melody's hand twitch beneath her fingers and she turned her attention from the detectives back to her younger sister. She saw the flutter of eyelashes as Melody fought the medications the doctors had administered and struggled to wake up.

"Melly, baby, it's me, Morgan. Melly, honey, wake up," she stood up and leaned over the bed. But, her hand stilled and an alarm next to her bed started beeping.

Morgan felt hands on her shoulders gently but firmly moving her out of the way. A nurse took her spot by the bed. A team rushed into the room headed by the on-call doctor. Despite Morgan's protests, Kurt and the police officers ushered her out of the room.

She stood with her back to the wall by the door, desperate to get back in there. Impatience made her snappy when Detective Suarez resumed the questions. "What do you know about your sister's activities in the last couple of days."

"Look, she's been gone to London for two weeks. I don't know anything."

"Was she there for work, or on vacation?" Roberts asked.

Morgan shook her head as if to clear it. "What? Oh, she was supposed to be on her honeymoon."

Suarez waited then said, "But she left him at the alter?"

"Yes," Morgan whispered, feeling the blood drain from her face when the doctor stepped out. "Doctor?"

He shook his head. "She's stable for now but it isn't good. I've ordered a bed for her in the ICU just in case she takes a sudden wrong turn, and the head neurologist is on his way. There is some pretty serious swelling of her brain right now. Until I see the head CT, I really can't tell you anything else. Is your sister a fighter?"

"What?" Morgan said, the words the doctor said somehow not making any sense.

"Is she tough? Is she a fighter?"

Morgan thought about the question, actually considering it. She remembered how Melly had held up after their parents had died on the Atlanta highways. She remembered how Melly had kept her back up after her brother-in-law killed himself, how Melly had pulled Morgan out of her depression spiral and self-pity. Yes, Melly was tough. She had an inner strength that few women could honestly claim. Morgan slowly nodded in response to the doctor's question.

"Okay. That's good. So what I can tell you is that it's pretty bad right now. I'm not going to lie to you. But she's a fighter, okay? So hold onto that."

Morgan put a hand to her mouth and felt Kurt's arm go around her shoulders. Not caring that she barely knew anything about her date, she turned her face to his chest and cried, fear washing over her in waves. She heard the doctor saying some things to the police but she didn't really listen to his words. Then she heard him walk away before she heard the tattoo beat of high heels running down the hospital corridor.

Morgan knew who she would see before she even looked up. She stepped away from Kurt and opened her arms as her best friend, Ginger Patterson, rushed to her. "I just heard. Daddy's parking the car. Oh my goodness, the world isn't safe anywhere anymore."

The comforting smell of Ginger's stupidly expensive perfume filled Morgan's nostrils. "I knew you'd come."

"Of course we came! Who do ya'll have besides me and Daddy?" Ginger stepped back. She wore her blonde hair piled high on her head with ringlets escaping everywhere. Her black pantsuit outlined her dancer's body and a gold belt highlighted her slim waist. Ginger stood well over six feet tall in her cheetah patterned heels. She narrowed her eyes at Kurt. "Who are you?"

Kurt smiled. "Kurt Lawson. Morgan and I were having dinner when the ambulance ..."

"Dinner?" Morgan watched as Ginger looked Kurt up and down. Her best friend was incorrigible. Morgan actually grinned as she swallowed a chuckle.

"Yes, with me," Morgan said, looping her arm through Ginger's. "Let's go sit. They're moving her to ICU."

♪ ♪ ♪ ♪

JERRY Roberts and Jonathan Suarez waited in the outer office of Mike Redman, head of security at M & L Technologies.

The secretary responded to a buzz from her desk phone. "Mr. Redman will see you now. Please go in."

The two detectives walked through the double doors and into another outer office. Sliding doors to the left were open to reveal security panels and walls of monitors. Three uniformed employees milled around the room, and one sat in one of the three swivel chairs while he typed something at a monitor station. From the interior of that room, Mike Redman came out.

He did not wear the suit and tie that Roberts remembered him wearing six months before. Instead, he had on a red golf shirt with the Atlanta Police Department logo on the chest. His biceps muscles bulged out from under the sleeve. He had salt and pepper hair, cut military short, and a tanned face that framed icy blue eyes. Roberts remembered those shirts from the last golf fundraiser. "Mike," he said, holding out his hand. "It's good to see you."

"Jerry," he said, shaking his hand with genuine warmth. He looked at Suarez and gave him a sideways grin. "Detective Suarez, congratulations on your promotion."

Suarez was surprised he remembered him. He worked for Redman when he was a rookie in the department, but ten years had easily passed. "It's good to see you again, sir."

Mike waved a dismissive hand. "Please, it's just Mike, now." He gestured to the sitting area off to the side from his desk. "Come, sit. How can I assist Atlanta's finest today? Is this about Angela?"

"I wish it were," Roberts said with a grim look. "I want to close that case so badly."

"Me, too. Almost enough to rejoin if they'd let me." He sat on the edge of the couch but did not sit back and relax. Instead, he leaned forward, his hands forming a steeple, and rested his elbows on his knees. "So, what do you need, guys?"

"We had an incident two weeks ago with a passenger on a flight coming in from Newark."

Mike raised his eyebrow. "An incident?"

"Yes," Suarez said, "a woman was badly beaten and is still in a coma."

"And what does that have to do with M & L?"

"Mr. Montgomery was on that flight," Roberts said. "Passengers think they saw him interacting with the assault victim."

Mike shook his head. "I don't know anything about it, gentlemen, and I debriefed the boss personally the day after his return. Mr. Montgomery is currently in a closed door meeting but I can clear time if it's important."

Suarez pulled out his notes, "No problem Mike. Can you account for his whereabouts on the night he arrived?"

Redman sat straighter, picking up on the all business tone. "All right, guys, level with me. There's other private sector jobs I can do. Is my employer a suspect?"

Jerry Roberts shook his head. "No, Mike. We're just chasing leads. Person of interest. You know the deal."

Mike sat back, visibly relaxed. "He came into the office that night around 15 'til 6. I've got video of him coming and going if you need proof. We store it forever. Before that he was at his hotel. Probably they have footage too."

Roberts said, "The perpetrator messed this girl up pretty bad. Kind of like that Lawrenceburg Mall thing a few years ago."

Mike let out a low whistle then clicked back into investigator mode. "I can tell you for sure that Mr. Montgomery showed no signs of being involved in any kind of struggle. He had no fight bites, no abrasions or contusions on his hands or knuckles, and no visible scratches. Also, and this is important I think, he looked happy for the first time since his wife was killed. Said London was good for him. You know perps. If the boss had just beat up some random woman he met on a plane, he would have been manic or just, 'off' somehow. Not the case. The boss was mellow."

Suarez flipped his notebook closed just as his cellphone vibrated. He checked the incoming message and stood. "Looks like she's trying to wake up."

All three men stood. "Let me know if you still need to talk to Mr. Montgomery after you interview her," Mike said.

Roberts nodded and shook his hand. "I'm certain we won't. But, I'll call you if something comes up."

Suarez shook Mike's hand. "Thank you, sir."

"Anytime, guys. I'm here five days a week. Sometimes four."

Roberts grinned at the dig while trying to remember his last full day off. "Thanks for everything, Mike. See ya soon."

♪ ♪ ♪ ♪

WHEN Melody heard Morgan calling her name, and heard tears in her voice, Melody knew she had to get to her, to comfort her. Fighting the mist, the pain in her body became tangible, and she started to understand what Morgan was saying. *I think she's waking up ... Kurt, get the doctor ... Melly, honey, open your eyes...*

Suddenly, she found herself on a bed in a hospital room. That realization took a back seat to the pain that crushed her. Her entire body ached and specific areas throbbed.

People stood all around her. As they came into focus, she saw Morgan standing next to a man she didn't recognize and a doctor standing at the foot of her bed. She felt so thirsty. What had happened? She looked over and saw her sister, tears streaming down her face, gripping her hand.

"Morgan," she managed to get past her dry lips.

"I'm right here, baby."

"I'm thirsty."

Morgan looked at the doctor for consent. At his nod, she grabbed the cup of water from the table next to the bed. She held the straw to Melody's lips. Melody took a couple of sips, swallowed, then leaned back, strangely exhausted from the effort of drinking.

"Melly, do you remember what happened?" Morgan asked as she grabbed her sister's hand again, "Someone attacked you outside of your house."

Melody closed her eyes, wanting to escape from the pain in her head. She started to drift away, when Morgan's words registered. She squeezed her eyes in concentration, trying to remember. Driving home, she had a song on her mind she needed to put on paper, when ... Her eyes flew open, the memory suddenly and terrifyingly clear.

"Richard. Oh, Morgan, Richard was at my house when I came home." She squeezed Morgan's hand tighter. "He was so angry, and he ... and he —" she couldn't finish as the sobs tore through her.

The first sob wracked through her chest and she felt her broken ribs give a little bit. The unbelievable pain when she felt her broken bones grinding against each other made her gasp at the end of her sob. Ironically, the gasp made her want to cry even harder.

Morgan stood, then carefully sat on the side of the bed. She gingerly wrapped her arms around her baby sister.

"It's all right, Melly. You're safe now." She looked up as Roberts and Suarez came into the room. She demanded, "Did you ever find Richard Johnson? She just said Richard did this to her."

"The person who called himself Richard Johnson does not exist." Suarez said as he pulled a phone out of his jacket pocket. "All the contact information Patterson had was bogus. There is nothing on him in any system we can access including the NCIC database."

Melody put a hand over her mouth. "I think I'm going to be sick," she said.

The doctor intervened and gently guided the men out of the room. "Gentlemen, she's been in a coma for two weeks. She identified her attacker. Can a formal statement wait until tomorrow? Give her a little bit of time to get her feet under her?"

♫ ♫ ♫ ♫

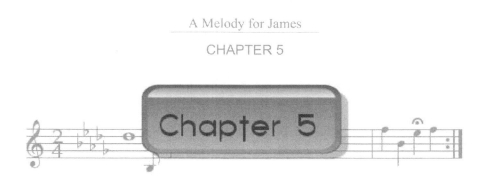

FOUR YEARS LATER

Nashville
December

"NEXT up on *WKIB the Kibble* is Melody Mason singing her eighth top ten hit, 'Not Until You'. She's managed to hold the number one spot for four weeks with this song, folks. Be sure to tune in tonight and listen to the countdown to see if she can hold onto that number one spot for week number five." Melody smiled as she heard her voice coming over the radio. She thought that she would eventually get used to listening to herself sing, but she still felt a tinge of startled pride whenever she saw one of her videos or heard her voice coming over the airwaves.

The last four years had passed like a dream. After several months of recovery from her beating, she decided to move from Atlanta and make a fresh start. Over dinner one night, she told David Patterson her dreams. He confessed that he had an old record label that he hadn't put to any good use for a long time, and offered her a contract. Within weeks of her move to Nashville, with David's help, she finished recording her first album. By the end of the first year, two of her songs had made it to the top ten of the country music charts. She had won the Country Music Association's Horizon Award for best new female vocalist, and then watched her first album go platinum before it went double platinum.

After recording her second album, Patterson Records, a fast-growing label in the country music scene thanks to her help, started crossing her songs over to the pop music stations, and week after week her singles landed in the top ten of both the country and pop charts. Her third release hit number one in record time — "number one with a bullet" as they said in the industry — and after that, there seemed to be no stopping her.

Flying into the parking lot at the warehouse that served as the on location set for her latest video, she screeched to a stop in front of the door. She recognized the vehicles of the members of her band, knowing they had been here for a few hours already shooting scenes that didn't involve her.

She grabbed her bag out of the car and walked in, hearing "Our Love Song" playing over the speakers. It was her favorite song she had ever written. She wrote it with one man on her mind. The same man who was always on her mind, who made her heart ache even after four years. She told herself it was ridiculous to squeeze so much emotion out of a coffee, a breakfast, and a lunch with a man whose last name she didn't even know, but she woke up almost every morning with him on her mind, and went to bed every night with him in her heart.

She'd written a fun, comedic song for him that very quickly became her fourth number one hit titled, "Dating an International Super Spy." This new song, though, had nothing funny about it. It was nothing more than her baring her soul, and she prayed he'd get the message and find a way to contact her.

Her manager, Hal Coleman, met her at the back door. "Melody! Girl, we were about to send out a search party." He stood a full head taller than her. His ebony face usually looked at her with a gentleness that defied his professional wrestler size, but today his forehead wrinkled into a frown.

"What do you mean?" she asked all innocence and cheekiness.

"After your jaunt to Cancun last week, when you're five minutes late I don't trust that you're actually gonna show anymore." He folded his arms over his massive chest and tried to look stern.

"I needed that jaunt to Cancun." She stopped in front of him, only because he blocked the door.

"Maybe, but we needed to get this video shot. And one cannot shoot a video with a crew and extras scheduled if the star is in another country sunning her skinny white behind on a Mexican beach."

Melody sighed, admitting defeat. "You're right. And I know it cost us a lot of money. I've already offered to pay it."

"That's hardly the point."

"Isn't it? Isn't that why everyone is here today? The almighty dollar? If I've offered to pay the added expenses for the rescheduling of this video, then why does everyone still care and why are we still discussing it? Move, Hal. You're blocking me and it's rude."

Irritated, she pushed by him and entered the warehouse. The stage manager, a short woman with frizzy black hair and crooked glasses, rushed toward her, directing her to the space they'd designated as her dressing room. While the stage manager talked to someone on her bluetooth, she gave Melody the printed outline of the filming schedule and directed her as to which outfit to wear first.

Melody finished dressing then looked through the boxes of boots for the pair that matched the outfit. Keeping in line with her trademark, she always wore brightly colored, flashy boots, and owned hundreds of pairs of them in every color and style imaginable. More than a few times she had to get a pair custom made because the color combination she wanted had never been made before.

This Christmas season she had launched her own line of boots, and they'd found out this morning that the demand was much greater than the supply. People were buying up Melody Mason Brand Signature Cowgirl Boots in greater numbers than they had ever purchased Cabbage Patch Kids or Tickle Me Elmos.

Success.

What the people in her crew used to tease her about was now a huge fashion craze. Teenage girls all over the country begged their mamas to buy them overpriced brightly colored glittery boots for Christmas, and those very mamas often begged their husbands for the same.

When she opened the box that contained the turquoise boots studded with silver, she spotted the single yellow rose lying inside. Her heart skipped a slow beat while her hands started to shake. She picked it up and read the note attached to it.

I'M WATCHING YOU

Always the same message. With a sob, she flung the rose into the wastebasket, and sat down in the chair.

The yellow roses had shown up off and on for the last year, just at her concerts in the beginning, with the notes always identical. At first she thought an obsessed fan had placed them, but then they started to appear almost everywhere she went. So far, she had told no one about them, but she knew she needed to soon. They terrified her, which made her angry.

She shook off the feeling of dread, slipped her boots on, and went to find Lisa, her makeup artist. She had work to do. She wanted to get this video wrapped up today, then she had to perform tonight at an awards show, then it was off to Atlanta to help her sister with the final preparations for her wedding.

It had taken Kurt three and a half years to convince Morgan to get married again, and Melody wanted to be there to make sure Morgan didn't change her mind and bolt at the last minute.

♪ ♪ ♪ ♪

JAMES bustled into the pub and brushed the wet snow out of his hair. His glasses immediately fogged up in the warm interior, so he slipped them off and pulled a handkerchief out of his suit pocket to wipe them off while he worked his way through the crowded room. He reached his usual table and saw the figure of a man already seated there. He smiled before he even slipped his glasses back onto his face. "Mark, my friend. It's good to see you."

Mark Knight, the vicar of the church James attended while in London, offered his hand in greeting. The two men shook hands as James sat. "I thought you were leaving tonight. Don't you have Kurt's wedding?"

"I do, but this weather has us stalled. I'm going to give it a go again in a few hours."

"The fowl is good today. Not at all dry," Mark said, sliding an empty plate toward the waitress.

"Sounds good," James said with a smile. He warmly winked at the daughter of the pub owner and said, "I'll have the chicken."

"In a tick, Mr. M." she said. She picked up Mark's empty plate. "Anything else for you, Vicar?"

"Perhaps another pot of tea," he said. "This one's gone cold, and it looks like my friend could use a hot drink."

She grabbed the half empty tea pot as well and worked her way back to the kitchen.

"You sure you want to wait until Christmas to come visit?" James asked.

"I don't want to miss the hanging of the greens. It was Laney's favorite time at the church. Helps make missing her at Christmastime a little easier. Besides, my show premiers you know."

"Oh, your time-traveler show." James nodded, only intellectually understanding that other people actually enjoyed watching silly science fiction dramas, or reality shows, or sporting events on television. He had little to no practical experience with it, personally.

The Vicar smiled, "How Laney loved that show. Can't miss it. And you Yanks won't have it available in the colonies for another half a year."

James nodded again. No one knew more than he what it was like to face holidays as a widower. Mark had guided James through that first year. Without him, he didn't know what he would have done.

But as much as he thought of Angela, despite his best intentions, he also often thought of the singing heiress, Melody. She had completely disappeared after she drove away that afternoon.

He'd sent her a text the evening they met just so she'd have his number, but he'd never heard from her again. He called her several times leading up to their planned dinner Thursday, but she never returned his call. After a few months, he felt desperate and tried one more time. The number came back disconnected.

He had never mentioned Melody to anyone, except Vicar Mark. In explaining his feelings and talking it out, James had realized that the reason he had never talked about her was because the singing heiress represented something that he couldn't confront. She represented hope.

He and Angela had so many hopes for the future. They hoped to make enough money that they could sponsor ministries and charitable foundations around the world together. They hoped to spend a lot of private time together shutting out the rest of the world. They hoped, secretly and in their own ways, for children. They hoped to be parents.

The loneliness after Angela's murder, the dashed hopes, the constant ache in his heart, crushed him. Some nights alone in his bed he would stare at the untouched pillow beside him and the gigantic hole in his life where his wife should be threatened to swallow him up.

If he admitted that he felt a new hope based on a chance meeting in an airport, that he felt a momentary relief to the constant distracting grief, that he desperately wanted — needed — to bring a new best friend and confidante into the intimacy of his vulnerable and lonesome heart, that would make the hope real. In Melody's presence he felt he could share anything, all of his deepest feelings and dreams for the future. And she had never even called him back.

No. He knew better than to hope. That kind of hope left unrealized would make him feel a thousand times worse every waking moment than he currently felt. Better to keep it to himself and simply feel anger.

Except the anger gave way to despair. Then the despair gave way to emptiness.

Needing to fill the emptiness, he gave in to Kurt and went to church with him and Morgan — the same church Angela had started attending right before her death. And that is how it happened. That is how his life changed forever.

One Sunday morning as he sat in the pew next to the haunting memory of his late wife, he felt the presence of God. It was absolutely nothing he could explain to an unbeliever. He couldn't have even explained it to his former self in any meaningful way.

James felt a very real and very tangible God — the great I AM, Creator of all things, Jehovah, A'doni — he felt Him enter his heart and, for the first time, felt real healing begin inside. It was just as real as real could be.

He wondered how he had missed God speaking to him during all that time. Had he truly been that blind? On his knees at the altar, James fully handed his life over to the Creator of the universe.

Not long after, he moved out of the hotel and into an apartment near his office. He started reading the Bible in earnest and finished it, then read it again … and again. Three times in three translations that first year. After that, he studied and studied, learning all he could about God and the life offered by following Him. He took on the task with the same passion he had once poured into learning about technologies.

During his commutes to London, he found a flat, found a church, and became very close to Vicar Mark, who happened to be his age and also a widower. The two bonded almost as closely as James had with Kurt. Vicar Mark taught him more about healing and learning to let go of the pain and opening his heart to God's plan for his life.

He had only started dating again this year. Try as he might, though, no one sparked much of an interest. He quickly tired of any woman, American or British, within a few dates, then was left dealing with bad feelings and inevitable tears.

He had decided that the cultural notion that men cannot handle rejection was nothing more than a myth. A lie. Men handle rejection routinely. He had discovered, by and large, that women were completely unequipped to cope with it, though. He had nearly decided dating just wasn't worth it.

He couldn't replace Angela, and he refused to continue to search for someone like Melody, the coffee drinking cheese grit craving singing heiress bound for seminary. He decided that jet lag and loneliness must have been the things that sparked his imaginary feelings for her at the time.

Returning to his table companion, he said, "Signed the contract renewal this afternoon."

"Ah, congratulations I suppose. Tell me. Do you think you will ever tell me what it is you actually do here?"

James frowned. "Not really, no. I can't. Not honestly, anyway. You know that."

Mark laughed and shook his head. "Jimmy, lad, you are an extremely literal person. It must be that genius mind you have in that very American noggin of yours." He glanced at his watch. "What time did they tell you to arrive back at the airport?"

"They said there's a 2:25 flight. I'd still be back in Atlanta by 7:00."

"Not awful, I suppose. At least it's a direct flight."

"True. I hate stopping in Newark."

Mark raised an eyebrow. "Indeed."

He enjoyed his lunch with Mark, then made his way back to the airport. The clerk at the ticket counter assured him that the flight would leave on time, so he went ahead and worked his way through the intense security at London Heathrow International Airport. No matter how often he came and went, the sight of policemen with fully automatic machine guns scrutinizing the passengers still unnerved him.

Once in the terminal, James discovered that the flight had been delayed by at least an hour. Annoyed with himself for not rescheduling his travel plans for the storm, he realized that he didn't want to sit for an hour. He had a 9-hour flight of sitting in front of him, so he wandered through the newsstand at the airport in the international section.

While looking through business magazines, he found a tabloid magazine out of place. He started to look behind it when the picture on the cover made his stomach drop.

His singing heiress seminary student with the vivid blue eyes and the curly black tresses stood there clutching the arm of a tall, black haired man wearing a white cowboy hat. The headline boldly proclaimed "Bobby Kent Marriage Maybe?"

His eyes trailed to the body of the story below the fold.

    International superstar and Country Music's most
    eligible bachelor, Bobby Kent, was rather
    tellingly 'unavailable for comment' when asked
    about the reported budding romance with
    sensational phenom, Melody Mason. Will Mason have
    to change her name to Kent? We hope so! In fact,
    we think this is a Duet best sung to the sound of
    wedding bells …

As he snatched the tabloid, the cover of the weekly television guide caught his eye. There she was again; this time wearing blue jeans, a purple and orange western style shirt, and sporting vivid orange and spectacularly purple sequined cowboy boots. She stood surrounded by four western clad men. Below some headline about an award he had never heard of before, he read:

> Who will come out on top this year? Magnetic Melody Mason spurs UK's growing interest in Country Western music. Dare we hope Miss Mason crosses the pond for an international tour soon?

He snatched the television guide as well. Then he noticed the American fashion magazine.

> These boots were made for … walking to the White House! Exclusive interview! First Lady admits she secretly loves wrapping her size eights in Country Music's to-die-for designer leather.

And there she stood on the cover of the magazine, arms linked with the First Lady of the United States. They wore identical looking brightly colored boots.

He pushed his way through to the cashier and tossed a twenty pound note on the counter. With a muttered, "Keep the change," he grabbed his purchases and rushed out of the newsstand.

♫ ♫ ♫ ♫

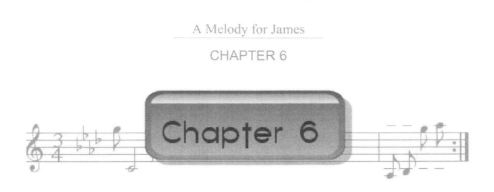

JAMES rolled his head on his shoulders and waited for Morgan to answer her door. "Hi," he greeted. He hadn't seen Morgan in six months, maybe longer. Kurt had done some traveling to England while they worked on the negotiation with the contract renewal, so James hadn't been traveling like normal.

Her eyes widened. "Hi stranger. What brings you to town?"

"Well, turns out a beautiful and talented woman is marrying this guy I know." He pulled the collar of his coat up. "May I come in? This rain is killing me."

"Of course!" She stood to the side and he stepped into her foyer. "Let me take your coat." She gestured toward the back of the house. "Kurt's here. Is everything okay?"

"I actually came to see you."

Morgan raised an eyebrow. "Okay." She looked at her watch. "But you either need to talk fast or wait until after the awards show I'm watching. Melly is on it."

"That is exactly what I want to talk to you about." He pulled the cover of one of the magazine's he'd bought hours ago out of his pocket. "Is this your sister?"

Her eyes glanced to the page and she smiled. "Of course."

"Of course? What do you mean of course?"

"Seriously? You didn't know Melody Mason is my sister? How long have we known each other, James? Five years?"

"Four," he corrected. "Apparently, I didn't know." He released a sigh. "Your last name is Hamilton but your sister is Melody Mason, not 'Melly' Hamilton?"

"I'm a widow, James. My married name was Hamilton. I never changed it back. My sister Melody goes by our maiden name, Mason, and her nickname is Melly." Her brows came together in a frown. "What's going on with you?"

James felt like he couldn't breathe. His eyes shot from Morgan to the magazine cover and back again. Just then, Kurt strolled into the foyer.

"Hey, buddy. Welcome back to American soil. Want some sweet tea? You know, with ice and such. Served cold and all. In a glass. Not like the tea we tossed into Boston harbor a few years back."

"Yeah. Sure." James paced into the living room. As he walked, he tried to recall all of the conversations he had with Morgan concerning Melody. He had always listened with only half an ear to her comings and goings because — truth be told — he didn't really care.

He allowed himself an ironic laugh. What a hoot. He cared, all right.

What he did recall with absolute clarity were the days that followed his first ever meeting Melody. The days when Kurt came and went from the office sporadically, because his new girlfriend's sister had been in the hospital in a coma after having been battered nearly to death. While James had grown more and more frustrated with 'Melody' for not returning his calls, 'Melly' had lingered in a hospital bed fighting for her life while recovering from a brutal beating.

"Did Melody ever mention meeting someone, a man, on the day that she —" he hesitated, unsure of the words to use. "The day that she was assaulted?"

Morgan frowned. "Maybe. There was something she was talking about in delirium one time. Something about a date she couldn't miss."

His lips thinned. "Thursday dinner?"

Morgan paused, her eyes locking with James. Despite the years of personal knowledge, she looked at him with a little bit of suspicion and demanded, "How did you know that?"

"It was me, Morgan. I was the man she met. Her date was with me." He released the air in his lungs.

Kurt's eyes widened in curiosity. "What?"

"We were both returning from London. A northeaster grounded all flights in Newark for several hours. We started talking, then kept talking. I waited for her outside baggage claim hoping to talk her into going to dinner with me that night. The guy she broke the wedding off with, Richard, was waiting for her, too. She was scared, Kurt. Like, beaten dog scared. I've never seen anything like it.

"I acted like we were a couple, called her darling, and whisked her off in a cab away from the creep. We ended up spending the entire day together and made plans for dinner that week. Except she never called, never returned any of my texts, and her phone always went straight to voice mail. Then the number came back disconnected.

He loosened his tie and looked at Morgan, who had a wide-eyed shocked look on her face. "I was broken, wishing I could die. I remember sitting in that airport, exhausted, wishing I'd been with Angela when it happened so I could have died, too."

He saw their eyes widen slightly. He looked at Kurt. "Melody made me forget Angela. She made me feel. For the first time in months I felt something other than raw pain. That was priceless to me at the time. For those few hours —" He felt defeated and leaned his head back, closing his eyes. "I tried to get in touch with her for weeks — months even — but to no avail. I know why, now. I remember you saying she was in the hospital because she was attacked. But I was so angry and hurt I just gave up on her."

Kurt said nothing through the whole exchange — he merely sat back and listened. When James finished, he didn't respond right away, obviously letting it sink in and processing all the information before speaking.

James broke the silence. "I have thought of her every single day since. Every day. I wake up thinking about her and fall asleep thinking about her. I cannot fathom the connection between her and Morgan right now."

"This is the most incredible thing I think I've ever even heard of!" Morgan exclaimed. She checked her watch. "Hey! It's almost time."

Morgan rushed to the coffee table and picked up a remote control. Pushing a series of buttons, a large flat screened television the width of the massive mantle came on, and the logo of the music association spread across the screen to signal a commercial break.

♫ ♫ ♫ ♫

MELODY took a sip of water, hoping her stomach would keep it down, then leaned back and started her deep breathing exercises, trying to force her body to relax. She loved her job. She loved to write songs. She loved to hide away in the studio for days and record her albums. Above all, she loved interacting with her fans and the press.

But she hated to sing in front of a live audience. Where once she would take to the stage as naturally as rising from bed each morning, now it terrified her. In college she had no problem with all of her required performances. But, now, all she could think about was that *he* might be watching her.

Once she took the stage, once she found herself actually up there and singing, the terror faded. But to actually willingly walk out onto a stage with thousands of eyes on her — she almost had to be forced out every time.

This came as quite a shock to everyone involved in her first concert appearance. Melody probably felt more surprise at the stage fright than anyone in her entourage. Until the very second before she had to walk out in front of the audience, she was mentally prepared to confidently strut up to the microphone. That had been a very, very bad night.

Feeling a little better after the breathing, she sat straight and let Lisa put the final touches on her makeup. Her eclectic makeup artist with the hot pink pony tail and thick black eyeliner popped her gum to signal that she had finished her work, then stepped back to give Melody access to the mirror. Melody stood and began her inspection.

She'd opted to wear her hair down tonight, letting it fall just past her shoulders. She wore a long black gown with subtle sequins sewn throughout the fabric, designed to catch the lights just so. The sleeves started just barely off her shoulders, leaving her neck and most of her shoulders bare, then fit her arms tight all the way to the wrist. The dress fell to her ankles, but had a slit up one side to mid-thigh. She'd chosen a diamond choker and matching earrings to complete the outfit.

Now for shoes. "No boots tonight," she declared with a nervous chuckle that she judged a shade too close to hysteria for comfort. Lisa handed her the plain black heels. As Melody slipped into them, Lisa popped her gum again exactly at the same time a knock sounded at the door.

Melody jumped then smiled nervously. "You're always right on time," she said, making Lisa smile.

With hands that started to shake again, she opened the door and stepped out into the orderly chaos of the awards show backstage area. She stepped over cables and around technicians, and brushed shoulders with the host of the show, a popular comedian. Men all along her path, from technicians to the host, paused to stare and watch her progress to the stage. Melody fought so hard to make herself keep walking that she barely noticed.

She knew her band was already in place and forced herself to walk up the steps to the darkened stage. *It's only one song*, she told herself. *Just one song then I'm done.*

She found her mark and waited for the curtain to rise. She could hear the host introducing her, and felt her stomach turn to water.

Wait a minute, she thought, *I can't do this. What am I doing? This is insane!*

In a panic she took a step back, ready to flee, when the curtain started to rise. Taking a deep breath, she stepped back to the spot, folded her hands in front of her, and forced herself, through the inner turmoil and fear, to look calm.

A single spotlight shone down on her, the bright light obliterating her ability to see the crowd. Her band was set up behind her, hidden by another curtain, back lit so that they appeared as a tableau of black shadows to the audience. Silhouettes. Through the applause she could hear fans in the back chanting her name, "Mell-y! Mell-y! Mell-y!" and waited for the noise of the audience to ebb at least slightly before starting to sing.

She sang the first verse *a cappella*, her voice strong and sure, flowing through the building. The song she chose to sing was a simple love song, the words painting a beautiful picture of the joy of true love. This was the song that had played in her head while driving home from her wonderful day with her James, the song that made her itch to get to her piano. She'd entitled it "My Love Song." The lyrics were touching and poignant, and those accompanied by their loves in the audience reached over and held hands as the words soared through them.

As she began the first chorus, very softly in the background, a flute joined in, slowly followed by a fiddle. One at a time the members of her band added their own instruments, until by the beginning of the third verse, they reached full tempo. Melody strengthened her voice to compete with the music, singing with all she had. For a brief moment, even the activity backstage stood still, as the full power of Melody's voice hit them. At the end of the last verse, every instrument suddenly stopped, the building fell perfectly silent for a heartbeat as the chords faded away, then Melody began the last chorus as she had begun the song, with no musical accompaniment, singing softly. She reached the end of the song, holding the final note for a full count of ten, lifting her arms above her head to keep her voice strong. Then, she slowly lowered her arms and bowed her head, breathing heavily.

No one moved at first, afraid to break the silence. But as she lifted her face back to the light, she heard the audience surge to their feet and a tidal wave of deafening applause washed over her in more and more intense waves. Tears came to her eyes as she peered beyond the lights and saw her fans and her peers standing for her. She gave a small bow, like a curtsy, as the spotlight went dark and the curtain began to descend.

The host of the show ignored the script on the tele-prompter, barely able to see through the unexpected tears in his eyes. He waited for the ovation to die down and had to clear his throat twice to speak. "Well, only an idiot would follow that act. We'll go ahead and take our next sponsored break now," he said roughly, then stepped back from the podium.

Melody stood in her spot in the dark for a moment, shaky and weak from the effort she put into the song before slowly making her way across the stage. She knew she had to make room for the next band to set up in the short time between performances.

As she stepped from the stage, she got bombarded with people hugging her, everyone around her talking at once. She looked up and caught Hal's eye as he started making his way toward her.

"Get out of the way. Move. Let the girl breathe," Hal said, using his huge frame to bodily move a few people who weren't intelligent enough to listen.

Hal enveloped her in a hug, nearly snapping her spine, then set her away and wiped his eyes. "You did real good, Mel. Real good." With one massive arm, he sideways hugged her again.

"I did, didn't I? It isn't every day a woman can bring Hal Coleman to tears, is it?" She smiled up at him.

"Miss Mason! Over here! They're announcing Performer of the Year!" This came from somewhere around the monitors. Hal grabbed Melody's hand and dragged her over to the group standing around a monitor, and held his breath. Melody was nominated this year — the only woman nominated and competing against some really well established male stars.

♫ ♫ ♫ ♫

JAMES stared transfixed at the television as the curtain rose on Melody. She looked so at ease, so beautiful. Then she began to sing. His stomach muscles clenched at the sound of her voice rising and falling with the song. He felt the song weave through him, felt like she was singing just to him and not to millions of people around the world.

He couldn't move after the song ended. Somewhere in the back of his mind he heard Morgan and Kurt talking, but couldn't make out their words. Suddenly, he was staring at a commercial for dish detergent, and he came out of his reverie. He shook his head to clear it, then stood.

"I need to go." Did his voice sound odd to them? Anxious to be alone so that he could analyze all of this, he started toward the door but stopped. "I don't have a car. I'll need a cab. Can we call the gatehouse?"

Kurt looked at Morgan. "He could take your sister's car. You have it ready for her to drive tomorrow."

James watched her weigh her options then nodded. "Sure. Take Melly's car. But, please have it back here after lunch. Her plane arrives at eleven."

"Her plane?"

"She's coming in for the wedding." Morgan stepped forward and put her arms around his waist, hugging him. "I try not to think about what happened four years ago. I'm sorry that somehow, in the process, you were hurt."

"I found God back then, Morgan. Or He found me. Don't forget that. Above all, I needed that." She squeezed him tighter.

Kurt left the room and returned with James' still wet coat and the keys to Melody's little white Mercedes. James vividly remembered spending that morning riding in her car with her. "I'll see you two tomorrow."

"Good to see you, brother," Kurt said, walking him to the door.

James held out his hand and they clenched hands as they hugged. "Likewise. Goodnight."

Morgan called from the front room. "Don't leave yet, James. They're about to announce Performer of the Year."

The two men returned to the room with the television. Morgan grabbed Kurt's hand, watching the screen intently.

♫ ♫ ♫ ♫

"AND the winner is … Melody Mason!" The crowd went crazy. No one in the building doubted that she deserved the award after the performance she had just delivered.

Melody almost fell down. Hal pushed her to the stage, and suddenly she found herself walking toward the podium. When the presenter handed her the award, she shook so badly that she feared she would drop it.

"I, um … I had no idea I would win tonight, so I have no speech prepared. I have to say I'm just floored. Wow, y'all," She stopped for a moment to breathe, then continued.

Her voice sounding worn out, and getting harsher and more hoarse with each word, she said, "Sorry about my voice. I think I overdid it back there." The audience started applauding, and she had to wait a moment to speak again.

"Okay, I want to thank my band. They're the best. And I have to thank Hal, y'all know Hal don't you? I swear he's about as popular as I am." The audience laughed and cheered. "I also want to thank my sister, my fans, and Patterson Records for an amazing year."

She started to step away, then stepped back up to the microphone. "Oh, and, one other thing. I don't know if this person is watching tonight or not, but I was a damsel in distress a few years ago, and a knight in shining armor came to my rescue. If you hadn't done that, I wouldn't have had the courage to even be here tonight. So to you my handsome hero, I say thank you. I hope you liked your song. Buy me a coffee sometime."

♪ ♪ ♪ ♪

RIKARD Šabalj stared at the television set as Melody finished her speech. The phone rang.

"Yeah," he answered, turning the television off as the MC started into his canned closing. He listened to the voice on the other end. "Team is already prepared for that one. We move tomorrow."

He listened some more. "You know I'm ready for it. The question is, are you?" He smirked while the caller paused. "It's up to you. Just give me a go."

At the affirmation, he disconnected the call without another word. A new note was attached to the stem of a rose, this one with a much clearer message.

♪ ♪ ♪ ♪

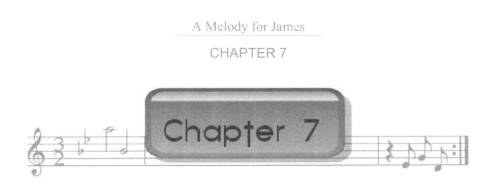

JAMES entered his office through his private elevator. At five-forty in the morning, he expected an empty office, but he could see Rebecca's light on. She normally came in at six so that their schedules didn't vary too much when he was in England, but she must have anticipated his early arrival this morning.

Not wanting to bother her for coffee, he decided he would make it himself. He secured his laptop to the docking station and brought it out of hibernation. His office door opened and Rebecca Lin walked in, carrying a steaming mug.

James glanced at her as he logged in to his computer. Even at this early hour, she still looked smart and crisp in her gray pencil skirt and white blouse. She had her straight black hair cut to her chin, making her petite frame seem even smaller. As a second generation Chinese woman, she could speak either Mandarin or Georgia southern drawl with equal fluency.

"Good morning, Mr. Montgomery," she said, handing him the cup. "Welcome home. Burroughs called earlier and asked if you could try to call him if you got in before the conference call."

"Thanks."

It took him a long time to fall asleep after hearing Melody's speech, and once there dreams of her had haunted his slumber. He'd decided to work out at four in the morning, thinking that sweat and muscle strain would purge her from his system.

Obviously it didn't work, he thought to himself, *because you're still thinking about her.*

He took a sip of the coffee. "See if Kurt is in yet. I'll need to brief him before the seven-o'clock call."

"Yes, sir."

"Then come back in here to take down some letters for me." As Rebecca turned to leave, he added, "Oh, and get me the cell number for that Steel Hill guy. I want to touch base with him about the off-site data warehousing later this morning."

"Yes, sir." She pulled a phone out of her pocket. "Here is your U.S. phone. It's charged and ready to go. I went through the latest texts yesterday afternoon and wrote messages for you, so it should be clear."

"Thanks." He turned it on as he sat back in his desk. While it powered up, he went through his written messages, making notes in his calendar as needed. "Go ahead and grab yourself a cup of coffee. We have quite a bit of work to do."

Four hours later, Rebecca sat down wearily at her desk. Her boss was in rare form this morning. Usually, upon his return from England, he holed away and worked at the site in Albany, catching up on the latest with the data warehousing project. She didn't usually have to worry about this kind of workload for at least a week after his return to American soil.

She picked up the phone to schedule yet another meeting, while she started another memo. Her inner office door opened, and Julie, her part time assistant, stuck her head through. Julie was a nineteen-year-old college student, perky and cute, with long, curly red hair. She had yet to be in a bad mood, as far as Rebecca could tell, and she lit up any room she entered.

"I'm here, Rebecca. Need any help with anything?" Julie asked.

"Yes. Thank goodness you're here. Mr. Montgomery is back. We have a pile of work. Go make these calls, then come see me for some memo distribution," Rebecca said as she handed Julie a stack of notes. "I have to go to a lunch with him today."

Julie came all the way into the room and put a hand to her heart, "I wish Mr. Montgomery would ask me to go to lunch with him."

"Trust me, speaking from experience, it's not all it's cracked up to be. I'll have to eat before I go because I'll be so busy taking notes for him that there's no time to eat," Rebecca said, hitting the button to tell the computer to print the memo she just finished. "He will slow down a little bit. It's just been so long since he was here."

James' office door opened, cutting off anything else she might have said. "Rebecca, are the department heads in the conference room?" he asked as he rolled down his shirtsleeves and put on his suit jacket.

"Yes, sir."

"Good. You're with me. I need you to keep minutes." James headed toward Julie, who still stood in the doorway. "Good morning, Julie." He stopped in front of her, waiting for her to move.

"Ah, g … g … good morning, Mr. Montgomery." Her face turned almost the same shade as her hair. James stepped around her and Rebecca followed, shooting Julie a warning look over her shoulder.

Outside the conference room door, he stopped abruptly and turned. "Exactly where is Kurt?"

"Eve told me he left a little while ago. Something about having to pick up a friend from the airport," she answered.

Melody.

He'd managed to get through the last two hours without thinking about her. New emotion surged through him at the thought of her. He suddenly felt disoriented and out of sorts. His tightly held focus fled. But, he had a meeting, a room full of department heads who hadn't seen him other than via teleconference for six months. He needed to keep working. "All right, let's go in."

Forty-five minutes later, the department heads practically scurried out of the conference room, grateful the ordeal had ended. James Montgomery was a hard, demanding boss on a good day. Everyone who had been in that room today learned very quickly not to draw attention to themselves. Most left feeling thankful he had planned on vacating the area for the Albany office for the next few days.

In the conference room, Rebecca finished jotting down a note before her eyes met James'. He sat leaning back in his chair, rubbing his face. She'd seen enough to know that something was really bothering him.

"Mr. Montgomery, sir. If there's anything you want to talk about you should know by now that it would be kept in the strictest confidence," she said, almost sorry she'd said the words as soon as they came out of her mouth.

He looked at her startled for a moment, before he smiled. "I'm that bad?"

She cleared her throat and nodded.

"I appreciate the offer, Rebecca, but I think I'll just go home, before you or someone else runs me out. Finish up what you have to do, then take off early. It's Friday, and with Kurt out, too, and the Albany team at that conference, nothing should come up." With that, he got up and strode out of the room. By the time she'd made it back to her office, he had already gone. Now she really worried about him. The only time off work she'd ever seen him take was after his wife died. Not only had he just left early, but told her to take off early besides.

She finished giving instructions to Julie, then mentally shrugged. *Well*, she thought, *take advantage of it while you can.*

"I'll see you Monday morning," she said as she passed Julie's desk on her way out the door.

♪ ♪ ♪ ♪

MELODY ran down the escalator from the secure area of the terminal and launched herself into her sister's arms. Both women laughed and cried at the same time, while the paparazzo's cameras flashed and fans cheered. Her security team worked with airport security to try to keep everyone at bay, while at the same time trying to usher the sisters out of the terminal. Within minutes, they sat in the back of a limousine, speeding through the city.

Melody leaned her head back and closed her eyes, feeling herself really relax for the first time in a couple of years. "I haven't slept yet. I was so wired from the awards there was no way I would have been able to sleep last night if I'd tried," she said, her voice hoarse.

"Did you go to any of the parties last night?" Morgan asked.

"A couple, but I started to lose my voice, so I just went back to my house."

"You sang your rear end off last night," Morgan grinned.

"I know. That's why I have no voice left." She opened her eyes and looked at her sister. "I plan on singing that song for your wedding."

Morgan smiled. "We would be honored," she said, reaching over and grabbing Melody's hand.

When they got to Morgan's house, Kurt went into the study to call his office while the two sisters followed the chauffeur, who carried Melody's bags up to the guest room.

Melody loved this room. Maple wood floors made the room feel light and airy. The walls were a deep peach color trimmed in white, and double doors opened onto a small balcony that looked out over Morgan's beautifully landscaped back yard. A large four-poster bed sat centered to the wall, covered in a cream and brown colored cover. Throw pillows in peaches and browns covered the bed, and a dark brown blanket lay folded at the foot of the bed. Against the far wall, a chaise lounge, a low chair, and a small table formed a sitting area.

While Melody hung up clothes, Morgan went into the adjoining bathroom to put toiletries away.

"I can't wait to see your dress," Melody said.

"I have a fitting scheduled next week. I tried so hard to keep this simple, since it's my second wedding, but it just kind of got away from us."

Melody smiled. "That's okay. This is Kurt's first wedding, so it all works out."

"That's what he says," Morgan said, coming out of the bathroom with an empty bag. "It's been fun. Ginger's been totally indispensable."

"Well, parties are her thing," Melody said with a snort.

Morgan gasped then laughed. "You are horrible."

With a shrug, Melody said, "I've been having a hard time with her dad, is all. David's been an absolute terror with whom to be bound by contract. Don't tell anyone, but I don't think I'm going to stay with him."

Morgan sat on the end of the bed. "After everything he's done for us since dad died?"

"Trust me, that's the only thing that's kept me from buying out my contract. When I turned 25 and had access to all of my trust fund, I really struggled with it."

"Maybe you should pray about it," Morgan said gently. She knew the crisis of faith that Melody had suffered at the hands of Richard Johnson and her near death experience. She knew that much of Melody's lifestyle no longer reflected the faith that used to be so strong that she once wanted to write praise music for a living. But, for now, she had her sister home, under her roof again. She would gently persuade her for as long as she possibly could.

Melody nodded. "So you say." She zipped the empty suitcase and tossed it into the closet. "Let's round up something to eat," she squeaked out. "Maybe food will help my voice."

She hooked her arm into Morgan's and they started down the stairs. At the bottom of the staircase, Morgan said, "I'll go start on lunch. I have to tell you though, that I have an enormous surprise in store for you. I can't believe I've kept quiet this long. I have something to tell you that is going to completely blow your mind."

Curious, Melody inquired, "What?"

Before she could answer, Morgan's phone rang. She looked at the number. "I have to take this. It's a big client. I'll tell you at lunch." She answered the call as she walked toward the kitchen. "Morgan Hamilton."

Melody started toward the study in search of Kurt, but the sound of the doorbell ringing stopped her. She hesitated before opening it, until she remembered her security team at the gates of the community, so she felt safe opening the door.

♪ ♪ ♪ ♪

JAMES Montgomery had to have possessed a great deal of physical and mental strength to have survived his childhood, succeeded in his adolescence, put himself through college, and to have taken a company and risen it to the ranks he had in such a competitive field.

These thoughts went through his mind as he sat in Melody's car outside of Morgan's house, acknowledging a weakness in him that he neither wanted nor appreciated. He worried about ringing the doorbell, worried about what her reaction to him might be. He worried she might reject him, like some pimply high school boy about to ask the head cheerleader for a date. His fear was that she would reject him entirely and if that happened, he just didn't know what he would do with himself. He worried ... and it made him angry.

With a scowl, he got out of Melody's car and slammed the door. It felt like a very long walk to the front door and, once he rang the bell, the wait felt interminable. Then the doors swung open.

♪ ♪ ♪ ♪

JAMES and Melody stared at each other for hour-long heartbeats as the world stood still around them. James stared at her, remembering her beauty and her cool blue eyes, remembering the feel of her smooth forehead beneath his lips. He remembered watching her on the television the previous night. She looked even more beautiful than she had four years earlier.

Melody stared back at him, feeling transported back in time, back to the feelings she'd felt that day, back to the irresistible attraction. She thought about all of the times she couldn't seem to get him out of her mind. And, here he stood, on her sister's front porch?

"How did you —?"

Misunderstanding the question, James held up her keys. "I brought your car back."

"My car?" Looking past him, she could see the Mercedes parked next to Kurt's car. "I don't understand." Wariness made her take a step back, and worry made her frown when he followed her into the house.

"I picked it up last night."

"How?" Her voice, nearly gone, came out in a half croak, half whisper.

It was James' turn to frown in confusion. "From Morgan."

She sensed Kurt come into the foyer more than heard him. His leather shoes made no sound on the ceramic tile, but her senses were heightened with a flight instinct.

"Hi bro," Kurt greeted.

James nodded back before saying, "I'm getting the feeling that neither you nor Morgan mentioned our discovery last night," James said dryly, nodding in Melody's direction.

Kurt looked from James to pale and wide-eyed Melody and back to James. "I imagine your arrival here this morning driving her car is kind of a shock for her, then."

"What are you talking about?" Melody said, feeling like maybe she'd totally lost her mind.

"Melly, I'd like to introduce you to my business partner and my lifelong friend, James Montgomery. James, my future sister-in-law, Melody Mason."

Melody felt her eyes widen. "You can't be serious. What are the odds of this?"

James gave her a wry smile. "I could tell you, but the number is so great it exceeds Borel and Meyer's definition of mathematical impossibility. The result is imaginary."

She felt like the air had been sucked out of her body. Putting a hand to her chest, she willed her heart to slow down and quit threatening to beat itself out of her chest. A domino effect of feelings assaulted her, closing in on her — remembering that day all those years ago, how happy she was as she drove home, the love song in her head, then the pain of Richard's fist as it plowed into the side of her head.

Unable to breathe, she leaned back against the wall. "Melly?" Kurt said, putting a hand on her shoulder.

At his touch, her head stopped spinning and she quit feeling like she might collapse. "Sorry," she croaked out. "I must be more tired than I thought."

James put his hand on the doorknob. "I think I'll go."

"No," she said, grabbing his hand. "Please don't go."

"You're clearly uncomfortable…"

"I'm not. I'm just shocked, and exhausted, and a little bit on edge. And I just got here from the airport so I'm a bit of a mess which is not how I ever wanted you to see me." She gestured with her free hand toward the door. "I was remembering that day so long ago, and I couldn't help but remember how it ended."

"Melody, I'm so sorry," he said.

She shook her head. Her voice only came out in a whisper now. "I have to overcome that terror every day. When I'm tired, it's harder."

Kurt looked between the two of them. "Why don't you two go get reacquainted? I'll go check my e-mail."

She pulled on James' hand and led him into the living room. She gestured at the couch and sat at the same time he did. James spoke bluntly. "I guess it would probably be easier to recover if he'd been arrested."

Melody shrugged around the burn of tears in her eyes. She forced them back. "Probably," she squeaked.

Morgan came into the room, carrying a coffee mug that had a tea bag string dangling over the side of it. "Tea and honey with lemon. Sister's orders." She paused when she saw James. "Oh. I guess it's a little too late to tell you about our amazing discovery last night."

Melody's lips thinned. "It would have been nice," she said in a whisper, taking the tea from her sister.

"I thought I had time." She walked by the couch and squeezed James' shoulder. "It's nice to see you, James, even though you're early. Are you staying for lunch?"

He shook his head. "I don't think so, but I appreciate the offer."

"You're sure?" With his affirmation, she said, "Okay. I'll go finish up." Morgan left the two of them alone.

Melody ran her finger over the design on the couch. "I am so sorry about us losing contact."

"Or never really having it?"

"We had something." Her eyes met his, and the warmth in them as they stared back at her from behind his glasses made her heart skip a beat.

He smiled and nodded. "We had something." He looked around. "I often wonder what life would have been like if we'd actually had dinner that Thursday night."

"I think about it all the time." She felt her face fuse with color at her admission.

With a smile, he reached for her hand. "Regardless, I'm happy to find you again. Are you too tired to have dinner with me tonight?" James asked, noting the shadows under her eyes.

"I would rather not go anywhere tonight. I don't feel up to being mobbed, and that typically happens."

James raised an eyebrow. "Mobbed, eh?" She felt a little heat in her cheeks. "Perhaps we could eat in."

Melody cocked her head and smiled. "I think that's brilliant. Maybe just get some takeout."

"Why don't you come to my apartment? I'll cook you an early dinner there."

Kurt came into the room, pulling on his suit jacket. "If you need a ride, I have to go. I'm late for a meeting." He pulled car keys out of his pocket. "Melly, welcome home. I'll see you later."

James pulled his phone out of his pocket, checking an incoming text. "I do need a ride to my apartment, thanks." He stood, and Melody followed the men to the front door.

Kurt opened the door and stepped out. "I'll meet you at the car."

"Be right out," James said. He stepped closer to Melody and took her face in his hands, rubbing the shadows under her eyes. "Go take a nap. I'll see you at my place." He broke the contact and opened the door. Before he left, he turned to her and held out a set of keys. She recognized her car keys and took them from him.

"'Til tonight, then." she said. After he left, she shut the door, leaned back against it, and sighed.

Morgan walked into the foyer. "Are you seeing James tonight?" she asked.

"Yes, I am," she said with a squeak. She pushed herself from the door and hugged her sister, giggling. "I can't believe it's him."

Morgan smiled, praying for this connection between her fiancé's best friend and her sister to strengthen and bloom. "I can't wait to hear all about it. I love James so much and am happy for you." She hugged her back and stepped away. "Lunch is ready."

♫ ♫ ♫ ♫

MELODY Mason, as in THE Melody Mason, walked herself right into the building and straight up to the security desk, looking just as pretty as a picture with her purse over one arm, a shopping bag in the other, and her trademark boots clicking on the marble floor the whole way. The security guard manning the desk in James' apartment building already knew his wife would never believe this.

She took off her sunglasses and directed the full force of her smile at him. "Hi. Melody Mason, here to see James Montgomery."

That lucky dog, thought the security guard.

He made a show of glancing through the list of expected guests, but of course he knew exactly where he would find her name on the list. "Of course, Miss Mason. Follow me, please. You need a special key to reach his floor." He guided her to an elevator, and using a key from the big ring of keys attached to his belt, he accessed the proper floor. Then he stepped out of the elevator. "Enjoy your visit, Miss Mason." He wanted desperately to ask for her autograph, but policy wouldn't allow it. Maybe if he was still on duty when she came back down, he'd bend the rules just a little.

As the doors closed, Melody dropped her bright, worn only in public smile and rolled her head on her neck. She continued to stretch her neck muscles while watching the numbers light up as the elevator rose to the top floor. It surprised her to find only one door in the hallway when she stepped off. Before she could knock on it, it swung open, and James stood there, filling the doorway. He'd removed his tie and jacket and rolled his sleeves up, exposing the tanned muscle of his forearms. He flashed her a quick smile as he stepped back and held the door open wider.

She retrieved and held up the bottle of Cabernet she'd carried up in the shopping bag. "I brought wine," she announced as she stepped into his apartment.

James raised an eyebrow. "Melody," with an ironic grin, he shook his head and he said a little uncomfortably, "I don't drink."

She stopped with the bottle halfway extended to him, then quickly pulled it back. "Oh. Okay. I'm sorry."

"No reason to apologize. We did have our first conversation in a bar." She reached into her bag again and he was surprised, and more than a little touched, when she handed him a bouquet of flowers as well.

At his surprised look she said, "I would expect nothing less if I had spent the afternoon preparing a meal for you." With a laugh she added, "Not that you would want me to. I am not Morgan in any sense."

He led her through the apartment. One entire wall was made of glass and looked out at Atlanta. Wall to wall and floor to ceiling bookcases with sliding ladders on either end made up the opposite wall. Near the bookcases, two wing-backed leather chairs crouched near a round table topped with a large chess set. The teak floor was broken only by a large blue rug near the windows. On the rug, two brown leather couches formed a sitting area around a low coffee table. A flat screened television hung above the fireplace. It was an extremely tastefully masculine room. Melody immediately fell in love with it, and if her voice had any strength to it at all, she would have sung a tune to get a sense of the acoustics.

They went through the room into the kitchen. A table that could seat six sat next to a large window. On the table, a beautiful woven ceramic basket held apples, adding a nice homey touch Melody hadn't expected. A large bar separated the dining area from the cooking area, and that's where James headed. A big gas stove sat against the far wall, and on it two pots simmered.

James set the flowers near the sink and started looking through the cupboards for something in which to put the flowers. "You don't cook?" he asked, locating a vase.

"The things I can do to a few helpless ingredients should be labeled a crime. In fact, I think they might be criminal acts in certain regions of France. I am, however, pretty good with a frozen meal and a microwave. I know my way around a coffee maker. And I can order take-out like no one's business." She went over to the sink and rescued the flowers from him.

"I'm surprised. Morgan is a fantastic cook. I guess I always thought your mother taught both of you."

"My mother taught me how to plan an intimate dinner for sixty, and a formal party for three hundred. Her philosophy about cooking, however, was to hire caterers to do it. Morgan is self-taught. It was one of my mother's biggest woes that she couldn't keep her eldest daughter out of the kitchen. After all, that's where the servants belong." She set the arranged flowers on the counter, and pulled up a stool, wishing she had something else to do with her hands. "What about you? You don't strike me as the domestic type."

He lifted the lid on a pot on the stove, sending wonderful aromas — the tang of tomatoes, the heartiness of garlic, a mix of spices — throughout the kitchen. "The house mom at the home where I grew up taught all her boys how to cook."

How had she forgotten that James was an orphan?

He opened both doors on the refrigerator and disappeared behind them, reappearing with an arm full of salad vegetables. He saw the sympathy on her face, and decided to stem it. "I barely remember my parents, Melody. And my group home was a safe place. Don't feel sad."

So much pain for one man, Melody thought sadly, remembering his wife. "I'm just sad for the you that was a little boy."

"That little boy was an awkward little boy who was way too smart and thought too much and went into his own head way too often. But, he had Kurt, who kept bullies off his back and reminded him to sleep when he got too involved in learning something new, so it worked out for him." Wanting to lighten the mood a little, James handed her a tomato and a knife. "Think you can handle slicing this?"

"As long as it doesn't require mixing ingredients or applying heat, I can handle it just fine." She grinned as she set to work on her task.

"Your voice sounds almost normal," he remarked as he lifted the lid on a pot of boiling water.

"Morgan pampered me all afternoon. I have ingested so much honey that I'm surprised I'm not buzzing like a bee."

"When you find some honey, eat just enough ..." he began.

"... for too much can make you sick." They quoted in unison.

He smiled at her recognition of his reference before he concluded, "Proverbs 25:16." Noticing how she handled the knife, he stopped her and said, "Whoa, whoa. Don't cut like that. You'll slice your fingers off."

With a tiny little grin, Melody said, "It's okay. They're insured."

After he let out a little bark of laughter, he took the knife back and said, "Let me show you how."

They worked in companionable silence for a while, James concentrating on cooking, and Melody concentrating on watching him cook. He looked so at ease here, she thought, in the kitchen with the late sun coming through the window. James Montgomery struck her as a man who was sure of himself in whatever situation circumstances placed him.

In no time he dished up plates of pasta and red sauce then warm bread fresh from the oven and salad, and they carried their plates and glasses of sweet iced tea to the table.

"Would you like to bless the meal?" He asked as he set his plate down.

Melody blinked in surprise. "No. You go ahead." She bowed her head on cue and closed her eyes.

"Heavenly Father, thank You for all of Your gifts. Thank You for bringing us back together that we may fellowship together. We ask that You show us Your will tonight. Bless this food and bless our bodies by these, the gifts of Your generous hands. In Jesus' holy name, Amen."

Melody tried to remember the last time she had blessed a meal without the prompting of her friend, Bobby Kent. Maybe last Thanksgiving day? She listened to the simple prayer of thanks before releasing his hand and picking up her fork. Then she sighed in ecstasy at the first bite. "Okay, this tastes amazing," she said.

James smiled at her reaction, surprised to feel so pleased. "I haven't cooked for a woman since Angela died," he said, then stopped abruptly when he realized what he just said. "Sorry. I realize that it is probably bad manners to mention one's late wife while on a date."

She wasn't offended. "I'm glad to hear less pain in your voice now than the last time you mentioned her to me. As hard as it is to admit, time does heal all things." She took a nervous sip of her tea.

He stared at her for a long time. "No," he said, "time doesn't heal everything." Tension suddenly replaced the casual air at the table.

Melody delicately wiped her lips with her napkin. "Can I ask you something?"

"Of course."

"Why have you never tried to contact me, James?"

James sat back and ran his finger down the dew that collected on the outside of his glass. "I did at first and never heard from you. I know why, now. I remember Kurt's coming and going right after we met. But since then, until yesterday, I didn't know your last name and I didn't know how to find you."

Defensive, she crossed her arms. "How would you not know how to find me? I'm everywhere. I was at the White House last month posing for pictures for the entire press corps for goodness sakes."

He ran his fingers through his hair. "I don't know what to tell you, Melody. I don't watch television. I don't listen to the radio. I only read publications that are directly related to my field. And, six to nine months out of the year, I'm on another continent." He raised a hand and shrugged. "It may seem odd to you that I don't know you, but I'm oblivious to pop culture."

She slowly relaxed. "I guess I'm so bombarded by people who feel like they know me, that I just assume everyone does."

James nodded and took a sip of his drink. "Fair enough." The tension had dissipated. "My turn to ask a question. Why do you do what you do?"

She considered the question for a while, wanting to give him a heartfelt answer instead of the blurb on the back of her CDs. "Do you hear music in your head?" she asked.

"You mean as a constant presence?" James asked.

"You know, like a movie soundtrack. There's almost always music in the background of the movie, and unless it picks up tempo or suddenly stops, you are hardly aware that it's even there."

He shook his head in answer to her question, and she continued. "I hear music in my head all the time. Sometimes it's really clear and I have to stop what I'm doing and write it down. Sometimes it's just in the background, and I'm not even aware that it's there."

She leaned back in her chair, comfortably full, content to just sit there for a while. "When I was a little girl, I made the mistake of telling my mother about my music. She panicked and sent me straight to a topnotch therapist. Her advice to my mother was to put me into music lessons and let me work it out of my system. After that, I never mentioned it to her again, knowing she would never understand me, glad that I got the music lessons out of it."

She leaned forward again, passion for her career evident in her face. "I write songs, and people laugh at them, or cry at them, or dance to them. I sing the songs I write, knowing that I am putting the right emotion with the right song, not really trusting someone else to do it exactly as I envisioned. And I do the videos, translating my songs into visible stories, helping some people understand it who otherwise wouldn't."

"I think I'd like to see your videos." James mused.

"A lot of artists have sold out. They do product placements and stuff so their video is about soft drinks or a line of clothing instead of about the story the song is actually trying to tell. Mine are true to the song. I think that's partly why I became so popular so fast. That kind of integrity was refreshing."

She sat back again. "I am glad every day that my rug was ripped out from under me four years ago. If that hadn't happened, I would probably have ended up frustrated and unfulfilled, with a cheating abusive husband and very few friends. My music might have just faded away."

"No more thoughts of seminary?"

Melody felt a puzzled frown mar her face. "Seminary?" Then she remembered. "Oh yeah! I'd forgotten about that." She waved a dismissive hand. "I never thought I'd love the limelight, but I find that it's kind of addicting."

That remark intrigued James. "I would love to watch you perform live sometime, too. I watched you last night for the first time, and even through the television I was swept into the song."

"The first of the year, we kick off my tour right here in Atlanta, so you should come to the concert. I've been told that it's almost sold out, but I'm sure that I could finagle some tickets for you." Melody stood up to carry her plate to the sink.

"I'll count on it." He got up, went to the refrigerator, and pulled out a cheesecake. As he sliced it, the telephone rang. He'd told his answering service not to put any calls through unless there was a verified emergency, so he knew he had to answer it. He gave Melody an apologetic look. "Excuse me a moment," he said, and picked up the extension in the kitchen.

Melody spotted the coffee maker in the corner of the counter, and decided to make some coffee to go with the cheesecake. As she looked for coffee, filters and the like for the machine, she couldn't help overhearing the conversation. She felt a chill at the tone in his voice.

"Rebecca, slow down and tell me one more time." She watched a muscle begin to tick in his jaw. "Who called you?"

He ripped the glasses off his face. "Do you know any details?" he asked as he rubbed his eyes then put his glasses back on. "All right. Call Redman and have him meet me down there. Have him pull all the security video first, before he does anything else. I'll start driving now. Try to find Kurt, if that's possible. I know he and Morgan had plans tonight."

He hung up the phone without giving time for a response. When he looked at Melody, he appeared almost surprised to see her still there in the room.

"Someone broke into one of my facilities. I have to drive down to Albany." He put the cheesecake back into the refrigerator. Gesturing to the kitchen door, he walked through the kitchen and into the living room. Melody followed him. "I'm afraid we'll have to postpone the rest of our evening for another time. Excuse me a moment." He disappeared down a hallway.

Worried, Melody gathered her purse and keys. James returned and laid a suit jacket on the back of one of the couches before he began putting on a tie. "I am incredibly busy this week. I've been gone for six months and once I get down to Albany, I'll probably stay for a couple of days. But, I would love to see you again. Soon." He finished knotting the tie then picked up the jacket. "Do you think we could maybe have a late lunch or dinner Wednesday?"

The transformation amazed her. He was no longer the personable soul who had tossed pasta and salad. Everything about him screamed business right now. Serious, concentrated business. She shook her head and tried to focus on his question, mentally reviewing her own itinerary. "Yes, Wednesday's fine. The weekend will be full of wedding stuff, but as far as I know, until the rehearsal dinner Friday night, I'm free in the evenings."

James helped her into her coat, grabbed an overcoat off the stand next to the door for himself, and then held the door open for her. "Good. If for some reason I don't make it back in time, I'll call you. What's your number now?"

Remembering what he said about his memory, Melody rattled off her number as they stepped into the waiting elevator. "Okay. I'll call you soon."

The elevator reached the ground floor. As he steered her out of the building, he asked, "Where did you park?"

She pointed the way and he walked her to her car. It was still light outside, the world turning red and orange from the setting sun.

Melody felt a pang of regret at the interruption to their evening, and when she turned from unlocking her car, James surprised her by framing her face with both hands and giving her the lightest of kisses. She stared straight into his eyes and she felt herself drowning. She thought maybe she could stand there all night and just stare up at him. But, the rest of the world waited. He kissed her one more time, then stepped back. "I'll see you in a couple of days," he said, then turned and walked away.

♪ ♪ ♪ ♪

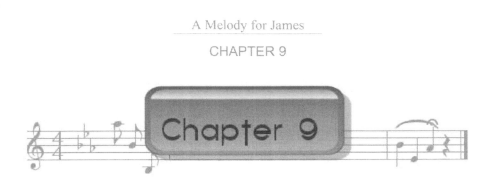

"THE smoke from the filing cabinets set off the alarms. Whoever set the fires made sure they were contained to just the cabinets, so it took a long time for the smoke to sound the alarms," Mike Redman said as he and James surveyed the damage to the lab. "The video from the surveillance is gone — wiped from the main discs, and so far, the police haven't found even one fingerprint."

James had barely said a word since he walked into the building. Normally, he enjoyed the Albany site. Because it was remote, it could be made "posh" for his engineering teams. He had installed video games, Ping-Pong tables, and putting greens in the break rooms, for example. Whenever he could spend a weekend here, there was a popular church not far from this facility that he immensely enjoyed attending as well.

Someone had messed with his perfect little facility. The lab was completely destroyed, along with all of the prototypes stored there. The police officers who had responded to the call asked him several questions before they conferred with Mike for a while. Kurt came in about half an hour after James arrived, and the two of them tried to take inventory of all that had been destroyed. Company policy required that electronic copies of everything be made at the end of the workday, and the electronic files were stored in another part of the building. A quick check confirmed that everything there was intact giving them the opportunity to cross-check the information, but the rage remained. He struggled desperately against the violence sweeping through him, and only the constant prayer in his head helped him hold onto self-control with a thin thread.

"Why was no one working? It's still relatively early. Someone should have been here when this happened," James said to Kurt. They walked to the secure section of the lab. James swiped his badge and keyed in a security code.

"Electronics R & D had that seminar they all went to up in Atlanta that started yesterday so no one was here in this department." He knew the electronic security could detect two people and would not unlock the door until Kurt also swiped his badge and keyed in his code. As soon as he hit the last button, the doors unlocked.

"Lights, full." The lights in the outer office came on. James walked to the keypad next to the far door and punched in the number to unlock the door to the interior office. Here is where Angela's work continued.

"We should have the police check in here, just in case," Kurt said.

James shrugged. "As long as Redman keeps an eye on them, that's fine."

In no time, police officers arrived with their crime scene kits and began processing that room, too. With everything being handled and checked, no one noticed the female officer who took covers off of three power outlets and installed tiny but powerful listening devices in three different areas in the room. The devices would work so long as no one tampered with the power.

Several hours later, James, Kurt, and Mike all sat in James' office, weary from the evening. The three men were discussing the obvious flaw in the security.

"Mike, the point to all of this is that we need to figure out how someone was able to get into the building to do this, alter video surveillance, and manage to do it at six o'clock on a workday" Kurt said.

"I'll start an investigation into it in the morning. It happened so early that someone had to see something out of the ordinary. Whoever did this knew what he was doing. I'd guess it all points toward an employee." Mike busily typed in notes about the events into his laptop. He'd review everything several more times tonight, he knew, to make sure that he didn't miss anything.

"Get ahold of me tomorrow night, and let me know if you're able to come up with anything." James looked at his watch. His body burned with exhaustion from the lack of sleep. "Mike, I have a feeling the destruction was a way to mask something else. That lab needs to be gone through with all of the engineers to discover what, if anything, happened. I don't believe this was mere vandalism."

"I'll get with everyone here first thing in the morning," Mike said, correctly interpreting that he was being dismissed.

James took his glasses off and rubbed his face. "I hadn't planned on coming here until Monday morning."

"You going to head back to Atlanta?"

"I don't think so. If I start working now, I'll feel good leaving Wednesday. I still get the feeling that something else happened here tonight." He leaned his head back and closed his eyes. So tired.

"Why don't I drive you to the hotel? You can get some sleep and get a fresh start first thing in the morning." Kurt stood and pulled his car keys out of his pocket.

James sat up and retrieved his glasses. "You ever get tired of mothering me, Kurt?"

"Not if it means that genius brain keeps churning. I'm looking at a comfortable retirement in my future." He opened the office door. "Let's go. I know if I leave you here, you won't sleep."

As he stood, James buttoned his suit jacket. "Can you arrange for some clothes and toiletries to be delivered in the morning?"

"Of course. I'm sure Rebecca will love to have something to do. Would she even know what to do with her time if she weren't hassled on a Saturday?"

They left the building, confirming that all of the locks were secure and the security enabled. "She's used to it and gets paid pretty well for it."

♩ ♩ ♩ ♩

MELODY let herself into Morgan's house, feeling loose and limber after a relaxing jog. She loved Nashville, but nothing beat her little secure neighborhood in her corner of her daddy's city.

She lifted her arms and stretched, unzipping the sweatshirt she wore, and thought about how much this house felt like "home" more than her big ranch outside of Nashville. She smiled and made her way to the kitchen to drink the water she'd left out and get some coffee started.

Morgan sat at the table composing a text message. She wore a sweatshirt with her college emblem on the front and a pair of shorts. "Ah. You beat me to it. I was about to go out and run a couple miles myself."

"Wish I'd known. We could have gone together." Melody grabbed her water bottle and twisted off the cap.

"My short legs have never been a match for yours in distance running. I have to take two strides for every one of yours."

"Maybe, but you could get twice the workout."

"Har har."

Melody took a big drink and eyed her sister while she swallowed. Deciding to plunge forward, she said, "Tell me what you know about James."

Morgan raised an eyebrow. "Like what?"

With a shrug, Melody pulled out a chair and sat down. "That man has been through so much in his life. He's incredibly intense. I get the feeling that I'm battling demons that I don't even know about."

"You don't even know half of it. It's amazing that men with James and Kurt's background have become as successful as they have." She stared at Melody. "Is this going to go anywhere?"

"Don't know? I've probably spent twelve hours total with him in my life."

"Yeah, but how were those twelve hours?" Morgan teased. "I knew I wanted to be with Kurt before I ever even spoke to him."

"Maybe, but it took him years to get you to trust him enough to marry him." Morgan nodded sadly and Melody put her elbow on the table and propped her chin in her hand. "I met him in the airport coming back from London and we spent the whole day together. I didn't want to go home. I wanted that day to just go on and on. After Richard —" She stopped, remembering the pain of the beating, the time in the hospital, the therapy, the recovery, the lingering fear. Her hands turned cold and she shuddered. "My phone was destroyed by Richard. By the time I got out of the hospital and got my new phone, it was too late. James had quit trying, and I didn't have his number or even his last name."

She pushed away from the table and walked to the counter, opening the bread box and pulling out a loaf of bread. "I've never been able to get him off of my mind. If I'd have known his name, I would have found him."

"It's crazy how he's been in my life this entire time." Morgan shook her head when Melody held up a slice of bread, silently asking if she wanted some. "Every time you've been home in the last four years, James has been in London. Your paths just never crossed." She stood and pulled a hair band out of her pocket. "God's timing must not've been right with it."

Melody felt her mouth twitch. "What makes you so sure God has anything to do with this?"

Morgan studied her sister. "What makes you think He doesn't?"

Melody decided the question deserved honesty. "The truth is I haven't considered God in a long time."

With a nod, Morgan said, "I can tell. Why don't you think on that for a while and see where your thoughts lead you?"

"Maybe." Melody waited for her toast while Morgan pulled her hair up and prepped herself for her run. As soon as the toast popped up, she spread butter on her toast, but did not sit back at the table. Instead, she grabbed her water and started out of the room.

"It seems to me that if God wanted me to be happy, He could have made our paths cross sometime in the last four years," Melody opined.

Morgan said, "Well, I guess I'm glad if that means you're happy now. You deserve it. But your argument doesn't hold water."

"Meaning what?"

"Meaning God doesn't promise we'll be happy in this life. In fact, Jesus promised that believers would have troubles. That's kind of the opposite of happy. But we take our joy in our salvation."

Melody took a big swallow of her water and said, "Wow, Tammy Faye. Thanks for the sermon."

Morgan smiled sweetly. "Don't be snotty, baby sister."

Melody glanced at her watch. "I have to meet my choreographer at Ginger's dance studio in an hour. I think I'll go up and get ready."

"I thought you were on vacation."

"I am. But I'm also on tour in four weeks. I have to get in shape, work with the dance routines."

"You told me you were going to take the next three weeks off completely." Morgan pointed a finger at her. "You can't keep up the pace you've been keeping. You'll end up collapsing."

Melody walked over to her sister and hugged her. "Morgan, I'm going to work out for a couple of hours a few times a week. That won't cause me to collapse. In fact, it will probably be really good for me." As she left, she paused at the kitchen door, toast in one hand, water in the other. "Are we still planning on trimming the tree tonight?"

"We have to. I have a magazine coming Monday morning to photograph it." Morgan said, raising her arms and stretching her lower back.

"Okay. I'm really looking forward to it."

"Me, too, Melly. Hey," Morgan caught her. "Say hi to Ginger for me. Tell her I'm looking forward to seeing her Friday."

Melody winked at her as she shoved the kitchen door open with her shoulder.

♬ ♬ ♬ ♬

Chapter 10

"**MELLY**, pick up your feet. We aren't doing a 'shuffle'. Good … good. Now, turn, two three four. Kick." Melody finished the dance routine, every muscle in her body screaming. "Okay, Melody. Take five." She collapsed against the wall, too tired to open the water bottle sitting next to her. She managed to raise her head long enough to see Ginger bounce over wearing a hot pink body suit.

"Turn off the suit, Ginger." Melody teased as she let her head fall back to the floor and threw her arm over her head to shield her eyes. "Where in the world did you find that color?"

"Aw, don't be that way, Melly. I've seen you wear boots this color. Except they had sequins on them. Real flashy." She sat down next to Melody and opened the water for her. "You're pretty good you know."

"I'm a musician, not a dancer anymore," At Julliard, she discovered that her passion wasn't truly dancing. But she knew she had to dance to put on a good show. She pushed herself to a sitting position and took the water. "How do you do this for a living?"

"You should know. You're the one who went to Julliard."

"Yeah, but my love is not this. My love is the black and white notes on the page."

Ginger shrugged, "My mother was a professional dancer before she met my dad. I guess it's in my blood."

Melody's choreographer, Clarissa, stepped back into the room. She stood taller than Melody by a good three or four inches, with light brown skin and a face so beautiful that she often stopped conversations when she entered a room. A broken ankle ended a very successful dancing career on Broadway. Now she was one of the most sought after choreographers in the business. "Break's over. Let's get another hour in before we finish the day." She walked over to the sound system and started one of Melody's songs.

Melody groaned and rolled to her feet, prepared for more torture. Clarissa paused the song and gave Melody time to find her mark and get herself into position.

For now she worked out alone. After Christmas, the background dancers would work with her. Because they had more complicated steps to perform, it wasn't necessary for Melody to practice with them every day, just the week before the tour began to make sure they were all in sync and to give Clarissa a chance to work out any kinks in the routine.

When her body could take no more, Clarissa decided to call it a day. Melody collapsed again, laying down on the floor and breathing heavily. Clarissa sat down next to her, a notebook in her hands. "We need to sit down and go over three more of the songs."

She wearily sat up and grabbed the towel that Ginger threw her. "Let's get together for lunch tomorrow, Clarissa. We can talk about them then. I still hate you right now, so give me a few hours."

Clarissa tapped her pen against her lip. "Okay, Melly. That sounds like a good idea." She cleared her throat and tried her very best to keep her voice even and nonchalant. "How's Hal these days?"

With a knowing smile, Melody said, "Hal's just fine, Clarissa." She ran her towel over her face. "He's totally blind, of course, and I guess a little stupid about certain things, but other than that he's fine."

"It's so frustrating. It's like he doesn't even know I'm here."

"There has to be a way to make him see you." She pushed herself up onto all fours, trying to find the energy to stand so she could get to the showers. "He'll be here after Christmas for the full week. Maybe I can throw a dinner party or something."

"I would love that." With a grunt, Melody made it to her feet and limped from the room. Clarissa called after her, "You look good, Melly. Your audiences will be impressed with the show."

She waved behind her as she walked away, too tired to speak. In the dressing room, she stripped on her way to the shower, and stood under as-hot-as-she-could-stand water for as long as she could take it. Feeling moderately better, she pulled on her clothes, opting for the same outfit she'd worn that morning, draining a bottle of water while she dressed.

Her driver and security guard, Peter Glasser, waited for her outside. He drove them back to Morgan's house. Melody knew Morgan had an appointment with a client and would not be home, so she decided to take a nap to make up for such an early morning.

After sleeping for an hour, she woke up sore, but refreshed. The house was still quiet, so she went down to the kitchen and diced some fresh strawberries and pineapple for a smoothie. She added some yogurt and ice to the blender and turned it on. When she turned it off, she heard a noise at the back door.

Her hands went cold, and she felt sweat break out on her upper lip. She put a hand to her chest to try to still the sudden furious pounding of her heart. Noises sounded amplified and her ears started roaring with fear. Feeling like her vision was closing in on her, she picked up the large chef's knife lying by her cutting board and slowly walked to the door, nausea swirling in her stomach.

Reaching for the door handle, she saw her hands trembling. She ripped the door open and jumped back at the same time, screaming out loud when she saw a raccoon digging through Morgan's recycle box. At her scream, the raccoon paused, looked up at her, then rambled away.

As tears burned her eyes, she pulled her phone out of her pocket. Sweaty fingers had her push very hard as the touch screen barely responded to her swipes. She managed to look through her address book and find the number she needed.

Despite four years' time passing, she recognized his voice when he answered. "Detective Roberts?"

"Yeah, speaking."

"This is Melody Mason. Do you remember me?"

Without hesitation, he replied. "Yes, ma'am."

Overwhelmed with being afraid all the time, she sat down at the chair at the table. "I need help," she whispered.

♫ ♫ ♫ ♫

MELODY saw the car pull up, so she didn't hesitate to answer the door. "Detective Suarez. Detective Roberts. What a pleasure to see you again." She grasped each man's hand warmly and sincerely.

Roberts' face turned a light pink, uncomfortable with her attention. "Miss Mason. I wish we were here under different circumstances."

"I know. Me, too." She led the way to the study and gestured to have them sit on the couch across from the wing-backed chair she claimed.

Suarez pulled a notebook and pen out of his jacket. "Why don't you tell us what's been happening."

Melody told them about the roses with the notes, trying to give as much detail as she could. Then she added, "I wish I had kept the notes when I received them. In the beginning, I thought they were just pranks, and lately I just throw them out to get them away from me. I know that isn't much help to you, but if I get anymore, I'll make sure I keep them."

"If you get another rose, you need to make sure that you touch as little of it as possible, and if you can, put it in an envelope or a paper bag. Don't put it in a plastic bag. The humidity you lock in with the paper destroys any shot we have at getting a clean set of prints," Roberts instructed. Then he continued more quietly, "This has been going on for a year. What made you call us today?"

She sat back and crossed her arms. "One thing that has kept me from contacting the police before is the publicity," Melody said. "You can imagine the fodder this would be for the tabloid rags."

"You don't have to worry about either one of us letting this information out, and I think we can convince our Captain to let as little people in on this as possible," Suarez said. "I would worry that if the press started reporting this, we would start getting copycats, which would muddy up our investigation. But that's not it, is it? Something happen today?"

Melody had fully recovered from her scare, or so she thought. She felt pinpricks of fear moving up her neck. "I'm afraid all the time," she whispered. "Whenever I forget, whenever I think I have it beat, he leaves me a rose. Receiving one at my video shoot the day of the awards show, it totally threw me off my trip here."

Suarez inclined his head toward the front of the house. "Your security is tight. I don't think you need to worry about your sister's home here."

Melody nodded and tried not to burst into helpless tears. "Yes. My team is top notch. I don't travel without them."

Suarez spoke again, "Do you think Richard Johnson is leaving you these roses? That why you're afraid?"

"What?" The idea spoken aloud made her head spin with panic. Somewhere in the back of her mind, she'd feared that, but she'd never faced the idea. Could he be? "How?"

"That's the question." Suarez stood and Melody walked them to the front door. Suarez paused with his hand on the door. "We haven't quit trying to locate Richard Johnson."

Melody took his hand and kissed his cheek. "Thank you, for everything in the past and for now. I appreciate you two working so hard for me."

After they walked out and Melody shut the door behind them, she rubbed her arms with her hands, trying to ward off the chill that had settled around her. She hugged her arms to herself and slid down the door. She wrapped her arms around her legs and buried her face in her knees, trying to contain the terror that settled around her like a cloak.

♫ ♫ ♫ ♫

"**MOVE** it over about one more foot." Morgan directed before once again hearing the sound of male grunting under muscle strain behind the giant Douglas fir. Morgan stood back, her hand rubbing her chin. "Actually, I think it might look better back where it was. What do you think, Melody?"

Melody sprawled across the couch in Morgan's front room, amusement dancing in her eyes. "I think if you make Kurt move that tree one more time there might not be a wedding next week."

A voice came from behind the tree. "Listen to your sister, Morg."

Morgan sat down next to Melody. "Actually, looking at it from this angle, I think it's perfect where it is. Thanks, honey."

Kurt came out from behind the 14-foot tree. "Where did you get that tree, honey?"

Morgan snorted, "Are you kidding? I'm an interior designer. I have all sorts of sources."

"Well, as heavy as that tree is, I thought you might have gotten it from the petrified forest."

Morgan decided to press her luck one more time. "Now, if you can go up to the attic and bring down all of the boxes marked 'Christmas Tree', us girls will get this tree decorated."

It took six trips for Kurt to bring down all of the boxes. When he set the last one down, he said, "Before you put me to anymore work, I'm leaving." He kissed Morgan. "I'll see you tomorrow."

Morgan walked to the first box and opened it. "I think I scared him off." She laughed as she pulled out a string of lights.

Christmas carols played in the background and a fire burned invitingly in the fireplace. Morgan and Melody worked side-by-side, conversations coming and going, until late into the night. Morgan viewed the tree as a painter would view a canvas, and created art from nature. Melody let

Morgan do what she did best, and simply followed directions, offering little decorative input.

Hours later, the two women stood back and viewed the tree, a beautiful creation of festivity. "I think you need to call *The Journal* again this year and have them feature your tree," Melody said.

"They'll be here Monday afternoon, after the magazine folks leave." Morgan draped her arm over her sister's shoulders. "For the last two years that I've been featured, the response for my business has been amazing."

"You deserve it." The clock in the hall sounded the hour, stopping after one chime. "Let's go to bed. We can do the rest of the house tomorrow."

♫ ♫ ♫ ♫

MELODY spent the next few days working with Clarissa on her dance steps and helping Morgan decorate the house. She claimed exhaustion to avoid going to church with Morgan Sunday morning. Sunday and Monday dragged on and on and she found it hard to sleep at night. She tried to tell herself it was because she was used to a much more demanding schedule, but she caught herself counting the days until Wednesday more than once. James called once while she was out, but she didn't hear from him again.

Tuesday brought a cold rain. Melody felt clumsy, restless, and didn't feel like working out. Despite Clarissa's objections, she called a halt to the workout an hour early.

After she showered, she stepped out of the studio. Peter held an umbrella above Melody's head. She got in the car and wiped the rain from her face. She looked over as Peter's door opened, then noticed the rose lying on the front seat. It was a red one. She reached over the seat back and snatched it out of the way before he sat down, holding it by the end of the stem. Her hand shook so badly that she almost dropped it.

"Drive to the police station, please," she whispered.

"Ma'am?" Peter looked at her face, then his eyes moved down to her hand holding the rose. As one of her security agents, he had been briefed as to what was going on. Without another word, he started the car and drove the few blocks to the police station watching carefully for signs of someone following them, of danger. They sat outside while he called Rogers from his cell phone. He quickly explained why they were there. "I don't want to bring her in. Someone might recognize her, then there'll be no way we can keep this contained." He waited while Rogers responded, then hung up the phone. "Rogers will be out here momentarily," he said, checking the mirrors and windows.

A tap on the front passenger window startled Melody, but Peter was already unlocking the door. Suarez slid into the front seat. Seconds later,

Rogers entered and sat next to Melody. He held his gloved hand out for the rose and Melody handed it to him, thankful to no longer have to touch it. He read the note, and passed it over to Suarez. "Did you read the note?" he asked Melody.

"No. I don't know if I want to know what it says."

"You need to. It says, 'Now the fun begins.' Do you have any idea what this means?"

"No. No I don't. That's new. The rose is a different color, too."

"What it means is that you need to stay as contained as possible for the time being, Miss Mason," Suarez said as he put the flower and accompanying note into a large evidence bag.

"That isn't completely possible, Detective. My sister's wedding is in less than a week. And that is nothing compared to the exposure I'll receive after the first of the year. I go on tour then."

"You run the risk of something happening if you don't."

"This has been going on for over a year. Why do I need to be cautious now?" She knew she risked sounding like a spoiled brat, but most of her didn't care.

Suarez answered in a very serious voice. "Because he's changed the pattern. For a year he's sent the exact same message. The exact same color of rose. Now we have a different note and a different flower. It means he's decompensating. It tells us he's going to do something that might put you in jeopardy."

"I can contain myself while I'm here, but once the tour starts, I won't be able to."

"Mr. Glasser, what type of security is involved for a tour?" Roberts asked.

Peter thought for a moment. "There's good security, but we'll make arrangements to really beef it up."

"Good." Both men opened their doors simultaneously. "We'll call you if there is anything useable on this one, Miss Mason. You were smart not to touch much of it."

"Thank you."

Peter drove Melody back to the house, each quiet and locked in their own thoughts.

♫ ♫ ♫ ♫

MORGAN had an appointment for the final fitting of her dress, along with those in her bridal party. The seamstress met everyone at Morgan's house. They made a party of it. By early that evening, the house had filled with women, all laughing, trying on dresses, and generally celebrating Morgan's upcoming big day. Melody wanted to have fun, but the rose that day had deflated her joy. She couldn't coax herself into a party mood so she made her excuses early and went upstairs.

She tossed and turned for a while, eventually falling into a restless sleep. She dreamt of faceless men chasing her through a rose garden, and woke up soaked in sweat and breathing heavily. She turned on the lamp beside her bed, trying to chase the demons away, then shakily got up and went to the bathroom. She splashed her face with cool water and drank a big glass of it. The eyes in the mirror still showed a bit of panic and she didn't want to try to go back to sleep.

She threw on some comfortable clothes and went downstairs in the quiet house. The living room showed the remnants of last night's party, with cups and plates everywhere. She rolled up her sleeves, and in no time had the house put back in order. She left the gleaming kitchen behind her with the dishwasher quietly humming.

In the study, she turned on the television and surfed channels, but nothing was on at that time of morning. She settled on the country music video channel, and watched the new video by her good friend and country music heartthrob Bobby Kent. The tabloids had been trying to put her and Bobby together for over two years now, and the two of them had shared several laughs over some of the headlines.

Restless, she went back into the living room and turned on the lights to the tree. She sat there for a while, watching the colors twinkle on and off, feeling lonely and edgy. Finally, she went into the kitchen to make a pot of coffee, for no other reason than to give herself something to do. She passed the hall clock and saw that it was four o'clock. She would have to wait at least another hour or two before her sister got up.

As she sat down at the table to wait for the coffee to perk, she pulled out her cell phone and scrolled through the numbers, finding the missed call from James.

Because she hadn't heard from James for a couple of days, she felt very nervous about texting him. But, she did it anyway.

> **Hi. Restless, awake. Thinking of you. Looking forward to dinner tonight.**

She nearly jumped out of her skin when the phone in her hand rang about ten seconds after she sent the text. "Hello?" She said.

"Hello, Melody."

Strange how her heart rate accelerated with the sound of James' voice. "Hi. I hope my text didn't wake you."

"I should warn you about something," he said.

Curious, she said, "Oh?"

He cleared his throat. "When I work, I … work. I honestly don't even know what day it is right now."

That made her smile. "I get the same way on tour."

"Don't we make a pair then?"

"I sure hope so." She licked her lips, surprised she'd said that out loud. "It's Wednesday, by the way."

"I got that from the text."

"Are you still in Albany?"

"Yes, but I'll head back this morning." She heard him yawn. "I can't remember when I slept last. I may need to do that, actually, before I drive back."

Melody rubbed her lip with the back of her thumb nail. "I'm glad you're just a workaholic and not avoiding me."

After a long, audible pause, James said, "I am not avoiding you. I'm actually really looking forward to dinner." She heard some rustling. "Is it seriously four?"

"Yes."

"Okay. I'm going to close up and get some sleep, then drive up. I'll see you later. Thank you for texting me, Melody."

Melody grinned. "Thank you for calling me, James."

♫ ♫ ♫ ♫

Chapter 12

"THERE you are. I just got back from Nashville," Hal said when Melody came downstairs several hours later. "Did you see the news reports this morning, Mel?" She'd gone back to bed and had risen after noon.

"No, why?" She headed into the kitchen, straight for the coffee.

"We released *My Love Song* Friday." That was the title of the album, with the single of the same name that Melody sang at the awards show. "It went platinum before noon on Saturday. It went double platinum before 8 Saturday night — record breaking sales of the CDs — the digital downloads of the singles are crashing servers all over the world."

She set the coffee pot down and stared at him with her mouth open. Unable to contain himself any longer, he picked Melody up and whirled her around. "You sold out the stores, Mel. There's now a huge demand for them to restock for Christmas."

Melody laughed and hugged Hal. "How is that possible?"

"You're just that good, girl."

She wanted to call James and tell him. How did he become so important so quickly? "James will be thrilled," she said out loud.

"James?"

Melody laughed. "Remember my speech at the awards show?"

"Of course. You left the gossip rags tittering about who your mystery man could be."

"In the strangest of coincidences, he happens to be Kurt's business partner."

Hal's face marred in a confused frown. "Run that by me again."

She told him about meeting James and losing touch with him. "We're supposed to have dinner tonight," she said.

Hal lifted her chin and examined her face. "I like this glow you got, girl."

Melody laughed. "I like the way I feel inside. I can't believe Melody Mason is all jittery about a dinner date."

She left Hal to handle publicity calls about the record breaking sales and went in search of her sister, wanting to spread the good news. She found her in her bedroom, staring at the dress hanging on the back of the closet door. "Hey, sis." Morgan looked pretty melancholy. "Everything okay?"

Morgan shrugged and a tear slipped down one cheek.

"Oh honey, what's wrong?" Melody said as she sat down on the bed and put her arms around her.

Morgan started crying. "I miss dad," she said. She sniffed and wiped her eyes with a handkerchief. "I know I'm being silly. I'm thirty-two years old, about to get married for the second time, and I'm crying because my Daddy isn't here."

"That isn't silly. Every time I reach some pinnacle in my career, I wish Daddy were here, too."

Their father had been a wonderful man who had showered his two girls with love. Their mother had been a cold, demanding woman, more concerned with her social status than with the children she'd conceived. "I'm sure Daddy will be there. He just won't be able to walk you down the aisle."

"I know. David Patterson will have to do." She sniffed again, and asked, "So, did you come in here for a specific reason, or were you looking to have a good cry?"

Melody lay back on the bed next to her sister and said, "Oh, it's nothing. Just that my album just flew off the shelves at the stores so quickly that they all sold out. It went double platinum in less than 24 hours. There's like this big demand now for the record company to get more out before Christmas."

Morgan flew up. "Oh Melly, that's wonderful! We need to celebrate!"

Melody sat up, too. "That's what Hal said."

Morgan was already walking out of the room. "We'll have a big celebratory lunch. I'll run out and get some pastries from that café on the corner, and we'll make big fat omelets to go with them. We'll put on a few pounds, but who cares?"

"Um, will your wedding dress care?" Melody teased.

"Oh, shoot." Morgan reconsidered. "Okay, let's skip the pastries and do fruit instead."

An hour later, the three sat back in their chairs. Morgan asked Hal, "So what happens now? Will the record company be able to get more CDs out?"

Hal drained his orange juice, and answered, "Sure. They don't send their entire production in one load. There's more en-route to the stores now. But, now that it's hit the news, it has become the next must have consumer item. When people think there's a shortage, and they think there's a huge demand, the demand becomes even greater. We'll probably have a hard time keeping up with the demand."

"Just think, Melly, just over four years ago you didn't even have plans to be a star, now look at you."

"I know. Sometimes the press gives me a hard time about it. In the music industry, the longer you struggle, the better a success you are. I just recorded an album one day with the help of my rich daddy's friend, and all of a sudden, I had a record contract and a hit song. A lot of people don't like me for it, accusing me of buying my success."

"Well, Miss Rich Superstar, roll up your sleeves and do the dishes. I cooked."

Melody leaned back and batted her eyes, exaggerating a southern belle's accent, "Excuse me, Miz Hamilton, but I'm afraid that you must not be aware of my social status."

"Yeah, I'm fully aware of your status. You're six years younger than me, so get to work."

Hal brought in one of Melody's new compact disks and loaded the stereo in the kitchen before turning the volume up loud. The two of them cleaned the kitchen while Morgan went to her office to prepare her business for her absence during her honeymoon.

From her office, Morgan heard the doorbell ring and figured that the two in the kitchen couldn't hear it, so she got up to answer it. To her never ending joy, James stood there looking tired and worn out. "Hi," she greeted.

"Hi Morgan." She stood back and let him in, taking his coat from him. "You wouldn't happen to have any coffee made, would you?"

"You came all the way from Albany, across town from your office, to see if I have any coffee? How many coffee shops must you have passed along the way I wonder?"

When James looked sheepish and answered her with a shrug, she said, "I think what you're looking for is in the kitchen." She left him in the foyer and went back to her office, feeling a silly grin cover her face.

James smiled and made his way to the back of the house. The song he thought he heard when he stepped into the house got louder, and when he pushed open the kitchen door, he stopped short. Melody and the man he recognized from all of the press he'd read about Melody as her manager Hal two-stepped around the kitchen. He twirled her around as if she were a rag doll, performing the complicated footwork with grace that a man his size shouldn't have, and Melody kept up with him just fine. James leaned against the door frame, and watched the odd couple. He recognized Melody's voice singing the song, but had never heard the song before.

Melody saw him and grinned. "James!" she said with a huge grin.

Hal looked over at him and executed a turn and twist that swung Melody in his direction. James automatically caught her. At her look of surprise, he felt his heart leap. He felt his unshaven cheeks stretch into a slow smile. She felt amazing in his arms.

Melody tossed her head back and laughed in pure joy. Suddenly, he found himself moving with her, letting her lead him in a dance that resembled a two-step but had a few extra steps thrown in for some reason. Melody had to raise her voice to a near yell to be heard over the blaring music. "They invented this dance for just this song. It's all the rage in the clubs for the past few months now. I do something like this kind of footwork on stage. I'm thinking this song is going to be my encore next year."

They didn't notice Hal leave the kitchen. When the song ended, *My Love Song* filled the room, and they changed the pace of their dance, eventually just swaying there, looking into each other's eyes. James slowly lowered his head, keeping his lips just a whisper above hers. She moved her hand up to the back of his head, applying pressure there, trying to close the distance. Finally, he couldn't take it anymore, and with a groan he crushed her to him, devouring her mouth with his. The song soared around them, enveloping James in a world where nothing existed but Melody's voice and her lips.

The song was the last one on the CD, and when it was over, they slowly ended the kiss. James framed her face with his hands and raised his head to look in her eyes, pleased with the dazed look on her face. He kissed the tip of her nose, and stepped away from her. "Do you have any coffee made?"

"What?" She had to grip the back of a chair to steady herself.

"Coffee?"

"Oh, yes, of course," she said as she ran her hands through her hair, and tried to get a handle on the emotions swirling through her head.

She poured James a cup of coffee as he sat down at the table, and decided to pour herself one, too. He waited until she sat down. "Kurt told me about your roses." He sat back in his chair and calmly met her gaze. To someone not staring into his eyes, he would have appeared completely relaxed. But Melody could see the intensity shining at her through his glasses.

"Did he? Should he have?" Melody pushed her cup away.

James took a sip of his coffee. "I think he should have. I think he is about to leave on his honeymoon and he's worried about you. And I think he knows I care about you."

She tried to wrap her mind around how comfortable she felt with him, how she felt like she'd known him her whole life. His words, despite the short amount of time they'd spent together, made sense and she accepted them. "Okay. That's understandable."

"He told me about the most recent rose you received. He said that the police haven't been able to get anything useable off of it."

"I didn't really expect them to," she said. She began to draw designs on the table with her finger.

"He told me that Detective Roberts volunteered to talk with your security people to step up security for your tour."

"I wish it wasn't necessary." Her cell phone buzzed at her elbow. She had received hundreds of messages of congratulations that morning. "But since there are so many people on tour, more than half of whom I don't know when you add the crew of the opening act, it's probably best if there were people all around me, watching out for me." She scrolled through a text and set her phone back down. "Hal only has two eyes."

"Are you going to keep the added security a secret?"

"We'll give them cover jobs that put them in the places they need to be, but I'm sure eventually people will figure out that these people don't really know what they're doing and the press will smell blood in the water." She took a sip of coffee.

"What are you planning on doing while your sister's on her honeymoon?" James asked, switching the subject when he could tell the other conversation started to bother her.

"Just bum around, basically. I've never really taken a break before, so I'm not positive." Melody laughed. "The sad thing is that I'm actually looking forward to the workouts with my choreographer these days because it gives me something to do. I used to come up with any excuse so I wouldn't have to go."

He leaned back and hooked his foot on his knee. "Why do you workout with a choreographer?"

The question surprised Melody. "There's more to a show than just standing there and singing pretty. People expect to be entertained. A good number of my songs are choreographed, with background dancers doing more complicated steps."

"Isn't that tiring, to sing and dance for an entire concert?"

"Between that, and the rush of changing outfits in ten seconds about six times each show, it's exhausting. But, I sit at the piano and play every fourth song, to give myself a break. The slow songs aren't choreographed, either. The lighting sets the stage for those."

James stopped with the coffee cup half way to his lips. "You change outfits in ten seconds?"

She waggled her eyebrows. "Boots and all."

"How?"

"Trade secret. If I told you, I'd have to kill you." She laughed and got up to rinse out her cup.

James saw a stack of CD's on the table. "Is this your new CD?"

"Yes!" She grabbed a paper towel to wipe her hands as she came back to the table. "Didn't they do a fantastic job with the cover?"

"You're very beautiful." He tapped one. "My assistant likes country music. Could I get one from you?"

"Sure. Of course." Melody went to a drawer by the sink and pulled out a black marker. She wondered if she should offer one to James, too, but decided against it. "Hal left me those to sign for some group, but he can get more. What's her name?"

"Rebecca. She's brilliant and absolutely irreplaceable. I think she'd enjoy getting this on release day. I've had her working since about 5:30 this morning, so I know that she wouldn't have had time to go get it."

As Melody sat down and removed the plastic wrap on the CD to sign it, he looked at his watch. "I have a meeting that is absolutely unavoidable in about twenty minutes. If I leave now, I might not be late." He carried his cup to the sink and turned around. Melody stood there right behind him, holding out the signed disk.

He took the disc from her and reached out, brushing a strand of hair off of her forehead. "Are we still on for dinner tonight?"

Her heart started beating double time. All of her senses were full of him and she suddenly wanted nothing more than for him to kiss her again. "I, um, I promised Morgan I'd ask you to eat here tonight," she said in a breathless whisper. She stared at his lips.

He put a hand on the back of her neck and was lowering his mouth to kiss her just as his cell phone rang, breaking his stride. He sighed as he pulled it out of his pocket. "Montgomery." All laughter faded from his eyes, and he straightened up.

"All right, Rebecca." He paused and glanced at his watch again. "If they're waiting there now, then they're early and they can continue to wait. I'll see you in about twenty to thirty minutes."

He turned toward Melody, clearly thinking of something else. Then his expression softened back up. "Problem?" she asked him.

"Clients. Early clients who will now have to be entertained. Hopefully, Kurt is there. I work. He talks to people. Things work better that way." She followed him to the front door. Obviously at home in her sister's house, he pulled his coat out of the closet by the door.

"Will you come to dinner tonight?" Her eyes sparkled. "I promise I'm not cooking."

"In that case," he said as he pulled her to him, "I will sacrifice a night alone with you, only because they're leaving Saturday." He gripped her waist and pulled her to him quickly and passionately. In that single movement, he put her exactly where he wanted her to be. Then he gave her a hard kiss that made her knees feel like two helium balloons and made any thoughts in her mind evaporate like a morning mist. "I'll be back as soon as I can."

♪ ♪ ♪ ♪

HAL stayed long enough to officially meet James and attempt to grill him much like a father would a teenage boy before a daughter's first date. But, before dinner was served, he departed for the drive back to Nashville, leaving just the two couples for dinner.

Morgan outdid herself with the meal. The beverages perfectly complimented the sumptuous food, and the conversation stayed light and cheerful.

After dinner, Morgan and the men sat in the living room watching the lights on the tree while Melody sat idly playing tunes at the grand piano that sat near the large bay window. Every once in a while, she would enter the conversation, but mostly she just played. At one point in the evening, she started playing a very complicated classical piece that required her full concentration, so she didn't hear James remark to Morgan, "She's very good."

Morgan stretched out on the couch and propped her feet in Kurt's lap. "Yes, she is. She minored in piano at Julliard. I always figured she'd become a concert pianist because our mother never let her play anything that wasn't classical, but as soon as mom died, Melody started writing her own stuff. The magic she can create with those ivory keys is amazing sometimes."

"Does she write all of her songs?" James asked.

"Yes. She won't even consider a song someone else wrote. She hears them in her head, or something." Morgan waved her hand in the air. She didn't have to understand her sister to love her and appreciate her talent. "She's stopped in the middle of a conversation with me more than once to go write down lyrics. And if any kind of major event happens in her life, she'll sit at the piano for hours on end and just write. She wrote some of her best songs after our father died, and again after Richard attacked her."

Melody came to the end of the song, and for added flare, gave the grand finale a flourish. When she finished, James looked at his watch. "I need to go, before I fall asleep where I sit."

"It's nice to know my playing is putting you to sleep," Melody teased, lowering the lid to cover the piano keys.

"I assure you, it's the only thing keeping me awake." He stood and set his cup on the table next to his chair. "I'm not certain how many hours of sleep I had in the last several days, but it's not a lot. Morgan, as usual, thank you for the wonderful meal."

"Always a pleasure to cook for an appreciative man," Morgan said, earning a light slap on the soles of her feet from Kurt. "Not to imply that you're not appreciative, darling," she added.

James met Melody's eyes as he stood. She slid off the bench and followed him from the room. At the door, James put on his coat and brushed a strand of her hair off her cheek. "I wish I wasn't so tired," he said, pulling her close.

She wrapped her arms around his neck and kissed him, pulling away when he started to deepen the kiss. "Go home and sleep. I'll see you soon."

"What are your plans tomorrow?" he asked, trying to delay his departure.

"Todd and Gina are coming in town. I have to work with them for the wedding."

"Who are Todd and Gina?"

"Todd plays fiddle in my band," she said as she kissed him on the chin, "and Gina is a back-up singer who also happens to play the flute."

"And tomorrow night is the rehearsal." He mimicked her kiss.

"Tomorrow night is the rehearsal and dinner, and afterward you have to keep Kurt away from this house, and I have to keep Morgan here, away from Kurt." She kissed him one more time, hard on the mouth, and pushed him away. "I'll see you at the church tomorrow night. Go."

"I'll leave in a minute." He pulled her back to him. "I'm not done yet."

♪ ♪ ♪ ♪

"WE aren't going to do anything different than we did last week, guys, except the rest of the band isn't here," Melody said. She stood in the church, waiting for some men to move the podium aside. "I start singing as they're lighting the candles."

"Where will we be?" asked Gina.

"You two will come in through each one of those doors in the choir loft. You'll get the full idea of the timing tonight at the rehearsal," she said, gesturing with her hands.

"I wish there was just one more instrument accompanying," Todd said. "That packs so much more of an impact for the song." His hands busily tuned his fiddle.

"I'm not going to sing it the same way. It's going to be softer. " She stepped onto the platform and checked the microphones. "All right, let's get started."

The church bustled with people busily decorating and cleaning. Morgan marched from one end to the other much like a drill sergeant, issuing orders, approving decorations, arranging flowers. Melody and her team ignored the busyness. This was nothing compared to the stage during sound check prior to a concert.

They finished the first run without flaws, but Melody wanted to go over it at least one more time. She looked at her watch. They had at least an hour before the rest of the wedding party showed up for the rehearsal. "All right, let's try it again. Todd, can you play more classically than country? I don't know which sound I'll like better yet."

♫ ♫ ♫ ♫

"YOU need to leave in an hour, Mr. Montgomery," Rebecca said, gathering up the letters that were on his desk.

"I know. I'm trying to get out of here."

"Oh, Diane Simmons called. She said to tell you that her sister's hip replacement surgery went well, but that she would not be able to come to the wedding."

James' hand paused in the middle of signing the letter in front of him. Angela's mother had become his and Kurt's surrogate mother after Angela's death. "Does she need anything?"

"She said she knew you'd ask that, and to tell you she didn't need anything and that she hopes to be home right after Christmas."

He nodded and finished signing the last document, then remembered something. He grabbed his briefcase from the floor and opened it. "You listen to country music, right?"

"Of course, sir."

"I thought I remembered correctly. Melody Mason gave this to me for you," he said, and pulled out the *My Love Song* CD. Melody had added a personal note and autographed the cover.

How did her boss know Melody Mason? She bit her tongue on a dozen different questions. "Oh, how sweet. I went to buy one of these when it was released, but everywhere I went was sold out. Please thank her for me."

"You can thank her yourself tomorrow," he said.

"What do you mean?"

"She'll be at the wedding," James said as he put reports in his briefcase.

"Why?"

He stopped and looked at her. "She's Morgan's sister."

"I had no idea. I knew she was from Atlanta, but I didn't realize there was a connection." She grabbed the last letter he'd signed. "These will go out today. The restaurant is prepared for your full party and a seven-thirty arrival time." James was hosting the rehearsal dinner since Kurt had no family. "The caterer should already be at your apartment for Mr. Lawson's private party, and I called the guard after their shift changed and reiterated that there are to be no women allowed to your apartment, regardless of the excuses given to him."

"Good." James didn't trust some of Kurt's more worldly friends not to send a stripper to the bachelor party. "I'm going to go ahead and go. It's already close to five. Traffic is going to kill me as it is." He snapped his briefcase shut.

As she left the office, she stopped at the door. "I'll see you at the wedding."

"Rebecca." She paused, ready for the typical last minute tasks that usually ended up wiping her Friday plans clean. "Thanks for all of your help with this wedding. I would never have been able to do my part without you."

The smallest, lightest feather could have knocked her down. "You're welcome, sir." She couldn't help smiling. She went back to her desk and looked at the brand new Melody Mason CD. She wondered if the star had anything to do with Mr. Montgomery's new more relaxed attitude.

♫ ♫ ♫ ♫

GINGER stretched out on the sofa lounger in Morgan's bedroom wearing blue silk pajamas. She held her phone next to her face, texting like crazy. Melody sat cross-legged on the bed, wearing cotton pajama bottoms and a loose thermal top, looking through a photo album of Kurt and Morgan's engagement party. "How did I miss this party?"

"You were still avoiding Atlanta," Morgan said, pulling a flannel nightgown over her head. "I think you were afraid you'd walk around a corner and run into Richard."

"That's ridiculous," Ginger said, sending a text and setting her phone down. "There are, like, a million people here."

Melody rolled her eyes, "Or, you know, like five million."

Morgan gave her a quick glare and a harsh shake of her head, silently telling her to not make fun of Ginger. Ginger just picked up her phone again. "I'm checking the last census."

Feeling chastised, Melody said, "It's still kind of scary to walk around here. It's one of the reasons I have a driver wherever I go."

"You have a driver because you're *über* rich and famous," Ginger said, pushing herself up on her elbow. "Comes with the whole big star package."

"I never use a driver in Nashville."

"Maybe you don't want to look so snotty in Nashville." Ginger hypothesized.

"I beg your pardon?"

Morgan stepped between them. "What is up with you two?"

Melody shrugged. "I don't know. I'm being argumentative. I'm sorry, Ginger."

Ginger lifted a shoulder. "No prob." She fluffed her hair and slid off of the lounger. "I'm headed to bed. Big day tomorrow," she singsonged, running her finger over Morgan's dress. "I totally can't wait."

She hugged Morgan and waved at Melody. "Sweet dreams, girls."

After she left, Morgan climbed onto the bed next to her sister. "Why this sudden antagonism with Ginger?"

Uncomfortable, Melody shrugged. "No idea. I haven't seen her in years. Maybe it's just from having to deal with David Patterson so much."

"Ginger is not her father. What she is … is my best friend."

Melody nodded. "I know. I apologize."

"Just chill the tension." Morgan lay back against the mound of pillows and held her hand up, studying her engagement ring. "I can't believe I'm going to be married tomorrow."

Melody set the picture album on a table by the bed and lay back next to Morgan. "Again," she laughed.

"Right. Again." Morgan turned her head to look at Melody.

"We haven't had the best luck with men, have we, Morg?"

With a wistful smile, Morgan said, "I don't know how much luck has to do with it. I think listening to God works more than anything."

Melody frowned. "You think? After what happened to me, after what I went through, when all I did was talk about and think about and talk to God?"

"Is that what happened? Are you blaming God?"

Melody shrugged. "He didn't do anything to stop it, did He?"

"We have no idea what He did or didn't do. Maybe if James hadn't been there, Richard would have abducted you. Maybe he was meant to crush your skull but God protected you. Maybe you shouldn't have ever gone out with him in the first place. Maybe all of this was meant to happen and God is going to do good things with it. You can't know. You don't have the omniscience needed to know or understand. You simply have to trust and have faith."

With a shake of her head, Melody pushed herself off of the bed. "Maybe you're right. I don't know. Here's what I do know. The world loves my music and my fans adore me. That's what's real."

Melody struggled with her next words, her jaw clenching before she finally spoke. "Putting my faith in the same God who couldn't get down off of His throne long enough to keep a con artist from putting me into a coma for two weeks…" Melody ran her finger over the scar near her hairline. "I feel like He betrayed me, and I don't know how to reconcile that."

"Maybe it isn't meant to be reconciled."

"If that's the case, then that's just wholly unfair." Melody tossed her hair over her shoulder and sat on Morgan's side of the bed.

"You could try talking to Him about it." Morgan sat up and crossed her legs.

"I just don't know if I know how anymore." She reached forward and put her hands on her sister's shoulders. "Enough about that. I'm so happy for you. Kurt is amazing, and I think Daddy would approve."

Morgan's smile was a little sad. "I think even mother would approve of

Kurt."

"You're right. He is entirely a people person. He would have convinced her that his marrying you was her idea."

Morgan laughed and leaned forward, hugging her sister. "You're absolutely right."

♪ ♪ ♪ ♪

JAMES leaned back against the couch and closed his eyes. Party debris lay scattered all around him, but Kurt had followed the last guest out the door about twenty minutes earlier. James ignored the mess and just allowed himself to drift inward.

He found it peculiar just how much Melody Mason occupied his thoughts. For a week now, every time he really found focus in whatever he was working on, her face would suddenly swim across his mental landscape, or her voice would fill his ears. He wondered what that meant. Was it obsession? Lust? Something more? Something deeper?

After giving this singular mental phenomenon what he felt amounted to adequate analysis, he reached a conclusion. He believed very sincerely that it was something deeper. He believed God brought them together in the Newark airport and he believed that, for whatever reason, God kept them apart for four long years. He trusted that God had a plan concerning all this. What frustrated James was his inability to envision the full plan and understand it so that he could implement it more efficiently and effectively.

Intellectually he understood how controlling that thought sounded, and he didn't mean it in a worldly way, he simply didn't like the danger hovering over Melody. He didn't like this inability to make it go away. His heart's desire was to shield her and protect her.

What were these feelings? He knew what he felt, but none of these powerful emotions made logical, rational sense. After all, true love wasn't something built on a few cups of coffee and the bluest eyes he'd ever seen. True love, sacrificial love, that kind of love grew out of respect, similar interests, mutual goals. What he had with Angela was love built on a foundation of their shared education, their company, and their science. What he had with Melody couldn't compare to that.

Could it? Certainly, they respected one another. Could God, who *is* Himself love, have orchestrated events already with infinite wisdom and infinite knowledge and predestined them to be brought together despite a lack of common interest or experience?

Or could he in his lonesome flesh simply be reacting to his best friend, his brother, finally becoming one with the love of his life? Could he just be missing that special kind of relationship he had known before? Was he selfishly struggling to try to replace what he lost with someone he cared about? How fair would that be for Melody?

He took off his glasses and gently tossed them onto the table in front of him. He couldn't objectively analyze feelings. Maybe that was the problem. Feelings didn't come with numbers and parameters and formulas. They just existed in a sea of constant and maddeningly dynamic variables. And, in this case, they apparently possessed the power to hold one's heart and mind hostage.

Surging to his feet, restless, he scooped his glasses up and slipped them back onto his face as he walked across the room to his floor-to-ceiling bookshelves. Running his fingers across the leather-bound spines, he found *The Brothers Karamazov* by Fyodor Dostoevsky. He put his finger at the top of the spine and gently pulled. Immediately and silently, the bookshelves parted and slid back to either side like the silent opening of a stage curtain, and revealed the most sophisticated personal computing system M & L Enterprises had developed to date.

Unable to restrain himself, James had enhanced the prototypes with personal touches here and there over the years. Panels of flat screen monitors covered the wall and keyboards stood ready to respond when voice commands became too cumbersome. James felt lazy tonight, so he pulled the ergonomically designed preacher's bench out from beneath the console, propped himself on it, and just spoke.

"Function voice." At the audible command, he heard the very quiet fans whir to life, moving airflow over the solid state storage and memory chips. "Display overview. Albany site. Angela project."

With each new parameter the system drilled down in real-time. On the central monitor panel, the computer displayed a floor plan of his highly secure Albany site. "Display security cameras CAD overlay. Night vision. Zoom R&D lab insider threats."

Atop the wire-frame schematic, a real time view of the lab at midnight overlaid it like a cartoon texture. The security cameras at all of his secured sites where equipped for both starlight ultraviolet recording as well as infrared night vision. James' proprietary artificial intelligence extrapolated the red-blue-green values of each green-red mixed pixel into hues and saturation levels that a human eye could appreciate in the visual spectrum. The technology was similar to that employed to transform old black-and-white film into color versions, just orders of magnitude more sophisticated and accurate.

The computer extrapolated and, in near real-time, James viewed the lab in very sharp and fine detail including all the elements that human eyes could never ordinarily see. Specifically, he could perceive the three glowing dots behind three electrical outlets. The glow represented the encrypted electronic signal the listening devices transmitted every few milliseconds. These bugs had been placed in his lab during the inspection of the arson and vandalism a week ago.

James felt a muscle in his jaw tic at the sight of them. He had turned over recorded images of the female crime scene investigator planting the devices to the FBI and Mike Redman had quietly been coordinating with InfraGard. But in perfect opposition to his own policy, he had not removed the bugs from the lab. He wanted to trace the signal and find the people who planted them, first.

A backup generator test had provided the opportunity he needed. He made sure the facilities UPS was off-line before the test and the lab had lost total power for seven minutes on Monday morning. That gave him all the time he needed to get to one of the devices, photograph it, and closely examine it. The technology tool marks of the military grade microelectronics looked far too similar to the burned up bugs they had also found in Angela's lab for him to interpret this as mere unrelated coincidence.

He had an inner circle of people trying to run careful traces, trying to intercept and decrypt the signal of the person or people listening, trying to back-trace and give him a location — anything. So far, very limited success.

In the meantime, his team continued to work. James didn't want anything to tip off the people listening to the fact that he knew. He just prayed that he could find them before any kind of useful breakthrough happened. He aided that by working closely with the manager there, a man he trusted implicitly. They had forced each employee to endure mandatory "trauma counseling" and follow-ups in the wake of the break-in which resulted in hours spent outside of the lab. This strategy worked so well, that James got creative.

He had planned for mandatory certification training and use-it-or-lose-it leave time for vacation. He had already hired a "workplace stress" counselor and suggested weekly putting, foosball, and table-tennis tournaments to relieve "stress." He would soon require fulfillment of a series of mandatory compliance briefings and tests covering every subject from export laws to OSHA and FISMA requirements. Every few days,

Mike Redman planned to disable one of the key engineers' access cards or logon credentials and blame it on patches or system upgrades.

All these efforts would add up. His team of engineers would spend a great deal of time outside the lab. James felt certain they would also remain fairly distracted with other issues by the time they actually accessed the lab to perform potentially useful work within range of the bugs. It would cost him a small fortune, but if he caught those responsible — Angela's killers — he would consider it money well spent.

Angry, frustrated, confused about Melody, James shut it all down and closed the bookshelves. He had to let it all go for the next 24 hours — the bugs, the roses, the threats against his company and Melody. He had to focus on Kurt's big day, on Morgan, and, hopefully, on dancing with Melody at the wedding tomorrow.

♫ ♫ ♫ ♫

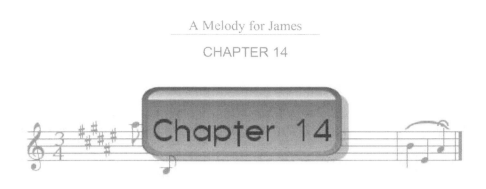

"YOUR second wedding is supposed to be the quiet, simple one. You know, run off to a wedding chapel in Vegas or go to a Justice of the Peace on a Tuesday during your lunch hour," Morgan complained as she applied mascara. "Why I ever let Kurt talk me into this, I'll never know."

"Probably because you love him, and it's *his* first wedding," Melody answered with a rough voice. Melody had booked a room next door to Morgan's, and had fully moved in not intending to go back to Morgan's house while she and Kurt were on their honeymoon. She had no desire to be alone in that big house while someone intentionally tried to scare her with the roses and notes.

While Morgan fussed with her makeup, Melody lay sprawled across the bed of Morgan's hotel suite, trying to calm her stomach. She hadn't given a thought to her stage fright, thinking that for her own sister's wedding it wouldn't hit her. But she'd woken up this morning sick as a dog, and once she emptied her stomach, she'd fought the rest of day to keep from throwing up again.

"Are you going to be okay?" Morgan asked, concern for her sister evident in her voice.

"Yeah. I just took some medicine that's supposed to settle my stomach. Maybe it'll help." She sat up slowly. Morgan didn't know about Melody's stage fright. Very few did.

A knock sounded at the door of the suite. Melody carefully stood and moved through the bedroom and the main room to the door. As she opened it, Ginger came bouncing in, looking bright, sunny, and otherwise perfect.

Morgan had very carefully picked out the dresses for her attendants, knowing the extreme differences between the appearances of each woman, but Melody and Ginger in particular. The style she'd finally settled on looked impeccable. The red velvet dresses matched the winter theme, square cut at the neck and back, and came to just above the girls' knees. Simple diamond chokers, a gift from Morgan and Kurt, added the perfect complement to the image.

Excited, Ginger hugged Melody hard. "You look wonderful!" Ginger exclaimed. "Where's the bride?"

With a genuine smile and wave, Melody gestured toward the bedroom.

"Why aren't you dressed yet?" Ginger demanded from the doorway, putting her hands on her hips.

"Because I still have an hour before I'm supposed to be ready," Morgan said.

"Goodness gracious, Morgan, you should be saying I only have an hour to get ready. You also don't have on nearly enough makeup. You're going to look washed out in your pictures."

Morgan tried to struggle, but Ginger became an irresistible force. Forty-five minutes later, Morgan looked like a fairy tale princess. The other three attendants had shown up, and all five women stood back commenting on how beautiful she looked. Somehow, during the process, Melody forgot about the feeling of panicked sickness that had threatened her all day.

Right on cue, Kurt sent Melody a text, letting her know the cars had arrived to drive the wedding party and musicians to the church.

"All right, let's get this show on the road," Morgan said, and grabbed the box containing her veil. She whispered a quick prayer. "Dear God, before I leave, please let me know if I forgot anything. Amen."

♫ ♫ ♫ ♫

MELODY stood in the back of the church, waiting for her turn to walk down the aisle, surprised the flowers she held still had petals since her hands shook so badly. She turned around when she heard Morgan grumble, and went to help her arrange her train. By the time she finished, some of her nervousness had passed and it was her time to go. She slowly walked down the aisle of the church, passing about 600 guests, trying to forget that she would have to sing in front of them.

Come on, Melody, she said to herself as she smiled and nodded to people in their wedding best, *you've packed stadiums filled with tens of thousands. You can do a wedding of 600.* Stomach rolling and flipping, heart pounding, panic overtaking her and causing her vision to gray, she fought and won the battle to keep walking forward.

She made eye contact with James and felt a little balance return. He stood next to Kurt, hands crossed in front of him, looking so handsome in the black tuxedo that it nearly took her breath away. His dark hair was just long enough that it curled on the ends. His hazel eyes flashed from behind the lenses of his glasses, and he gave her a small smile and a nod.

She took her place at the front as the music changed to the bridal march and the audience came to their feet. Feeling almost as if she had to tear her gaze away from James, she turned her body toward the back of the church. Morgan appeared in the entrance on David Patterson's arm, and Melody forgot herself and her own fears as she saw how truly beautiful and happy her sister looked.

As Morgan set her hand in Kurt's, Melody felt her heart give a wistful tug. She found herself making eye contact with James again. He made her wish and he made her want. His eyes seemed to reflect her desires, but her head spun so that she couldn't cognitively say exactly what she wanted.

The beginning of the service passed quickly, and suddenly the time came for Melody to sing. She braced herself for the thrust of panic, but this time it felt very low-grade, very manageable. Her hands felt steady as she handed Ginger her bouquet. She went up the steps smoothly and took her microphone like joining hands with an old friend.

Melody began singing the song unaccompanied, *a capella*, as she had the week before, and heard Todd and Gina joining perfectly on their cues. Morgan and Kurt lit the candles in the middle of the song, and the timing worked out so that they resumed their places just as she began the last chorus.

As she resumed her position and took her flowers back from Ginger, she glanced at James again. She wondered if he realized that she wrote that song for him, with him and him alone in mind. Did he hear the dedication to him during the awards show last week?

The rest of the service went without flaw, and in no time Kurt gave Morgan a long, passionate kiss. When they turned around for their first introduction to the audience as husband and wife, the guests surged to their feet, cheering and clapping. The newlyweds walked arm and arm, back down the aisle amid cheers with their five pairs of attendants following.

♫ ♫ ♫ ♫

THE Viscolli Atlanta Hotel hosted the reception. The chosen decorations helped emphasize rather than overpower the luxury and taste of the bride. Elegant centerpieces of white and red roses graced the tables, candles in the burgundy of the gowns cast each table in a soft glow, reflecting the crystal glasses. Gold trimmed china held delicate morsels and tender food in different varieties.

Morgan opted for a buffet rather than a sit down dinner and the staff stayed busy keeping the chafing dishes stocked. People stood talking in small groups. Many couples took turns on the dance floor while others sat at their tables eating. Through all of this, children darted between adults' legs, hid behind table cloths, and chased each other around the room.

When the wedding party first arrived, James excused himself and left Melody talking to Ginger. She listened with half an ear to her friend who kept tearing up while describing the whole wedding for what had to be the fifth time when Melody felt a tap on her shoulder. She turned around, and found James standing there with a beautiful, petite woman on his arm. She had straight dark hair cut to her chin, with features that showed a strong oriental background.

James introduced them, "Melody, this is Rebecca Lin, my secretary. Rebecca, Melody Mason." He extended the introductions to Ginger.

Melody smiled her warmest smile, "I am so very glad to meet you," She took both of Rebecca's hands in her own.

"The pleasure is mine," Rebecca said. "I promised myself I wouldn't get star struck, but I must tell you how much I enjoy your music."

"Thank you." She squeezed Rebecca's hands and released them. "I hope you enjoyed the CD."

"Yes, I absolutely did. Thank you so much. Your tour starts in a few weeks?" Rebecca asked.

"It does. The first concert is on New Year's Day here," she said.

"The radio is really hyping it. As far as I know, if it's not already sold out, it will be soon."

"I'll make sure that we reserve you some good seats and backstage passes. It's going to be a great show. My choreographer has outdone herself. And Ginger, here, will be dancing with us on opening night." Melody said.

Rebecca looked at Ginger, who shrugged and said, "I've never had the guts to go out and try to 'make it.' Melody is giving me one of the rare opportunities I've had to perform in front of an audience."

"What do you do now?" Rebecca asked her.

"I own a dance studio, and teach everyone age three to sixty. My mother was a professional ballerina before she married my father, so he was sentimental enough to buy me the building and fund the studio for the first few years," Ginger said.

"I seem to be surrounded by talented women. I'll just slink back into a corner so that no one notices how clumsy I am or that I can't carry a tune," Rebecca joked, making all of them laugh.

James returned and passed out the glasses he carried. Until Melody took a sip of her tea, she had no idea how thirsty she felt. She drained half the glass. "Morgan often says how much she admires you and Kurt's assistant. Don't cut yourself short."

"Speaking of," James said as he turned to Rebecca, "did you bring my phone with you?"

"Yes," she said as she pulled it out of her purse, "I just checked the messages, and there wasn't anything important on them. They're all stored."

"Thank you," he said.

Someone stood up on the stage and tapped the microphone. "If I could have everyone's attention, please. It's time for the best man to give his speech."

James looked up and said, "That's my cue." He put a hand on the small of Melody's back. "If I have to do it, so do you."

Melody put a hand on his arm, stopping him. "No. I'm not giving a speech."

"Of course you are. You're the Maid of Honor."

"No, I don't want to." James started moving again, putting pressure on her back to make her step forward. Real panic set in, clawed at her throat, rolled at her stomach. "James, stop! I don't want to give a speech!"

He turned and looked at her, the shrill note of terror in her voice making him realize she was serious. Putting a hand on her cheek, he said, "Okay. I'm sorry. I didn't realize. I'll take you to your sister." Making a quick detour, he took her to the head table before he walked up to the stage. He stepped in front of the microphone, his glass in hand, and waited for the room to quiet down. "I have no speech prepared for tonight. To be honest, between all the other things she had to do, my secretary probably just forgot to write it."

Laughter flowed through the room like a wave. "I'll just say the things that come to my mind, and the closest thing to my heart." He looked in the direction of the bride and groom. "Morgan, when I was a little boy, I met Kurt Lawson, and immediately knew I had found a lifelong brother. Now, because of his love for you, I consider myself lucky to have also gained a sister." He raised his glass in her direction. "Welcome to the family."

As the night wore on, the hotel wait staff took down the dinner buffet and replaced it with a dessert buffet. Kurt and Morgan cut cake, danced, ate fruit, and danced some more. Melody never had a moment to sit down and enjoy any of the luxurious looking food. She danced every dance, with men aged everywhere from eight to eighty, and loved every minute of it.

More than once, she danced with James, surprised at how naturally he moved and how much fun he appeared to be having. She would have never pinned him as a dancer. At one point in the evening, she found herself wrapped in his arms during a particularly slow song, her head on his shoulder, doing almost nothing more than swaying with the music.

Relinquishing Melody to his 70-year-old choir chairman to partner with her in a group line dance, James worked through the crowd and made his way to Kurt. He found the groom sitting at his table, jacket off and tie loosened, feet propped up on the chair next to him.

"What a party, eh?" Kurt observed with a grin. "Morgan outdid herself."

"She really did." James smiled. "This soiree will be the talk of Atlanta for years to come." He sat in a nearby chair. "What time are you supposed to head out?"

Kurt look at his watch. "Our flight leaves at six a.m."

"Where are you going when you leave here?"

"I got us a room here so that we could just take their airport shuttle in the morning." Kurt narrowed his eyes. "Problem?"

James rubbed the back of his neck. "No. Just making sure you don't need a ride anywhere in the morning."

Kurt rolled his head. "I'm not comfortable leaving with police investigating a stalker who is sending threatening notes to my wife's sister."

"I understand. I'll be here, though."

Melody came to the table and sat down. Without a word or a look to either man, she pulled her bag out from under the table and dug through it until she found a small notebook and pen. She bent her head and started writing something down. After a while, James leaned forward. "What—?"

Kurt interrupted him before he could finish his question, "She's writing a song. Don't break her train of thought, or she might lose it."

James moved closer and saw that she wrote on miniature sheets of blank music paper which he would later learn is called staff paper. Melody's pen moved swiftly, and musical notes filled the pages, her other hand tapping on the table to a beat only she could hear. He looked at Kurt. "How can she do that with the band playing?"

Kurt shrugged. "She doesn't hear anything but the song in her head."

"Fascinating." He leaned closer, trying to see the notes, but her hand moved too fast, continually blocking his vision.

Melody finished transcribing her thoughts into musical notations, capped the pen, then stowed everything back in her purse before looking up again. "I have had so much fun tonight."

Kurt smiled. "Me, too."

"It feels good to dance for fun instead of for work."

James raised an eyebrow. "Wasn't that one of your concentrations in school? Dance?"

Melody shrugged. "The workouts I do for dance can suck all of the fun out of it. I will say, the end result is well worth it and I'm not complaining. I'm thankful that I have that as a background."

James wondered at the feelings stirred up inside of him at the sight of Melody in the red dress, her black curls falling out of their up-do to dance around her shoulders, her cheeks a little flushed from the constant dancing. He wondered at the furious pounding of his heart and the ache in his soul. As he examined and dissected and contemplated his thoughts, he struggled to find some balance.

Antsy, he stood. "I'm going to step outside," he said to Kurt. "Be right back," he said to Melody, putting a hand on her shoulder as he walked by her chair.

Melody looked at Kurt. "What was that about?"

Her new brother-in-law shrugged. "It's hard sometimes to know what he's thinking. He's a little intense at times."

"He looked almost angry."

"Not really. Let him be. He'll be right back, like he said." Kurt waved at Morgan who was dancing a line dance. "James internalizes a lot of things. He clearly needs to process something."

Not satisfied with that answer, Melody stood and followed James from the room. She walked through the corridor of the hotel and came to the lobby, where she saw him going out through the big turnstile doors. She rushed after him and stepped out into the cool night. Scanning the street, she found him with his hands in his pockets gazing up at the night sky.

Rubbing her arms against the chilly air, she walked up to him.

"Everything okay?"

He looked down at her, his eyes glittering with intensity behind his glasses. "I think so," he said with a smile, sliding his tuxedo jacket off of his broad shoulders. "I'm just processing a lot of information."

"Oh? What kind of information?" She wanted to protest him draping the jacket over her shoulders, but it was still warm from his body and smelled like his after shave.

He ran a finger down her cheek and smiled. "Maybe another time. I did come to a surprising conclusion. I'll share it with you one day." He glanced at his watch. "What say we blow this joint and go get a waffle and a cup of coffee? There's a 24-hour place across the street. They might even have cheese grits."

The thought of some alone time with James after a week of sharing him with Kurt and Morgan held such tremendous appeal. "I'd love that."

"Is your car here? Kurt picked me up. I was just going to take his car home for him."

"Sure." She turned to the doorman who stood a discreet distance away. "Can you have my car brought around? I don't have my ticket with me."

He stood stiff and crisp in his dark green uniform, but as soon as she spoke to him, he relaxed and nodded. "Absolutely, Miss Mason." He lifted a finger to the valet, who took off at a jog. "Be just a moment."

"Thank you." With a smile, she turned toward James. "You'll have to buy coffee. I don't have my purse with me."

James put a hand on the small of her back and walked toward the valet stand with her. "I think I can swing a cup of coffee."

Seconds later, the valet pulled up in her little car. "Thank you," she said as he slid out from behind the wheel.

"Sure thing, Miss Mason." He held the door for her as she took his place. "Have a good evening."

James got into the passenger's seat and, smiling, Melody turned to speak to him. "Ready fo—?" she began, but she didn't finish the word as her peripheral vision picked up something red in the back seat. Her heart felt like it froze in her chest and the breath abandoned her lungs.

James' eyes searched her face. "What?"

Afraid to look, but knowing she had to, she slowly turned her head. There, on the back seat, lay a single red rose with a note tied to the stem. Hot tears burned her eyes as James pulled his phone out of his pants pocket and dialed Suarez's number.

♫ ♫ ♫ ♫

"THE longer we wait, the higher she beefs up security and the greater the risk of getting caught," Rikard stated.

His companion shrugged. "I don't think anyone will suspect us. That's paranoia."

"It isn't your life on the line, either." He struggled to keep his voice accent-free, practicing even in private.

"You never know whose life is on the line."

He raised an eyebrow. "Certainly, you're not threatening me. After everything I've done."

"Of course not. You should know me better than that."

With a wry smile he said, "I know exactly what you're capable of." He paused, making sure that sank in. "If we wait, I may not be able to move."

"She's careless and arrogant. She thinks she's a god. You'll have ample opportunity, and if what you're saying is true, we can make other arrangements. If we wait until closer to the new year, there will be much more publicity. Publicity is what is going to matter."

"You are, of course, the boss." He waved his hand, mentally dismissing his earlier words. "I just hope I don't have to say, 'I told you so' someday."

With narrowed eyes, his companion said, "You wouldn't dare. If you hadn't failed the first time —"

A flash of white anger burned through his chest. "Do not bring that up." His accent was back, full force, and he didn't even struggle to contain it. "I lost good men because of bad intel. I had no way of knowing about the thermite. No one did. You were inside, too. You saw everything I saw."

"That's right. You're right." The voice became calmer, intended to deflect the anger. "No worries. How is the monitoring going in Albany?"

"So far, no progress. They do a lot of talking as they work, which is good. We're able to keep up with them so that if a breakthrough happens, we can make it to the patent office first."

"The concept of that much money —"

He smiled. "Years of planning and hard work will finally pay off."

"Exactly. So, don't get impatient now."

♫ ♫ ♫ ♫

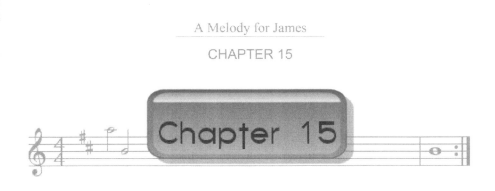

MELODY replied to the text she'd just received as she stepped into the hotel elevator, letting James know she was on her way down. She still wasn't exactly certain what she was doing up this early. The only thing she could think of was that it was because James wanted her to be.

Since when in the last four years did I ever cater to others' wants or needs? she asked herself.

Her whole life she'd bent and twisted to suit others, but stardom had brought out a selfish side of her personality that she didn't know for certain she liked. Everything was accomplished on *her* time according to *her* needs and wants and to *her* standards.

Now suddenly some man she'd taken a shine to wanted her to go to church at ten AM on the morning after the exhaustive wedding, meeting with the detectives about some maniac stalker, the rose in the car, and then a late coffee with James, just so she could go to church for the first time in over four years and … she just complied?

Melody smiled as the elevator doors closed and she began her descent. Yeah, she complied. Every minute she could spend with James felt like heaven on earth.

She knew instinctively that he'd do what he could to protect her, and consequently, she felt safe with him. No fear of notes or roses. No fear of surprise attacks and beatings so bad they required lengthy hospital stays and surgeries and weeks of therapy. Just time spent with that man who gave her happy little butterflies in her stomach and filled her head with beautiful love songs.

Love songs? Is this love? Could it be love?

She thought so. She thought so that endless day four years ago, and time never diminished the memory. Melody felt the smile turn to a silly grin on her face as she stepped out of the elevator and into the busy lobby of the hotel.

Every minute spent with James the last few days only confirmed it. Every song she'd ever sung about the emotion paled in comparison to how her heart wanted to burst from her chest at the sight of him lounging on the black leather couch near the lobby's welcoming fireplace.

"Good morning," she greeted, the grin never fading. "How are you?" *Other than heart stoppingly handsome in your blue suit*, she mentally added.

He stood when he saw her approaching, and she stopped, the toes of her red heels just inches away from his leather shoes. He reached out his hand and brushed a strand of hair off her cheek. Instead of releasing her hair, he slipped his fingers around to the back of her neck and pulled her close, brushing his lips over hers in a silent greeting.

Before she could sigh and step closer, he released her and stepped back. "Good morning, beautiful," he said while his eyes took her in from the top of her head, down her black sweater to her red and black houndstooth skirt, and ending at the toes of her bright red heels.

The look made her blush as much as his words. "Thank you."

He gestured toward the door. "I have my car waiting. Traffic should be moderately light this morning."

She raised an eyebrow. "This is still Atlanta, right?"

He laughed. "True. But at least it should be manageable."

They stepped out of the hotel into the crisp morning. Melody rubbed her arms through her black cashmere. "I'd have worn a jacket, but it's supposed to be warmer today." James held open the passenger door of his green sports car.

"Little different from Nashville, huh?" James asked as she slid in.

"Winters are slightly harsher, but not too bad." The seat warmer worked divinely, and Melody immediately forgot the chill of the outside air. James slid into the seat next to her and drove forward.

"I never look forward to going to London during the winter. It's a much wetter, colder climate than here."

"You've spent a lot of time there?" She watched him and admired the way he maneuvered the little car through the downtown traffic.

"The day we met, I was returning from brokering a deal and signing a contract for a four-year project in London. We just recently renewed the contract. Seems like I spend more than half my time there. I have a flat in the city, a church family, and a fully staffed office."

"Wow." She felt the pull of centrepital force as James accelerated onto the on-ramp of Interstate 20. "Is renewing it good?"

"It's wonderful. I have really been challenged by the project and hope that our government here will incorporate some of the technology we've designed and implemented."

"Can you talk about it?"

He shot her a grin as he changed lanes. "Not unless you have a pretty impressive security clearance."

Her heart skipped a little beat watching his handsome profile. "I understand."

When he moved over lanes to exit, she said, "We aren't going to Morgan's house, are we?"

"No. Didn't you know? I attend the same church as Kurt and Morgan."

"No, I didn't know."

"My house was about a mile from there. When Angela first went to church, it was to go to a women's dinner with a friend of hers. She started going to that church and begged me to go with her."

James darted forward when the light turned green. He continued, "I went with her Easter Sunday. Kurt went, too. It was beautiful and inspiring." He paused and his eyes grew dark before he murmured, "After that, she was killed."

Melody reached over and lightly touched his upper arm. "It's okay. You don't need to continue."

James glanced at her as he slowed down for the next light. "No, I'm good. Anyway, after she died, I didn't go back for a long time. But, Kurt kept going. He'd found a relationship with Christ and fell in love with God. Not long after, he met Morgan and fell in love again. When you —"

Melody raised an eyebrow. "Didn't call you back?"

With a wry smile, James said, "Disappeared. When you disappeared, I felt lost. Angela was gone. You'd stirred up some feelings that suddenly had no outlet. Work overwhelmed me at times. I knew something was missing. Kurt kept bugging me so, I went to church with him, and discovered exactly what I'd been missing."

"I'm so glad." Melody's smile felt fake, but she couldn't conjure genuine joy for him. Her heart started beating a frantic, panicked rhythm. They'd just strayed into a conversation she didn't want to have. Thinking of her own life and how it contradicted his rather than paralleled it, she looked down at her lap. "I'm glad you found direction."

She saw the familiar steeple of her home church — the church her father had helped build — appear and James pulled into a parking space in seconds flat. He shut off the ignition, but turned to look at her instead of getting out of the car. "It's more than direction," he said with a smile. "You should know that, Miss 'I want to go to seminary and become a worship leader.'"

"Hey, that's a lot of water under the bridge now. Like an ocean, really."

She watched his eyebrows draw together in a frown. "What do you mean?"

"I mean," she said, turning her entire body to face him, "that the last time I was in church, discounting Morgan's wedding and rehearsal, was at this church, four years ago, in premarital counseling with the man who claimed to be Richard Johnson."

"Seriously?"

"Yes."

"Why?"

Melody shrugged and ran her finger over the pattern of her wool skirt, unable to really keep eye contact with him. "I don't know. I just got busy. Then religion became less important to me."

"Religion." He repeated, as if tasting the word and not really liking the flavor. "So, why'd you agree to come with me this morning?"

"Because you are becoming important to me." She felt her cheeks burn. With a huff, she raised her head and looked at him. "I want to spend time with you. I want to be with you. Here, there, it doesn't matter to me."

She reached out and took his hand, sandwiching it between hers. "For four years, you've been in the forefront of my mind and heart. Everything I've done, I wanted to share with you. I was so frustrated at not being able to find you, at not knowing your whole name."

"And why do you think that is, beautiful? Why would someone you just met — why would someone I just met and spent one endless day with — why would that person take up so much of your energy and thoughts?"

"Because I —" her breath hitched.

James ripped his glasses off of his face and tossed them on the dash of the car, then reached forward and framed her face with his hands. Her cheek tingled from the touch, her head felt light. "Say it. Say it so that I know

I'm not absolutely insane."

The words tumbled out of her mouth before she could stop them. "Because I fell in love with you that day, and that has never, ever gone away."

"It's never weakened," he whispered, lowering his mouth, bringing her closer to him.

"No. Never diminished." She didn't know if he finished closing the distance, or if she did. She fisted her hands in the lapels of his suit jacket and tried her best to drag him even closer as his mouth covered hers.

Beautiful music exploded in her head as his lips moved over hers. Her heart threatened to beat itself out of her chest. Four years vanished in a breath. Years of dreams and wanting, wishes and desires. Her heart opened and the flood of emotions and longing nearly overwhelmed her.

James ripped his lips away, but did not break contact. He kept his hands on her cheeks, rested his forehead against hers. Eyes closed, just enjoying the feel of him, the smell of him, Melody felt some sanity return, felt her skittering pulse slow a bit.

She felt his thumbs brush under her eyes, felt the cool air hit the wetness on her cheeks. She pushed away and put her hands to her face, feeling the streak of tears. "I —" Her breath hitched and she dug in her purse, hoping to find a tissue. "This is so overwhelming."

James reached over and squeezed the back of her neck. "Yes. But it's real. I'm just glad I'm not the only one feeling this way. It occurred to me last night, and I had to work it out in my head."

"Is that when I followed you outside?"

"Yes. But, I decided that the timing was bad. First, you have a stalker threatening you, then a man you've only technically known for a few days claiming his undying love for you. That would be a lot for any star to take."

He released her neck and retrieved his glasses from the dashboard. Cold air swirled into the car when he got out and in seconds, he had her door open. She checked her reflection in the mirror under the visor, and seeing no real damage done by the tears, she allowed him to help her out of the car.

"Are you sure you don't want to go somewhere and just talk? Catch up?" She slipped her purse over her shoulder as he shut the door and took her hand.

"I absolutely want to do that," he said, bringing her hand to his lips and kissing the knuckles. "But first, I want to worship here with you. Is that okay?"

She forced a smile. "Sure."

She had blocked the pang of stepping through those doors for the rehearsal and the wedding. They'd had so much to do to prep for Morgan's big day that she didn't have time to face it. Now it was time to face it. What had happened? When had God become the last thing on her mind?

Her mother had attended church because that's what one did in society. Her father went along with his wife in matters of proper behavior and etiquette. When the old, established, long attended by all the "right" people church determined they needed a new building, her father, as was his way, built one. Melody and Morgan grew up in that building, attending all of the right functions so that they would be seen regularly.

Despite Melody knowing what motivated and drove her parents, she fell in love with worship. The music poured over her and lifted her spirit. When the music leader and the head pastor worked together with a theme, his message would just implant itself in her heart and she would walk out of there on air, ready to be an active and functioning member of God's kingdom.

But something happened inside of her soul when Richard's fist plowed into the side of her head. Something broke. Finding out he was a fake, a con artist, and the subsequent shame that followed broke her even further. How could God have allowed that to happen to her? Her heart had always only been for Him, and He left her to be used and beaten.

She worked through those thoughts and feelings for weeks, and instead of turning back to Him, she ran off to Nashville. Instead of feeding herself on the Word of God, she fed herself on the cheers of crowds and adoring fan mail. The faster she rose to the top, the further from God she felt, until He was just a memory, a part of her childhood. God became as unimportant to her as she had felt to Him.

Now she walked through the doors not for a wedding or a function, but to supplicate herself and worship. She assumed the time had come for a reckoning.

She recognized half of the people milling around in the lobby. Many more recognized her. She stepped a little closer to James and slipped her hand into his as a long time family friend approached them.

"Melly, what a pleasant surprise," Beatrice Stuart said.

"Mrs. Stuart," Melody replied, holding out her free hand. Beatrice and Melody's mother had worked several local charities together, always putting on some ball or function for fundraising. "how nice to see you."

The older woman squeezed Melody's hand gently and released it. "I saw you at the wedding yesterday but didn't get a chance to make my way to you and say hello. In fact, I saw you and James here dancing several times."

"Excuse me," James said, releasing Melody's hand. "I need to speak with someone momentarily." He looked at Beatrice and smiled a heart-stopping smile. "Nice to see you, Bea."

She smiled and a faint blush tinged her cheeks. "You as well." She stepped closer to Melody as James moved away. "I think it's been several years since I've seen you. Of course I see you on TV and so on but that isn't the same, is it? How have you been?"

"Busy." Two decades of etiquette training by her mother forced a return question when all she wanted to do was escape into the sanctuary and away from the people starting to gravitate toward them. "You?"

The older woman patted her well sprayed hair in a nervous, habitual motion. "This time of year with Christmas and all the charitable needs, it is always very hectic."

"Indeed." With a smile, she stepped toward James. "It was good to see you again, Mrs. Stuart."

"Melly, wait." Beatrice opened the clasp on her purse and pulled out a piece of paper. "I'm glad to see you. I have a children's home that seems to have fallen through the cracks this Christmas. One of my charities has donated to them regularly over the years, but this year they don't seem to have much in the way of Christmas gifts. Would you like to help?"

Melody looked up and saw James' profile as he laughed at something someone said to him, then shook the man's hand and turned toward her. She thought about the little boy whose parents died, leaving him to be raised in an orphanage. How many people could have given to them but didn't for whatever reason they told themselves at the time? Sadness for that little boy brought a sharp sting of tears to her eyes.

"I'd love to help," she answered, feeling her discomfort at being back in this church start to slip away. Memories of Beatrice always happy, always joyful, constantly encouraging her mom to give and do flooded her mind and she realized that this woman didn't do it for the same reasons her mother had done it — for show, for tax write-offs, for a resume filled with a laundry list of charitable causes she supported. Beatrice Stuart did it because giving and doing, helping and serving, lifting up her fellow man during times of hardship was simply how she chose to live her life.

The grin that lit up the older woman's face brightened the whole room.

"Oh, wonderful. Here is the information of the children and their ages. If you will just let me know how many you can sponsor and I'll mark them off my list."

Melody's eyes skimmed down the list of names and ages, sizes, wants, and needs. "No. I'll take care of them all."

Beatrice's eyebrows rose. "All?"

"Yes. All of them. I'm happy to." Melody re-folded the sheet of paper and put it in her purse. "And thank you so very much for asking me."

Beatrice reached forward and grabbed Melody's hand. "God bless you, child. Thank you. The address and number for the home is on that paper. Can I just leave it to you to coordinate?"

Melody smiled and nodded. "I'll contact them soon. Thank you for giving this to me."

James returned and put a hand on the small of Melody's back. "Ready?"

She smiled up at him. "I think I might actually be."

♫ ♫ ♫ ♫

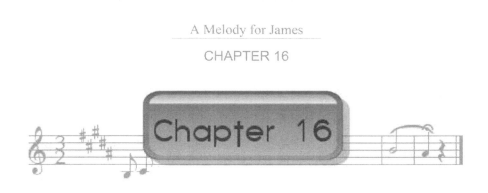

Chapter 16

MELODY had forgotten how much she loved worship music. Over the last four years, her focus had been country music with a largely secular ambiance. As she sang and clapped and worshipped with James, she felt a little door to her heart she had long ago slammed shut start to nudge open.

It felt natural and right to stand next to him. She loved the sound of his voice lifted in praise. It surprised her, actually, how much she enjoyed it. He didn't have a particularly great voice, but she could feel his love of the worship and it didn't seem to matter his lack of skill or talent.

When the congregation sat, he slipped an arm around her shoulders and she scooted in closer to him, feeling at home for the first time in a long time.

She listened to the pastor's sermon, but only with half an ear. Instead, she doodled on her worship bulletin, not paying attention to what she was writing, letting her mind wander. Before long, she realized she was filling the white space on the bulletin with song lyrics.

As she read the words, it occurred to her that the song was a worship song. She quickly opened her purse and pulled out her notebook and a fine tipped black marker before finding a blank page. As she uncapped the pen, the notes sprang forth, and she started translating what she heard in her mind onto the paper.

She worked fast. It had been years — years since she last felt this close to God and she didn't want to lose the song. The notes flowed around her, the chords, the melody. With one foot, she tapped a beat in tune to the one in her head.

The atmosphere surrounding her changed. She could feel movement and hear chatting. She paused and looked up and suddenly realized that service had ended. She glanced toward James, who remained sitting next to her as other congregants rose and made their way out. He sat silently just watching her. Her face flushed with heat.

"Sorry," she mumbled, putting the notebook and pen back in her purse.

"Not a problem. It's amazing to watch you do that." He ran a hand down her arm before he slowly grinned and his eyelids lowered. "Ready?"

Melody slipped her purse strap over her shoulder as she stood. "Sure."

James kept a light, steadying hand on the small of her back to guide her through the crowd. He smiled and nodded to people he knew, but could sense that Melody didn't want to linger. He hoped that many of the people she knew had talked to her yesterday at the wedding. Protectively, he preferred Melody not be bombarded with greetings and questions from old friends and family this afternoon.

The pastor was engaged in a conversation with a young family, so rather than stop and speak to him as was his typical habit, James walked by him, through the milling crowd, and out one of the side doors.

"Thank you for the hasty retreat," Melody said, smiling up at him. "I'm just not up to socializing for some reason."

"I understand." He stopped at his car and opened the passenger door for her. Once she had slipped into the seat, he shut the door and walked around to the driver's side to slide behind the wheel.

"Anywhere special you'd like to go for lunch?" He asked as he revved the engine.

She rubbed her face with her hands and said, "I have lunch waiting for us at the hotel. I hope you don't mind. I'm just so exhausted and don't really want to deal with people."

As he left the parking lot, he turned the car in the direction of the hotel. "I don't mind. I obviously have no experience with being recognized everywhere I go."

He shot a glance at her. She smiled as she leaned her head back and closed her eyes. "It's the price I pay, I reckon. It's different in Nashville. I'm one among many, and most people are used to singers popping up at the coffee shop or grocery store. They're all over the place. Here, not so much."

"I have the opposite problem. I'm gone so much, that most of my employees don't even know what I look like."

Her purse suddenly erupted in music - *The Barber of Seville*. It made him recollect an old Bugs Bunny cartoon and that thought made James almost laugh out loud as she dug it out of her purse. "Hello?"

He shot a glance at her profile and watched her frown. "No."

She toyed with the edge of her sweater. James could hear the other voice, but could not make out who was speaking or what was being said, exactly. "I appreciate that, but I need to be here." She huffed out a sigh as James accelerated onto the Interstate and drove toward downtown. Traffic had seriously picked up in the last ninety minutes. "Hal, I get that we can practice there and move everything there. Point is, I want to be here. This is my home. I'm not going to be run away from it. I'm not going to run from anything."

She started talking business then, naming names and places he didn't know, so he let his mind wander, thinking back to the conversation they'd had in the car that morning. Where had that come from?

He knew, deep down, buried under four years of life, that their meeting four years ago had sparked a small flame. He'd never been able to escape it. To hear the words out of her mouth — that she'd felt the same way, that she had fallen in love with him the way he had with her — that absolutely floored him. How he'd managed to get through the church service without jumping up on the pew and shouting for joy, he didn't know.

What now? Where did they go from here? He knew the answer his heart wanted — they'd go in the direction of a happily ever after. But, he wondered if she felt the same. He knew they both needed to digest it all first.

He pulled in front of the hotel and left the engine idling. The uniformed valet opened his door for him and handed him a valet ticket. "Good to see you again, Mr. Montgomery."

It fascinated him how much of the staff who had worked at the hotel while he lived there could still remember his name. "Eddie," he said, pulling the name and details from his eidetic memory. "It's been a while. How's college going?"

"I start the last semester in January, sir. I will be thrilled to be done."

"Did you ever determine a major?" He glanced inside and saw that Melody was still on her call, so he slowly made his way around the car.

"Yes, sir. I took your advice. Computers are obviously our future, so I will be graduating with a degree in Information Assurance."

James gave him another look. "Got any certifications?"

"I just got my Security Plus and I'm already studying for my CISSP."

Hand on the passenger door, James paused, considered, and stepped forward on faith. "I have an intern program at my company. Contact me tomorrow and I will be happy to set you up." He reached into the inner pocket of his suit and pulled out a business card. "Tell Rebecca I said to put you through to me."

Eddie stared at the card for a long second before taking it from him. "I can't thank you enough, sir."

"I'm not offering a free ride. Work hard. That's all the thanks I need." He saw Melody disconnect her call and opened her door. "Everything okay?" he asked her as he helped her out of the car.

"Hal thinks I should go stay in Nashville until it's time for the tour to start." They walked together through the hotel lobby and to the bank of elevators.

He didn't necessarily want her so far away again so soon. "Oh?"

"He feels like everything got intense when I got back home. He feels like I'll be safer back there."

She pressed the button for the sixteenth floor. "What do you think?" James asked.

Melody looked up at him, her bright blue eyes trapped him, stopped time. "I think we've spent enough time apart, don't you?"

Surprised by her directness, he laughed. "I absolutely concur." The elevator came to a smooth stop and he gestured for her to lead the way. They walked past doors until they came to her corner suite. She produced a key card from her purse and swiped it.

As they walked all the way into the room, James noticed the room service tray next to the table. "What does a singing heiress pre-order for a late Sunday lunch?" he teased, lifting the silver dome off of one of the plates on the cart. "Cheeseburger and fries?"

"My comfort food," she said with a grin, slipping her shoes off and pulling out a chair at the table. She put one of the domed plates in front of her and the uncovered one at the place next to her. James pushed the cart out of his way and sat down next to her. "I remembered that you liked sweet tea," she said, gesturing to the pitcher next to the ice bucket.

Touched by her thoughtfulness, he held out his hand. "May I bless the meal?"

She smiled and placed her cool hand into his warm one. His prayer of thanksgiving was quick and simple.

As Melody swallowed her first bite, she said, "I remember that after my parents died, one of the first things I did was buy a cheeseburger and fries at a fast food restaurant." She grabbed a hand-cut French fry off of her plate, and dipped it in the ketchup that she had poured onto the side of her plate. "One of my mother's rules was no fast food at all. She used the excuse about it being unhealthy, but I think that what she was most worried about was that someone would see us there. A Mason would never have cause to eat fast food." She took a sip of her drink. "It was one of the best meals I had ever eaten, but I kept looking over my shoulder expecting my mother to be standing there."

"I lived on fast food in college," he said. "Well, and Vienna sausages and Ramen noodles."

"I went to a performing arts college in New York. Most of my friends there were earthy vegetarian types, and almost every meal was eaten at this little café around the corner from my apartment." She shrugged, "I also didn't have to worry about budgeting money. My dad made sure my allowance was pretty high, then Mr. Patterson did." She thought back for a moment. "I did eat some pizza from one of those chains at a study party one time. That was pretty good."

James wiped his mouth with the cloth napkin. "How different our lives have been," he said.

Melody saluted him with a fry. "Morgan and Kurt seem to get along okay with their differences."

James laughed. "You're right. You almost forget they're from two different worlds. The mermaid and the squire."

"That's because they were meant to be."

With a nod, James said, "I believe you're right. I hope they're having a great time." They ate in companionable silence for a while. As he polished off his last fry, he said, "Tell me about the song you wrote this morning."

Melody sat back, full and content, and smiled. "I can play it for you if you'd like," she said, gesturing to the baby grand piano on the platform by the huge window. "I loved what I was hearing as I wrote it down."

"I'd love that."

Melody tossed her napkin on top of her plate and stood. "Let me grab the notebook." As she opened her bag, her phone rang. The number looked weird — an international number she didn't recognize. She thought of a couple of friends on European tours, so she answered without caution. "Hello?"

The voice on the other end was unrecognizable, heavily accented with maybe a Russian accent. "There is only one reason to send you messages."

Not quite comprehending the call, she said, "Oh?"

"Yes. It is so that I can put you on edge. It makes the end so much sweeter to know that you're afraid, rather than oblivious."

Tingling fear swept her limbs, leaving her weak. "Who is this?" she whispered with an outward breath.

"You will never know. And that makes it funny." After a long pause he said, "I knew his wife, you know."

"I beg your pardon?" Uneasy, Melody shifted her eyes to James. He clearly saw something wrong because he immediately came to her side. Melody pulled the phone away from her ear as if it hurt to have it touch her skin. With a swipe of her thumb, she put the phone into speaker mode.

"Unlike you, she didn't know she was going to die."

No sound preempted the line going dead. One minute the call was connected, the next it wasn't. With a cry, Melody dropped her phone. She put her arms around her middle and hugged herself tight. She felt James' arm come over her shoulder.

"We need to call the police," she said. James pulled his phone out of his suit pocket and dialed the number for Detective Suarez. He answered on the first ring as James handed Melody the phone.

"Mr. Montgomery?"

"No." Her voice didn't work properly, so Melody cleared her throat. "This is Melody Mason. He called me."

There was a slight pause. The detective did not ask for clarification. "Tell me everything he said."

♪ ♪ ♪ ♪

WHEN Melody finished talking to the detective on the phone, she went to the couch and curled up into the corner, pulling her knees up to her chest. James followed her, not sure what to do or what to say. As he sat down, she turned to him. "I'm so scared. What is happening?" Her last word ended on a strangled cry and sobs shook her body. He didn't hesitate to put his arms around her.

Confused, scared, James whispered, "I don't know." He swallowed the anger that welled up from his chest, temporarily choking him. He wanted to stop this, to lash out, to protect. But he felt helpless, and he didn't like that feeling.

While Melody cried, he rubbed her back and spoke in a soothing tone, sensing that she needed to do this, and fought the ache her tears generated in his gut. She cried for a long time, the sobs gradually easing. When she grew quiet, he tilted her head back and kissed each eye, tasting the salty tears. Then he gave her a gentle kiss on the mouth. "You need to rest," he said.

Melody nodded. "Can you stay with me?" She whispered.

Need surfaced, surprising him. He fought back against a baser instinct. "Sure. I'll just get my laptop out of my car and work in here. Go lie down."

She put a hand on each of his cheeks and kissed him again. Her lips felt soft, tasted of her tears. "Thank you," she said, standing and going toward the suite's bedroom.

"You're welcome," he said, standing to clear the table. "Don't worry about anything. Go rest."

♪ ♪ ♪ ♪

SHE gently shut the bedroom door. Mindlessly, he cleaned up from lunch, purposely forcing his mind not to churn on the last hour. Instead, he finished stacking the dishes and rolled the service cart back to the door. He called the kitchen to have it removed and ordered a pot of coffee. Then he quietly opened the bedroom door and looked in on Melody. He found her sprawled across the bed on her stomach, still in her clothes, breathing deeply in an exhausted slumber. He pulled a blanket out of the closet and covered her with it, then shut the door quietly.

He put the palm of his hand flat against the door and bowed his head. "God," he whispered, "please help me." He cleared his throat as anger tried to be the first emotion. "Help me protect, and help me to guide Melody. Lord, You know everything in your omniscient wisdom, so I'm desperately trying to hand this one over. But, honestly, the man in me wants to be in control here."

Feeling more centered, he used the suite's land line and called the front desk, asking to have the valet retrieve his briefcase from his trunk.

He rushed downstairs to the valet stand just as Eddie walked up with his laptop bag. He took it with a smile, worried room service would arrive before he did and wake Melody. When he got back to the room, he was relieved to find the old cart still there. As he set up a temporary office at the desk in the corner of the room, a brisk knock at the door announced the arrival of the coffee and the retrieval of the lunch cart.

He tipped the waiter and poured himself a cup of coffee. Before getting to work, he checked in on Melody one more time. She hadn't even moved since the last time he checked. He took off his jacket and draped it over the back of the couch, loosened his tie, and got to work.

Every time the door in his brain tried to nudge open to analyze the words of Melody's stalker, he slammed it shut again. What did he mean, he knew Angela? How did that relate to Melody?

He couldn't think about that now. He had to digest it first, to mull it over and chew on it. Instead, he would do what he did best — drown himself with technical specifications and industry jargon that meant nothing to anyone not in his field.

♫ ♫ ♫ ♫

THE citrus smell of gun oil filled the room. Rikard sat in the dim space. He ran his hands almost lovingly over the cool metal and black plastic of the high powered rifle.

He knew the risk associated with calling her, but the taste of the terror in her voice was so appealing to him. As he savored the memory of the sharp intake of her breath and the shaking in her voice, the ringing of his phone nearly startled him.

"Yeah?"

"Am I to correctly assume you received my package?"

Through an appreciative grin, he answered, "I did. It's very nice."

"Remember," the voice on his phone chided, "to aim carefully."

"Oh, you don't have to worry about my aim," he assured before disconnecting the call without another word. He chuckled and ran the oily rag over the muzzle of the weapon. "No worries."

♫ ♫ ♫ ♫

MELODY spent the next two weeks at the hotel. During the day, she stayed holed up in the suite, sitting at the piano for countless hours, writing her fear away. Evenings, she spent every spare moment with James. They talked, played games, watched movies, attended a few Christmas parties, and spent hours and hours just talking.

Every night when he would leave, she would have to stop herself from begging him to stay. Then she would fearfully toss and turn in the bed until she finally gave up and slept fitfully in a chair in the suite's living room. When she finally gave up on that, she'd move to the piano and write and write until James came back in the evening.

After breaking the ice that first Sunday, her apprehension at attending her old church disappeared. She attended two different Christmas parties there with James, and four services, renewing old friendships, meeting new friends, and worshiping. Every second in those two weeks, she felt the foundation of her faith begin to repair itself and start to grow. Gradually, she began praying with James, praying for James, and talking with him about spiritual matters.

Neither one of them mentioned the stalker. When she was with James, she felt safe, and as the days rolled into each other and the holiday approached, she thought maybe James felt like she did — just maybe calling had been her stalker's end game. She had received no further notes, roses, or phone calls from him. The police had not been able to glean anything from tracing her phone calls, and had hit a wall in trying.

Instead, they just enjoyed each other. Melody felt her feelings for James grow every minute of every day and hoped - and prayed - that he felt the same. Neither mentioned love again. No long confessions of deep abiding feelings happened, and as the days wore on, Melody worried maybe he regretted being so open with her that Sunday. But, as much as she wanted to be the first one to broach the subject, every time she started, she stopped herself. They'd only technically been together for a few weeks. Despite her mindset of forever, she thought she'd give him a little more time before pouncing on him with eternity.

On December twenty-second, Melody sat next to James in his car while she gave him directions. "Turn here, and go over the railroad tracks," she said. He shot her a questioning glance as he carefully maneuvered the sports car along the potted road and over the railroad tracks. She laughed and patted the hand he had resting on the gear shift. "Trust me."

"What Christmas present could you possibly have for me out here?" He approached a T-intersection and Melody pointed to the left. "Go that way, and at the second warehouse on the right, pull into the parking lot."

Large metal buildings stood in rows on both sides of the road. The area appeared largely deserted. Melody prayed that she had followed the directions properly and that they were in the right place. Her secretary had made all of the arrangements, and she couldn't wait to see what she found inside. She was so excited that she didn't even wait for James to open her door and instead bounded out of the car the second he put it in park.

She pulled the key out of the pocket of her red leather jacket and unlocked the glass door to the office. James came in just as she hit the light switch. Light flooded the empty interior, allowing her to see the door at the end of the room that led to the warehouse.

She grabbed James' hand and turned to look at him. "This is my Christmas present to you and Kurt."

He smiled down at her and tucked a strand of hair behind her ear and his eyebrow quirked up. "An empty office attached to a warehouse. What we both always wanted."

With a laugh, Melody pulled him to the door. Another key unlocked this one, and she stepped carefully into the cold, dark warehouse. "There should be a switch…" she felt along the wall, shuddering at the feel of a spiderweb before her hand brushed the light switch. "There it is." She flipped the lights on, illuminating the room.

Pallets of toys stood near the big metal rolling doors. Melody walked toward them, her red boots clicking on the concrete floor. She saw the controls for the door and flipped them on. With a screech and a groan, the door rolled up and daylight illuminated the interior.

James walked around the pallets and looked at the boxes of toys, bikes, and scooters. "What is all this?"

"Beatrice Stuart told me about a children's home here in Atlanta and that it had been overlooked this Christmas season. She gave me some information on it, and I found out the charity that normally adopted them had struggled against closing its doors last year. She asked if I'd help. I told her I'd take care of it all."

She approached him, and felt emotion burn her throat. "When I got all of the information, I e-mailed Kurt and found out that it's the home where you both grew up." She ran her fingers over a box that contained a boys' bike. "I can't imagine what life was like for you. My heart breaks for the little boy with no parents. Imagine how much worse it would be without Christmas."

She stopped in front of him and looked up at him. The intensity of the look on his face made her worried. Had she acted out of turn? Was he upset? "James?"

He cleared his throat and looked up at the ceiling. "It never occurred to me —" When he looked back down at her, she could clearly see the tears glistening in his eyes. "Sometimes we had Christmas, other times we didn't. It just depended on the hearts of people that year. All this time, it never occurred to me to help them this way."

He reached out and put a hand on the back of her neck, pulling her forward. She gladly went, laying her face against his chest as his arms came around her. "My love for you has done nothing but grow every minute of every day." At his words, her heart started beating a little faster. "What a beautiful gift. Thank you."

She tilted her head back and looked up at him. He took the opportunity to run a finger over her cheek and lower his head to kiss her with the sweetest kiss. Tears fell down her cheeks as emotion overwhelmed her. When he ended the kiss, she took a step back and scrubbed her cheeks with her hands.

"I'm glad you like it," she said. "I don't think the toy company would be overly thrilled with us returning everything."

James threw his head back and laughed. "I imagine not." He looked around. "What all do you have here?"

"Bikes for every child, scooters, lots of books, Christian music albums, stockings with stocking stuffers for everyone..." Melody listed while pointing to various shelves. "I think there might be a crate of candy in here somewhere. Lots and lots of clothes and socks and underwear and warm coats."

"Do you have a list of the children?"

Melody nodded. "I do." She walked to a box and tapped it. "This should be wrapping paper and accoutrements." She looked at her watch. "Morgan e-mailed me their itinerary this morning. They're due in at three."

James walked toward her and took her hand. "Any plans this afternoon?"

Melody spread her hands and gestured at the boxes. "I guess we need to get busy wrapping and labeling presents, and putting stockings together."

"Weren't you going to do that with Morgan and Kurt helping?"

"Sure, but there's a lot to do, and I have the afternoon free."

"How are you going to get the presents there?"

"I have a truck coming on Christmas Eve."

"I think I might have a better idea for the afternoon," he said, slipping a hand into his suit pocket.

"What?"

She knew. Something about the look on his face, part happiness, part nervousness, tipped her off as to his intentions. When he pulled his hand out of his pocket and slipped the ring on the ring finger of her left hand, she thought her heart would beat itself out of her chest. The diamond caught the light from the afternoon sun and sent a splash of rainbow reflection through the warehouse.

"Marry me. Today. Before another minute of our lives goes by. Marry me. Be my wife."

She licked lips suddenly dry. "Marry you?"

"Yes. My good friend, Mark Night, arrives from London in an hour. Let's see if he'll marry us."

"Today?"

"Sure. Why not?"

She held her hand up and looked at the ring. Married. To James. Excitement fluttered in her chest. The grin that stretched across her face seemed to appear on its own. She looked up at him and laughed. "Okay. Let's do it."

"Really?" He cupped her face with both of his hands, running his thumbs over her lips. "I'll take a yes, let's wait, if you don't want to do it now. As long as it's a yes."

Melody gripped his wrists. She could feel the furious rhythm of his pulse. "Nothing would be more wonderful than becoming your wife."

♫ ♫ ♫ ♫

MELODY called Hal on the way to the hotel to collect her passport. Strangely, he didn't object. Instead, he said, "This is going to cause a media uproar."

Melody sighed. "I know. But no matter what, that would happen. A big wedding would just drag it out and be a bigger uproar."

"True. Are you going to change your name? Tell me you're keeping your name. You're a brand, you know."

That stopped her. "I don't know. We haven't talked about that yet. I'll let you know." She had always imagined that she would become her husband's wife in every way. She once thought she would be Melody Johnson. What would James want, she wondered? She sounded out the name Melody Montgomery then Melody Mason Montgomery in her imagination and decided she liked it.

Hal sighed. "God bless you, girl. I would object, strongly, if it were anyone but James."

She smiled and reached over in the car for his hand. The ring on her finger felt good. It felt right. "Me, too." She smiled as he took his eyes off the road momentarily to look at her and kiss her hand.

As soon as she hung up with Hal, his phone rang. "Mark!" James said as he pulled up to the hotel. He put the car in park and waved the valet away. He nodded as Melody slipped out and said she'd be right back. "Are you on the ground?"

"I am. The pilot made good time. Something about wind currents."

"That's fantastic. I'm looking forward to seeing you."

"Likewise, brother. I still have to clear customs."

"Considering the holiday season, I'm sure that's going to be a bear."

"Certainly. The flight was full."

James checked the clock on his dash. It was just after two. "She said yes, by the way."

James could hear the smile in his friend's voice even through the thick Scottish accent. "Congratulations!"

"Can you marry us?"

"It would be my honor. When do you think the big day will be?"

"How long do you think it will take you to clear customs?"

Mark paused for several heartbeats before laughing. "No time like the present, is that right?"

"That is absolutely right." James couldn't help but smile.

"Then we shall pray that nothing holds us up. As you know, I usually like to enjoy a wee bit more premarital counseling."

James knew he was only half joking. "I really, really appreciate it, Mark."

"All right, then. I'll see you at your flat in just a tick."

"Do you need a car?"

"Not at all. I have one reserved. I learned the last visit that Atlanta's public transport is not as user friendly as London's. I'll just have to ensure that I drive on the wrong side of the road."

James grinned, "Mark? It's Atlanta. Everyone drives on the wrong side of the road."

As he hung up, Melody came out of the hotel. She still wore her red boots and red leather jacket, but had traded the black jeans and black sweater for a white sweater dress. Her black hair tumbled down her back, curls bouncing as she walked. He felt his breath catch in his chest. He had never met anyone more beautiful. As the valet rushed to open her door, he whispered a prayer of thanksgiving to God for bringing them together — not once, but twice.

"You are so beautiful," he said as she slid into the seat next to him.

He watched color tinge her cheeks. "Thank you," she said.

"All set?"

"Yes. I have a passport and driver's license. I hope that's enough."

James shot out of the parking lot. "It should be." He only had to go a few blocks to the courthouse, and prayed they'd be able to find parking. "Mark just landed. He said he'd marry us today."

"Do you mind if we wait for Morgan and Kurt?"

James reached over and took her hand. "I wouldn't dream of doing it without them. I've already sent Kurt a text asking him to come straight to my apartment when they get home. As soon as he turns his phone on when they land, he should get it."

They found parking in easy walking distance to the probate court where they could obtain the license. At two in the afternoon on the week of Christmas, there was little activity in the building, and no wait applying for the license. The man who helped them was older, a gray-haired man with skin the color of rich cocoa. He did not seem to recognize Melody. She was thankful that they might actually have a few days before word of her nuptials reached the press.

License in hand, they went back to James' apartment. Melody had been there a couple of times in the last two weeks, and felt comfortable shedding her jacket and going to the kitchen to make some coffee while James went into his home office to conduct a conference call with a client. She put dark roasted beans in the grinder, poured some filtered water from a pitcher into the well, added a clean paper coffee filter to the basket, and hit "Brew."

She arranged a tray with five cups, some cream, and some sugar, and carried it back into the main room. As she set it on the table in front of the couch, James came out of the back room, hanging up his phone as he walked.

"My afternoon is now clear."

"I'm glad," she said, moving forward and slipping an arm around his waist. "What about tomorrow?"

"All the way to Christmas." He put a finger under her chin and lifted her face so that he could look into her eyes. "How are you feeling?"

She smiled and put a hand against his cheek. "In love. And excited."

His eyes turned serious as he stared into hers. "We can slow down."

A knock sounded at his door. Melody stood on her toes to kiss his mouth. "No need," she said, and moved to answer the door.

A dark haired man with a goatee stood there with a leather satchel in one hand and a coat draped over his other arm. "Hello," he said, "I assume you are Melody." He spoke with a strong Scottish accent.

"I am. And you are Mark," she said, stepping back to give him room to enter. "It's a pleasure to meet you."

"The pleasure is all mine." He set the bag at his feet and hugged her before turning to James. "Brother, it's good to see you." The men shook hands and hugged. James took Mark's coat and hung it in the closet by the door. "I saw Kurt and Morgan in customs. We waved across the room, but did not get a chance to speak. Something about them already being U. S. Citizens I'm sure."

"He called while I was on a conference call, so I didn't speak to him. I did leave him a message to meet us here."

"Ah. So the ceremony will happen once they arrive?"

"That's the plan," Melody said. "Can I offer you a cup of coffee?"

"That would be lovely." Mark sat on the sofa while Melody went to the kitchen to get the brewed pot. "She is beautiful," he said to James.

"Inside and out," James agreed. He fielded a text from Kurt.

ALL OK? STUCK IN CUSTOMS.

With a smile, he replied.

MEL & I GETTING MARRIED. COME TO APT NOW.

He knew Kurt and Morgan would be beyond jet lagged, but he knew they would want to be there, too.

"Kurt and Morgan should be here within the hour," he said to Melody when she returned with the carafe of coffee.

"Awesome. " She poured three cups of coffee then sat in a chair facing the couch. "I wouldn't want to do this without them."

"Nor I." He looked at Mark. "How is everything in London?"

"Cold and wet. It's nice to escape for a bit."

"James said you're here for two weeks. If you'd like, I can get you tickets to my concert."

Mark shook his head and smiled. "I am actually here just over a week. I will be leaving the 31st. I conduct an annual New Year service that I don't want to miss."

Melody smiled. "I understand. I'll be in London later in the year. Hopefully, it will work with your schedule."

With a nod, Mark said, "I look forward to it."

She chatted with Mark, happy to get to know this man that James loved so much. When the doorbell rang, her stomach did a nervous flip. What would Morgan say?

Before James could even get to the door, it flew open. Morgan rushed in, arms up, and headed straight for Melody. "I can't believe this! I'm so excited!"

Melody laughed. "I was so worried you'd say I was moving too fast."

"If it was anyone but James, I probably would." Morgan hugged her tight, then turned to James who had just greeted Kurt. "You've given me the best wedding slash Christmas present on the planet," she said, hugging him.

Kurt shook hands with Mark. "Brother, it's good to see you. I saw you at customs, but didn't want to relinquish my place in line to come over and say hi."

Mark laughed. "Understood." He looked around at the small crowd. "Are we ready, or do we need to wait?"

Melody moved over and stood next to James, slipping her arm around his waist. "I'm ready."

James hugged her, tight. "I think we're both ready."

♫ ♫ ♫ ♫

MELODY rolled over on the bed and realized, through the haze of sleep, that she was alone. She reached further and did not feel James' body. She slowly opened her eyes and looked around the bedroom of her hotel suite. His clothes still lay draped over the chair in the corner, but the gym bag he'd packed before leaving his apartment last night wasn't sitting next to the chair anymore.

She looked at the clock. Six? Who woke up at six?

Apparently her husband. With a groan, she sat up, automatically clutching the sheet against her bare chest. The silly grin that covered her face the entire day before returned. She slapped both hands against her cheeks, rubbing the tired muscles, aching from such a bright smile. Could she be happier? Honestly, she didn't think so. And after the first good night's rest in weeks, she felt energized.

With a giggle, she bounded out of the bed and rushed to the shower. Married! She and James were married!

After the beautiful ceremony conducted by Mark, she and James had ordered Thai takeout then spent the evening with Morgan, Kurt, and Mark, celebrating long into the night. James had packed a few bags and they left Mark at the apartment and went back to the hotel.

James had been so patient with her. She was nervous, and he understood that. But he had slowly and patiently made love to her with such beauty and gentleness that it had taken a long time to quiet the songs in her head enough to fall asleep.

She tried to summon some tiny bit of apprehension at marrying a man she'd known for such a short time, but nothing came. She knew a lot of that had to do with Morgan and Kurt and their closeness for this man she now called her husband. She also knew that it had a lot to do with the fact that she had abided in him every day for four years, even when she didn't know his last name. She hoped every day that he would find a way to get in touch with her. And now they were bound in matrimony — one in the sight of God and their friends.

Love filled her heart, overflowed and spilled through her entire soul, giving her a sense of completion, of oneness that she couldn't explain.

They'd slept all night long, wrapped in each others' arms. Blissfully slept. Solidly slept. Melody rubbed her cheeks as she smiled again.

Married! Melody Mason Montgomery. Mrs. Montgomery! Married!

♪ ♪ ♪ ♪

JAMES kept a steady six-minute-mile on the treadmill while he watched C-Span on one television and the European stock market on the other. The mood of his company had quieted down. The work pace had slowed a bit with the approach of the Christmas holiday.

He had cleared his schedule on what would otherwise be typical work days so that he could take time off the rest of the week and celebrate his nuptials. He wanted to spend every minute he could with Melody before the real world reasserted itself — before her tour started and before his business once again demanded his nearly constant attention.

He took a moment and intentionally thought about Angela. Doing so no longer brought a pang of hurt or longing, just a momentary missing of her presence. He felt certain she would be happy for him. Melody filled his heart in ways he didn't think would ever have been possible again.

He had planned on proposing to Melody on Christmas Eve, not in a warehouse surrounded by toys and clothes for a children's home. He certainly hadn't planned to propose and then get married that very same afternoon. He'd thought they'd get to know each other even more, move slowly, with more sure footing. But, it all felt so perfect and not for a second did he feel like they'd done anything they weren't supposed to do.

It surprised him how strongly he felt for her, how he longed to protect her and make her feel safe no matter what the outside world threw at them.

A small part of him felt apprehensive about her super stardom. He didn't know exactly what that would bring. He knew she anticipated they would have to weather a lengthy media storm. She'd promised him that Hal would work at keeping it as minimally disruptive as possible.

At four miles, he slowly started cooling off. He rolled his head on his shoulders and looked at the weight machine, but felt absolutely no desire to spend the next forty-five minutes lifting weights. Instead, he wanted to find himself back in bed beside his bride.

His wife. What a thought. He missed her for four years, thought of her every single day. Now she was his. Bound by love and in the presence of God and their closest friends.

He grabbed a towel and wiped the sweat from his face. Checking to make sure he still had the room key, he slung his gym bag over his shoulder and left the hotel gym.

This early, the hotel was still quiet. He rode alone in the elevator and encountered no one in the halls. Moving as quietly as possible, he unlocked the door with the key card and slipped into the main room of the suite.

He was surprised to see Melody up, wearing a white cotton robe, curled up on the couch, feet tucked under her, hair piled on top of her head scribbling away in her notebook. She didn't look up at him when he came in, so he assumed she was so focused on transcribing the music in her head that she didn't hear him.

He went to the refrigerator to get a bottle of water and chugged half of it while standing in the small kitchen area. Then he recapped it and put the half empty bottle back in the fridge.

She looked up when he sat next to her. For a moment, her eyes were dazed and unfocused. Then she smiled a slow sexy smile that made his heart start pounding hard in his chest.

Melody put the cap back on her pen and tossed the pen and notebook onto the coffee table in front of her. She turned her body so that she faced him, on her knees on the couch.

"Hi, you," she said, moving toward him. She swung a leg over his lap so that she half straddled him. "How was your workout?"

He could smell the scent of the soap on her skin. He slipped his glasses off and set them on the end table next to the couch. He put his hands on her waist as she leaned forward and looped her arms around his neck. "I just ran a few miles. I didn't feel much like working out."

She leaned forward and gave him the briefest whisper of a kiss. "Oh?" Heat surged through his body as her lips ran across his jaw line and down the side of his neck. "Not up to it this early?"

"No," he growled, scooping her up as he stood. "I think I might need to go back to bed."

"Marvelous idea," she said, then laughed as he carried her back to the bedroom.

♫ ♫ ♫ ♫

AFTER breakfast, Hal called to tell Melody that he'd arrived at Morgan's house as they arranged. The newlyweds dressed and headed to meet the rest of their family at the warehouse, where they spent the entire day with Kurt, Morgan, Mark, and Hal assembling bicycles and scooters, sorting clothes and toys, and wrapping gifts for all the kids in the home. Morgan purchased twenty-seven Christmas stockings and employed fabric paint to carefully label them with each child's name. They filled stockings with apples, oranges, candy canes, and chocolate bars, as well as fun little toys. Hal placed neatly folded single one-hundred dollar bills in little gift boxes and put one in each stocking.

They worked until late that night. Back at the hotel and bone weary, Melody and James fell asleep in each others' arms close to midnight. At nine o'clock Christmas Eve morning, Kurt and Morgan woke them with strong coffee and fresh pastries.

After picking up Mark, they all rode together to the warehouse and supervised the loading of the pallets and boxes onto the truck. Kurt drove Morgan's SUV, and the truck followed as they made their way through town to the children's home. As they rounded the last corner before reaching their destination, Melody felt her heart sink.

Somehow the press had gotten wind of their plan and a crowd of reporters and photographers waited for them at the gate to the home's drive when they arrived. Melody tried forcefully to stifle her irritation, but the last thing she wanted was for this to turn into a publicity stunt. She saw Hal in his car and called his number. "Was this you?"

"We have a tour starting in a little over a week, Melody. This was Patterson's idea. He knew what you were doing this morning."

"How?"

"I don't know. I swear I didn't tell him, but he already knew. Let's put a positive spin on this. This is a good thing. Slow news day. You could top the human interest stories nationwide. Now, turn that frown upside down, paint on your public smile, and get out there and throw the sharks some chum."

Cameras whizzing and recorders whirring, a group of reporters descended on the SUV. Melody grimaced at James. "Some days I really wish people would mind their own business," she said.

He squeezed the back of her neck. "The price of fame, I imagine."

The truck sat idling behind the vehicle, unable to move forward due to the crowd. Melody fluffed her hair, eased into a practiced smile, and opened the back door. She felt James get out of the car behind her.

Microphones were shoved at her, and questions hit her like raindrops in a hurricane. With an inner sigh she decided the only way to get rid of them would be to appease them. The first question she heard and decided to answer came from a local reporter. "Miss Mason, what made you decide to do this wonderful deed?"

"A long time friend and fellow charity supporter of my mother's approached me at my home church a few weeks ago. When she told me about the home, I could not help but do my part. This home is full of children who can't be with loving parents, for whatever reason, during Christmas. My heart almost broke in two when I thought about it. I realize that material possessions can't replace a family, but it might make this one day a little brighter for these boys and girls. God sent His son as a gift to us, as a sacrifice and redemption for the bondage of our sins. My small act pales in comparison to what God did for me and for you. I just want to give back."

Melody told James once that a lot of people didn't like her because she hadn't had to struggle to make it in the business, but he wasn't prepared for the viciousness in the tone of the reporter who asked the next question. "Melody Mason, don't you find the timing of this expedition suspicious? Hoping the coverage of this staged little charity event might spur next week's concert ticket sales to be completely sold out?"

James' hand tightened on Melody's waist, but she squeezed it in silent warning. "Why Ryan Haggarty. I didn't realize the terms of your release allowed you to travel outside of Nashville. When *did* you make bail?"

Some of the other reporters chuckled at the outsider in their midst, well aware of the libel charges Haggarty faced from the owner of the Tennessee Titans.

"Well, Miss Mason, I heard there was some hot story about you, and couldn't wait to come in person to report on it. Do you intend to answer my question, or are you going to ignore it like you do so many?"

"Yes, I intend to answer it." She walked up and stood in front of him, the toes of her red and green rhinestone boots hitting the toes of his wingtips. "In the first place, I didn't call you — someone else did. I did this for someone I love, and am sorry and a little ashamed that I didn't think to do it every single year all of my life.

"Second, the timing of this little charity event, as you so graciously put it, couldn't be helped, because it happens to be Christmas Eve. Thirdly, I don't need to boost my ticket sales. It's my understanding that the New Year's show is already sold out and has been for days, now. Fourth, the only reason I stopped to talk to any of you is because you are all blocking the street and keeping us from delivering these presents we brought for these children. I figured the only way to get you to move out of the way so these little boys and girls can have their Christmas would be to give you what you came for since you don't seem to have the decency to just let us deliver these gifts."

She stepped back, dusted off her hands, and smiled at the other reporters just as sweetly as she'd been taught by her southern belle mama. "Now, I'd like to introduce y'all to my husband, Mr. James Montgomery."

She turned around, facing James, and grabbed his face in her hands. She kissed him long and full. Cameras rolled and flashes went off. He pulled her close and whispered in her ear, "What was that for?"

"I just wanted to give them something to report other than me losing my temper," she said before she kissed him again. "That Haggarty over there really gets my goat. Hey! Let's get these gifts delivered."

After that, it took little effort to get the reporters to clear the entrance. James and Melody slipped back into the back seat and Kurt moved the SUV through the gates. The big truck followed behind. The Director met them outside and gave the truck driver directions to the back of the home where a back porch could be used as a temporary loading dock. In no time, they had the truck unloaded and distributed the presents to the kids.

Melody and Morgan teared up spontaneously as they watched the joy on the children's' faces as the presents kept coming inside. Melody watched the interactions between the children and the adults. The staff at the home were kind, loving people, and it was obvious that the children who had been there for a while trusted them.

Leaving everyone to their reveling, Melody pulled the director aside at one point in the afternoon to smuggle in the stockings. Those would wait, so that the children would have something to open in the morning.

By the time they left, the reputable press had mostly given up and gone home. A few paparazzo lurked on the corner, perhaps hoping Melody or someone in her party would stumble out in a state of intoxication or half dressed, despite the fact that it wasn't Melody Mason's style.

Morgan and Kurt went back to their house while Melody, James, and Mark went out to dinner. She told James what she wanted to eat, and while he raised a questioning eyebrow, he followed her directions and they ended up at a barbecue restaurant that advertised the best beef brisket in

Atlanta on the neon sign.

"Aren't you worried you're going to get mobbed here?" he asked her. "I'm sure that the clientele at this establishment knows who you are. And, you've always been so careful not to go out much in public."

Melody held her hand up to be helped out of the car. "If I'm careful and low-key it should be okay. By the time anyone gets up the courage to ask me if I'm who they think I am, we'll be gone. Besides, I'm not dressed for anything else," she said, indicating her jeans and Christmas sweater with the green and red boots. As she spoke, she twisted her long black hair into a loose bun at the base of her neck, and pulled a pair of large dark framed glasses out of her purse.

"American barbecue," Mark said with a grin. "Yum."

"See? Mark's good with it." She slipped on her glasses, and the shape of them completely obscured the shape of her face. She tapped the lens. "No prescription. Just clear."

James kissed Melody's hand. "If you're sure."

People dining in the restaurant looked at Melody several times, but as she predicted, no one approached them. The beef ribs were tender and juicy, and they ate potato salad and drank iced tea that tasted approximately as sweet as maple syrup while they tried to talk above the din. James felt completely relaxed, and realized that this was the first Christmas Eve in a long time that he didn't feel a looming depression. He worried for Mark, though. He didn't want his personal happiness adding to his friend's sorrow.

"I know this didn't turn into the trip you expected," he said at one point.

Mark smiled and swirled the ice in his glass. "This has been the best Christmas I've had in years. Thank you for letting me be a part of it."

James nodded. "I had worried —"

"Brother," Mark said as he cut him off, "you know as well as I that life goes on despite the big hole in our lives that the death of a spouse brings. Do you even remember when we first met? You were crushed, sinking in despair, but reaching out to God to save you. I was the same and couldn't figure out why God had put a broken man in my path when I was so broken myself. But God in all His wisdom knew that the two of us would come together and heal together, strengthen each other with a bond of brotherly love."

He reached across the table and took James' hand in one hand and Melody's in the other. The couple had already been holding hands, and

now the trio formed a circle. "Now look at you. Your love, your peace —
those things give me a renewed spirit, encourage me for what God might
hold in store for me in my future."

Melody blinked back tears. "You are a wonderful man, Mark. I believe
that there is someone really special out there for you."

Mark squeezed their hands and released them, leaning back in his chair.
"Maybe. Maybe not. There was someone tremendously special. Ah, my
sweet Laney was so very, very special. I had special until sickness took it
away. But, I do now know that it is possible to love so deeply again."

He picked up a French fry and popped it into his mouth. After he washed it
down with tea, he said, "What you did today was fantastic. I hope you
inspire others to follow your example."

Melody nodded. "I'm embarrassed to say that charity work was my
mother's forte. She didn't do it for love, though. She did it for glory. I
think that made me turn away from the concept. But, when I found out
about the home, I didn't think twice about it. As I worked out the details
and ordered the clothes and toys, I feel ashamed about all of these years I
simply didn't do anything. I intend to make sure that never happens
again." She turned to James and smiled, feeling a glow of love for her
husband that just seemed to keep getting bigger and stronger. "Did you
like your present?"

James opened a wet wipe to clean the barbecue sauce from his fingers. "I
loved my present." He leaned forward and ran a finger down her cheek.
"And I love you. Thank you."

"It will be hard to top next year," she said with a smile.

He laughed. "You know the best thing about next year?"

Melody cocked her head and said, "What?"

"We will be celebrating our first anniversary and the birth of Christ at the
same time. I don't think a gift could top that."

Melody grinned. "Do you want to go to church? I think there's a service at
seven."

After glancing at his watch, he nodded. "I think that's a great idea. If we
leave now, we'll might make it a few minutes early." He looked at Mark.
"You?"

"Absolutely." The two men stood. James held Melody's chair while she
followed. "It's always nice to sit in the pew while someone else does all
the speaking."

James reached for the bill, but Melody snatched it up. She went to the register by the door and pulled out her own credit card. The waitress ran it without looking at the imprint, and when Melody signed it, she wrote with a flourish, "Thank you. Merry Christmas. Melody Mason." She added a hundred-dollar tip, then grabbed James' hand and pulled him from the restaurant. She laughed and looked behind her as the waitress looked at the receipt. "Hurry up, Mark!"

They piled into James' car, Mark taking the back seat. As James peeled out of the parking lot, he said with a laugh, "Why in the world did you do that?"

"Why not?" She leaned her head to rest it on his shoulder. "Did you get me a Christmas present?"

"Of course," he said as he took her hand and laced his fingers through hers, bringing it to his mouth for a kiss.

With a silly grin on her face, she reached back and brought the seat belt forward, latching it.

♫ ♫ ♫ ♫

MELODY giggled as James opened the hotel room door. They'd gone to Christmas Eve services, then dropped Mark off at James' apartment.

"We made that waitress' night," she said as she breezed into the room.

"You're an awful lot of fun, you know?" James said, grabbing her by the hand and whirling her around and into his arms. He kissed her long and slow. As her thoughts melted and turned into one beautiful melody, she let her purse slip from her hand. James pushed the jacket off her shoulders. As soon as her arms were free again, she wrapped them around her husband's neck.

He cupped her cheeks with his hands and backed her into the bedroom, kissing her the entire time. Her head spun. She felt the bed hit the back of her legs seconds before she fell back against the mattress.

"Ouch!" She said. She tore her mouth from his and put a hand on his chest. "Something poked me." Pushing against his chest, she lifted her shoulder off of the bed. Something sharp dug into the skin on her shoulder.

"What?" James moved aside as she sat up and felt behind her. Nothing protruded out of her shoulder, but the look on James' face as he looked on the bed scared her.

"What is it?"

She whirled around and felt her blood turn to ice. A white rose lay on the bed, slightly crushed, a note attached to it. With a shaking hand, she reached forward to pick it up, but James stopped her. "Don't touch it." He took her hand and pulled her off of the bed while he pulled his phone out of his pocket like drawing a gun. From memory, he dialed Roberts' phone number. He initiated the call, ignoring the late hour on Christmas-Eve. "Roberts, James Montgomery. We got a gift today." He held Melody's hand and led her from the bedroom. "I'm at the Viscolli downtown, room 1216." He sat in the chair and pulled Melody into his lap. "Oh? I am very

154

sorry to interrupt your party. Yes. Great. See you in ten."

Melody listened to his conversation with half an ear. How had he gotten in? "Can we move out of here and into your apartment?"

"Sure. I'll get Mark a room. I think it's a good idea." While he spoke he ran his hands soothingly over her back. His voice washed over her, calming her. In his arms, close to him, she felt safe. She knew he wouldn't let anything happen to her. "Roberts said the department is having a party across the street at Trader Vic's. He also told me he was bored to tears and glad I called."

"I don't understand what's happening," she said after several minutes.

"Neither do I. I feel like there's a piece of information missing." He squeezed her tight and shifted out from under her to stand. "It's like I'm trying to solve the puzzle, but all the pieces don't seem to match and I don't know what the final picture is supposed to look like." He scooped his glasses off of the end table by the couch and slipped them on.

Melody rubbed her arms. "I'll get some coffee going," she said, moving into the kitchen area.

As the coffee brewed, a sharp rap of knuckles on the door startled her. James went to answer it, looking through the peephole before opening the door to Detectives Suarez and Roberts.

Despite her fear and anxiety, years of politeness browbeaten into her had Melody smiling and stepping forward. "Detectives. So good of you to come so late on Christmas Eve."

"Ma'am," Roberts said, taking her hand. "We were across the street. It's really no trouble at all. We hear that congratulations are in order."

Despite the fear and anxiety, she smiled. "Thank you." Melody shook his hand and then turned to Suarez. "And thank you all the same for coming. James insisted on calling you."

"He was right." Suarez pulled out his ever present notepad. "What happened tonight?"

"We were out all day," Melody started.

James interjected. "We left around nine-thirty and returned right before I called you."

"When we came back, there was a rose on the bed with a note." She rubbed her shoulder. "I landed on it and it poked me."

Suarez cleared his throat. "Landed on it?"

As heat flushed her cheeks, James explained, "We, ah, didn't see it until a thorn poked her."

Melody gripped her hands together. "We didn't touch it. It's on the bed." She gestured with her chin. "In there."

Roberts went into the bedroom and returned, gingerly holding the rose with a gloved hand. He set it on the table and gently opened the paper attached to the stem.

A ring fell out. He picked it up and held it up. "Is this significant?"

Memories flashed across her mind, of Richard kneeling on one knee on a busy Atlanta sidewalk, proposing to her without a ring. She remembered Richard slipping that ring on her finger after they picked it out and she paid for it. She had felt so special and so happy. Certainly, she had fancied herself in love with him. Then she remembered the terrible feeling of utter betrayal when she took the ring off and gave it to the airline attendant on what should have been her wedding day. "That was the engagement ring Richard Johnson recovered from the Atlanta airport four years ago," she said, barely above a whisper. "I gave it to an airline attendant at the airport right before flying to London. At some point that week, he must have shown up at the airport and claimed it."

Roberts nodded and unfolded the paper. It was a printout of a computer screenshot of a news story about Melody and James' marriage. The news screen was frozen on the photo of Melody kissing James outside of the children's home. In angry, black letters, he had written:

REMEMBER WHAT I SAID WOULD HAPPEN TO YOU IF YOU EVER FLAUNTED HIM IN MY FACE AGAIN?

Melody remembered lying on that driveway, fading in and out as Richard kicked her over and over again. *Don't ever flaunt your lover in my face again, or you won't live long enough to suffer.*

That was what he'd said. With a gasp, she covered her mouth. Sobs felt like they would burst out of her chest. "Why?" She wailed. "Why is this happening? What does he want?"

Her knees felt like rubber. She fell onto the couch and pulled her knees up to her chest, wrapping her arms around her legs, getting into as tight of a ball as she could get. Cold shivers, deep bone cold shivers ran through her so that she clenched her jaw to keep her teeth from chattering. She rested her forehead against her knees and just started praying, a whispered prayer that barely had any words that made sense to her, a pleading prayer for protection, courage, strength, understanding.

She vaguely heard James speak more to the detectives, vaguely heard them say their good-byes. James sat next to her when they were gone and she shifted so that she curled up against him. The knees of her jeans were wet from her tears.

After several minutes of silence, James said, "I think you should postpone your tour."

Defensiveness sprang up from some unknown place inside. She pushed away and sat up, scrubbing her hands against her face to try to get rid of the tears. "I'm not postponing my tour."

"I really think you should."

Melody pushed off of the couch and stood, rounding to face him. "I really think it isn't up to you."

James raised an eyebrow. "Oh? I beg to differ."

Her back straightened so quickly she thought her spine would crack like a whip. "So that's it, huh? Married two days and you suddenly get to dictate what I can and can't do? Let me tell you something, husband, I decide what Melody Mason is going to do." She stuck her thumb in her chest. "Me and no one else. You have no possible idea what goes into planning and arranging a tour, or you wouldn't be so *blasé* about postponing it."

"So it's Melody Mason, now, not Melody Montgomery like a few minutes ago?"

"My name is a brand, James. You know what I mean."

"I'll tell you what I know. I know that a stalker is out there threatening Melody Mason Montgomery. Someone who threatened you with death, and alluded to having something to do with Angela's death. Therefore, I get to have a say in your actions. That's what I know." James stood so that they were face-to-face.

"If you really believe that," she waved her left hand in his face, showing him her ring, "then we seriously need to rethink this." Marching over to the table, she scooped up his keys. "I'm taking your car. See you later."

"Where are you going?" He was right behind her and grabbed her wrist, whirling her around before she could get to the door.

"Let me go," she said, ripping her hand free. "I can't stand to be here where he's been."

"Then I'll drive you."

"No. I'll send Kurt with it tomorrow. I love you. Merry Christmas." She slammed the door in his face and rushed down the hall, eternally grateful when the elevator doors opened right away.

♪ ♪ ♪ ♪

JAMES sent Kurt a text the second Melody left. Thirty minutes later, his friend replied that she'd arrived safely.

As soon as he knew she was safe at Morgan's house, he relaxed. A little. He didn't really understand what just happened, but somehow, the rug had suddenly been ripped out from under his perfectly steady feet.

He felt a little panicked, like he knew he needed to fix this but he didn't know how to even start. For a moment, he considered getting a cab and going to his apartment. But, Mark was there and he had no desire to face him after that beautiful speech about his marriage and love.

He wanted to throw something, but reigned in the unexpected temper that surfaced, knowing most of the negative feelings had to do with circumstance rather than Melody. In all honesty, he was scared. Scared out of his mind that this madman would get to her and he wouldn't be able to protect her. He would kill her just as surely as he had killed Angela.

Fear. Fear paralyzed men, made them weak, useless. James froze in the midst of pacing the length of the room and thought for a moment, mentally thumbing through the verses in the Bible that dealt with fear. "Fear not." "Do not be afraid." "God has not called us to have a spirit of fear." "You are my strong tower. Whom shall I fear?"

Humbled, he sat down on the couch, took his glasses off, and pressed his palms against his eyes. How could he have been played so effortlessly? God constantly spoke about not being afraid, and yet here he was, pushing away his wife, his lover, the other part of his one, because he felt afraid of what a mere man might do.

He turned and slid off the couch, landing on his knees. "Dear God," he began, "I'm sorry I reacted with fear and without prayer. Please forgive me…"

At some point someone knocking on the door broke him out of his prayer. Momentarily disoriented, he looked around and found his glasses under the coffee table. He slipped them on as he went to the door. When he opened it, he felt astonished to find Kurt on the threshold.

"I brought your car," Kurt said, holding out the keys.

"Thanks." James stepped back and held the door wider. "Is she okay?"

"She is not really okay, no." Kurt came in and went to the kitchen and laid a hand against the cold coffee pot. He dug around in the cupboards until he came across the makings for coffee. "She's terrified, emotional, and very worried about you."

"Interesting." James scrolled through the messages on his phone while Kurt made coffee.

"Is it?" While the coffee brewed, Kurt said, "There's something about Melly you might not have picked up on yet."

James felt his lips thin. "I'm sure there's a lot about her I don't yet know."

"No doubt. But this is something that you really need to be aware of."

"What's that?" James sent Rebecca a reply to a text she'd sent him two days ago, then remembered that it was nearly midnight on Christmas Eve and immediately replied again to tell her not to worry about it. He put his phone on the counter and pulled two mugs out of the cupboard.

"Melly's mother was a heartless, controlling woman."

James turned around and leaned against the counter, crossing his arms over his chest. "And?"

"And, I'm not exaggerating when I say 'heartless'."

"What are you talking about?"

"She controlled every single movement those two girls made, everything they consumed, every emotion they publicly exhibited, everything they learned … everything. They did nothing without her express permission and criticism or approval, and they suffered terrible consequences if they did not comply."

James splashed coffee as he poured it into the cups. He grabbed a napkin from the coffee service and wiped the counter as he handed Kurt his cup. "Terrible consequences? What? Were they beaten?"

Kurt shrugged. "Only to an extent. She played mind games with them, locking them in their rooms, withholding food, taking away anything they considered precious. As long as they complied, they had peace. The second there was a perceived sidestep, she came down on them hard and without remorse."

James silently considered this information and when he had taken it in, said. "I understand."

"I thought you would." Kurt pulled his phone out of his pocket and called for a taxi. When he hung up, he said. "Melody's band comes in town tomorrow evening to start getting ready for their tour that kicks off next week. That will take her away for nine or ten months. You've only seen her while she's been on vacation, and other than working out a few times a week to get ready for her dances, she's taken a complete break. Once her band is here, she will no longer be Melly Montgomery. She'll *be* Melody Mason. There's a reason she shot to the top as fast as she did, and the fact that she can sing like no one else on earth is only part of it. That woman is a workhorse that makes you look like some lazy fisherman living in Iowa drawing unemployment. She will eat, sleep, and breathe the branded commercial success that is known in Nashville as Melody Mason, Inc. On top of that, she's going to be on tour. If you don't fix this now, you probably won't have a chance any time soon."

Kurt put his cup down and slapped James on the shoulder. "I'm sorry this is happening. I look forward to the day you don't have to look over her shoulder."

James rolled his head on his neck. "Me too. Anything else?"

"Just one last thing," said Kurt. "You're a complete moron and I can't believe we had to have this conversation you big dummy."

James grinned. "I love you, too."

Kurt grinned back. "I know. Now go home. I doubt she'll come back here after her stalker was here."

James nodded. "Thank you, brother."

"Merry Christmas. Let me know if you need anything."

James cleared his throat. "There is one thing."

Kurt raised his eyebrows and waited.

"Will you pray with me?"

Kurt swallowed and pursed his lips. "Of course I will."

♫ ♫ ♫ ♫

THE telephone rang. Rikard sighed as he answered it. "You risk much when you call."

"I've waited weeks. It's time to move."

"I'll move on Monday. That will be the perfect time."

"And the other?"

"Your little bugs are picking up every word. I have programs analyzing every keystroke. They're close. Better be ready to move."

"You be ready to move."

He looked at the high powered rifle. "You don't need to worry about that. I am looking forward to this."

♪ ♪ ♪ ♪

MELODY sat in the chair in the corner of her room and watched the sun come up, heralding Christmas morning. Her eyes ached and her head throbbed. She had cried until she could cry no more.

Why had she overreacted so badly? Why had she left her husband on Christmas Eve, when all he wanted to do was protect her? It wasn't unreasonable for him to suggest that she postpone her tour, especially when he wouldn't fully know all of the planning and preparation that went on months in advance prior to a tour.

She lifted her hand to cover her burning eyes, and remembered the pain his whole body emanated six months after Angela's death.

This … man … Richard she would call him for lack of another name … wanted to kill her. Of that she had no doubt. It didn't take a computer engineer to figure that out. James was a smart man — probably the smartest man Melody had ever met. He knew. And in knowing, knew that he stood a very real chance of becoming a widower twice over.

How terrifying for him.

But the second the one person in the world who loved her more than Morgan suggested a plan of action she didn't think of herself, it had her putting her back up so fast she was surprised she didn't break it. Where had that come from?

She thought she'd gotten over her childhood by now, had gotten over the way Richard manipulated and controlled her just like her mother had. Surely, she didn't actually think James would try to control her life. She knew, deep down, she knew he didn't mean that at all. Yet, here she was, watching the dawn of the morning of their first Christmas Day as a married couple, and they were miles apart.

Determined to rectify that, Melody pushed herself out of the chair. She would go to James' apartment, and, until they found a house, that would be their home.

She dressed in a pair of jeans and a black sweater. After she called for a cab, she went to the front porch and settled into the porch swing in the corner, wrapping up in her jacket.

The opening of the front door didn't surprise her. She looked over as Kurt stepped out onto the cold porch. "Merry Christmas," she greeted.

"I hope so," he said in reply. He wore a gray sweatshirt with a yellow jacket on the front of it. "Need a ride somewhere?" He asked hopefully.

"No." He raised an eyebrow. She continued, "I didn't want to interrupt your morning. I called a cab."

Kurt nodded and put his hands into the pockets of his jeans. He leaned against the porch railing. "He's at the apartment. Not the hotel."

Melody nodded. "I figured he would be. I told him I couldn't be in that hotel room anymore."

After a few minutes of silence, Kurt spoke. "His relationship with Angela was really amazing," he said without preamble.

She raised an eyebrow. "Do I want to hear this?"

With a shrug, he continued. "Depends. Want some insight into how your husband ticks?"

She didn't answer, merely thinned her lips. He continued his story. "They met in college. They worked on some project that I can't begin to comprehend, and by the end of the late nights and early mornings, they weren't so much dating as they had already transformed into a couple. They were an absolute match made in heaven, and I don't mean that lightly. It was like they did everything in one accord. If they ever got into a single argument, I didn't know about it."

"This is supposed to make me feel better somehow?"

"Don't let yourself get in the way and miss the point. Just hear me out." Kurt continued, "We all lived in that farmhouse of hers. Some uncle left it to her in his will, and we were all so broke getting through college that after they got married, we just pooled our resources. The two of them had a business plan, and I had the personality and know-how to get some investors lined up and get the work done. Between the three of us, we had some serious potential. Once Angela started in on that data storage endeavor, there was nothing in our future that couldn't be ours for the taking. It gave us confidence to make risky business decisions that really panned out in the end. In hindsight, I truly believe God was directing us even then."

Melody stared at him, but didn't speak.

He continued. "I loved them. I love him, I loved her, and I loved the two of them together. They were the only family I'd ever known. I couldn't imagine James with anyone else. Ever. The last few years, he tried dating here and there, but I didn't encourage it because I knew there was no one else for him. Angela was the beginning and the end for him."

Her lip curled into a snarl only to hide the desolation his words caused. "Gee, thanks."

Kurt looked at her with surprisingly stern eyes. "Hey, Melly. Didn't you hear me? Are you listening to me? I'm not comparing the two of you because there's no comparison. Angela was my friend. One of my best friends. She was beautiful and funny and she loved James like nothing I can even explain. And oh-my-heavens was she smart. Smarter than all of us combined. And she loved God. She would work and work and work and just hum or whistle old hymns the whole time … *Old Rugged Cross* or *Amazing Grace*. There are days I still miss her."

Kurt's sincerity forced Melody back out of her bubble of self-pity. "I'm sorry. I didn't mean any disrespect."

Kurt nodded. "I know. You just never met her. You don't have any context. For all you know, Angela's just this hole in your husband's past labeled 'irreplaceable love of my life.' And the funny thing is, ever since Angela died…" He swallowed and his eyes grew hard. "Since that sick psychopath murdered my very good friend Angela, my best friend's wife … ever since that day I would have agreed with you. No one could take her place. How could anyone?"

Melody heard herself smother a sob. She had never really considered the impact that terrible violent act had on everyone who had ever known her husband's first wife. Clearly, Kurt still mourned the loss of that remarkable woman.

"Then I saw James with you. Whatever I thought of Angela … seeing him with you wipes the slate. He is so enamored of you. He's going to have a hard time saying it. He is a man of few words, and not many elaborate ones. But, he loves you. He loves you, Melody, like something I've never seen before. The way he loves you is like, it's like something everyone around him feels, like the wind in your face."

The offense that had started to take root in her heart immediately dissolved, and though she thought she'd cried her last tear, she felt wet trails racing down her cheeks.

Kurt cleared his throat. "When he killed her, I thought maybe he'd killed some part of James, too. Maybe his soul was murdered and burned down to the ground along with her. For a long time, he just hurt so much."

"When I met him ..." Melody said, but then stopped speaking. She couldn't explain the man she had witnessed all those years ago, but then Kurt glanced at her and slowly nodded.

"Yeah, that's right. You met him about six months later. So you know what I mean." He turned his face away from her and stared at the flaming southern sky as the sun crawled slowly higher over the rooftops. "If he loses you, if this psycho gets to you, he won't just be murdering you. Losing you will kill James once and for all. It will kill everything about him. He will just go through the rest of his life waiting to die."

He stood as her cab pulled into the long drive. Before she got up he bent and gave her a hug. "Just remember something I'm sure you know already: Every single minute of every single day, he is afraid to lose you, and that's going to make him difficult to deal with because he knows what's on the other side of that kind of loss."

Melody sniffed and then put a hand on his cheek. "I'll keep that in mind. Thank you."

"You're welcome." He straightened and gestured as she stood. "Looks like your ride's here."

♫ ♫ ♫ ♫

MELODY'S cab pulled up outside of James' apartment building. The doorman opened the cab door for her before she could finish tipping the driver.

"Merry Christmas, Mrs. Montgomery," he said. Melody wanted to ask him how he knew who she was, then she remembered that most people in Atlanta would recognize her after the recent media frenzy.

"Thank you. Merry Christmas to you as well."

She walked through the door he opened and the security officer at the desk smiled at her. "Merry Christmas, Mrs. Montgomery."

"Thank you," she said, smiling. "I'm afraid you both have me at a disadvantage."

"I'm Cliff, ma'am and your doorman is Montez. We work most mornings, six to early afternoon."

"Well, Cliff, it's a pleasure to meet you. Were you expecting me?"

"We expect all of our residents at all times, ma'am. That way, we're never surprised."

Despite everything, Melody laughed. "That's very Biblical you know."

Cliff merely inclined his head. "Indeed, ma'am."

With a smile, Melody said, "Have a blessed Christmas."

"Oh, here's your key. Mr. Montgomery asked me to have it made for you, but didn't collect it yesterday. It will work on the elevator and door."

Melody took the small silver key from the palm of his hand and closed her fingers around it. "Thank you," she whispered.

Desperate now to get upstairs, she rushed to the elevator. The ride up seemed to take forever until it finally stopped on the appropriate floor. She went to the door and felt her stomach twist with nerves before she slipped the key into the lock and it effortlessly turned.

She took a deep breath to calm her nerves, pressed a hand once to her fluttering stomach, and walked into the apartment. James stood at the large bay window across the room, looking out at the city, his hands in his pockets, his stance a bit tense. He turned at the sound of the door closing, and she felt a twinge of sympathy about how horrible he looked. "I was kind of hoping you would show up last night," she said by way of greeting.

"I thought you might need time alone last night." He jingled some change in his pocket. "Kurt came by and we chatted."

"Oh?" Melody crossed the room.

"He called me a moron."

Melody could not reconcile that but assumed it was some male thing. "He and I chatted a bit this morning."

"Is that so?"

"Yes, but he didn't call me a moron."

James grinned. "Very chivalrous. What did you chat about?"

"Angela." James frowned. "Anything else come up in your conversation besides questioning your intelligence?"

"Your mother."

Melody stopped in front of him and reached up to cup his cheek with her hand. He closed his eyes and leaned in, as if trying to get her hand even closer. When he opened his eyes, the strength of the emotions swirling around their hazel depths made her gasp.

"I've been praying about it," he said, "and I realize now that I was reacting fearfully and acting on that fear. I was wrong to do that. God says we should not live in a spirit of fear. I withdraw my opinion that you should postpone your tour and instead simply request that I be a part of the talks with your security team. You are a highly successful businesswoman, and I am not going to ever again try to tell you what you should and should not do in your career." He stopped. "Unless you ask."

Melody smiled. "Funny you should say that," she said, "because I've been praying too, and realized that I need to trust you enough to submit to you." She lowered her hand, intending to step back a step, but he grabbed her wrist and held her hand to his chest. "So if you really want me to postpone the tour, I will abide by your decision. I'm your wife and you're my husband and that is just the way it's going to be."

James grinned, "Begin as you mean to go on? That right?"

"That's exactly right. I love you and I know you love me. I really, really don't want to mess this up."

James kissed the top of her head, "Oh, honey, neither do I. And I don't want you to postpone the tour. I don't."

Melody said, "I'm sorry I reacted the way I did. I was overwhelmed, and scared, and felt defensive."

"I don't know how to do this," he said gruffly. "It seemed so easy before."

Unexpectedly, her eyes welled up with tears. "It doesn't have to be hard," she said.

Suddenly his arms came around her. She rested her face against his chest and breathed in the smell of him, listened to the beautiful rhythm of his heartbeat in her ear, relished in the feel of the strength of his arms around her. She slipped her arms around his waist and squeezed tight.

James said, "I think we should make up for arguing, now."

Melody sniffed and giggled at the same time. "Make up, huh?"

James nodded and said, "Definitely. I think we should begin as we mean to go on."

♫ ♫ ♫ ♫

MELODY slept until noon. She smiled, eyes still closed, when she felt the bed give under James' weight. Reluctantly she pried one eye open and saw him sitting there, freshly showered, wearing a pair of jeans and a worn-out Georgia-Tech sweatshirt. The most beautiful sight, besides her husband, was the cup of strong coffee he held in his hand.

"Merry Christmas," he said, bending over and kissing her cheek. He had not bothered to shave, so the rough scrape of more than a day's worth of beard scratched her neck and shoulder.

"Merry Christmas." She pointed at the cup. "Is that for me?"

"Maybe, for a kiss," he said, then laughed and set the cup aside when she launched herself into his arms and kissed him all over his rough face. She snatched the cup off of the night stand before scooting back and leaning against the headboard, pulling the blankets up with her.

She took a sip of the delicious brew but something about the flavor startled her. "What's in this?"

He grinned slowly. "Honey."

She grinned back and took another sip, deciding she liked the unexpected flavor. "When you find some honey …"

His grin became a smile. "Exactly."

She pushed her hair back from her face, the coffee warming her middle. "What are your plans today?"

He ran a hand down the shape of her leg under the blankets and peered at her over the rims of his glasses. The gleam in his eye made her giggle with joy. "I have no specific plans," he growled. Then he laughed with her and said, "But I do think we're supposed to be at Kurt and Morgan's at some point tonight to celebrate the holiday. I'm sure she's cooking up a storm."

Melody took another sip of the coffee. "Actually, she's having dinner brought in. But we do have to be there. At six."

James raised an eyebrow. "What's six?"

"My crew is all due in tomorrow. Some of them are coming in tonight. Morgan is hosting her annual Christmas dinner slash open house slash come to get leftovers if you get in too late for them that she always throws for my crew."

James nodded. "Right. I remember. She invited me weeks ago, but I declined because I had Mark coming in town."

Knowing his plans to visit Mark's late wife's family in Savannah, she said, "Did he mind you not going with him this morning?"

"Not at all. I think he figured out when I got married a few days ago that our Christmas plans would change."

Melody ran her tongue over her teeth. "Right. Good point." She reached out and ran a finger over his muscled forearm. "I am looking forward to introducing you to everyone."

"And I am looking forward to feeding you." He leaned forward and kissed the tip of her nose. "Brunch is ready in ten minutes. If you want to take a shower, I packed your stuff for you at the hotel yesterday. Your bag filled with your clothes and various mysterious gadgets and potions is in the bathroom closet."

"Thank you," she said.

He plucked a flat box gaily wrapped in Christmas paper off of the corner of the night stand and handed it to her. "Merry Christmas, Melody. I love you."

She grinned and snatched it from him. She ripped open the paper and opened the box, a gasp escaping when she saw its contents. "Oh, James, how beautiful." It was a choker made of sapphires, and after every third stone was a small diamond encrusted music note. She pulled it out of the box to look at it in the light, then launched herself in his arms. "It's perfect," she said with a smile as she pulled his head down for a kiss.

♫ ♫ ♫ ♫

CHRISTMAS lights tastefully decorated the exterior of Kurt and Morgan's home. Evergreen wreaths accented with large red bows hung from every window facing the street. The brick mailbox at the end of the drive even had wreaths on each side of it. Welcoming smoke puffed out of the chimney, promising a warm relief from the cold Georgia night.

James parked behind a pickup truck on the end of the lawn. "Looks like a few people beat us here," he said before getting out of the car to open Melody's door.

"That's Stevie's truck. He's my lead guitarist." She gestured at a red Ferrari. "And that belongs to Ray Porter, my drummer. He's a hoot."

James smiled as they walked up the drive. "A hoot, huh?"

"A constant source of entertainment. I think he originally wanted to be a stand up comedian." Excitement nearly burst her open. She couldn't wait to see everyone.

Morgan met them at the door. She wore a cream colored sweater and blue slacks. Her heels made her come to eye level with Melody. "There you are," she said, grabbing her sister and hugging her. "I missed you this morning."

"I wanted to be with my husband," Melody laughed. She stepped back as Morgan hugged James and wished him a merry Christmas.

"Good. That's where you belong on Christmas day," she said. "With the nature of ya'll's careers, you're going to be apart enough."

Melody frowned. What a sobering thought. "You're right. I hadn't even thought of that."

James put a hand on the small of her back and gently rubbed. "We'll make it work," he promised.

Melody smiled up at him. "Absolutely." She looked past Morgan and spied her lead guitarist. "Stevie!" She rushed toward him and gave him a hug. "How's Tiffany?"

"Big as a house and beautiful as ever," Steve said. "Only four weeks now."

She tucked her arm through his and turned him around, guiding him back toward James while she spoke. "We have a backup lined up for when she goes into labor. He's going to travel with us so there will be no delay. We also have the pilot on call so whenever you need to leave, you can."

"You're the greatest, Melody. I can't imagine not being able to be there when the baby's born." He held his hand out to Hal, who was talking to James. "How's it going, big guy?"

"Definitely not boring, Stevie. How's your beautiful wife?"

"Happy to have made it through today without going into labor."

Hal's laugh boomed through the room. "I bet."

"She's been eating a ton of mayonnaise. It's weird."

"Mayonnaise? On what?" Hal asked.

"On everything. It's weird, man."

Melody released Steve's arm and slid next to her husband, slipping an arm around his waist. "Stevie, I'd like you to meet James Montgomery, my husband. James, this is Steve Masters."

James and Steve shook hands. "It's a pleasure to meet you," James said.

"Likewise. I'd hoped we'd get to meet you tonight." He gave Melody a significant look before adding, "Music City has been abuzz."

"I bet." A uniformed waiter approached with a tray of eggnog. She grabbed one for her and one for James. "They'd convinced themselves that Bobby Kent and I would announce our nuptials any day."

James raised an eyebrow. "Who's Bobby Kent?"

Stevie looked at James like he had just asked who Albert Einstein was. "Seriously man?"

Melody took a sip of her drink and stifled a chuckle at her very disconnected husband. "A dear friend, fellow singer, and good man. We are always coupled in the tabloids. They often fake my photos to make me look pregnant and run headlines like 'Bobby Kent's Love Child', etcetera, etcetera. It's highly annoying."

"But good press," Hal said. At James' sideways glance, Hal laughed. "I don't condone it. But, every time her face is on the cover of a tabloid, her name is there with it. Name recognition is, pardon the pun, the name of the game in branding."

Melody saw a shock of bright red hair through the archway into the dining room. "There's Ray. Come on, I want you to meet him."

James held his hand out to Steve. "It was nice to meet you. Excuse us."

Steve laughed. "Go ahead. Todd just walked in, anyways."

Melody spent the evening introducing James to a good portion of her band, crew, backup singers, and dancers. He watched her with them, watched their reaction to her, watched her interaction with them, and realized that what she had was a very close, very large family. He felt a sense of relief at their signs of an initial acceptance of him, though he expected, and therefore didn't feel phased by a little skepticism.

At one point, Ray, the drummer with nearly orange-red hair and shocking green eyes suggested that they all go caroling. And somehow, James let Melody talk him into it. So the group of entertainers with a few spouses and significant others, bundled up in coats and scarves and set out to carol their way through Kurt and Morgan's gated community neighborhood.

The professional musicians made amazing music with their voices. They stomped booted feet for rhythm, and others hummed melody and harmony to accompany those who sang. The beauty of the experience moved James.

Walking back to the house, following behind Melody and Hal, James was startled when someone rushed up behind him and took his arm. He looked down at Morgan's friend, Ginger. "Hi there, Ginger. I didn't see you earlier."

"I got here late. Caught up with ya'll as you started. Wasn't that fun?"

"It was. I've never caroled before."

"Seriously?" He glanced down, certain she batted her eyes at him. "They always go caroling. It's like a thing with them or something."

"I can see that," he said with a smile.

"Last time I saw you was Morgan's wedding. I was, like, totally shocked when I saw the cover of the local section in the newspaper this morning."

"You were?" He kept an eye on Melody as she rushed away from Hal and jumped on the back of one of her male dancers. He laughed and twirled her off of him, then spun her around like a top. James' heart stopped when she looked back at him and grinned, blowing him a kiss. "I guess Melody and I are on it?"

"All over it. You'd think she would have called a certain someone."

"We've had a lot going on." James disengaged his arm as Melody twirled back to him, launching herself into his arms. She laughed with joy as her legs went around his waist and her arms around his neck. He easily caught her and kissed her, warming her cold lips. He couldn't help but smile as she slid off of him.

"Ginger!" she said, excitedly. "I'm so happy you decided to come."

They walked up Morgan's driveway and the group made their way back into the warm interior. "I was just telling James it would have been nice to get a phone call. Daddy's not too happy about it either, Mrs. *Montgomery*."

Melody slipped out of her gray coat and straightened her back. "I don't care if he's happy about it or not. Morgan didn't even find out until the day of. And yesterday we were a little busy."

Ginger's eyes filled with tears. "I thought I was your friend."

"Honey, you are." Melody put her arms around her. "I'm sorry you felt left out."

"I did feel left out. Just, " Ginger sniffed, "next time when you're making calls, at least call me after calling Hal."

Melody smiled. "Deal."

♫ ♫ ♫ ♫

HOURS later, curled up with Melody on the sofa in their apartment, sipping mugs of hot spiced cider, James kissed the top of her head. "Will you be free for church on Sunday?"

"Definitely." She sat forward. "We'll invite everyone and arrange transportation to get them all there. Then we'll have a catered lunch afterward before getting back to work."

"I think that's a great idea."

Melody leaned back against him. "Maybe. We've never been a churchgoing crowd, but I have several believers in the crew so they might like the chance."

"Are you always with your crew on Christmas?"

She took a sip of her drink and snuggled further against his chest. "So far. I always start my tours on New Year's Day. This is the third year in a row I've done it. We have so much work to do in the final stages of the launching of the tour that we start on the twenty-sixth. That might change after next year. My five year contract is up. Why do you ask?"

"The caroling was fun. Has anyone ever told you you're a pretty good singer?" He overlaid the question with understatement.

Melody laughed. "I think a few folks might have mentioned it on rare occasions. But, thank you. I appreciate it."

"And the party at Morgan's house was also a lot of fun. You work with some really talented people."

Melody leaned forward and set her cup on the coffee table. "I always kick my tour off in Atlanta and she has that party every year. I can't believe we didn't meet until now."

"For the last two years, I was in London during Christmas. Before that, I went with Mark to his wife's parents' in Savannah for Christmas. I guess God's plans were for us to meet this year."

"I guess they were. Aren't you curious about that?" Melody nervously spun the ring on her left hand. "Why now? Why the missed meetings year after year until now?"

James picked up her hand and brought it to his lips, kissing her right above the ring. "His timing is perfect. We have to trust that."

"You're right." She leaned back under his arm again, feeling content and sleepy. "What does your schedule look like next week?"

"I am considering a totally confidential merger with a Japanese firm. I'll be behind closed doors with them starting Monday morning." He slipped a hand under his glasses and rubbed his eyes with his fingers and thumb. "I should have spent the last week preparing for that, but I've been a little, how shall I say it, occupied."

Melody playfully slapped at his arm. "Occupied? Is that what you kids call it these days?"

He smiled and kissed the top of her head. "Engaged."

Snuggling even closer, she sighed and closed her eyes. "Last few hours of vacation."

He ran a hand over her arm. "How can we avoid the crushing boredom?"

Melody laughed. "I don't know. Surf the internet? Read a book? Watch reruns? I could probably unearth a deck of cards from my suitcase."

With his raised eyebrow, she grinned and lifted her face for his kiss.

♫ ♫ ♫ ♫

"**WE** can't do that song until the encore." They had gathered at the Philips arena. Hal had arranged to have it for the entire week in order to get her band and crew ready for the upcoming tour, and this Monday afternoon, she and Steve sat on the edge of the stage, busy debating the order of the songs after the first full practice. All around them people tuned instruments, or ran cable, or adjusted lights, or tested the sound system. The arena crew prepared the flooring and the overhead stanchions and the seating. Melody loved the chaos of it all.

"Melody, you can't do it last. That song is shooting up the charts. Everyone will be waiting for you to sing it all night."

"If it was any other song, I would agree with you. But the last time I sang it live, I almost lost my voice completely. We can't risk that happening again." Someone handed her a bottle of water, and she took it with a smile of thanks.

"Then don't sing it the same," he said, watching her roll her eyes. "Look, all you have to do is tone down the ending. You probably lost your voice hitting that high C."

"By the end of the show, my voice isn't going to be in the best shape as it is. I'm not singing that song in the middle of the show. The fans might get upset that I do it last, but they'll be even more upset when I have to stop half way through because I can't sing at all."

Hal walked up and touched her shoulder, which made her check the time on her phone. "I have to get to the dance studio to practice with the whole group. I'll come back here when I'm done."

"When does the fill-in get here to work with me?" Steve asked.

"He's supposed to be here in about ten minutes."

"I keep meaning to ask. Who'd you get?"

She winked as she stood and brushed off the seat of her pants. "Max Warren."

Steve's eyes bugged out of his head. "You got Max?"

"Don't worry, Stevie. I'm not replacing you." Melody teased.

"How did you get Max?" It was amusing to hear the deep respect for Maxwell Warren's talent in Steve's voice, mainly because Max had spoken equally highly of Steve Masters' musical talent.

She patted his cheek as she walked past him. "Because I'm Melody Mason," she said with a laugh. She left him staring at her with awe as she headed to her dressing room. A glance at her watch told her just how late she was running, so she hurried in to grab her bag.

In the process, she didn't see the rose that she knocked off the table. It fell to the ground and she stepped on it, crushing the delicate petals under her boot.

She found Hal backstage with David Patterson looking over the schedule for the tour. David's white shirt stretched tight against his large stomach and his tie looked too small for a man of his girth. He wore his thinning gray hair slicked back from his forehead. "Hi, David."

"Hello, Melly. I've hardly seen you since you've been in town," he said, taking her thin hand in his large, warm grip. "You should come to dinner one night this week while you've still got the chance." His eyes narrowed. "Bring your new husband."

Dismissing his tone, knowing he felt left out in the wake of her impromptu marriage, she absently waved her hand. "I'll see what I can do. Ready, Hal?"

"Yes. I'm going to go take her to Ginger's studio, David. Want to ride along, see the routines?"

"No, not today. I'll arrange to be here Thursday to see the full show," he said, turning back to Melody. "Thank you for giving Ginger the chance to dance with you, she's very excited."

"She's good. I wish she could work it into her schedule to do the entire tour with us."

"Well, you know, commitments and all. You two better get going before you're late. We'll go over those dates again, Hal. Call my office tomorrow. See when I'm free."

Hal and Melody walked to the back exit. Once out of earshot, she asked, "What problem does he have with the dates?"

"There's not enough of them," he said, reaching to open the door.

"How many different ways do we have to point my contract out to him? There is no way my body will take performing every night. I'd end up in the hospital." She stopped, angry. David Patterson was a good friend of her late father, but doing business with him was like being put through a wringer.

"Maybe if he knew why, it would be easier to explain things to him." He put his hand in the small of her back to guide her along.

They stepped outside and a brisk winter breeze instantly chilled her cheeks in stark contrast to the bright noonday sun illuminating the empty expanse of concrete. A few dozen rosy cheeked fans and bundled up reporters waited behind a roped off area. When they caught sight of Melody, cameramen started filming and fans started screaming her name. It would only get worse as the week wore on and the concert date approached. As they neared the car, Peter Glasser opened the door of the limousine.

"We can't do that, and you know it. We're still in the early stages of negotiating the deal with Marathon records. I can't risk him using that as leverage to stay with his label." She glanced up at the crowd and waved as she started to get in the car, when she spotted a man showing a pass to the security officer assigned to the barricades. "Hey, there's Max! Let me talk to him before we go."

She started toward him. Hal stepped in front of her to block her path. "Melody, we're already late—"

Hal stopped his sentence midway through a word in the exact moment Melody felt something hot and wet splash against her cheek and neck. A split second later, Melody heard a distant explosion like thunder and the sound echoed around the mostly empty parking lot. Hal just stood there with a shocked look on his face, staring down at her chest, his mouth moving, unable to speak. Melody slowly looked down at her white shirt and, to her instant horror, saw her chest covered with bright red blood. It began to steam in the cool December air.

Her world became very small as her peripheral vision evaporated. Oddly, she felt no pain, none at all.

Is this what it feels like to die, she wondered?

Hal grabbed her and threw her into the car, yelling at Peter to go. The crowd screamed in fear, now, while people dropped to the ground or ran for cover and the television crews filmed everything. The limousine peeled out of the parking lot, the rear end fishtailing as it headed in the direction of the nearest hospital.

♫ ♫ ♫ ♫

KURT'S secretary stuck her head through the doorway of Rebecca's office. "Hey there. I know you're standing guard. You need a break to go to the girl's room or anything?"

"Eve, you're a Godsend. Give me fifteen minutes to go grab a snack and I'll be right back," Rebecca said.

"Take your time," Eve said as she sat at Rebecca's desk.

Rebecca had been unable to leave her desk for the last two hours. James and Kurt were in deep negotiations with a Japanese firm, discussing a buyout that would allow Montgomery-Lawson to own a large electronics manufacturing company in Japan, thus opening a toehold in the Asian market. No one was allowed in the office, and no phone calls were permitted through, so she'd been afraid to leave her desk for any reason. Very few people knew about the meeting.

She went to the break room on her floor. Several people sat around the table in the middle of the room. She got a container of yogurt out of the refrigerator and joined the group. "Hey guys. What's up?"

"I read the paper yesterday," an intern from R&D said. "Our boss has apparently tied the knot."

Rebecca smiled. "She's a lovely woman. I got to meet her at Mr. Lawson's wedding."

A secretary from the engineering department put a hand on her forehead. "That's right. I guess Lawson and Montgomery are brothers now. What a riot!"

Rebecca started to respond, but her eyes glanced over at the silent television on the wall by the door. A breaking news report interrupted whatever medical human interest piece usually ran on the 24 hour news station this time of day. The headline in the graphics sent a cold chill through her. "Country Diva Melody Mason Shot".

"Beck?"

"Quiet!" She rushed to the television and turned up the sound.

The announcer spoke, "…outside of the Philips arena. Melody Mason was rushed to Westwood hospital…" The footage showed an explosion of blood all over Melody's chest about one second before her manager, Hal Coleman, bodily shoved her into the back of her limousine. Then the footage looped. The look on Melody's face in that split second was an expression of complete surprise followed by terror.

Rebecca's pulse started pounding and she could only hear a roaring sound in her ears. She didn't even hear the gasps of the other people in the room. The yogurt fell forgotten from her hands as she ran from the break room. She impatiently kicked off her high heeled shoes and sprinted down the hall. She knocked someone over as she rounded a corner, but she regained her balance and burst into her office. Eve looked up, shocked. Rebecca yelled as she headed toward the big oak door at the other end, "Go to Kurt's office and find his car keys. Try to find that pass he got from Melody Mason's people. Go now, hurry — it's an emergency. Run!"

She threw open the door to James' office, going straight to his desk to look through the stack of mail she'd placed there before his meeting began. James sat at the conference table with Kurt and five other men, three of whom were the representatives from Japan. "What in the world, Rebecca?" he asked, startled.

She faced down the table of men, putting her hand to her chest. She panted so hard it took a moment before she could speak. "Melody's been shot — she's at Westwood." James and Kurt bolted out of their chairs, almost to the private elevator doors before she even finished her sentence. Desperate, she looked through the stack again and finally found what she was looking for.

"James, wait. Here's the pass Hal Coleman sent over this morning — you're going to need it to get in the hospital. Eve is bringing Kurt's keys and his pass," she said. She ran to the coat stand in the corner of his office and grabbed his coat, making sure his phone was in the pocket before she handed it over to him.

Eve ran into the office and handed everything over to Kurt, then the two men stepped into the elevator and began their descent to the parking garage. Rebecca and Eve turned and looked at the shocked gentlemen at the table, and Rebecca gave a weak smile. Eve turned to her and said, "You want to tell me what's going on?"

♫ ♫ ♫ ♫

JAMES tried Melody's cell, then Hal's. When he got no answer at either number, he mentally flipped through the information pages of the clients who used his technology and pictured the number to the Westwood Hospital. He dialed while Kurt drove onto the shoulder to pass an out of town driver who was driving a mere five miles over the posted speed limit. James ground his teeth when he got a busy signal. "It's busy."

"Keep trying," Kurt said. He used his own phone to try to call Morgan. When there was no answer at the house, he called her mobile. "Morgan," he said.

"Oh, thank God almighty, Kurt," Morgan prayed a brief relieved prayer of thanks. "I just tried to get you at your office. Did you hear?"

"Yeah, I'm on my way to the hospital now," he said, careening onto the exit ramp and passing another car.

"I'm almost there. I'll see you when you get there," she said, and disconnected the phone.

James hung up the phone and then threw it with some force to the floorboard. "I can't get through." His stomach turned to a hard knot of fear.

"Half the free world is probably trying to get through," Kurt said. "Turn on the radio, maybe they know something."

He scanned the stations until he found a country channel. A song by Melody was just finishing, as the disc jockey came on the air. "That was *Red Roses and White Lies* by Melody Mason. Once again, for those of you just tuning in, there is an unconfirmed report that Melody Mason has been shot outside the Philips arena while leaving rehearsals for her upcoming concert tour. We have no information to report to you at this time, and we would like to stress that these are unconfirmed reports. We'll keep you updated as we learn anything but let's keep that little lady in our prayers."

He scanned the stations and ended up on the local talk radio channel. Some anonymous caller was expressing her opinion that "… probably that new husband has something to do with it. I read in the *Journal* his first wife was murdered, too."

James stabbed the button to turn off the radio and barely clamped down on a curse word before it could escape from his lips. Kurt skidded into the hospital parking lot. A huge crowd had gathered outside and the police worked at setting up barricades. Kurt pulled into the grass in front of the emergency entrance. The two men jumped out of the vehicle. As they passed the uniformed security at the scene, one held out a hand to stop them. "You two can't go in there," he said.

James pulled the pass Rebecca had given him out of his coat pocket. "I'm Melody's husband."

Immediately, the security officer opened the barricade to let them pass, handing the paperwork back over to James. "I apologize for the delay, sirs. This gentleman will take you in." The crowd protested someone gaining entrance, while paparazzo snapped photos of the men important enough to enter through the barricades, and still more people arrived to take up the vigil. They started lighting candles in little paper cups.

Kurt looked out at the gathering crowd and mused, "Don't these people have jobs?"

The guard took them past the waiting room, straight to a room off the emergency room guarded by a uniformed policeman and Melody's driver, Peter Glasser. Peter opened the door and stood back to let them go inside.

When the door opened, Melody immediately looked up. James felt his breath catch when he saw Melody sitting next to the bed.

"It's not my blood," Melody announced, her voice pitched high on the edge of panic. Rust colored blood covered her once white shirt. There was blood in her hair and spatter on her neck and cheek. A doctor worked on Melody's arm, applying a white bandage.

When what she said registered, James realized she was sitting next to the bed holding Hal's hand. The big man lay unconscious, hooked up to IV's and monitors, his normally dark chocolate brown skin looked nearly gray. A stark white bandage covered his shoulder and part of his massive chest.

James went to Melody and knelt beside her chair, putting his arms around her. "I love you, baby." He looked over at Hal. "Is he going to be okay?"

The doctor answered, "Yes, he'll be really sore, but he'll be okay. The bullet went through his shoulder and nicked a vein which we sutured. Don't ask me how, but it missed arteries and bone. Someone was watching out for him."

He handed a tube of medicine to Melody. "Put this on twice a day, and keep it clean. The residue on the bullet could cause a nasty infection. I'm going to keep Mr. Coleman overnight at least. I want to keep him on the intravenous antibiotics for a few more hours and observe him. He lost a lot of blood. You're wearing most of it."

Melody felt James tense. "It only scratched me. It went through Hal and grazed my arm." As she continued to explain, her voice came out in an even monotone absent of emotion, as if analyzing a spreadsheet or discussing historical events. "He stepped in front of me. He stepped in front of me to make me get in the car. If he hadn't done that, the bullet would have hit me in the chest."

She buried her face in his neck and sobbed, "He's always blocking me like that. I always tell him it's rude."

The doctor gathered his supplies. "I'm going outside to make a statement. Everyone thinks you're the one who was shot, Miss Mason." Melody nodded as the doctor left.

"Has Morgan been in here yet, Melly?" Kurt asked.

"She went to find a signal to try to call you to tell you I was okay. She wasn't sure how much longer you'd be, and she knew you two were frantic about me."

They all looked up as Detective Roberts walked into the room. "Mrs. Montgomery, Suarez just called and said that another rose was in your dressing room." He cleared his throat, "The note read, 'bang, you're dead.'"

"I didn't see it," Melody said in a panicked voice. "I'm about to go out of my mind."

James stood and looked at Roberts. "Did anyone see anything this time?"

"No one so far. We're obtaining copies of the news footage now, and we have a request in for a warrant in case the stations give us a hard time. We'll want your wife to look them over, see if there's anyone around she recognizes." He looked at Melody. "I'm going to go help Suarez interview your crew, see if we can find out how he got into your dressing room," Roberts said.

Morgan came into the room, saw Kurt, and went straight to his arms. "I've never been so scared in my life," she said.

Hal opened his eyes and frowned at the crowd in his room. Melody reached for his hand again, and gave it a squeeze. He turned his head to look at her. "You okay, Melody?"

"Yeah, Hal. You took my bullet. I never thought I'd say that to anyone," she said as she smiled at him.

"Sounds like a good song title." Hal constantly teased Melody about country song titles. "You took my bullet and I gave you my heart?"

"Don't make me laugh right now. I'm trying to maintain my composure."

"What's all that blood?" he asked her, indicating her shirt.

"Yours," she said, her eyes welling up again. "You passed out on me in the car."

Hal's eyes slowly closed as if his lids were very heavy. "Better me than you, baby girl," he whispered as he fell asleep again.

James remembered the men he left in his office. "I have to call Rebecca," he told Melody, "I'm going to step outside."

"Will you go to my car and get my bag? Peter can get it for you. That way, he can take the car to get it cleaned up and not have to fight to get back through the crowds." She stood and went to the door.

"Where's your car?" he asked.

She stuck her head out the door and spoke quietly with Peter. She turned back to James. "He'll take you."

"You want some coffee, too?" James asked, running a finger down her cheek. She nodded and watched him walk away. She went to the sink in the corner of the room.

"Oh, man. No wonder everyone keeps reacting the way they do when they see me," she said as she looked in the mirror. She ran water on a paper towel, added some soap, and started to scrub at the dried blood on her face.

Morgan went to her and took the paper towel from her, then held her chin in her hands and took over the task. "Let me do this before you rub your skin off." She worked for a few minutes, going through several towels, then lifted a strand of Melody's hair, looking at the blood matting it. "There's nothing I can do about this right now."

"Do you have a clip or something?" Melody asked her. Morgan shook her head. "That's okay, I have one in my bag." She wrapped her arms around her sister. "I'm scared, Morg."

"So am I, honey," Morgan said as she hugged her back.

♫ ♫ ♫ ♫

JAMES followed the security guard out through a back entrance to the hospital and pulled his phone out of his pocket. He dialed his office number and Rebecca picked up on the first ring. "She's fine, Rebecca," he began without preamble, "Hal Coleman was shot, but he's going to be all right, too."

"I've been so worried. The news footage was awful," Rebecca said.

"What happened after we left?"

"At first they were highly offended, but I explained everything to them. Apparently, Melody Mason is a big star in Japan, too, and with your marriage and Kurt's family connection, they understood and said that they would wait at the hotel for you to complete your personal business."

"Good. I'll be in first thing. Have a car at the hotel at nine to pick up our friends, and call to let them know what's happening now." They reached the car. When Peter opened the back door and pulled Melody's bag out of the back seat, James saw the amount of blood on the seat, and thought that it was a good thing Hal was such a big guy. "And get me Redman."

"Yes, sir."

Frustrated and angry — more angry than he could ever remember feeling — he slammed the door of the car much harder than he needed to. He whirled around and leaned against the car door. He had to get a grip on his emotions or else he was going to make a mistake or do something he would regret.

Mike Redman was on the phone in seconds. "Heard what happened, James. Is Melody okay?"

"She's fine. Her manager was shot, but it's not life threatening. I need you to arrange protection for Melody."

"I'm on it. I actually know someone who will be perfect."

"Have him contact me immediately."

"Her."

James paused. "Her?"

"Trust me."

He internally debated, considered, and decided in the span of two heartbeats. "Have her call me immediately."

He disconnected the call.

Peter Glasser narrowed his eyes at him. "I am Miss Mason's protection."

"Understood. However," James straightened and did not flinch from the anger on the other man's face. "*Mrs. Montgomery* needs more than someone trained at keeping the crowds of adoring fans at bay." He slipped the strap of the bag over his shoulder. "Unless you think I'm mistaken in light of where we're presently standing."

The younger man's face fell. "You're absolutely right. I'm sorry, sir."

"Don't be sorry. Help us be diligent. Now we know this is real."

Without another word, he left the driver at the car and walked back to the hospital.

♪ ♪ ♪ ♪

DAVID and Ginger Patterson came to the hospital and left after a short visit. Kurt and Morgan left at dinnertime, promising Hal that they'd come back in the morning. It took James another three hours to convince Melody to leave. Hal finally intervened, telling her that he wasn't going back to sleep until she left, no matter how much the doctor said he needed to rest. She finally conceded and asked James to drive her back to the hotel so she could talk to her crew.

He watched her as she had them all gather in one of the suites. She was obviously well liked, but more importantly, well respected. It was apparent that she was their leader, and he felt proud to be her husband. She explained to everyone what the doctor had said to her, then answered as many questions as she could, not giving any detail about the roses or threats.

"Are we still performing Friday?" Todd asked.

"Yes. Nothing changes. The band needs to continue rehearsing, as well as the dancers. I'll be back to work Wednesday, going first to the dance studio then to the Philips arena. I've not danced with everyone yet, so that needs to be the focus of my practice. We'll still have a full show rehearsal on Thursday, but the songs that don't require dancing aren't going to get played more than the intro and end. We've all done the songs enough times that we could do them in our sleep, so we don't need to practice doing them, we just need to practice the stage movements for them. There's that complicated entrance for *You Got Me Tied in Knots* that we're going to shelve until Jacksonville. I can't focus on that right now."

"How can we perform with Hal shot?" someone asked her.

"Listen, ya'll. You know Hal will blow a gasket if we cancel the show. Besides, I know Hal well enough to know that he's not going to stay in bed if he's not tied down. He'll be up and around by Thursday."

She answered more questions until the questions started repeating, then dismissed everyone. "Get some rest tonight. I'll see all y'all tomorrow." James stayed in the back of the room until the last person left, then went to Melody and pulled her into his arms.

"There's someone here you need to meet," he said.

Melody felt more exhausted than she'd felt in her life, but she didn't protest as James took her hand and led her to the room on the floor that had been turned into Hal's office. She walked in and stopped short when she saw a tall, thin woman with brown hair that brushed her shoulders, dark eyes that sized her up like a predator, and only one arm.

"Jennifer Thorne, I'd like you to meet my wife, Melody Mason."

"Montgomery," Melody said, correcting him.

Despite the day, James smiled. "Montgomery. Melody, this is Jen."

Melody stepped forward with her right hand extended. "Nice to meet you, Jen."

The woman was classically beautiful, but her hazel eyes looked hard, mean. It detracted from her beauty and threw Melody off. "Likewise. You know why I'm here?"

She looked at James and back at the woman. "I'm going to guess, by the shoulder holster and the gun, that you're to be my bodyguard."

Jen raised an eyebrow and her eyes momentarily softened. "Personal security."

"Are you law enforcement?"

"I am not. I worked for the government until —" she paused, shrugging the shoulder on the side with the missing arm. "— recently. Anyway, I contract privately, now."

"May I ask what happened to your arm?"

"It was a freak accident. I was chopping carrots and just didn't want to stop." Her delivery was perfectly deadpan.

Melody, likewise, kept a straight face, "So you'd rather not discuss it then."

"I like to keep that subject at arm's length."

Despite herself, Melody smiled. "Okay, then. What do you need from me?"

"Mostly, I'm going to be invisible and quiet. If that ever changes, I need you to listen to me the first time I speak and never argue with me or second guess me. About anything. Be where you say you are and go where I tell you to be. If something happens, you don't have to understand it while it's happening. Just take direction and you'll come through it. We can vacillate in chains about the details and minutia over coffee a week later. We'll have that luxury because you'll be alive to buy it for me." Jen looked at her watch. "What do you need from me?"

"Other than the obvious?" Melody decided immediately that she liked this woman. She didn't know why, but she very much did. "I need you to be obscure. I don't want my crew afraid."

"I will do what I can under the purview of keeping you alive," Jen said. "Are you staying here?"

"No. We have an apartment." Melody turned to James. "Are you ready to go home?" she asked in a tight voice. Reaction was starting to set in.

"I like that," James said. "Home." He pulled her into his arms and hugged her tight.

♫ ♫ ♫ ♫

MELODY woke up to the sound of James' voice coming from the other room. She heard another voice that she almost recognized, then heard James again. She rolled over and found the clock. To her dismay she discovered it was four-thirty in the morning.

Moving slowly, she rolled out of bed and rubbed her temples. The headache there felt slight, and she knew it wasn't worse because James had her so relaxed by the time she fell asleep. Her arm ached where the bullet grazed it, but it was just an annoying pain and nothing major.

He'd brought her to his — to their apartment and made her eat a bowl of soup, then he ran her a hot bath, lighting scented candles in the bathroom. She'd sipped on a cup of spearmint tea while she soaked, and when she found herself nearly dozing off in the tub, he'd made her lie face down on the bed while he gave her a gentle massage. At some point during his ministrations, she'd fallen asleep.

She turned on the lamp by the bed as she stood, feeling slightly wobbly. After she dressed she went to the bathroom and splashed her face with cold water. The cool splash of the water eased some of the headache, but she went ahead and took two headache pills from the nearly full bottle in the medicine cabinet.

She found James in the living room with Roberts and Suarez. The bookcases that covered the wall were slid back, revealing a very intense and high speed electronics system complete with a large wall-sized monitor and several smaller monitors. James held a wireless keyboard in one hand and typed something very rapidly on it with his free hand while Suarez loaded a disc into a DVD player.

"Hi," she said. All three men looked up, surprised. "What is this? A command console?"

"Just some toys." James looked up, distracted.

She realized that at that moment, her love for this man doubled. "Is that the news footage?"

James set the keyboard down and his eyes cleared. He walked to her, taking her face in his hands and looking at her closely. He rubbed his thumbs across the shadows under her eyes and said, "You should have slept for at least another hour."

"I'm fine, James. I'm not going to collapse on you," she said.

"Let me hear you say that after you finish your dance rehearsal today," he said, kissing the tip of her nose.

"*Touché.*" She sat down on one of the leather chairs near the chess set, drawing her legs under her. "Where's Jen?"

"Sleeping while these guys are here. She made a pallet in my office."

She looked at Roberts. "Were you gentlemen able to find anything out at the Philips arena yesterday?" she asked the detectives as James went into the kitchen.

"Anything about this note strike you as odd?" Roberts tossed an evidence bag on the coffee table. Inside and visible through the clear bag was the note from the rose. It read:

BANG! YOU'RE DEAD.

Melody nodded. "Looks like the same handwriting and same kind of paper."

Suarez said, "Right on both counts."

James returned with a cup of coffee which he offered to her. She gratefully accepted it.

Suarez pulled out a notebook and began to flip through the pages, but Roberts spoke before Suarez found what he was looking for. "Nothing from any witnesses. However, we did pull the footage from the hidden security cameras we installed. One of them points directly at your dressing room door. We have that with us now. Someone left that rose and that note for you. That someone had to go into your dressing room."

James said, "Perhaps he's made his first mistake."

Roberts answered him, "We can only hope. He might have guessed they were there, but we know for a fact no one could see them."

"The first tape is from Channel 4 News. They were on the scene from twelve until the shooting, which puts them there for approximately thirty-five minutes," Suarez said.

James turned one of the couches around and pushed it across the room closer to the console, then gestured at it for the detectives to sit. Then he sat adjacent to Melody and hit the 'play' button on the remote. They watched a young newscaster give a brief synopsis of Melody's career as the cameraman made a sweep of the parking lot and the building. She stopped halfway through a sentence a few times and started over, rather tediously. Then she went on.

They watched as the crowd grew, and the police continued to monitor the entrance into the building. Melody gave the names and jobs of those coming in that she recognized. For the people she didn't know by name, she told the men that Hal would know. Then the sound picked up the excitement of the crowd as Melody and Hal emerged. They saw Hal guide Melody to the car, saw her wave to the crowd then start toward it before Hal stepped in front of her. They watched the red stain suddenly cover Melody's chest then they heard the shot. In a heartbeat, Hal had Melody picked up and shoved in the back of the car while Peter jumped into the front and the car tore away.

The cameraman scanned the crowd and behind the crowd, but his movements were so jerky, and he did it so late that they weren't able to see anything. He apparently calmed down and redid the scan, waiting for the anchor to get up off the ground. The sound picked up her sobbing then getting herself under control before she ordered the camera to be trained back on her. She gave an accounting of what she saw, then she said, "cut," and the tape was over.

"Wow," James said in a hoarse voice.

A tremor rushed through Melody's body. "No wonder everyone thought I'd been shot," she said, running her hands through her hair and taking a sip of her coffee with jerky movements. "I just thought I was shot." She couldn't sit still so she surged to her feet to pace. "Play the next one," she said as she waved a hand in the direction of the screen.

The next one was similar to the first, without the big preamble and a slightly different angle of the shooting. This cameraman didn't panic, and immediately swept the area behind the crowd, but they saw nothing out of the ordinary.

"Look up," James said.

Melody took her eyes off of the screen long enough to look at him. "Why?"

Suarez was the one who answered. "With a crowd that size, he couldn't have been coming from behind them. And Mr. Coleman has a good eight inches on you. The bullet went through his shoulder and nicked your arm." He gestured with his hands. "Obviously moving at a downward angle. The time between impact and the sound of the shot indicates that the shooter was between 1 and 3 hundred yards away. Close for a supersonic round from a high powered rifle."

There was nothing different in the beginning of the other two tapes, and by the end, Melody was trying hard to feel immune to the sight of Hal's blood spraying all over her. She concentrated on faces when the cameramen turned to scan the crowd behind them. The last one they saw, the camera jerked up accidentally, and for a brief moment, they saw a gleam coming from the upper window of a building. "Function voice. DVD, pause. Back ten frames, pause. Advance and pause by frame," James ordered.

To everyone's astonishment, the TV began to execute the commands James spoke. He replied to Melody's questioning look. "Sometimes it's easier to just talk things out." He looked back at the television. "Play. Pause." He walked over to the large screen and double tapped it several times then drew a box with his fingertips.

The image zoomed forward, refocused, zoomed forward, refocused, enhanced, and zoomed forward until an image clearly appeared in the window of a building behind the arena. "There," he said, pointing to the screen. "DVD, show count by hundredths of seconds." In the corner of the screen appeared 362.14 seconds.

Suarez jotted it down in his book and said, "We'll have the lab guys calculate the trajectory."

James nodded again. "Function voice. DVD compile all imagery and model for 3-D with wire frame. Build CAD. Texture light. Extrapolate at 30 percent. Execute and show count."

The last three DVDs worth of footage became wire frame three dimensional overlays of the area. The limousine became the central point of reference in an artificial world the computer instantly created, treating all the input as data. Before their amazed eyes, the computer James had in his living room built an entire world out of electrons. Each set of footage was represented by a different color and the overlays became textured with the participants involved. When the count reached zero, James said, "Calculate trajectory and force of projectile. Intersection-resection and zoom. Extrapolate at 50 percent. Execute and show count."

He nodded to his guests and explained, "This will take longer."

Roberts said, "Oh. Well, no problem, Mr. Montgomery. We have a minute."

After perhaps three minutes the computer had calculated the trajectory of the shot and compiled all available footage to enhance the area of the shot's origin. "I wonder if that could be further enhanced," James speculated.

"Maybe," Suarez said. "We'll definitely take it in to the lab and see what they can do with it."

"Mind if I keep a copy and give it to my guys?" James asked. "I probably have equipment that's a little more advanced than what you currently have."

Suarez stood. "That's evidence. I'm afraid we can't release it to you. Can you point me in the direction of your rest room?" James sighed and gestured in the general direction.

"Mind if I help myself to a glass of water?" Roberts asked on his way out of the room.

James lifted an eyebrow, but made no comment. Then, to Melody, it sounded like he said something like, "Function voice. Write full mem to waffle, 3 through 370 seconds layers all. Compile to bin and offload differentials in 240 hurts increments. Alarm upon complete." She could only imagine the technical acronyms and jargon if she were later forced to write down his words. In about twenty seconds, a box below the monitor made a low chime sound like someone ringing the doorbell on a dollhouse.

Roberts returned from the kitchen a second later, empty handed. "What does something like that cost?" he asked James, visibly impressed with the equipment.

"Right now, about two point six million dollars in R & D," James said, pushing a button to retrieve the micro-SD card, no larger than the nail of his pinkie finger, and pocketing it as Suarez returned to the room.

Roberts let out a low whistle then offered, "If you're ever feeling charitable, the Atlanta Police Department could probably use something like that."

"Find this guy, and you can consider it done," James said, meaning it.

"Let's look at the security footage," Suarez said as he took a sip of his coffee.

James loaded it in the machine and told it to play at fast speed. A period of about two hours was covered, and several people went in and out of her dressing room. They stopped it when they saw Suarez go in, showing that the shooting had already occurred, and backed up, beginning the process again. James left the room after the first run. Melody looked at her watch. It was seven-thirty.

"Who's that?" Roberts asked her, pointing to a woman with dreadlocks and a large bag going into the room.

"Lisa, my makeup and hair artist," Melody said tiredly.

"Why would she be going in?" Suarez asked her.

"Probably to catalog my outfits and boots for the concert. I have ten to twenty seconds to change clothes, and she needs to be ready for me when I step off the stage."

"Who is that?"

"David Patterson, owner of Patterson Records, my record label."

"Why would he be going in?"

"He was probably looking for me or Hal. There was some point that we were up in the lighting booth, talking with the tech up there."

"Who is that?"

"Steve Masters, my lead guitarist." She held up her hand to keep him from asking the next question. "I know the routine. He was probably going in to check e-mail. His wife is pregnant and due in a few weeks." She watched for the next person. "Gina Cobb, backup singer. She's delivering a pair of boots in Atlanta Falcons colors." Roberts slanted her a look out of the corner of his eye. Melody shrugged. "They probably have a shot at the Super Bowl this year if he plays deep in his bench in the early quarters."

Suarez looked impressed, "You get no argument from me on that point."

Melody continued, "I have a jersey the team signed and I'm going to sing that song they play before Monday Night football," she smiled. "It's a crowd pleaser." She continued, "That's a sound tech. Some wiring was delivered and accidentally stored in my room instead of the storeroom. Hal sent him in there to get it out. I don't know his name." She went on through the list, knowing most names, but not all. She did, however, have a reason for everyone who went in.

Suarez was frustrated. "You have a lot of traffic in and out of your dressing room," he said to her.

"Most of the people had a specific purpose for going in there."

"That's about all we have for you to review, now," Suarez said.

Melody felt frustration well up in her chest. "We didn't find anything!" she said.

"Sure we did," Suarez said, but Jen came into the room and interrupted him.

"Has the FBI stepped in yet?"

Roberts nodded. "Sniper shooting in this area is almost certainly going to be labeled as domestic terrorism. They're just advising at this point, though. Suarez and I are still on lead."

Jen handed her phone to Roberts. "Can you give me your digits? I'll need a POC."

"A what?"

Her eyebrows knitted momentarily. "A point of contact."

"That can be either one of us," he said. "We're pretty much on this full time as of yesterday."

James came back into the room, dressed in a gray suit with a dark green striped tie, fastening his watch. "I need to leave to finish a meeting I started yesterday. I'm going to take Melody to the hospital. There's still a police guard at the door, and she'll have Jen here to escort her wherever she needs to go."

Roberts and Suarez stood simultaneously. "We appreciate your time, Mrs. Montgomery. Mr. Montgomery. We'll take the other disc to the lab now. Hopefully they can get something useful from it."

Melody nodded.

"Keep me updated," James said, walking the men to the door.

Melody went into the bedroom and ran a brush through her hair. She looked through a drawer in the bedroom until she found her cap and glasses. She tucked her hair into her hat to get ready to go.

She turned and jumped when she saw James watching her from the doorway. "Do you want to get something to eat before we go?" he asked her.

"No. I can get something at the hospital. Knowing Morgan, she's probably brought a buffet for Hal to choose from."

He smiled, figuring she was right. "I called and spoke with Kurt. He's already dropped Morgan off there. The doctor said you guys can take him home anytime."

"I'm so glad they're releasing him."

They walked into the living room. Jen nodded toward the door. "I'm going to go secure the vehicle. Wait 8 minutes then take the elevator straight down. I'll see you in the lobby."

"We'll be right down." James looked at his watch as he turned to Melody. "Do you have any of your CDs here with you?"

"Yeah, in my bag. Why?"

James cleared his throat, looking a little uncomfortable. "Rebecca said that the gentlemen I was in a meeting with yesterday are fans. I just spoke with her, and she said that they are drilling Kurt with questions about you, impressed with our relationships with you." He rubbed the back of his neck. "Could you possibly autograph three of your CDs so that I can present them as tokens of apology for leaving yesterday's meeting?" He looked at the floor while he spoke.

"Of course." She dug through her bag until she found the CDs and went to his office, spotting Jen's rolled up pallet in the corner by a black canvas bag. She pulled a permanent marker out of a pen holder and sat at the desk. "What do you want me to say?"

James got a piece of paper and wrote something on it, then set it in front of her. She looked at it, paused, then looked at him. "What is that?"

"That's Japanese cuneiform. This says, '*Doumo arigatou gozaimasu*', which is 'thank you very much'. The last symbol is your name in Japanese."

"You speak Japanese?" she asked him.

"Yeah. I learned it when we knew we were going to pursue this deal."

She sat back and crossed her arms. "You learned it to do this deal?" She raised an eyebrow. "Do you speak any other languages?"

"Do we have to go into this now?" he asked her, color flushing his cheeks. "I'm already late."

"Then I suggest you answer my question."

He let out a big sigh, then looked at his hands. "I speak Japanese, French, and Spanish. I learned Greek to read the Bible. I tried to learn Mandarin but Rebecca is fluent so I only learned tourist Chinese. I have just enough of an understanding to get by with a conversation."

"Just get by, huh?"

"Well, it's a difficult language, and I haven't really had the time to study it. There are a lot of dialects."

"Well, in that case, you're forgiven." His humility at his genius absolutely floored her. "How do you speak all those languages?"

He tapped his temple and shrugged. "The memory, remember? It's almost perfectly photographic. It makes it a little easier for me. I watch movies with foreign language dubbing, and read the captions in the same languages. It helps me learn faster." He began to tap his fingers on the desk. "Can you just do that so we can go?"

"Why James, you're embarrassed." She laughed and put a hand on his cheek. "I love you and think you're remarkable." She gave him a warm kiss then said, "All right, let's see that paper. I'll write the thank you thing but I'm just signing my name. That way they know it's the real deal."

♫ ♫ ♫ ♫

MELODY found Hal sitting up in the bed, scowling. She smiled as she kissed his cheek. "Hi there. What has you so riled?"

"Clarissa was just here, blubbering all over the place. That woman seriously makes me uncomfortable," he said.

She sat down and narrowed her eyes. "What did you say to her?"

"I told her you weren't paying her all that money so she could hang out in my hospital room getting all weepy." He fidgeted as Melody's eyes narrowed further. For some reason, he felt the need to defend himself. "The tour starts in just four days. There were dancers waiting for her at the studio."

"Hal, how can someone with as big a brain as yours be such an idiot? She was here because she's so in love with you that she can't see straight, and probably wanted to see for herself that you were really okay."

"What exactly do you mean, she's in love with me?" he bellowed.

"She is full on, one hundred percent, head over heals in love with you. Everyone knows it. You'd have to be blind not to see it."

He looked down and began to pick at the blanket. "Did you bring me any clothes?" he asked, changing the subject.

"Morgan said she'd take care of that," she said, giving up.

"She went to call Kurt and update him on me." He looked at the doorway to his room, where Jen stood. "I see you had to get protection, since I don't seem to be capable."

Melody leaned over until her head was pillowed on his arm. "You're capable enough to be lying here instead of me."

The doctor arrived shortly after her, checked Hal's stitches, handed over some antibiotics and pain pills, then declared him free to go. They had to wait for a nurse to come in and remove the IV's, then Jen, Melody and Morgan stepped out into the hall to wait for a nurse to help Hal get dressed.

The doctor returned and stopped to speak to Melody. "Miss Mason, Mr. Coleman needs to have his stitches removed in two weeks. He told me you would be in Houston then. Here is a number for a colleague of mine there. I've already called him, and Mr. Coleman has an appointment for the tenth at nine o'clock local time that morning."

"Thank you so much. I confess that I hadn't thought about it."

"Here is my card with my cell number on it as well. If Mr. Coleman needs to seek medical attention between now and then, any doctor can contact me and I'll be happy to give whatever information I need to about his wound or treatment." He handed over his card, then added, "My wife and I are looking forward to the show Friday."

"I hope you enjoy it. If you'd like, I'll have someone send you some backstage passes. I'd love to meet your wife."

He smiled. "That would be wonderful. She's a big fan. She really likes that new one you do. The one you sang at the awards."

Melody held out her hand and took his between both of hers. "Thank you for your help."

As the doctor left, one of Melody's security guards approached. "We're ready for him, Melody." She had everyone on her crew call her Melody, especially in public. It was part of her brand image. "Hospital security is lending a hand. We shouldn't have any problems."

"Good. They're about out now. This is Jen Thorne. Start coordinating everything through her if it has anything to do with me." As she said that, the door opened and Hal slowly made his way to the hall. "Let's go."

♪ ♪ ♪ ♪

KURT and James sat in James' office after the men from Japan left. Kurt had his feet propped up on James' desk, his hands laced behind his head. "Can you believe we just did that?" Kurt asked.

"Especially after running out on them yesterday," James said, rubbing his eyes.

"Yeah, well, I think the CDs tipped the scales. They don't call you a genius for nothing."

James laughed. "Some people call me a moron."

"Only those who love you." Kurt quipped.

James sat back, contemplating the magnitude of human effort represented by the thin stack of signed documents atop his desk. "Montgomery-Lawson just became one of the biggest privately owned electronics firms in the world." He looked at the clock on his desk. "It's already three. What do you say the owners take the rest of the day off and go kiss our wives?"

"What good is being at the top if you never take advantage of it?"

James reached over and hit the button for the intercom for Rebecca's office. "Hey, Rebecca, come in here, please."

She opened the door almost immediately, pad and pencil in hand, and came up short when she saw James and Kurt, happily lounging back. "Yes, sir?"

"Am I done for the day?" he asked.

"According to my schedule, you are. Do you want your messages?"

"Not particularly. Is there anything urgent in them?"

"The only one I can think of came from Mrs. Montgomery. She said that she needs you or Mr. Lawson to come hold Mr. Coleman down. Apparently, they need to get him to take his medication." She referred to her book, trying to hold back the smile.

James laughed so hard he had to sit his chair back up. "Well, Kurt, I believe we just received our excuse to go home. Rebecca, if anyone calls, we had an urgent family matter to see to."

"Yes, sir." She smiled as she went back to her office.

♫ ♫ ♫ ♫

Chapter 25

THE next few days passed by in a flurry of activity. Melody worked with the crew during the day, and helped James entertain the three men from Japan in the evenings.

Wednesday, James and Melody attended a special prayer meeting at their church, praying for the coming year. Melody held onto James' hand as she sat next to him on the pew, then knelt with him during prayer, enjoying ending the year worshiping with him in their church, knowing that the coming year would have them going in so many different directions.

Thursday morning, they had breakfast with Mark Knight, who had returned from Savannah. He entertained them with stories of his nieces' and nephews' antics at Christmas, and they brought him up to date on the investigation. He spent some time in prayer with them, praying for Melody's safety during her tour and for the police investigation.

After an amazing meal in the hotel restaurant, they took Mark to the airport. He held Melody's hands in both of his. "God bless you, sister. I pray that you and James have a beautiful future. Keep God first with you two, and you'll not do wrong."

"Thank you, Mark. I can't wait to see you again." She kissed both his cheeks and hugged him.

He turned to James and held out his hand. "Brother, I'll keep the chair in the pub warm for you."

James smiled, pulling Mark to him for a hug. "I'll be there in a few weeks."

They left him at the security gate and walked hand in hand back to the waiting car.

Hal was up and out of bed by Thursday and watched the full rehearsal from a seat in the front row of the arena, throwing out insults and criticisms every other breath. Melody was surprised that half of the crew didn't quit by the time he finished with them, because she almost quit by the time that he was done with her.

At one point she left him in the middle of a tirade, stormed to her bag backstage, and came back with his bottle of prescription pain pills which she threw at him with all her strength from the stage. Her aim was his forehead, but he caught them with his good hand just before it hit its target. He didn't take any pills, but decided it'd probably be best if he kept his opinions to himself for a while.

Knowing that the next day would be the beginning of an exhausting marathon of tour dates and concerts, James and Melody brought in the New Year quietly at the apartment. Jen stayed in James' office, not interested in watching the ball drop. At midnight, James took Melody's face gently between his hands.

"I love you, Mrs. Montgomery," he said softly.

"I love you, Mr. Montgomery," she said. His kiss was warm, sweet, and full of the promise of their future.

♫ ♫ ♫ ♫

FRIDAY morning, Melody opened her eyes slowly. She lay there for a moment, listening to James breathing beside her, and thought about what she had to do that day. There was so much preparation involved in putting on a show, and it all came to a head on the day of the performance. All of a sudden, the nausea hit her full force and she barely made it to the bathroom. She vomited until her stomach muscles hurt, then leaned back and rested against the wall. Eventually, she stood on shaky legs to splash her face with water and brush her teeth. She turned to go back to the bedroom and nearly ran into James, who quietly watched her.

"I'm sorry I woke you," she grumbled, as she brushed by him to bury herself under the covers, suddenly very cold.

"What's wrong? Today's not a good day to have the flu," he said, concerned.

"It's not the flu." She buried her head under her pillow, wishing he would shut up.

"Are you pregnant?" Despite the intellectual knowledge that she couldn't possibly have pregnancy symptoms this early, a little spark of hope bloomed and carried in his voice.

"No, I'm not pregnant." That little spark sputtered out and died.

"Then, what's wrong?"

"It's just nerves. I haven't been on tour in a long time." She lifted her head and glared at him. "Leave me alone."

Not understanding the display of temper, but deciding to leave it alone for now, he thought he'd just go take a shower and give her some alone time. "What time will you be at the arena?"

"Probably about two." She heard the shower start, and groaned as another wave of sickness washed over her. Clutching her stomach, she bent nearly double and willed herself back to sleep.

♫ ♫ ♫ ♫

"**MELODY** sent these to you. She said she's sorry she couldn't get them to you sooner, but things have been a little crazy," James said, standing on Rebecca's front porch and handing her two backstage passes. "She said you might enjoy seeing the show from the wings rather than down on the floor, but if you want to, you can access the crowd from the stage without needing to use any tickets."

Rebecca was surprised. She didn't think Melody had remembered their conversation at the wedding. "Thank you," she whispered.

"Thank you." He started to walk away but turned around. "God has blessed me with you, Rebecca. I don't think I say it often enough."

Rebecca raised an eyebrow, knowing he'd never said it. Ever. "I could say the same, sir," she said.

"See you tonight."

♫ ♫ ♫ ♫

JAMES sat in Melody's dressing room watching her go through some deep breathing exercises. She was a mess. He didn't see how she was going to be able to perform tonight in this shape. She was shaky, nauseated, irritable, and so very pale.

After a few attempts at conversation, he'd finally given up, not willing to lose his head. He tried to mention it to Hal, but the giant completely brushed off his worry with the wave of his hand before he turned his back on him and yelled into a radio that seemed glued to his palm since that morning. James finally decided to just sit back and see what happened, and worked on trying not to worry too much.

When it was nearly time, Lisa came in and, under Jen's watchful eye, began to tease Melody's hair. She had on purple jeans that looked like they'd been spray painted onto her legs, a sleeveless black leather shirt covered with silver zippers, and her dreadlocks were tied back with a leather band. A silver band worn just above her elbow highlighted the tattoo that wrapped around her shoulder, and a naval ring glistened in the light from where her shirt ended just before her pants began. She had powdered her face to pale, lined her eyes with black, and smeared her lips with a color that impossibly matched her pants. Occasionally, she blew a pink bubble from the gum that she slowly chewed.

She never spoke a word.

James could hear the crowd, faintly, and heard the muffled tones of the opening act. When someone knocked on the door and announced ten minutes, Melody began to shake so badly her teeth actually rattled. Lisa just ignored it and continued with what she was doing. She spun Melody's chair and grabbed her chin, turning her face all around to catch the light. She added a little more makeup here and there, then stepped back and looked pleased with the result. Well, he assumed the frown instead of the scowl meant she felt pleased.

She snatched up Melody's hand, filed a nail here, added a touch of polish there, and then did the same to the other hand. She popped her piece of gum and put her stuff back in its case, silently.

Jen opened the door at a knock and Hal walked in. "Come on Melody. Opening act is just about done. You need to get in place." He looked over at James. "I may need your help," he said, gesturing at his sling, "I'm afraid it's not a hundred percent yet."

"Did you really expect to be?" James asked him.

"Well, I'd at least like to be able to move the thing." He put his hand on the doorknob, "Come on, Melody. Time to go."

She stood and put her hands on her stomach. Her ears roared and her vision started to gray. She stopped to look at the full-length mirror, removing the smock that covered her shirt. She looked at her reflection, but never saw the purple shirt lined with rhinestones or the black spandex pants. What she saw was the panic in her eyes and the sweat that began to bead her brow. Deep breaths weren't working and she feared she was going to pass out. Her vision grayed and her peripheral vision blackened.

Praying a whispered prayer and using all of the inner strength she had inside of her, she went to her closet and pulled out her purple and rhinestone boots. She slid them on.

She shambled like a zombie past Suarez who stood outside her door, through the chaos of backstage, shuffled down some steps to the area below the stage, and stopped at the platform where her piano sat. It gleamed white in the dim light, and at the sight of it her knees started to buckle.

Hal and Lisa stood right behind her, ready to catch her should she fall. Lisa slipped a microphone headset combination over Melody's head, fluffed her hair around it, popped her gum again, then grabbed the powder puff out of her makeup kit and stepped to the side, knowing what would come next.

Melody could hear the crowd chanting her name as they watched the opening act leave the stage and her band set up. She could feel the vibration of the noise in her chest and began to panic, losing the numbness that had gripped her the last hour. She turned to Hal, "I can't do it."

"Melody, I'm not in the mood to play this game tonight. Get up on that platform and get ready to play."

"No. I can't. I can't do it. I can't go out there," she said, hysteria bubbling in her chest. Her thoughts scattered, and all she could imagine was performing in front of those thousands of people. What if *he* was in the audience?

Hal heard the cue in his headset, and knew he had about thirty seconds. "Melody Mason Montgomery, get your fanny on that platform and start playing that piano, or else I'll have them turn your mike on so that the entire audience can hear this conversation."

James was lost somewhere between the laughing woman who went to bed last night and the pale, hysterical woman clutching Hal's shirt, begging him not to make her do what he thought she loved to do. "What in the world is wrong with her?" he asked Hal.

"Topophobia." At the blank look on James' face, Hal impatiently clarified. "Clinical stage fright. She's afraid of performing in front of a crowd. It goes away as soon as she starts to sing." He grabbed Melody around the waist with one arm and started to haul her onto the platform. "If I bust my stitches, I'm going to give you stitches when this is over," he threatened.

She began to struggle so James intervened. He framed her face with his hands and forced her to look up at him. "Listen to me," he said. She struggled against him. "Look at me." Finally, she stilled and stared up at him. Her breaths came in and out rapidly, and her eyes darted here and there before looking into his again. He could see the signs of absolute panic. He put his forehead to hers and closed his eyes. "Father, calm

Melody. Relax her nerves, help her let go of her fear." As he spoke, she relaxed slightly, but tremors still shook her body as she took a seat on the piano bench.

Lisa jumped up onto the platform and put fresh powder on her face to counteract the cold sweat that broke out there. Melody started to stand again, but James put a hand on her shoulder.

"Start playing, Melody. No one in the crowd can see you right now," Hal said in a gentle tone. He heard the band start the song, and watched as Melody automatically came in on cue, playing with stiff fingers at first, then starting to warm up. James stepped off the platform when he felt it begin to rise, and Melody began to sing. The crowd went nuts when they heard her voice, and when James didn't think it was possible, got louder as the platform crested the stage. Melody Mason took over now, and she began to play for real, keeping up with the fast-paced song, her voice rising above all of the sounds in the building.

James and Hal went back to wait in the wings by Jen and to watch Melody do her thing. James was completely blown away by her stage presence. She worked the crowd like the pro she was, and never let the nerves that had attacked her all day surface. He was absolutely mesmerized.

After a few songs, one of the male dancers spun her off the stage into the wings. Before she even quit spinning, she kicked her boots off and tossed them behind her. She tugged on a yellow pair as her people went to work. Two pair of hands grabbed the sides of her pants and ripped. There was hidden Velcro flawlessly sewn into the seam, and the pants came off in one second, while she whipped her shirt over her head. Underneath she wore a pair of flesh colored spandex shorts and a flesh colored sports tank that barely covered her breasts. A yellow dress that ended at mid thigh went over her head, then she ripped the headset off, bent at the waist and Lisa pulled her hair together, twisted it, turned it, and one clip later, her hair was stylishly put up in a fancy twist. Lisa took the last second to quickly dab her face with a powder puff, and Melody grabbed the cordless microphone from a tech and strutted back onto the stage amid the screams of the crowd. The whole thing had taken less than ten seconds.

Melody smiled a flirty smile at the audience. "A little slow on the change this time, but this is the first concert in a while, so we're not quite warmed up yet." The crowd cheered. "I want to take this opportunity to thank y'all for allowing me the opportunity to kick off my tour in my home town." How the crowd kept getting louder was a wonder to James. His body vibrated with their cheers.

A few songs later, he heard Hal slam his phone down on the floor. James turned and kicked it out of his way before Hal could stomp on it. "What's up?"

"Steve's wife has gone into early labor, and is apparently having complications. We've been waiting for Max to show up before we let Steve know, but he just got into a fender bender on the 400. I can't keep Steve waiting, but he's lead guitar."

"Where is his wife?" James asked.

"Columbus. It will only take him about thirty minutes to get from here to there." Hal turned around and yelled. "Someone get me a pen and paper, then get Melody's attention. Get one of those cops out there to be ready to drive Stevie to the airport. Give me back my phone, James. I have to call Melody's pilot." He yelled toward someone standing in the wings. "When is she due for a change?"

"After this song."

Melody continued to sing as she met a tech on the stage who handed her a note. She read as she sang, then nodded and handed it back to him and went back to the center of the stage. During an interlude in the song, she went and whispered into Steve's ear, who nodded and kept playing. She finished the song and ran backstage. She made eye contact with Lisa. "I need your manicure kit," she said as she pulled off her boots, pulled a pair of blue jeans on, then put on her new pair of Falcons boots. The dress was ripped off as the pants had been, and her signed jersey went over her head. "Someone find me something to eat during the next change," she said as Lisa handed over the manicure kit, and Melody ran back to the stage, going over to Steve and taking his guitar from him. A tech ran up and set a microphone on a stand for her while Steve ran off stage.

"We've had a bit of a situation," she told the crowd as she adjusted the straps on the guitar. "It seems that Stevie's new baby has decided to grace us with its presence a little early, so he has to go and tell his wife how to do it." The crowd cheered. Melody looked toward the wings, "Is Steve still in the building?" she asked. "Let him know that the good thing about a name like Mel is that it can be used for a girl or a boy." The audience loved it, as she'd known they would.

She pulled out a pair of nail clippers from the bag, then tossed the bag toward the wings. A tech darted out to pick it up. "Our backup guitarist is on the way, but he's not here yet. You know," she said coyly, "traffic in Atlanta. Hard to imagine." The roar of laughter washed through the building. She started to clip her nails. "These nails are the perfect length for my piano, but I'm afraid they'll get in the way with the guitar." She glanced up at the crowd, a sparkle in her eye. "Do ya'll like my outfit?"

Cheers. "How many of ya'll are Falcons fans?" They almost brought the roof down while she finished cutting off her nails, then she bent at the waist and slid the clippers along the floor toward the wings. "All right. It's been about three or four years since I played one of these things. Let me see if I can reintroduce myself."

Her fingers moved over the strings, making them sing with the rock-a-Billy fast tune. She was about halfway through it when James finally heard Lisa speak. "Man, she's jammin'." James grinned and felt that was an apt description. She was good. He caught himself wanting to tap his toes to the beat.

Max showed up under police escort about three songs later, and took over the guitar. Melody handed it over gladly, feeling the tiny abrasions on the tips of her fingers.

During her next change she managed to swallow three bites of some melon and chug half a bottle of spring water, still getting her clothes changed, and making it back on the stage in under ten seconds. She was tireless, riding the crowd's energy, giving them everything they came for, then blowing them away with more. There wasn't an inch of stage left untouched by her colorful boots, and there wasn't a person in the crowd left untouched by her songs. James decided watching her in full power was one of the most amazing things he'd ever witnessed.

She finished the last song, then went backstage for one more wardrobe change for the encore. Her hair was put back up and a black evening gown was shimmied onto her. She kicked off a pair of boots and slipped into a pair of heels while the crowd screamed for more. The microphone stand was brought back out, the lights dimmed, and a single spotlight shown down on her. She waited for the audience to calm down. They knew what they were about to get, so it took them a little while to completely settle.

Melody cleared her throat. "A little over a week ago, I became Mrs. James Montgomery," she said. The crowd surged to its feet and she had to wait a full minute before she could continue talking. "What most people don't know is that I met James four years ago. I wrote this song when I met him. It stayed in my head for a few years before I had the courage to actually record it. The best part of it is that through reacquainting myself with my husband, through falling in love with him, I fell in love with God again, too. The last few weeks have been the most amazing of my life." She paused and cleared her throat again. "This is my last song for the evening." She closed her eyes and took a deep breath.

And then she sang.

For the first time that night, the audience went quiet, letting Melody's voice work its magic. She let all the love she felt for James come out with it, and the song was twice as powerful as it had ever been. All throughout the crowd, cell phones lit up and swayed back and forth to the gentle beat, held high over head like lighters from decades before.

When she finished, the roar of the audience was beyond deafening. She stood there for a long time, letting them thank her before she blew a kiss. Her voice sounded a little hoarse as she said, "Thank you for spending New Year's day with me Atlanta. Good night."

She walked backstage amid the overpowering ovation, and Morgan ran up and hugged her. "Oh Melly, that had to be the best concert I've ever seen you put on. You were terrific!"

"Thanks, Morg." Someone handed her a bottle of water, and Lisa came up one more time to change her. The dress and shoes were stripped off, and a baggy pair of jeans and a loose button-down shirt slipped on. Her feet hurt too badly for boots, so she asked Lisa to find her a pair of canvas shoes. Ignoring everyone around her, she pulled James into a corner and kissed him as if her life depended on it. He held her close, still reeling from the night. From the song. She tilted her head up and looked at him, "I'm really hungry."

He threw his head back and laughed. "I bet."

"I wonder if we could find a waffle place open at this hour?"

James grinned, "Here in Atlanta? An establishment that's open 24 hours that sells waffles? I don't think so."

Hal stood back amid the chaos and beamed. His Melody was the best there was. His phone rang, and he fumbled with his good hand to get it answered. It took him a while to hear the voice on the other end, but his grin went ear to ear when he hung up the phone. "Hey everybody. Can I have your attention, please? Steve and Tiffany Masters had a baby boy, and they named him Steven Melvin." He found Melody in the crowd. "He said to tell you he heard you as he left the building, and he got the message. He barely made it in time, but Tiffany is fine, and the baby is great."

Everyone cheered. Ginger came from the hall leading to the showers, already dressed and made-up. She must have been showering during the last song. "Hey Melly. Man, what a night. It was like a dream come true. Plus, you were great."

"You were too, Ginger. The offer stands. Come with us for the entire tour." Melody reiterated.

"I wish I could, but I have commitments to the school." She grabbed

Melody's hand and squeezed. "I want to thank you. I would never have had a chance to do something like this if it wasn't for you."

"It's an open offer, Ginger," she said.

Hal got her attention to let her know that the audience members who had backstage passes were on their way. She nodded, kissed Ginger, and went to greet her guests.

♫ ♫ ♫ ♫

Chapter 26

MELODY had eaten steadily since she left the stage. Now she sat on the couch with a pint of ice cream in her lap, busy working her way through it. James sat in a chair with his feet propped on the coffee table, watching her. Jen had already retired for the evening, and they found themselves alone for the first time since they got up that morning, or, looking at his watch, yesterday morning. It was four o'clock.

"How much more do you actually think you'll be able to eat?" he asked her with a grin.

"You have to remember that I started on empty tonight, and I burned more calories out there than you'll burn in a month at your gym," she retorted.

"How are you going to hold up to nine months of this? It would be bad enough if you didn't go through all of the physical and mental stress beforehand."

"That's the problem David Patterson has with me. I only do one or at most two concerts a week. I couldn't handle more than that. Most stars do three or four. Plus, I fly instead of bus it. We have a trucking company that meets the plane in whatever city we're going to. That cuts back on a lot of the stress right there."

"Why does Patterson have a problem with it?"

"David was a good friend of my father's, and he's a good friend to us now. But, I am sorry I ever got caught up in business with him. His only goal is to make as much money as possible. I could be making more, but I won't. Thankfully, I have Hal, who was with me the very first night I ever performed, and almost had to drag me onto the stage and hold me there. My first contract was only for a year, then when we signed my four-year contract, Hal put a clause in it that I can set my own tour schedule. I was really starting to hit it big, and they were afraid they'd lose me, so they agreed to it, thinking they could get around it later. But I think that people look at Hal's size and forget the brilliant legal mind he has. Last year they took him to arbitration twice. They've tried everything in their power to break the clause, but nothing has worked."

James raised his eyebrow, amazed at the amount of energy she still had after the last 30 or so hours. "Knowing David personally, I really can't reconcile his professional behavior. It hurts my feelings and feelings have no place in business, you know? So, we're negotiating with another label right now." She took a big bite of ice cream. "I'm hyped up and babbling. I'm sorry."

"I'll let you know when it bothers me. Please go on," he prompted.

"Well, see, David gets a cut of the songs and he gets a cut of the ticket sales, but that's it. He has no claim to any licensed merchandise or sponsored public appearances. All that is the sole property of Melody Mason, Inc."

"What kind of things do you license?"

"Oh, heavens, all kinds of things. My name or face is on everything from key chains to post cards to coffee cups. There's a restaurant chain that named a sandwich after me. An auto manufacturer is coming out with a Melody Mason signature edition pickup truck with a leather interior that matches a pair of my boots. Oh. The big one is my boots. I visited the factory. It was about to go slap under. Now they're the biggest employer in that little town east of here. David doesn't get a cut of any of that. It all goes to my corporation."

"You really are a brand."

Melody nodded. "But that's not all. There's a publishing house that wants to do my biography. The cooking channel wants to collaborate on a cookbook with me and have me appear on some shows with that lady from Savannah."

James was frankly astonished. "You're kidding."

She shook her head and swallowed another spoonful of ice cream. "I know. But I won't be cooking. She will. My name is a brand. It's all about brand recognition. Anyway, David doesn't get any of it. But he makes a small fortune with every single I release and with every concert I put on. So it's a constant fight to try to get me to put more venues on my schedule."

"You know," James observed. "Years ago, after meeting with him a few times, I declined Patterson's offer to invest in Montgomery-Lawson. I prefer to be in control." He rubbed his eyes behind his glasses, tired. "Wouldn't Patterson rather have you perform less than collapse and not be able to perform at all?"

Melody took a bite of ice cream, then twirled the spoon around in her mouth. "Only a very few select people on my crew really know about my phobia. We kind of try to keep it hidden."

"How can you?"

"I'm pretty much off limits about two hours before show time. Before that, I mainly just have the nausea and a mean temper. A lot of people operate purely on nerves by then, so my temper goes unnoticed. The nausea I'm able to hide. We always try to find some way for me to get on stage hidden, like a trap door below the stage on the platform, or at the music show last month when I walked onto a darkened stage with the curtain down. No one really sees the panic."

"Have you ever been unable to perform?"

"No. Hal is relentless, and pretty big. I'm really glad you stepped in tonight, because he never would have been able to keep me down without hurting himself."

"My pleasure." He watched her as she put down the carton and stood. "So, where did you find Lisa?"

Melody laughed and walked over to him, crawling onto his lap. "Do you really want to talk about Lisa?" she asked him, wrapping her arms around him and kissing him.

♫ ♫ ♫ ♫

THE phone woke James late the next morning. He grabbed it off its base and went out of the bedroom so he wouldn't wake Melody.

"Montgomery," he answered as he went to the kitchen. He pushed a button on the coffee maker, and heard it fill with water and start to grind beans.

"This is Detective Suarez, Mr. Montgomery. The lab sent back the video from the day of the shooting, and we received the enhancement of the frames your company sent us. It's definitely a man, but the picture is still indistinct. We'd like Mrs. Montgomery to take a look at it, to see if maybe she can identify him."

"Make it late this afternoon. I think she'll be asleep most of today."

"I wouldn't be surprised after last night. I'm at home today. Call me whenever it's convenient for you to do so."

Jen appeared in the kitchen doorway. "Everything good?"

"Yes. Suarez has some pictures for Melody to look at when she's free."

"Did she plan on going out today or are they coming here?"

"She has plans this evening, but nothing until then. I'm going to do some work here. I'm sure Suarez will come here." The coffee maker signaled the coffee ready. "Would you like a cup?"

"No, thank you. Your office is free if you need it." She dug a bluetooth headset out of her pocket and hooked it over her ear and turned away.

He poured himself a cup of coffee then went to his office, hooking the laptop up to his docking station. After reading e-mails from the last several days, he made a note in his schedule to meet with accounting for the year-end, then opened the progress reports R & D had turned in on the data storage project. He read through the reports, frustrated to see that they were still stuck in the same rut.

He rubbed his forehead and thought. For the past few days something had nagged at his memory, something Angela had told him. He just couldn't recall what or even when.

Memory is a tricky thing, especially for someone with perfect recall. James could not help remember things like numbers or anything he read. But conversations he could filter. Every conversation didn't automatically end up in what he called his "permanent storage."

Angela often shared her work progress with him, but spoke as if she were drafting a thesis. More often than not, she simply verbalized her thoughts as they ran down one tangent and up the next. Occasionally, he didn't pay as much attention to the information she relayed as he ought to have done. At the time, he was more concerned about whether or not she felt happy about what she was saying. He leaned back in his chair and closed his eyes, trying to replay the last few conversations he'd had with her, but nothing popped out. If she had ever bothered to write some of it down, he would be able to recall it perfectly for the rest of his life.

He sat up and reached for his cup of coffee, realizing that it had gone cold. In the kitchen, he dumped out the old coffee, and poured a fresh cup, splashing his hand with the hot brew in the process. He dropped the cup out of reflex and watched it shatter on the ground. Suddenly, he felt as if he were in his old kitchen looking at another broken coffee cup on the floor.

It had been about a week before she was killed. They were in the kitchen that morning, and Angela was talking about the progress they had made the day before. James had mentally tried to reschedule his day to accommodate some men from London who decided to call a meeting at the last minute.

"So, I am sure someone had been going through them, so I sent them with the other things to my mom," she had said. She'd poured herself a cup of coffee, then held up the pot to see if he wanted some. He held his cup out to her, and as she began to pour, the phone rang. She'd jumped and spilled coffee on his hand, making him drop the cup. He'd watched it shatter on the floor.

She'd grabbed a dishtowel and wiped his hand, ignoring the phone.

"Honey, I'm so sorry. I've been so jumpy lately," she'd said, as she lifted his hand to kiss it, then placed her hand on his cheek and kissed his lips.

He winked at her, making her smile, then went to get a broom from the closet. "Anyway, what was I talking about?" she'd asked him, wiping up the spilled coffee.

"Something about your mother," he'd answered. She'd glanced at her watch then, and with a shake of her head said, "I can't remember. I'm sure I'll think about it as soon as I'm downstairs. I have to go, anyway. I'm late as it is."

She'd grabbed the key card that unlocked her basement lab, kissed him, and as she left said, "If you get a chance, pop your head into the lab before you leave. Love you, bye." She blew him a kiss and waved as she'd gone down the basement stairs.

Back to the present, James ignored the broken glass and went to the phone. His hand wasn't quite steady as he dialed his mother-in-law's number. She answered on the first ring. "Hello Diane, this is James. How are you?"

♪ ♪ ♪ ♪

"**WHEN** do all your mistakes add up to incompetence?" They risked much by meeting in person. Obviously, someone needed to make a point.

Rikard Šabalj felt something snap in his temple and his vision turned red. When he spoke, the words were so laced with a Serbian accent that they were hard to understand. "I cannot control everything."

"There's always an excuse and there's always a mistake."

"Enough!"

"You're right. It is enough. Leave her be for now. That was clearly a failed experiment. Focus on the project."

Rikard restrained himself from physically attacking the man. *He* would determine what he would focus on, not some self-important egotist with no practical experience in killing or death. "You and I both know you don't really make the decisions here."

"Is that a challenge?"

Rikard raised an eyebrow. "Not by me. But I'll leave her alone when I hear from the person who actually captains this ship." He poured tea into a small glass cup. "Unless you want to make it a challenge."

He watched the man's Adam's apple bob before he said, "Keep your phone nearby."

♫ ♫ ♫ ♫

Chapter 27

JAMES set a plate of chicken salad in front of Melody then took a seat directly across from her. They held hands as they blessed the meal. She groaned as she lifted her fork. "I can't believe how sore I am. I forgot I even had this many muscles."

"You'll probably be rather limber by the end of your tour." He smiled as he took a bite. "I'm looking forward to that."

Melody snorted and attacked her food with gusto. "What day are you planning to leave for Tokyo?" she asked him.

"Probably Thursday. I'm going to end up being there for the better part of a week."

"I leave on Wednesday," she noted.

"I know. That's why I'm going Thursday." He took a drink of his tea. "Where to next?"

"Jacksonville, Florida. I have a show there Friday night." She dished more salad onto her plate. "You know what I like most about you, James?"

He sat back in his chair, enjoying watching her eat with such enthusiasm. "Tell me what you like most about me, Melody."

She pointed her fork at him. "You probably think I'm going to say your good looks, your charm, or your mind."

"My minty fresh breath?" He added.

Melody shook her head. "None of that. It's what you can do to pasta that really has me hooked."

"You mean my looks have nothing to do with it?"

"Well, they're a bonus." She cleaned off her second helping, and considered a third, but decided to wait a while. "What did you do while I slept all day?"

"I read reports," he announced dramatically. "It was everything I expected. I laughed, I cried."

"You know something? My job is much less boring than yours."

"To you, maybe. There isn't enough money in the world to pay me to do what you do." He set aside his clean plate, and decided to come out with it. "Want to take a ride over to Pine Mountain?"

"Sure, why?"

"Angela's mother lives there," he said, waiting for — something.

"That's a great idea. Are we coming back tonight, or do I need to pack some clothes?"

He looked at her for a long time, feeling the pull of her eyes before he stopped himself. He shook his head. "Will you ever cease to amaze me?"

"I certainly hope not." She pushed away from the table and hugged him from behind his chair. Breathing in the scent of his after shave, she kissed the top of his head. "You haven't answered my question."

♫ ♫ ♫ ♫

"JAMES, what a pleasure. Please come in," his former mother-in-law greeted as she held open the door. She held her hand out to Melody. "Diane Simmons, dear, welcome."

"Melody Ma— Montgomery. It's nice to meet you," she said as she stepped into the house. Jen took a chair on the front porch.

"Sit down, sit down. I'm so happy you came," she said as she led them into her living room. "Would you like some tea?"

"That would be wonderful," Melody said. She looked around the comfortable room, liking the homey décor. The knickknacks were a mixture of priceless antiques and thrift store bargains, and framed photographs took up any extra space they could. One picture on the mantel above the fireplace caught her attention, and she got up to look closer. It was a picture of James and Angela standing with their arms around each other next to a rosebush. She looked back at James, whose expression was unreadable. "Angela was very beautiful," she said.

He didn't respond, just inclined his head, watching her. She walked around the room, looking at the pictures on the walls. "She was an only child. That's so sad. This house was made for grandchildren to run through it." She said it quietly, almost to herself, but James heard her anyway.

Diane came back to the room carrying a tray with a teapot and cups, and set it on the coffee table. She poured cups and passed them out, then sat in a chair and looked at James. "I looked in the attic and found several boxes that I didn't even know were there. She must have brought them by the week that I was at my sister's. The timing would have been right."

"May I take them with me?" he asked her.

"Of course. I should have looked through all the stuff I have and given you some, anyway. I know the fire destroyed everything you had. But you've never asked, and when I see you we get so busy just talking I always forget." She pulled a tissue out of her pocket and quickly wiped her eyes. "Melody, I enjoy your music. I had been hoping that James would bring you by while you were here."

"I have been so busy prepping for last night's concert that I never thought to see if we could meet," she said. "James has told me that you two get together as often as possible."

"James and Kurt kind of adopted me after Angela died. She was all I had. I would have been to Kurt's wedding, but my sister broke her hip and I've just returned." She took a sip of her tea. "You two were on the cover of *People Magazine* yesterday, kissing in front of that kids' home that you took all those presents to." She grinned before she dug through a stack of magazines on the table next to her chair. "Here it is."

She handed the magazine over to Melody, who saw the cover and started laughing. She turned to the page that held the story, and did a quick read of it. "Well, my plot worked," she said, handing it over to James. "There isn't one mention of me losing my temper to that reporter. Just bios of you and me, the story about our donations, and something about your Japan merger."

James frowned as he read the story. "No one knows about that," he said. "We don't announce it until tomorrow."

"Maybe someone leaked it," she said.

"Maybe." He finished reading the story, then handed the magazine back to Diane. "How have you been?"

"I've been much better, thank you. Will you two be able to stay for dinner?"

"Unfortunately, we have to meet someone back at my place in a couple of hours. We'll try to plan a time when we can come and spend the weekend." He pushed himself to his feet. "Let me see those boxes, Diane. I'll load them in my car."

They stayed another hour. When it was time to go, Diane hugged them both. "Take care of yourselves," she said as they walked to the car. Jen took the driver's seat, and Melody slipped into the back-seat.

James paused with his hand on the door. "Call me, Diane, if you need anything."

"I will, dear. Good luck finding what you're looking for." He opened the door and sat next to Melody. Jen started the car and drove away

♫ ♫ ♫ ♫

JAMES stayed quiet during their drive home. Melody watched his profile for a while, leaving him to his thoughts. Finally, she asked, "Is it hard to be there?"

James turned to look at her. "What? No, not anymore. I was thinking about something else."

Melody scooted down and propped her knees on the seat in front of her and closed her eyes. "I feel bad for her. She's all alone now."

"Not entirely. She has some family," he said as Jen exited the freeway.

"I guess. So, who are we meeting?"

"Suarez. He has the enhancement of the image of the shooter that he wants you to look at."

Her stomach started to tighten up. "You know, in a way I want to, and in a way I don't. I'm halfway afraid to confirm that it's Richard, and halfway afraid to find out that it's someone else."

Jen met Melody's eyes via the rear view mirror. "The more we know, the safer you'll be. Knowledge is power."

"And, the sooner we know, the sooner it's over," James said.

Jen pulled up in front of the apartment building, parking in the loading zone. They got out of the car, and Jen and Melody went on up to the apartment while he had the guard help him unload the boxes. There were four of them and they were big enough that three had taken up the entire trunk while one rode in the front seat.

Melody went into the kitchen and started coffee, knowing that James would be up all night looking through them. He'd told her about the remembered conversation. She hoped he would find whatever piece to the puzzle he sought in those boxes. She heard the elevator, and came into the living room just as Jen opened the front door.

James carried the first box in when the phone rang. He nodded to her to answer it, then went back to the elevator to get another box. She answered and Morgan's voice returned her greeting. "Hey there. We're almost to your apartment. I just wanted to make sure you all were back. And, before I forget, I wanted to see if you two wanted to come over tomorrow for lunch after church."

Melody slipped off her shoes and fell back onto the couch, letting her legs dangle over the side. "Sure."

"Oh, and let James know since I'm thinking about it and don't want to forget when I see him that Mike Redman called my house looking for him. Apparently, he's been trying to get in touch with him, and his cell phone was turned off."

"I'll let him know, and we'll see you in a few minutes." Melody hung up the phone as James brought in the last box. "Morg and Kurt will be here in a little bit. We're supposed to be at their place after church for lunch tomorrow."

"Okay."

"Mike Redman's trying to get a hold of you. He said your cell phone's been off all day."

Surprised, James retrieved his phone from his pocket. "I guess I didn't turn it back on." He set his phone down, and took the other one from her, putting it on the table, too.

Jen came out of the office. "I'm going to go coordinate with the guard for shift change."

"Are you hungry?" Melody asked.

"I just ate." Jen pulled a phone out of her pocket and checked a text. "Stay indoors until I get back. Don't go near the windows or balconies. I'll be back in twenty."

After the door closed behind her, Melody turned to James. "What could she possibly have eaten in the two minutes we've been back?"

James laughed. "Maybe she ate in Pine Mountain while we were inside." He put an arm around her and she curled up next to him. "How long do you think we have before your sister gets here?" His finger traced the skin along her neck.

"Just enough time for you to feed me." Her hands ran up his neck to play with his hair.

His grin made his eyes sparkle. "Do you love me or my pasta?"

She laughed. A knock at the door interrupted their play. He pushed himself off of the couch and moved smoothly across the room. Through the peephole, he identified Morgan and Kurt.

"Hi, James," she said, stepping into the apartment. "Melly said she was looking at police pictures today. Thought we'd come by and offer moral support."

James looked at his watch. "Good timing. I was about to feed your sister a snack. Hungry?"

♫ ♫ ♫ ♫

TWENTY minutes later, James came into the room just as Jen answered the door. He'd expected to see the detectives, and was surprised to see Mike Redman. "What's up, Mike?"

"Someone's hacked into our mainframe, James," Mike said as he took off his coat. James slung it on the stand by the door and followed him to the couch.

"How is that possible with the safeguards we have?" James asked.

"It means this guy either really knows what he's doing or has insider help," Mike said as Melody came out of the kitchen. She stopped short when she saw him.

"Hi," she said.

"Mike have you met Melody?" James asked.

"Yes, at the wedding rehearsal." He stood and held his hand out. "It's nice to see you again, Mrs. Montgomery. I enjoyed your concert very much."

She took his hand. "Thank you. Please, call me Melody."

With a straight face, Mike said, "I'm not sure that will be possible, ma'am."

James heard the elevator again and watched as Jen opened the door to let in Suarez and Roberts. Roberts saw Mike. "Hey, Redman. Good to see you."

"Roberts, my friend. Haven't you managed to loosen Suarez up any?" he asked with a smile as he shook their hands.

"I have. The change has been like night and day. Last week, he even ate a donut." Roberts handed the envelope he was carrying to Melody. "Here are the image enhancements. There were actually three frames they were able to pull from. Take a look and see if this is the guy you knew as Richard Johnson."

Melody's hands shook a little as she sat on the couch and pulled three pictures from the envelope. She laid them on the table in front of her. The first one was too blurry to see anything other than to tell that it was a man. The second one was a little clearer, but the rifle blocked part of his face. Her breath caught as she looked at the third one. It was a profile shot as the man turned, and was very, very clear.

In her mind, she could see the fist as it slammed into her face, feel and hear her ribs snap as they made contact with a boot. She stood quickly, knocking over her chair as she rose, and backed away, wanting to get as far from the picture as possible. The air burned her lungs, her breathing came very hard, very fast, and she concentrated on trying to get that under control. She couldn't take her eyes off his face. She hated — hated — that picture for confirming their theory.

James saw her reaction and immediately went to her. She was almost in a full-blown panic. He grabbed her by her upper arms and as soon as his hands touched her, she began to fight. "Let go of me," she said as she tried to twist away. "Don't touch me."

He gave her a little shake. "Snap out of it, Melody. It's me." She looked up at him and her eyes cleared. She began to sob as he wrapped his arms around her and held her close.

"I can't believe I was hours away from marrying him," she sobbed. She grabbed James by his shirtfront and looked up at him. "How can someone be this evil and I couldn't tell?"

He brushed the hair out of her eyes. "Sometimes you just can't tell, baby. Sometimes it's buried real deep." He pulled her back to him and let her cry. He met Roberts' eyes over her head while Suarez pulled a phone out of his pocket to call dispatch and have them put an APB out on the man they knew only as Richard Johnson. James sent Hal a text asking him to come over.

It took a few minutes for Melody to calm down. James sat her on the couch, and she curled up into a ball, leaning against the arm. Jen left the room and returned carrying a glass of water. The men pretended not to watch as she spoke in low, calm, soothing, feminine tones to Melody. Melody took a sip of the water.

After a moment, Melody nodded then suddenly shook her head. She'd vowed years ago that Richard would have no more control over her. She made eye contact with Jen, responding to the concern and care in her brown eyes. As soon as Jen saw that she was okay, her mask of businesslike indifference slid back into place and she stood and moved back to the back of the room near the door.

Roberts raised his eyebrows at her, as if to confirm that she had collected herself enough to answer questions, before he carefully asked, "Mrs. Montgomery, what does Richard have to do with the late Angela Montgomery?"

Melody suddenly remembered the message in the hotel room, the one in which Richard said he knew Angela.

"We've always operated under the theory that Angela's murder had something to do with their research breakthrough," Suarez said. "What we don't understand is what that has to do with you."

"Nothing!" Melody surged to her feet and paced the room. "It has absolutely nothing to do with me. I never even met her. I didn't meet James until six months after her murder and no one even knew we'd met." She looked at James. "Did you talk about it?"

He shook his head. "I didn't mention it to anyone."

"No kidding," Morgan said with a forgiving smile.

"Wait," Melody said, spinning around and rushing toward James. "One person knew."

"Who?" A frown marred his brow, then he remembered. "You're right."

"Who?" Suarez asked, pen poised and ready.

"Richard," Melody whispered, putting a hand against her stomach to quell the burst of nausea. "The man who called himself Richard Johnson was at the airport. He knew we'd met."

Suarez cocked his head. "That brings us back to the question. What does he have to do with the Montgomerys?"

"He told me he was an intern in a technology business, but I never really pursued that." Melody sat down carefully, feeling like maybe she would shatter if she moved too quickly. "He talked about a research breakthrough being just around the corner. I didn't really listen because I don't really understand it."

Suarez held his hand up. "Wait a minute. What you're saying is that the man who called himself Richard Johnson blew his way into a secured laboratory with military precision, inadvertently killed them before he could garner any information, so then wooed and courted you? For what purpose?"

Melody shrugged. "How should I know? I don't even know if he did it. I have no idea why he would. I was just an heiress with no direction in my life."

James put a hand on her knee. "That's right. An heiress." He smiled. "A singing heiress."

"And?" Melody asked, not amused by his trip down memory lane to their meeting in the airport. "What does that have to do with this?"

"How much?" Roberts asked bluntly.

"I beg your pardon?"

"What was your net worth before stardom?"

Melody frowned. "I don't —" She paused. "I'm not sure."

Morgan interjected. "Just over two billion."

Roberts' pen paused over his notebook. "Billion?"

"Yes." Morgan leaned closer to Kurt. "I know exactly how much money my late husband lost in a month of really bad moves on the stock market. Two billion, three million, nine hundred thousand." She took a sip of water. "And change. Melody had half of the inheritance."

James turned his body slightly to stare at his wife. "You're worth two billion dollars?"

Melody shrugged. "No. I think it's more now. Hal's really monitored my portfolio and helped it grow. Mostly mutual funds I think."

Kurt held up his hand. "So, you're saying that Johnson tried to get the information from Angela, but wasn't able to get it, so he decided he'd marry Melody and then take her money?"

James frowned then slowly nodded. "Likely. You and I both know the technology is conservatively worth a hundred times that. Assuming he thought he could steal what they'd backed up the day before and compile it, he likely hit the same brick wall my research and development team has hit for four years now. But if he had the funding of billions of dollars, he might have been able to, or thought he could have a chance of, breaking through."

"And then I broke up with him," Melody said. "And went on my honeymoon without him."

"He was waiting for you at the airport. Likely he intended to try to smooth things out, but ended up seeing you with me." James fisted his hands and surged to his feet. "Me. The husband of the woman he'd murdered. The president of the company developing that technology. Who knows what went through his mind when he saw us."

"You're right," Melody said. "When he saw us, he said, 'What are you doing with *him*?' I just assumed he meant with another man, but he specifically meant, what was I doing with *you*."

James slowly sat down again and took her hand. "What are the odds?"

Kurt shook his head as if to clear it. "This seems unfathomable."

"People have done worse for far less money." James sat forward and released Melody's hand to take his glasses off and rub his eyes.

"But why would he want to kill me?" Melody hated the way her breath hitched. "Why all of the roses and the notes? To what end?"

"Remember what he said?" Morgan asked. "He wanted you to be afraid. He fed off of that. But as for wanting to kill you, none of that makes sense to me."

Kurt rubbed his temple. "Now that we've worked it out, what are we going to do about it?"

Melody stood quickly, nervous energy fueling her pacing. "What can we do to make him come out? If he's actually been following me around for so long, I haven't seen him. I would have recognized him immediately."

"Not if he didn't want you to recognize him," Redman said. "He wasn't anticipating you being alive to be able to identify him in a picture, so he didn't disguise himself for the shooting. But, some people can change everything about themselves, including mannerisms and movements, accent, anything they need to change in order to not be recognized. Perhaps Johnson has that capability."

"He's right," Roberts said. "We need to take another look at that tape of the security camera outside of your dressing room. Now that we know who we're looking for, maybe you can point him out. If he's been disguising himself as a member of your crew, maybe that can be our chance to get him."

"But I know my crew. Don't you think that I would have been able to tell that a man I was engaged to be married to was on it?"

"Not if he was in a position you didn't deal with, like a lighting tech that only worked at certain times. There were some people going into your room that day whose names you didn't know."

"Was there ever a time that a rose appeared where you'd been that didn't require a good portion of your crew to be there?" Suarez asked.

Melody thought about it for a long time. "I've found them in my car, on my doorstep, and in my hotel room."

"What now?" Kurt asked.

"Now we catch him," Suarez said matter-of-factly.

Morgan felt like she had to do something, so she went to the kitchen and came out with a tray of cups and the coffeepot. Melody put an arm around her shoulders. "Thank you." She turned back to the group. "Maybe if I went somewhere by myself ..."

"No," everyone said simultaneously.

Melody felt like pulling her hair out. "Look, I haven't been alone since I got here. I've had Peter or Hal or James or Kurt with me constantly. Now I have Jen. Maybe if he saw that I was alone for the first time, he would jump at the chance to do something, worried he wouldn't get another one. He's arrogant enough to want to take that risk."

"The last time he tried to do something, he used a high powered rifle at two hundred yards. That isn't a risk that any of us are willing to take," Roberts said.

"You don't have to be willing," she said, "I do."

"We could put her in a situation where he would have to get close to do something," Redman said.

"No," James passionately insisted. "First off, my wife isn't bait. Second, there isn't a situation you could put her in and guarantee her safety. This guy's been on the run for nearly half a decade and he's doing just fine. He's probably too smart to fall for a trap."

Melody got her purse and pulled out a notepad. She drowned out everyone's voices and started writing, slowly at first, then with more speed. Within minutes, she had several pages filled. She zoned back into the conversation.

"There has to be a way to bring him out without putting her in any kind of risk at all," Redman said.

Melody chewed her lip. "What if we stroked his ego?"

Roberts looked at her. "How?"

She shrugged. "Obviously, he's obsessed with me. If in fact he's in my crew, he probably hears me sing." She picked at a thread on her pants. "What if I wrote a song to him?"

"What kind of song?" Kurt asked.

She looked at her notebook, and read from it, "'Even with him I think of you, you're never far from my mind, you hurt me once and I may be a fool, but can we give it one more try?'" She thumbed through the pages. "There's more, and this is really rough. The words might change a little once they're put to music, but if he felt no threat from me, if he doesn't think we suspect him at all, he might try to approach me. That will keep us from having to use me as some sort of lure somewhere alone, and we won't have to relax our guard."

They all stared at her, but she misread their expressions and spoke quickly. "Everyone knows I write all my songs. Most people, especially those with me all the time, know that all my songs mean something personal to me in some way, and most of them are based on experiences I have." She threw her notebook on the table in defeat as they continued to stare at her. "I'm sorry. Continue the Machiavellian brainstorming session. It was just an idea."

James spoke first. "You are absolutely brilliant. Can you write the song tonight?"

Everyone started to speak at once, interrupting each other with ideas for lyrics. Melody smiled as she picked up her notebook. "I appreciate the ideas, but I can do it without your help. Go to the kitchen and get a snack." She sat down at the portable electric piano she took with her for travel and drowned them out again.

Hal arrived just as everyone went into the kitchen. When he asked her what was going on, she just pointed to the kitchen door and kept writing. A few minutes later, she heard him bellowing at the group, causing her to smile. Then it grew quiet again.

♫ ♫ ♫ ♫

AN hour later, Melody sang the song she'd hastily written to the group. It seemed a little off to her because it didn't mean anything to her. It carried the theme they wanted, a woman with another man who couldn't stop thinking about her past lover, willing to forgive the pain he'd caused her if he would just come back to her. The line she thought of as the real grabber, and hoped would get Richard's attention, went, "You never even gave me a chance to forgive, you just left me alone to cry."

She sat on the edge of the couch. "Yesterday I introduced *My Love Song* by saying that I wrote it after meeting James. I'm going to repair the damage and say that this song was written right after I wrote *My Love Song*. Hopefully, Richard is arrogant enough to believe that after he beat me up, I wrote this one."

"How much will it mess up your schedule to add a song?" Redman asked.

Hal answered him, "If she won't require any dancers, it will be easy to do. This is a very slow song, and since we want to keep it as real as possible, I may stage a couple waltzing to it, which will be easy to light and choreograph."

"What about letting your band practice the song?" Morgan asked.

"I'll play it solo on the piano. That will draw more attention to me, which will draw more attention to the words. The more music and noise you add, the less the words mean, which is why I sing so much of *My Love Song* either *a cappella* or with very little accompaniment. You hear what I'm saying then."

"I still want you to look at the tape of the hall outside your dressing room, again. You might be able to tell us which one he is, which will give us the chance to get him without having to do this," Roberts said.

"I will, tomorrow night," Melody said.

Redman looked at his watch, then remembered something. "James, I meant to talk to you about the hacking going on."

"What tipped you off?" James asked.

"The IPSes we installed at Albany weren't able to prevent this guy from breaking in, but the IDSes in Atlanta logged it all and sent alerts on the VPN. The computer department hasn't checked the portal in the mornings very carefully for the last week, because of Christmas, and then the tech that does log review has been out with the flu. Nothing went above the tolerance because our black hat is very good. Our IAT went in yesterday, still sick by the way, and compiled the instances to an OLAP. He just called me this morning with the anomaly. All this activity was just below the radar so he obviously knows our thresholds and parameters. Apparently, our bad guy has hacked into Rebecca's computer four times in the last ten days and that caused a blip that a human being noticed."

James nodded. "I think he's also leaking information. There's an article in *People Magazine* this week that mentions the Japanese buyout. They used the wording, 'potential Japanese merger'. No one should know about it, but Rebecca has been typing meeting minutes."

"How did he get around the whole-disk encryption?"

Redman gave James a meaningful look, "He escalated privileges all the way to root level and created his own private key."

James suddenly felt very sick and very hot. "That's proprietary."

Redman nodded. "I know. Like I said, he's either remarkably good and superlatively patient, or this is an inside job. I've already had Rebecca disconnect her computer from the network. She's going to probably have to use her tablet in stand-alone mode until this thing is settled."

"Let's hope everything can still stay as quiet as possible before we announce the buyout tomorrow. It would blow the deal if it became too widespread," Kurt said.

"I'll meet you two in my office at eight tomorrow morning. The press conference is scheduled for eleven," James said. If it weren't for the expertise of Redman and his team, the breach would never have been detected in the first place. He turned back to Redman. "Are we ahead of this thing now?"

Redman grinned. It was sort of like when a shark smiles at a sea lion. "We followed protocol, so InfraGard has been notified. The FBI is involved and I'm keeping them in the loop. Internally, besides the people in this room, only four people in the firm know about this and they all have clearances. We're monitoring everything in real time, we set out honey pots, and he is completely surrounded. You want a call if we catch him?"

James nodded and put a hand on Redman's shoulder. "Great work, Mike. You have my gratitude. And yes, of course I do."

Redman left, and Morgan yawned in her hand. Kurt went to the kitchen to retrieve the phone he'd left there, and James walked Morgan to the door. He kissed her on the cheek. "How is life, Mrs. Lawson?"

"I love your brother-in-law," she answered as she put on her coat. "You two be safe." She kissed him quickly on the cheek. Kurt came back into the room and they left.

Suarez confirmed the time he would meet Melody back there the next day, and he and Roberts left, too. Hal stopped on the way out, and shook James' hand then rubbed Melody on the top of her head. "See you in the morning, kid."

"Okay, Hal," she said as she held the door for him.

James rubbed the back of his neck and walked over to look at the boxes in the corner. They could wait, he decided, then turned to Melody. "Where are you going with Hal tomorrow?" he asked her.

"Nashville. I have a meeting in the morning I forgot to tell you about," she said, slipping off her shoes.

"Does Jen know?"

"Yes. She's already coordinated with whomever at wherever about whatever it is she does."

James smiled. "When are you supposed to be back?"

"Probably about three or four," she said. "It's easy to hip hop when you have your own jet." She stretched, feeling her muscles protesting, deciding that she needed to dance and workout soon so that she didn't feel this way after every concert . "Why don't you have your own jet?" she asked.

"Never got around to it," James said. "Besides, some of us aren't worth two billion dollars."

Melody picked up an empty coffee cup and set it on the tray. "You are now."

James' laughter came out in a snort.

♫ ♫ ♫ ♫

Chapter 29

SUNDAY night, James ouldn't sleep. Every time he closed his eyes, his mind whirled with the way his life had changed in the last month, with the danger facing Melody, with praying that they stayed in God's will as they built their marriage.

Energized, James left a sleeping Melody in the bed and wandered into the main room. As he turned on a lamp, the door to the office cracked open. He spotted Jen checking to see who was in the room before shutting the door again.

Not really feeling like working, he decided he would go through the boxes from Angela's mom. He grabbed the first box off the stack and sat down on the couch, flipping the television to a country music video channel but turning the volume down low. He smiled at himself as he opened the box.

It contained everything from pictures to complex math formulas written on yellow post-it-notes. In a stack of pictures he found some shots of their ski trip they'd taken her last winter, mixed in with some prototypes of a long ago revolutionary flat screen television. Angela had been the most unorganized person he'd ever met. She put so much mental energy into whatever she worked on that little remained for any other details. That had been one of the things he'd found so endearing about his late wife. He set aside the pictures from the vacation to share with Diane.

He began to sort the personal from the business, creating two growing stacks that seemed about equal. After working his way through three of the boxes, he still hadn't found anything relevant to the last project on which she'd been working. Twice he stopped to watch his wife's music videos, remaining impressed with Melody's work.

He opened the last box expecting to find the same type of stuff, but found that it surprisingly contained several journals. He grabbed one out and quickly flipped through it, recognizing Angela's handwriting. He hadn't known that she'd kept a journal.

The sound of the bedroom door opening broke his attention from the book. Melody came into the room, stumbling, wearing a T-shirt and a pair of sweat pants. Since she neither spoke to him nor looked at him, he said nothing as he watched her dig through her bag and pull out her notebook and pen. The office door cracked and James waved at Jen that everything was all clear. The longer he was around Jen, the more he realized she neither slept nor ate. He wondered what kind of toll the constant hyper-vigilance took on her mentally and physically.

Melody sat down on the opposite end of the couch and began to write, never looking at him. He momentarily wondered if she was asleep or awake, then went back to the box. But after a few minutes, he decided Melody was more interesting.

Her pen flew across the pages, translating the music in her head to dots and lines on the paper. When she reached what he thought must be the end, she went back to the first page and began to put down the lyrics. With her free hand, she tapped a beat on her knee, and stopped only to turn the page. She paused only once, her pen poised above the paper, her hand stilled on her knee, and then she resumed. She reached the end again, capped her pen, closed her notebook, and threw them on the table in front of her.

She brushed the hair out of her eyes and looked at him. Her eyes cleared and she smiled as she crawled across the couch to him. "Hi," she said as she straddled his lap.

He hooked his arms loosely around her waist. "Hi."

She kissed him softly then sat back. She brushed a strand of hair off his forehead. Her eyes burned dark blue. "I love you."

He ran a finger gently down her cheek before cupping her face. "I love you, too." he whispered intensely.

♫ ♫ ♫ ♫

"WHAT'S your agenda today?" James asked Melody while she pulled on a gold pantsuit and, unbelievably, a pair of gold boots. Rather than looking tacky, the gold contrasted against her dark hair and tanned skin, making her look somewhat exotic. She went into the bathroom and he followed her, leaning against the door frame, watching her get ready.

Melody mentally clicked through her day. "At eight-thirty, I'm meeting a Realtor to sign the contract to sell my ranch there, then I have an appointment at Patterson Records with their marketing guy. At one, I'm having lunch with Bobby Kent to discuss a duet I wrote, then I have to go to my offices and meet with Hal's secretary," she said as she fastened a hammered gold and bronze necklace around her neck.

"On the plane coming home, I have an interview with a representative from some video channel because I'm their artist of the month for March. If I make it back to town before four, I have to meet David Patterson so he can complain to me about my tour dates, or what he calls the lack of them." She spun and looked at her outfit in the mirror. "Oh, don't forget we have to be at Kurt and Morgan's at seven."

"You really packed a day into a trip, didn't you?"

"Yep. Vacation's over." She opened her padded jewelry case to retrieve a pair of matching earrings. "Do you have a safe here, where I can store my jewelry?"

James frowned. "No, but I can store it in the office safe until we can get one installed."

"That's not a bad idea."

"You've mentioned him before, but who exactly is Bobby Kent?"

"Big time star, James. You really need to get out more." She laughed at his frown.

"I know who he is, but I don't know who he is to you."

"We are very good friends. Nothing more now or ever, despite the tabloids. We hit the scene the same year, and met at an awards celebration. We both won the Horizon Award from the CMA the same year, had a bunch of pictures taken together, and just clicked." She clipped the earrings on and ran a brush through her hair.

"What's that?"

"What's what?"

"The Horizon Award?"

She drew her hair up from the sides, added a gold clip, and turned to face him. "Best new artist."

"And what is ... "

"Country Music Association." She opened the drawer under the sink where her makeup kit had found a home. After she applied a bronze tinted lipstick, she stopped what she was doing and met his eyes in the mirror. "I'd like to buy a house. Maybe south or up north. This apartment is great for just you, but, honestly, it's a little small."

He raised an eyebrow. "Do you know how many square feet this apartment has?"

"I know exactly how many," she laughed. "But there's no room for my piano." She turned from the mirror and looked at him directly. "Do you want to look at houses with me?"

"I would when you get it narrowed down. Find what you want, or hire a Realtor to find what you want, then we'll look together. Because, honestly, I don't care where we live."

Feeling a flood of love and overwhelming emotion, Melody went to him and let him hug her to him. "I am ready for this stuff to be over. I feel like we can't start our life until it's over."

"Well, I'll admit that most marriages don't start under crazy stalker situations, but I love you and you love me and we both love God. You can't ask for too much more. We'll get through it."

She huffed out a breath and looked up at him. "You are incredibly pragmatic at times."

James raised an eyebrow. "Exactly what else should I be?"

"Even a little bit worried would be nice." Melody frowned and stepped back. "You can't possibly know what will happen next."

"I have some anxiety and I don't have a clue as to what happens next." James put a hand on her shoulder. "But I trust the One who does. That's what matters." He rubbed her arms up and down. "Would you feel better if we prayed before you start your day?"

For so long she had shut God out of her life. Day by day, James was teaching her how to bring Him back. She wanted the confidence in Him that he seemed to have, longed for it actually. "I think that would be wonderful. Thank you."

♪ ♪ ♪ ♪

JAMES and Kurt pulled into the parking garage at the same time, so Kurt rode up with James on his elevator, both men lost in their own thoughts. James set his briefcase down, took off his coat, and sat in one of the chairs at his conference table rather than at his desk. Kurt sat across from him and pulled the phone close, calling Eve to let her know he had arrived in the building. Then he used the intercom to ask Rebecca to bring them coffee, and sat back in his chair.

"What's up, brother?" Kurt asked.

"I've been thinking that it's time we invested in a corporate jet," James said.

"I said the same thing to you two years ago."

"We waste a lot of time sitting in airports, waiting on flights, changing flights. It would make more sense if we had our own."

"Yep. Same argument I gave you two years ago."

"We could lease or we could write off the majority of the expense …"

Kurt looked sharply into every corner of the room, "It's like there's an echo in here, but it takes two years to resonate."

James smiled, "I guess that concludes the monthly meeting of the stockholders of Montgomery-Lawson Enterprises."

Rebecca brought in a tray of coffee, and took Kurt's coat to take to his office. "Rebecca," James said, halting her exit. "See if Mike Redman is in the building yet, and send a car at ten to the hotel to pick up the Niroshim's reps."

"Yes, sir. Mike is here. I'll call his office. The car has already been arranged, and they should be in your office by ten thirty."

"Good. Thank you."

"Yes sir. Anything else?"

"Not until ten-thirty," James said. Rebecca left, and James poured them both a cup of coffee.

James propped his feet on his table. "I've been doing some research through Angela's career. Apparently, a student from Serbia named Rikard Šabalj gave a presentation on the same subject as Angela at a science symposium about six years ago. That subject, if you haven't guessed, was the storage model."

Kurt sat forward quickly. "What was his emphasis?"

James pursed his lips, "Apparently, he took more of an engineering solution based on hardware. You remember the early work IBM did with copper and germanium? This would have involved a carbon-copper substrate."

Kurt was intrigued. "As in diamonds?"

"Exactly. Fascinating idea, really. Heat wouldn't be a problem and he was working on a way to make a copper-osmium compound. The problem was etching the diamonds, of course."

"What about the software?"

"That's where it gets really interesting. He proposed a preliminary rewrite of the hex but he didn't go all the way to the new paradigm Angela proposed. His infrastructure work was Moore's Law heavy so he would have eventually topped out. But the infrastructure looked promising."

Kurt sat back, sensing he was missing something. "Go on."

James took a breath. "Apparently, they had both made about the same progress with a new paradigm, far more than anything published. She offered him an internship, and he accepted, but something made her decide to let him go on the first day.

"In hindsight, putting the presentations in context, what Šabalj demonstrated was identical information to Angela, just regurgitated to look fresh. My guess is that Šabalj was monitoring her work-in-progress. I'd bet he was the source of the bugs we found in the ashes and likely even had access to her nightly build backups — which is why the timing worked out for the attack and murders to happen simultaneously with her success."

Kurt nodded. "This is fascinating information. I wonder if there's a way to track a Serbian student."

"I already put Redman on it." Kurt leaned a bit further back, knowing that James would talk all the way through the process at this point in order to file all the data away in his highly unique mind.

"If he's the same person who hacked us over the holiday, then he's seriously skilled and we easily could have missed it back then when so many other things were going on. We hadn't even dialed up our monitoring back then."

Kurt nodded. "My thoughts exactly. Redman's sending some specialists back to the house on Wednesday to sift through the ashes. It's been years but maybe we'll get lucky and find something more we missed."

"If he heard her make the breakthrough, he probably broke in to get the information not realizing they'd incinerate the drives and erase the data. Blowing the lab door would have knocked over the incendiary devices and started the fire that couldn't be put out just like the fire marshal said. I bet he even bugged the lab that day he started as an intern." James took a sip of coffee, remembering the journals he hadn't looked through yet. "We're talking easily a hundred billion dollars the first year. And, every single minute that goes by without this breakthrough is another minute someone else working on it will succeed where we find we cannot."

James took his glasses off and pulled a handkerchief out of his pocket to clean the lenses. "My instinct says this is the same person, that Rikard is Richard. He must know how close we're getting. He's going to start taking bigger risks to ensure he doesn't miss anything."

"You're right. Hence the catching the hacking over Christmas. We need to continue to be careful about what progress is made and discussed at Albany in the range of the bugs," Kurt said. He took a drink of his coffee and changed subject. "Morgan's birthday's coming up next week."

"I know. What's the plan?"

"Big party at the house. Eve sent the invitations out last week. I don't remember if I had you on the list to receive an official invite or not."

"Let me know if you need anything from me," James said as Rebecca buzzed the intercom. "Yes, Rebecca."

"Mike is here."

"Send him in." They stood as the door opened and Mike walked in. He shook their hands, and they moved over to James' desk. "The main thing I'm concerned about is the security for the press conference," James said as he sat down. "This guy has already made it past our security systems at least once, and there's going to be a lot of people milling around later this morning."

Mike pulled out his laptop, ready to get to work. "We'll have a guard stationed in each of your offices, and at the door to each of the labs. All the engineers and developers have made off-line copies of everything to date, and all of the latest prototypes have been removed from the labs. Everything's being brought up to Rebecca's office, due to the tighter security here, and what doesn't fit will go to Eve. We'll have additional guards in their offices. We told everyone it was because we were going to give the Hiroshims a tour. We're all going to be able to communicate via mics and ear wigs."

"Keep an eye on Albany, too."

"Already taken care of. We have extra security there while the employees are here for the ceremony."

♫ ♫ ♫ ♫

MELODY thought about the schedule Patterson's marketing director had given her for her television appearances to promote her tour. She didn't like to do the talk shows, because they all put her in front of live audiences, but he'd arranged for her to do three of them. She tried to argue that people would come to the concerts without the exposure, but ultimately had no choice but to follow the orders David Patterson handed down.

All the way to the restaurant she complained to Hal. "Melody, we can't cancel them now. It would generate bad press," Hal said. "We'll just make sure you sing before the interviews."

"Not the point. We specifically said no live talk shows. Why is David being such a jerk?" The car pulled in front of the restaurant, and Jen opened the door so they could get out.

"Because he's always been a jerk. There's no use trying to change him now," Hal said. "Jen, will you be joining us?"

"I'll be here," Jen said.

"You want something to eat?"

"No, thank you. I'm good."

The *maître d'* knew Melody and showed her directly to her table where Bobby already sat waiting for her. Bobby Kent looked almost like a living caricature of a cowboy. He stood well over six feet tall, long and lanky with dark hair and ice blue eyes. He looked completely at home in his worn jeans, boots, and cowboy hat. Always the gentleman, he stood when he saw her, bent low to kiss her cheek and shook Hal's hand in greeting.

"How was vacation?" he asked as they took their seats, his voice a syrupy baritone drawl with a hint of deep south Virginia infiltrating his Nashville twang.

"Great. I almost got bored before I talked myself out of it," she said, then ordered some iced tea from the waiter. Hal ordered the same and they picked up the menus.

"So is boredom what drove you to your nuptials?" Bobby asked with a heart stopping grin.

Melody laughed and threw down her menu. "It was the most exciting vacation of my life. Watching Morgan marry Kurt, falling in love with James, and just jumping in with both feet. I cannot tell you what it's been like."

He reached over and took her hand. "I am so happy for you. As long as you're happy."

She winked and picked her menu back up. "I can't wait for you to meet him. He's amazing. What's been happening around here?"

"Same old thing. I finished recording *But Cowboys Don't Cry*. Threw in the steel guitar against my good judgment and it's actually better than I expected. Got a weepy sound, ya know? After this tour, that's it for my commitments to Patterson." He signaled to the waiter to come take their order.

"I just have one more. Who're you signing with?" Melody asked.

"Haven't decided. I can wait a month or two, look over my options." After they placed their orders, the three of them talked about the different record companies pursuing the two young stars.

"How's the shoulder, Hal?" Bobby asked.

"Still a little stiff, but better every day," Hal said, rotating his shoulder.

"I hear bullet scars do wonders for your reputation as a tough guy."

Hal grinned, "I wouldn't recommend it."

"Really caused an uproar here. They know who did it yet?"

Hal lowered his voice. "They know, but don't talk about it to anyone."

Bobby frowned. "What's up?"

Melody patted his hand. "Don't worry about it right now. When we can, we'll tell you the whole story." With deft slight of hand on the part of the wait staff, a plate of salad appeared in front of her. Knowing Bobby, she did not pick up her fork, but instead reached for his hand so that he could bless the meal.

After the three of them chorused an amen, she asked, "Can you come to Atlanta next week for Morgan's birthday?"

"Probably. I didn't know anything about it," Bobby said, picking up a knife to cut into his steak.

"I think Kurt said his secretary was supposed to send out the invitations last week," she said. "Check with your secretary."

He pulled out his cellphone and hit a speed dial. Melody said, "I didn't mean check right this second."

Bobby grinned. "I don't want to forget." Then he held up his finger. "Hey, it's me. Did I get invited to a party in Atlanta for next week. Sure. Okay. Yeah."

Melody saw his eyelids tighten very slightly. The rest of his features remained perfectly poised and collected. "Yeah, that's Melody Mason's sister. She's Lawson now."

He met Melody's eyes and grinned. "Why don't you go ahead and do that and e-mail me when the arrangements have been made." He disconnected without saying good-bye. That was the only outward sign of his clear irritation. "Oh, sorry. Montgomery, now, I guess."

"I'm going to have to rebrand myself I think."

Bobby gave her a sideways smile. "Well, at least it's Montgomery so your initials don't change." He cut his steak. "Anyway, looks like I can be there."

Melody grabbed her bag and pulled out several sheets of music. "Here's that song. We can put it on the album I start next week, if you want. I'd also like to perform it in Jacksonville, Florida, this week, if you can work it in."

"You really want to cut a record now? If you wait a few months we can put it under my new label."

"I think we can call this one a good start and do one every year under whoever we're signed with. It's really all about the fans."

He nodded. "Sounds good to me. I'll check my schedule and let you know." He took a bite, swallowed, then took a drink of his tea.

"I think the fans would flip if you came out on stage with me."

"That's a great idea. It would certainly be unexpected, since I didn't do it in Atlanta. As far as I know, I'm free, but I'll confirm and get back with you."

♫ ♫ ♫ ♫

"THEY'RE probably already there waiting on us," Melody said to James as Jen turned the last corner to the building, coming back from eating at Morgan and Kurt's. They had planned to meet Roberts and Suarez at the apartment five minutes ago.

"If they are, then they can wait," James said.

She couldn't stand to run late or keep anyone waiting. At her insistence, Jen dropped them off at the front door of the building before she went to park. She stepped into the lobby and saw the two detectives occupying chairs in the sitting area. She walked up to them. "I'm so sorry we're late. We had dinner at my sister's, and time got away from us," she said.

"We've only been here a few minutes, Mrs. Montgomery," Roberts said, standing and accepting the handshake she offered.

"Excuse me, Mrs. Montgomery," the guard said walking up to her, carrying a long gold box. "These were left for you."

She felt chills creeping along her skin, and didn't want to take the box from him. She knew. She knew what she would find in the box.

James put a hand on her shoulder. "Don't touch that," he warned.

Roberts reacted immediately and pulled a pair of rubber gloves out of his pocket and put them on before he took the box from the guard. "Where did this come from?" he asked.

With a confused and curious look, the guard shrugged and said, "A delivery boy brought it by about an hour ago."

Roberts carefully opened the box while Suarez pulled out his notebook and asked for a description of the boy. Melody looked inside as Roberts opened the lid and she gasped, taking a step back. Inside was a single long stemmed red rose, with a picture rather than a note attached to it. It was apparently taken from a video, and was an image of Hal's blood spraying over Melody. Written in marker across the bottom, was:

THOUGHT I HAD YOU. NEXT TIME YOU DIE

Jen came in and saw the box. "Exactly where did that come from?"

Roberts lifted the box and looked underneath it. "Busy Bee Florist," he said. "The address is just around the corner." He looked at his partner and recited the address. Suarez flew out the door before Roberts even finished speaking. He turned to the security guard. "I need a large paper bag," he ordered.

"Are you ready to come up to my apartment? We can get something up there." James offered.

"Yeah. The guard already told us what he knows," Roberts said as he put the lid back on the box and walked with James, Melody, and Jen to the elevator. "He said he takes deliveries from the same kid a couple of times a week. Apparently, they're open until ten."

Roberts' cell phone rang as they rode the elevator and he pulled it out of his pocket. "Yeah." His face paled then turned bright red. "I'll stay here with them. Find out what you can. I'll wait for you here." He kicked the side of the elevator wall as the doors opened, then stormed out. He spun to look at James, "The florist shop burned down about forty-five minutes ago. The fire department found two bodies inside, apparently the owner and her son, the delivery boy."

Numb, Melody walked past them and tried to open the door to the apartment. It was locked, and she rattled the handle a few times, then leaned her forehead against the door, wishing it would just open. Jen touched her shoulder to get her to step aside, and with stiff movements, Melody stepped back. James restrained her as Jen did a quick check of the apartment then gave them the all clear to come inside.

Melody walked into the apartment and went to the corner near the big windows. Leaning her back against the wall, she let herself slide to the floor, drawing her knees up and wrapping her arms around them. She started rocking. Hal had been shot, and now two people were dead because she wouldn't marry a man who had another woman in his apartment the day of their wedding.

James knelt on the ground in front of her. He reached a hand out to stroke her hair, and as soon as he touched her she fell apart. Her sobs felt like they would break her body in half. James shifted her and she willingly went into his arms. He let her cry as long as she wanted, and her whole body shuddered by the time she started to quiet down. "I don't think I can take anymore," she whispered.

He hugged her tight, not knowing what to say. They weren't the ones calling the shots right now. They'd have to pretty soon, if he had anything to do with it, but for now they just had to wait.

♫ ♫ ♫ ♫

RIKARD Šabalj stood in the crowd outside of the florist shop. He pulled his hat further down his head to shield his face and saw the cop come from her apartment and go to the florist shop.

He hadn't enjoyed killing them. He'd seen enough innocent death in his life. But, the mother had recognized him. She tried to pretend she hadn't, but he'd seen the look in her eye. The kid took the delivery and he could tell she was going to call the police the second he left. He'd had to take care of things.

It infuriated him how Melody Mason, superstar, constantly seemed to outsmart him by accident. She was like a bad luck charm. He had to find a way to just make her disappear.

♫ ♫ ♫ ♫

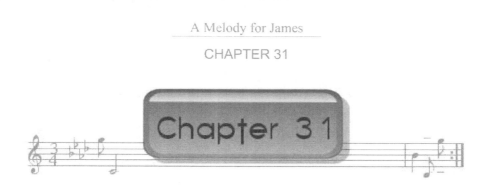

MELODY woke with a start early on Thursday morning, her pulse pounding, sweat breaking out on her body. She had the same nightmare that haunted her occasionally over the last four years. A pursuer caught up with her, and she relived the night Richard had assaulted her over and over again.

Her legs shook when she pushed herself out of her bed, and she stumbled on her way to the bathroom. She splashed her face with cold water and stared at her reflection in the mirror. The shadows under her eyes appeared darker every time she looked. Two or three hours of sleep at a stretch since Monday night had started to wear her down.

They'd watched the video of the hall outside her dressing room four times since Monday, and still hadn't been able to tell if one of the men going into her room was Richard. She felt jumpy, exhausted, and frustrated. This needed to end soon, or else she would have to find a deserted island and hide for the rest of her life.

She went to the living room, and turned a lamp on low. It was four, and she knew James would be up in an hour. On Thursday's he rose early to work out in the gym.

"You should call a doctor, see about getting some sleeping pills," James said.

Melody jumped and turned around. He stood in the entrance of the hallway, wearing a pair of sweat pants low on his hips. He had put off his trip to Tokyo. She knew why, and a little guilt nudged its way into all of her other feelings.

"You need to quit sneaking up on me until this is over with," she said. She stormed to the kitchen and pushed the button on the coffee maker.

James grabbed his briefcase off the table by the door, then followed her into the kitchen.

"Want to work out with me this morning?" he asked. "The physical exertion might help."

She shook her head. "I have to go workout with Clarissa this morning in Jacksonville. I need to conserve my energy until then."

"I wrote an app for our phones," he said.

Feeling like she was trapped in a foggy room, Melody shook her head to clear it. "You did what?"

"Our phones are different models, different suppliers, different carriers. I wasn't happy with the commercially available options so I wrote a custom app to connect us. May I see your phone?"

She went to the counter in the corner of the kitchen where she had her phone plugged in and charging. She turned it on and entered the pass code then handed it to him. He grabbed his glasses off of the counter and slipped them on, then pressed a series of buttons on her phone. "This will link us. It will link our calendars and give us an encrypted instant messaging system just for the two of us. A little more immediate and much more private than text messaging."

He handed it back to her. "Access your calendar."

She pulled up her calendar and saw strips of green across the current week. She turned the screen to show him. "What's that?"

He took it back from her and brought the week up, then leaned close to her so that they could both see the screen. "See? It says, 'James in Tokyo.' We can customize it to be total, like everything I have scheduled for work and private, or we can limit it to just the out of town trips. Any time you enter an event or appointment in your calendar," he said, pressing a series of buttons, "you just choose whether or not you want to share it with me by clicking here." After showing her how, he pulled out his phone and accessed his calendar. "See? There it is. And, with my calendar, it's linked up with my office, so you'd even be able to leave Rebecca notes about events."

"You wrote this?"

James shrugged. "Sometimes I like to play with simple code. There are similar apps everywhere, but I wanted something I knew would work with both our phones."

Simple code, she thought. *What would my husband consider challenging and complex?* Melody smiled. "Thank you, James."

He showed her some more features he'd written into the application, then drained his coffee cup and looked at the clock hanging on the wall. "I'm going to go. I'll be back in about an hour. What time are you leaving?"

"Hal will be here at seven to get me and Jen. Depending on how things go today, I might end up spending the night there," she said.

"If you do, I'll go ahead and come over tonight. Give Rebecca a call and let her know or update your calendar on your phone." He walked to the bedroom to change. She followed him and watched him get ready.

He grabbed his gym bag from the floor of the closet and she followed him to the front door. "I'll see you in about an hour. I have my cell phone with me if you need me," he said as he kissed her and left.

She locked the door. When she turned around, she saw Jen emerging from the office looking like she'd been awake for hours. "Coffee?"

♫ ♫ ♫ ♫

JAMES stepped off the elevator into the lobby and saw Suarez sitting in one of the chairs, reading the morning paper and drinking a cup of coffee. He walked over to him and sat down. "Melody might be spending the night in Jacksonville," he said without preamble. He looked up as Roberts came through the double doors, spotted them, and headed their way. "She doesn't have good mornings on the days of her performances, and I think part of the reason she wants to stay is so that she doesn't have to add traveling to her day."

"Jen arranged to have five men scattered among her crew. Suarez and I both have plenty of personal days saved up, so we'll be able to travel with you two wherever you end up going. The Captain is being decent about it. I think he's already preparing the speech he'll give the press when we nail this guy," Roberts said.

James looked at his watch and stood. "You still want to go work out with me, Suarez?"

He nodded, handed the paper to Roberts, and stood. "Let's go."

♫ ♫ ♫ ♫

"HEY, Morg. I was hoping you'd be up," Melody said, fiddling with her pen. Fresh song sheets sat next to her on the counter, but she had no music in her head today.

"Yeah, I just got back from my run. Are you okay?"

"I can't sleep."

"I'm sorry, honey."

"I'm sure it's normal. Are you going to be in Jacksonville tomorrow night?" She went to the bedroom and braced the phone against her ear with her shoulder. She pulled out her suitcase and started going through the clothes she had there.

"We're not sure yet. It depends on when some meeting that Kurt has gets over with. Are you staying overnight?"

"Probably. Days of concerts are bad enough without fighting airports, too. I'll let you go. I'll call when I get in on Sunday if I don't see you tomorrow night."

"Break a leg, or whatever you say to singers. I love you, Melly."

"I love you, too." Melody hung up the phone and finished packing.

Her limbs felt heavy and uncooperative, her head hurt, and she wanted nothing more than to bury herself under the covers and cry. But she couldn't. So she snapped the lid to the suitcase closed and stripped on her way to the shower.

♫ ♫ ♫ ♫

MELODY fell asleep on the plane, and slept through the short flight. She woke up with a worse headache than when she fell asleep and felt irritated at the nagging pain. She swallowed some aspirin as the plane landed and drank a cup of coffee as if dying of thirst. Hal gave her a concerned look, but she just patted his hand and said, "I'm just a little stressed, Hal. I'll be okay."

They went straight to the coliseum rather than heading to the hotel first. The dancers had already arrived and occupied themselves by warming up for the practice session. They would dry run through it first, then they would do it again with the band. Melody went to her dressing room to change, and recognized one of the security guys keeping guard outside her room. "Make sure Jen, Hal, and Lisa have complete access. Everyone else, you can give a hard time," she told him.

"No problem, Melody."

"My husband, knowing him as I do, will probably show up sometime this afternoon. He can have complete access, too," she said, opening the door.

"Got it," the guard said, tipping his chair back.

She changed into tights and a baggy T-shirt, then tied her hair into a ponytail and went out to get to work. As she passed an alcove just off the stage, a noise caught her attention and she spun her head around. She felt so jumpy. Her eyes almost popped out of her head when she saw Hal and Clarissa exchanging a very passionate kiss. Melody grinned as she slipped past the alcove quietly, then executed a series of cartwheels and flips across the stage floor, practicing a move they planned for her to do on her reentry after one of her changes. She finished amid the applause from the other dancers, and executed a graceful curtsey. Her headache had vanished.

♫ ♫ ♫ ♫

Chapter 32

MELODY lay on her back on the stage, not quite ready to move after the workout she just had, her arm thrown over her eyes to shield them from the lights above her. Someone sat on the ground next to her. She recognized the scent of James' cologne and felt his hand on her calf, and grinned. "Oh Marcus. You should hurry and get out of here before my husband shows up."

She heard James laugh, then moved her arm and sat up, noticing that none of the other dancers had moved yet, either. Crossing her legs, she spun until she faced him. "Hi."

He leaned over and kissed her, causing several catcalls and cheers from the crew around them, then sat back. "Hi, yourself."

"You're a little later than I expected," she observed.

"I wasn't going to be here until tonight."

"Yeah, right." Her eyes roamed over him. "You're going to get your pretty suit all dirty on this floor."

He leaned back on his elbows. "That's a risk I'm willing to take. You didn't look ready to move yet." He reached behind him and slid a bag toward her. "Unbeknownst to any die hard Atlanta fan that I come across in my business, I happen to own a small chunk of the local NFL team. Here's a present for you from them."

"This is just a day of presents, isn't it?" she said with a grin, ripping open the box she'd pulled out of the bag. She started laughing as she pulled out a jersey signed by the team and a pair of boots in their colors. "You are perfect," she said laughing. Then something occurred to her. "Hey! Is this why you drive a Jaguar?"

Before he could answer, Clarissa came from behind her and cleared her throat. "You need to do the reentry in boots to make sure you can, then you need to play the new song so we can work out the steps of the waltz,"

Clarissa said.

Melody huffed out a breath before she stood up. "You'd think that I would get a little more respect around here, seeing how I'm the star," she grumbled, going to the wings of the stage and grabbing a pair of boots from Lisa. They had fashioned them with a special rubber sole to allow her to turn flips on the stage floor.

James stood, brushed off his pants, and moved out of the way with the rest of the dancers. He found Jen in the wings.

"She's not just some pretty girl, is she?" Jen asked rhetorically, nodding toward Melody stretching on the other side of the stage.

"No. This job is incredibly physical."

"I never really thought about it."

The band stopped tuning their instruments, and at Clarissa's signal, played the beginning of a very upbeat song. Out of one side, Melody and three male dancers came out, tumbling and flipping, meeting three women and one more man that came from the other side. They all moved simultaneously, looking like mirror images of the other, and the final flip of the women landed them in the waiting arms of the men, with Melody and her partner in the front at center stage. Melody started singing, then Clarissa gave the signal to stop.

"That looked great. Let's not do it again. I don't want to risk someone getting hurt this close to show time," Clarissa said and clapped her hands in a perfect metronome rhythm. "Keep the beat. Don't anticipate. Make your timing absolutely perfect."

Melody went back to James, and someone passing by her handed her a bottle of water. "Where did you learn to do that?" he asked.

Melody stood up straight, throwing her shoulders back stiff as a board, and said in a smooth southern accent, "All proper young ladies must take gymnastics lessons. Now quit making a scene and go put on the proper outfit." She relaxed and took a swig of the water. "So said my mother every Tuesday and Thursday from right after my fifth birthday until my freshman year in High School." She grabbed a towel from the stack on the table next to them and wiped her face. "Morgan can do it, too. It's not very complicated stuff. It just looks flashy with all of us doing it in perfect sync," she said with a shrug.

"Melody, nothing that requires a musical beat is complicated to you. It's us mere mortals who have a problem with it," he said, taking the bottle from her and swallowing some water.

♫ ♫ ♫ ♫

JACKSONVILLE loved Melody. Even with the lack of sleep and the stress she'd been under, she was at her best in front of the crowd. The cheers pumped her full of energy and made her feel tireless.

She sang the song they'd set up with the same enthusiasm of all her songs, and no one who didn't know better would doubt the sincerity behind it. It made her ill to have to mix it in with her other songs, but it had to be done, so she grit her teeth and sang.

During one of her changes, she called out to Hal, "Did Bobby call?" The end of the sentence came out muffled as she bent down for Lisa to do her hair.

"He'll be here any time. We'll switch *Tears* for the duet." Hal answered her, turning when he spotted Bobby Kent walking up behind him.

"Signal me when he's ready," she said, "and someone find me something to eat." She didn't look back as she ran back onto the stage.

Hal shook Bobby's hand, and introduced him to James. "It's a pleasure to meet you. Melody bragged a lot about you at lunch the other day."

Bobby stood about two inches taller than James, but James looked a little less lean, a bit more broad in the chest and shoulders. The two sized each other up the way men do, and quickly and silently decided they would probably get along. James put out his hand. "I've heard a lot about you, too. Nice to finally meet you."

Lisa came up to Bobby, popped her gum, and pulled him toward a chair to apply stage makeup. He flirted with her, always trying to get her to say something, but she just worked, occasionally having to stop a smile from forming. "Lisa, you're going to break my heart one of these days," he said when she finished. She just winked at him and popped her gum.

Melody came backstage for another change, whipped off her boots, and spotted Bobby. "You all set?" she asked, all business as support staff ripped off her clothes and wiped her down with a towel.

"Yep. All set."

"Two songs. Enter after you start singing. I want it to be as big a surprise as possible," she said around a mouthful of melon while she pulled on low-riding black spandex pants and her rubber-soled boots. A shirt was held open to her and she put her arms through, then Lisa sealed it from behind. It was long sleeved and stopped at her midriff, fitting her tight. Lisa put the microphone headset on as Melody tipped her head back to swallow some water. She tossed the water bottle she drank from in James' direction and blew him a quick kiss, then ran to her spot, ready for the cue.

They performed the gymnastics perfectly. James wondered how she still had the energy to do it. She'd already performed for about an hour now. The crowd went nuts when they finished and she began to sing, and James knew why she'd done it so late in the show. She knew the crowd would be tired, too.

"Pretty fantastic, isn't she?" Bobby said at James' elbow.

James turned to study Melody's best friend, searching for anything more than genuine admiration in the other man's voice or expression, but finding nothing. He smiled and nodded. "Fantastic is a mild word for it."

Bobby slipped his hands into the pockets of his jeans. "Even in Nashville and throughout our industry, surrounded by the talent I see, I've never met anyone like her. God has truly gifted her."

James raised an eyebrow. "He has indeed." He gestured to the stage. "When we first met years ago, she wanted to be a worship leader."

"Really?" Bobby grinned. "Wow, can you imagine her leading praise? I'd pay to see that."

"She would be amazing. I pray she feels led to go in that direction again someday."

Someone handed Bobby a microphone. He held his hand out to James. "Brother, I can already tell it's going to be a joy getting to know you better."

As James shook his hand again, an understanding of spiritual brotherhood passed between the two. "Likewise."

The opening chords of the duet played, and Melody started singing. The audience was kind of quiet because they didn't recognize the song. Melody finished her verse, and on cue, Bobby began singing. A ripple of murmur went through the crowd. As he stepped onto the stage the murmur became a delighted cheer that rapidly rose to thunderous applause. Melody and Bobby grinned at each other and stopped singing while the band just revisited the refrain, waiting for the crowd to quiet down enough to hear the words.

After they finished, the crowd surged to their feet and cheered. Bobby waved, kissed Melody on the cheek, and walked off the stage.

He glanced at his watch as he handed a stage hand the microphone. He caught James' eye and had to shout over the noise of the crowd. "Tell her I have to run, but I'll see her at Morgan's party."

James didn't try to compete with the noise. He just nodded and threw a thumbs up. Bobby snatched some wipes from Lisa's station to remove the thick stage makeup from his face. He stopped one more time, putting his face close to James's ear and said, "I've been praying for Melody's safety. Please call me if you need anything."

James shook his hand and nodded, then yelled, "Thank you, brother. Your prayers are appreciated."

Bobby nodded, then left.

Once the show ended and the backstage pass holders headed home with autographs and smiles, Melody and James sat in the quiet of the inner room of her dressing room. Jen sat on a chair in the outer room near the door. Melody lay back with her eyes closed and her feet propped in his lap. He sat and watched her while rubbing her feet. A knock sounded at the door, and Hal came in, followed by Suarez and Roberts.

Melody opened her eyes, saw who stood there, and closed them again. "Can we go home tonight instead of tomorrow?" she asked James.

"If we can get a hold of your pilot, we can," James said.

"Hal has his cell number."

Hal sat down. "I'm going to stick with the crew. Send the pilot back tomorrow afternoon. I'll have him fly us to Houston, then I'll take a commercial flight to meet you in New York on Tuesday," he said.

"Sounds good to me," she said. She opened one eye and looked at James. "Do you think we can get a pizza delivered to the airport?"

He laughed and ran a finger up the arch of her foot, "Let me see what I can arrange."

"Make sure you get two, especially if Suarez and Roberts are flying with us. I know Jen's happy just eating fruit and nuts, but I don't want to have to share with those guys."

♫ ♫ ♫ ♫

MELODY flew to New York on Tuesday, with Jen accompanying her, and did the round of morning shows and talk shows. She did six that day, spent the night at a hotel there, then did two more in the morning. Hal arrived, and the plane came back to pick them up on Wednesday morning to take them to Houston. She fought Hal all the way to the doctor's office to get his stitches removed, then patiently listened to him complain all the way back to the arena. Wednesday night she did her sold-out concert in Houston, and went back to Atlanta on Thursday morning. She'd sung the song again, but still hadn't heard anything from the man who called himself Richard Johnson.

Hal watched Melody over the days since they met in New York, and decided to call the recording studio in Nashville and cancel the session they had arranged for Thursday afternoon and Friday morning. He decided that what Melody needed the most was a few days of pampering by James in Atlanta, and he would rather face her wrath over that decision than watch her collapse in exhaustion.

James entered his apartment building early Thursday evening, and nodded to Suarez who sat in a chair in the lobby. Suarez barely gave an indication of recognition, but he stood and folded his paper under his arm and left the building.

James paced the elevator the entire ride up to his apartment, anxious to see Melody. He didn't like having her away from him overnight while Richard Johnson remained on the loose. He smiled and mentally corrected himself, knowing he probably wouldn't want her away from him overnight regardless.

She lay asleep on one of the couches, the television tuned to a pop video channel. He set his briefcase and keys quietly down on the table by the door, then sat on the edge of the couch next to her. He brushed some hair off her face, and she stirred and slowly opened her eyes. As soon as her eyes cleared, she smiled and stretched, grabbing his tie as she brought her arms back down. She wound the tie around her wrist, and pulled him to her, giving him a long, warm kiss. When she broke the kiss, she stretched again.

"How was Houston?" he asked.

"Good show. Sold out," she said in a husky voice. "They didn't feed me properly afterward, though."

"You'd think Hal would know better," he said as he loosened his tie.

"Yeah, well he's a little distracted by Clarissa, lately. Is Tokyo still being understanding?"

"They really don't have much of a choice, but as far as I know, they're okay with the fact I haven't visited yet. I've sent people to check the place out and handle some preliminaries." He slipped his tie off and walked toward the bedroom, untucking his shirt as he went. "So, woman, what did you make for dinner?"

Melody didn't even laugh. "Take out."

♫ ♫ ♫ ♫

AFTER dinner at his desk in his home office, James checked e-mail. He immediately saw the message from Mike Redman flagged urgent. The subject line read, "INTERN."

He opened the e-mail and skimmed. Kurt and Mike had researched the intern Angela had briefly hired and fired. No electronic record existed, but he was able to dig through hard copies of files, through the hundreds of interns his company had employed over the last ten years, and find the hard file. He'd attached the photo from the security badge. James downloaded it and immediately recognized the man he knew as Richard Johnson.

He sat back and frowned at the screen. It looked like their theory was panning out. Richard must have tried to get the research, failed, then needed the capital that Melody's trust fund would provide. But, how? How did Melody become his target?

♫ ♫ ♫ ♫

RIKARD Šabalj sat back with the index fingers of each hand forming a steeple below his chin. With reptilian eyes, he watched the digital recording he'd made of Melody's latest show. Oh, he got her message. The question — was it a trap?

It didn't matter to him. She made him out to look like a failure. He wouldn't fail this time. This time, he would succeed and find redemption on her bloody altar.

♫ ♫ ♫ ♫

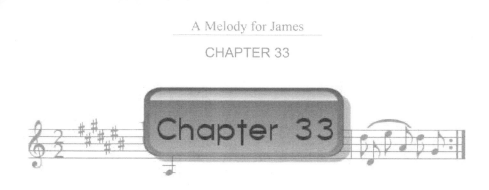

IT was Melody's duty to occupy Morgan before her surprise party. Knowing exactly what it would take to keep her sister out of the house for hours, Melody spent Friday with Morgan, Ginger, Suarez, and Jen, armed with a list and shopping for new clothes for the kids at the children's home. They hit the mall as soon as the doors opened, and shopped for hours. Melody used whatever powers of persuasion she had to get store managers to agree to deliver the clothes to the home. When that didn't work she took off her glasses and batted her eyes. As a last resort, she used her star status. Every store eventually agreed to deliver them.

While the women shopped, Rebecca and Eve, armed with an army of caterers, attacked Morgan's house, getting it ready for the party that night. They hung decorations, moved furniture, and supervised caterers in preparing food. Melody had orders not to allow Morgan back to the house until seven, and guests would begin arriving at six-thirty. Rebecca looked at her watch, frowned, and decided they needed to pick up the pace.

The plane flew to Dallas, where Melody was scheduled to perform Sunday night, to pick up Melody's band and her three backup singers. They had all been with her for four years and had become her extended family, and so were all invited to the party that night. When they arrived at the house, Eve sent the women to the hotel to get ready for the party, and put the men to work.

♫ ♫ ♫ ♫

"OH Melly, this house is beautiful!" Ginger said excitedly.

They got out of the car after Jen told them to go in without her, and looked up at the plantation house. Melody unlocked the door with the code the Realtor had given her. She felt excitement and anticipation all at once.

"How many bedrooms?" Morgan asked.

"Five or six, I think. What I want you to see is the music room," Melody said as she led everyone through the spacious entrance, up the stairs, and toward the back. "Check this out," she said, stepping into the large room and singing a quick version of the scales. "Do you hear those acoustics? This room was redesigned by an audio engineer just for music." She stood in the middle of the room and turned in a circle, singing one of her songs. "It's perfect."

Morgan folded her arms in front of her. "Have you even looked at the rest of the house, yet?" she asked.

Melody frowned. "I looked at some of the rooms, but then we came in here, and that was all I needed to see."

"Melly, where is the kitchen?"

"What difference does that make? Did you hear the acoustics?"

"What difference does that make? If you find out the plumbing doesn't work or the foundation is cracked or the walls are rotting and full of mold?"

Melody brushed Morgan off with the wave of her hand. "This is a nice house. Besides, I can hire someone to fix anything that's wrong. I'm not going to be able to find another room like this without building my own place, and between me and James, our schedules are too busy to worry about that right now."

"Why don't we look at the rest of the house, then you can let James look at it. You don't want to rush into this."

Melody crossed the room and hugged her sister. "James will love it, too."

She sighed knowing her sister was right. "Well, let's go see what needs to be done." Morgan pulled a notebook out of her purse, and they began to walk from room to room, the three women discussing furniture and colors and patterns. Suarez followed silently behind them, enjoying observing the way Ginger moved, and gallantly keeping his opinion about mint colored walls to himself.

♪ ♪ ♪ ♪

THEY would have arrived late for the party if Melody and Ginger hadn't practically dragged Morgan away from the house, promising to bring her back the next day to get some more ideas. Morgan stayed so busy taking notes and talking into her portable recorder that she didn't even notice all the cars around her house until Jen stopped the car and Ginger opened the door.

"What in the world is going on?" Morgan asked.

Ginger clapped her hands and danced with anticipation as Morgan climbed out of the car. "Happy Birthday, Morgan!"

Morgan was speechless. She followed them into the house, where Kurt and about sixty of her friends waited. "SURPRISE!" they all yelled, and Kurt handed her a glass of sparkling cider right before he swept her up into his arms, giving her a hug and a kiss.

"I had no idea," she said, wiping the tears from her eyes.

"You're not supposed to have any idea, silly. That's what surprise parties are for," Ginger said.

Suarez looked for Roberts and found him in the back yard with Jen, staring out at the blackness beyond the house lights. The three of them had help from Peter Glasser and his team of four. Considering the size of the house and the number of guests, they genuinely debated how they could keep the house secure.

"I'll take the inside," Jen said, "if you two can watch the perimeter."

"I wish they'd hired extra security for tonight," Roberts said.

"We'll just have to do what we can," Suarez said.

Jen answered, "I'll go ahead and do an inside sweep. You have my number if you need me."

Inside, Melody sought out James, spotting him in the corner of the room watching her. "Hi," she said.

He pulled her to him, hugging her to his side. "Hi yourself," he said.

"What an amazing party," she said.

James nodded behind her. "Rebecca and Eve did all the work. I'll go get us something to drink."

Melody turned and saw Rebecca. "You did a great job putting this thing together," she said, looking around the room.

Rebecca put an arm around Melody's shoulders. "We all have our own talents. I have been cursed with being organized. I think I would rather have been granted the gift of song. It is so much more poetic."

"Hey, Darlin'," a masculine voice said in her ear.

Melody turned around, "Bobby! I thought you wouldn't be able to make it!" She threw her arms around him, letting him spin her around before he set her down. She didn't have time to notice Rebecca's star struck look. "I'm so mad at you for leaving before the concert was over in Jacksonville last week. Oh, by the way, this is Rebecca, James' secretary."

"Nice to meet you," he greeted, taking Rebecca's hand and kissing it, causing a faint blush to tinge her cheeks. He turned back to Melody. "I told you I'd only be able to stop in," he said as James walked up.

James nodded his head and handed Melody a bottle of water, then pulled her close. "Good to see you, Bobby. How you doing?" James asked.

"Gearing up for my tour," he said. "Saw you on the cover of 'Newsweek.' Looks like you've been busy."

"Just another day in the life," he said dryly.

Voices, laughter, and music filled the house. Morgan always loved to throw a party, and slowly took the reins away from Eve and Rebecca, taking over the caterers and waiters. Kurt tried more than once to get her to stop and enjoy her guests, but finally gave up, deciding she was having more fun doing it her way.

Melody heard the sound of a fiddle playing, and dragged James into the front room, where Bobby Kent and Todd Rowlings stood, each of them holding a fiddle, a circle of people forming around them. Todd finished playing, then Bobby started, mimicking Todd note for note, then added his own flare. Todd smiled when Bobby finished, then played another set. Toes tapped all over the room.

"What are they doing?" James breathed the question close to Melody's ear.

"Dueling," she said. "They'll try to out play each other. They play everything that's been played up to a point then improvise the next refrain. It's like an extended game of concentration but with violins." While Bobby played, Todd kicked a fiddle case toward Melody. "Todd, I haven't played in three years. I couldn't keep up with the two of you," she said, protesting.

"Like falling off a bike, Melody." Todd taunted, then grinned at her as he played another round.

Bobby took a swig of ice tea then winked at Melody while Todd played. "I've never known her to back down from a musical challenge."

Melody sighed and took the fiddle from the case, putting it up under her chin. "Next time, the weapon of choice will be the piano," she threatened, then jumped in as soon as Todd finished. She played a little rough at first, rusty, but her fingers warmed up, and she played the complicated notes with ease, thankful she'd cut her fingernails the week before.

Bobby grinned, then played the same set, adding his own flare, challenging Todd to make it a little more complicated. Melody kept right up with them, the three dueling in a circle, finally playing together, until Melody laughed so hard that she had to stop. The crowd around them hooted, whistled, and the clapping turned to general applause.

She returned the fiddle to its case, turned to James, and said. "I'm thirsty"

He just shook his head and laughed, then went to get her some water. He no longer felt surprised about what was hidden inside Melody.

James came back carrying a new drink for Melody and found her talking with Morgan and Ginger. "Morgan? Are you having a good time catering your own surprise party?" he asked her.

"Oh, this is the best party. Don't you ever let Rebecca get away from you, James. She's a gem," Morgan said.

"Don't ever let her hear you say something like that," he said, "I'd never get any work out of her after that."

Ginger laughed, then someone in the crowd apparently bumped into her back, causing her to stumble, knocking her forward and into Melody. Ginger spilled nearly her entire full glass of red punch down the front of Melody's shirt. "Oh Melly, I'm so sorry!"

"It's okay, Ginger. It wasn't your fault," Melody said as she ineffectively brushed at her shirt with a napkin. Her imagination suddenly overlaid her punch spilled shirt with her other shirt, covered with Hal's blood. She involuntarily shuddered and blinked hard to try to rid her mind of that horrifying image. "Well, this is hopeless. I'm going to run upstairs and change shirts."

She wove her way through the party. Jen stopped her at the base of the stairs. "Everything okay?"

Melody gestured at her shirt. "I'm just going to go grab a shirt out of Morgan's closet."

Jen frowned and checked her watch. "I was just about to check outside."

Melody waved her hand. "Go. I'll be fine. I won't be gone a minute." She rushed upstairs and into Morgan's room, making a beeline for the closet. She took her shirt off, put the new one on, and then headed to the bathroom to rinse out the ruined one.

"Hello, Melody."

Startled, she turned around and saw Richard lying on the bed, his back propped up by pillows. A coppery taste of fear flooded her mouth.

♫ ♫ ♫ ♫

HE wouldn't do anything with all those people downstairs, would he? She wet her lips. "Hello, Richard."

He pushed himself off the bed and walked toward her, stopping directly in front of her. Her mind screamed to run, but her legs wouldn't listen. He brushed some hair off her face, and she tried desperately not to flinch or let her face betray the depth of her revulsion. "Rikard," he said, not bothering to mask his accent. "My name is Rikard Šabalj."

Panic made it hard to comprehend what he said. "I don't understand," she said around the driest mouth she'd ever had. "What is that accent?"

"I'm from Serbia." He reached out and picked up a strand of her hair. "My home is on the beautiful blue Danube River."

Keep him talking, she thought. Make Jen come look for her. "I don't know where that is."

"Of course you don't. You're American. There is nothing in your world except your sea to shining sea. The rest of the world only exists to amuse you on the evening news." He started winding her hair around his finger.

Melody licked her lips. "Why did you pretend to be American?"

"I was on a job. I needed to be Richard Johnson." His face relaxed and became more familiar. The next time he spoke, it was with the smooth southern voice she remembered. "Why? Is this easier for you?"

Melody shuddered, wondering again how she ever fancied herself in love with this man. Her stomach rolled with sickness when she thought about how close she'd come to marrying him. Trying to appear nonchalant, she shrugged. "It's more familiar."

"I heard your message in Houston," he told her softly. "Why don't you and I go for a ride and catch up?"

His eyes held pure evil. He wore his hair long now, down to his shoulders, framing his pale face like a retro rock star in a burned out boy band. He stood about her height, but after the way she had worked out for the last few years, she probably had him in the muscle department.

She had to find a way to let Jen downstairs know that he was up here with her, without him knowing about it. "Look, Richard." At his narrowed eyes, she quickly corrected herself. "Rikard. It's Morgan's birthday party. I can't leave in the middle of the party. Wait up here for me. I'll make my excuses and come back up as soon as I can."

The slap caught her off guard and knocked her to her knees. She put a hand to her throbbing cheekbone, and kept her head lowered, afraid he might hit her again. He grabbed more of her hair and hauled her back to her feet, keeping a grip on her hair. "I said, let's go for a ride." He put his face to her neck, and inhaled, letting a hand slide over her stomach. "You owe me so much. And, tonight, you're going to start paying," he said.

Bile rose swiftly to her throat. "Richard," Melody gasped, choking back the terror and the tears, "this house is full of people. You'll never be able to get me out of here."

His hand left her stomach, then she felt something cold and hard press behind her ear, heard the unmistakable sound of the hammer of a handgun cocking back. He laughed a laugh that sent chills running up her spine. "I want them to see us. I want *him* to see us. Especially him. I dare you to say anything to me again besides 'yes.' All I want from you is yes or the next thing you say will be the last thing you ever say."

His hand in her hair hurt so badly. A tear spilled out of her eye and she became furious for letting him see it. She realized that if he pulled the trigger, she wouldn't even have time to feel the pain. He tickled her neck with the cold steel barrel then spoke as if to a child. "Do you understand me?"

She said, "Yes."

Through grit teeth, he hissed, "Walk."

He pushed her from the room and at the top of the staircase, she grabbed at the rail, trying to prevent him from going any further. "You keep moving," he said, yanking on her hair.

She bit back a sob and started down the stairs. At the bottom, someone gave a startled scream, and she heard Rikard start breathing faster.

Dear God, she prayed, *he's enjoying this. Lord Jesus, please help me.*

She saw Roberts and Suarez appear at the base of the stairs, guns drawn and pointed up at them.

"I think we all know you run the risk of hitting her instead of me," Rikard said coldly.

Suarez slowly cocked his pistol and took careful aim. Rikard said, "How good are you, Detective Suarez? Very good? You have to make that first shot count. If I have even one heartbeat left, I squeeze the trigger. Understand?"

The muzzle of the detective's pistol remained as steady as if it sat in a steel vice. If it unnerved Suarez that the man knew his name, he didn't show it. He also didn't take the shot. Rikard kneed Melody in the back to keep her moving. Roberts and Suarez kept their guns aimed, but didn't make a move.

Suddenly, James was there, too. She locked eyes with him and felt fresh tears flood down her cheeks. For a slight instant, she saw fury in his eyes, then a blankness replaced it that she didn't recognize. He looked away from her and looked at Rikard, folding his arms across his chest, standing with his feet slightly apart. Rikard stopped three steps from the bottom. "Hand your little wifey number two your car keys, Montgomery."

James lifted an eyebrow, and Rikard raised the gun and brought it hard against the side of Melody's temple. Pain screamed through her head and she felt her knees buckle under her. Then Rikard jerked her hair again, causing her to stand back up straight. "I said, hand my former fiancé your keys, or I will kill her while you watch. You of all people should know I'm capable of that."

James took his keys from his pocket and held them up. "Good boy. Lay them on the post there, then step back."

James did as he was told, setting the keys on the post at the end of the staircase, and Rikard pulled Melody to the bottom of the staircase, keeping her in front of him. "Grab the keys." He hissed.

She hesitated a moment too long. Rikard raised the gun and pointed it at James. "No! No, don't!" she sobbed, grabbing the keys, afraid they would fall from her slippery hands.

He put the gun back to her temple, and turned quickly, so that they walked backward toward the door. Her eyes met Hal's, then Kurt's, then Bobby's, each of the men's faces showing the same cold rigidness, each of their bodies tense with rage. Jen stood next to James, her hand on his arm. Melody wondered if that was to restrain James or keep herself restrained. She could hear Morgan crying, and arguing with someone to let her go.

"Reach behind me and open the door," he ordered, giving her hair another jerk. Melody did what he said, fearing he would point the gun at James again.

She kept eye contact with James until Rikard slammed the door, then he ran and dragged her at the same time, stopping at James' little green Jaguar sports car. The door to the house opened, and she tried to keep him from pushing her into the car. He hit her again with the gun, stunning her, and pushed her in, from the passenger seat to the driver's, and put the gun back to her temple as he slid into the seat next to her. "Drive," he ordered.

She started sobbing as she started the car and drove away, knowing that Rikard was going to kill her and that she'd never see James again. He reached across her and grabbed her seat belt, fastening it. He did the same thing with his own seat belt. At the sound of the metallic click, he said, "In case you decide to try something stupid."

She tried to drive slowly, knowing they would follow. He placed the muzzle of the pistol onto the back of her right hand as she gripped the gear shift. "If you don't drive this car like I know you can, I'm going to shoot you in your pretty little hand. You won't be able to play your precious piano if I blow off one of your hands, will you?"

"What difference does it make, Richard?" Melody screamed. "You're going to kill me anyway."

He pressed the barrel down on the knuckle of her right index finger, "You have until the count of three. One … two … " She pushed the accelerator to the floor, slowing down only to take the curves and approach intersections.

♫ ♫ ♫ ♫

JAMES felt his world slipping away as the door shut behind Melody and Rikard. He grabbed the door handle, but Suarez pushed him out of the way, standing with his back against the door and one hand on James' chest. He pulled a phone out of his jacket pocket. Roberts held Kurt the same way. Jen Thorne and Mike Redman blocked Hal's access to the door.

"Get out of the way, Suarez," James breathed in an icy voice.

"We have to give him some room or else he'll kill her right now," Suarez said, then turned his attention to the phone, quickly summing up the situation. "Keep your distance," he said in the phone, "this guy's unpredictable." He hung up the phone, then let James go. They all poured out through the door, automatically pairing up as they went. James and Kurt ran to Kurt's Jeep, but a Porsche blocked it.

James kicked the tire of the Porsche. Jen pushed him out the way. A switchblade magically appeared in her hand and she struck the window of the sports car dead center and about an inch and a half above the door with the closed knife. The window shattered like porcelain into a thousand little bead sized gemstones of glass. She reached in and unlocked the car, then threw herself flat in the driver's seat. She opened the switchblade and used it like a crowbar to strip the ignition from the steering wheel column, then jammed it into the empty ignition well. Within seconds, the car started.

She stared at James, her lips a thin line. "I'm not waiting for you."

James whipped his head around as he heard the engine of his Jaguar come to life. As he ran around the Porsche, he watched his wife drive away, a madman with a gun in the seat next to her.

No time. He hopped into the passenger's side. "I may need help shifting," Jen said. "Just keep your hand near the shifter, be ready, and pay attention." As James slammed his door, Jen jammed the car into gear and expertly propelled them backward down the long drive. Using a knee to steer and her other leg to clutch or accelerate, she hit the brakes, spun the car, and slammed it into gear, pealing out after Melody. He could see the taillights of his car in the distance.

James looked back and saw two sets of headlights pull out behind them and knew for certain Kurt drove in one of the cars. After a few blocks, Melody shot ahead driving James' Jaguar, and Jen drove the powerful Porsche like the professional she was, keeping James' car in sight, but letting them keep their distance. They saw the Jaguar make a sharp turn, and Jen had to react quickly not to lose them.

"Get closer," James urged.

"Let me work." Jen darted in and out of the evening traffic, driving the low riding sportscar like a NASCAR driver. Driving with her knees, she fast-shifted up and punched the accelerator as she followed them onto the interstate. "Gas is low," Jen observed, gesturing with her chin to the gas gauge. "This isn't good."

He didn't respond. He couldn't. He felt fear start to work its way back to the top again, and tried to get a grip back on the rage.

Pray, he told himself. He wouldn't be any good to her if he couldn't think. *Pray, let God help.*

Whispering prayers to himself, blue flashing lights caught his attention in the side mirror, and he looked behind him to see two police cars slowly gaining on them. "We're getting some company," he said. "Suarez told them no lights. This must be highway patrol running radar or something."

His phone rang and he pulled it out of his pocket. "Yeah."

"Where are you?" Mike Redman demanded.

"Heading north on eighty-five, just about to go through downtown." He ended the call. "Get closer. They're getting away."

"I got 'em," Jen confirmed. She pushed a little harder on the accelerator.

♪ ♪ ♪ ♪

THINK, Melody told herself. *Pray. Slow us down so they can catch up with us.*

Rikard took his eyes off her to turn in his seat and look behind them, trying to see if they were being followed. He directed her to the interstate.

Once on it, Melody pushed the car up to ninety, weaving through the traffic, hoping to attract the attention of law enforcement. As they approached downtown Atlanta, she spotted the police lights in her rearview mirror.

Now's the time, she thought, while help can still get to me. Concrete walls lined the road, blocking downtown from the noise of the busy interstate. She'd always hated them, but now she blessed them as she moved the car to the far lane.

She put her hand on the gearshift. "You know what, Richard?" she said. He looked at her with a manic look in his eyes. "I think I'm going to try something stupid."

She reached over and pushed the release button on his seat belt, simultaneously downshifting and yanking the wheel, turning the car ninety degrees. She hit the accelerator again, flooring it. The rear tires squealed and smoked all around the car. When the tires caught traction, the car rocketed across six lanes of traffic as Melody drove James' sports car straight toward the wall like a dart toward a bulls-eye.

Richard tried to re-hook his seat belt, screaming at her to stop, and trying to grab the wheel from her at the same time. He didn't move fast enough. At the last second, she jerked the wheel, angling her side of the car away from the wall.

Instinctively, she shielded her face with her arms, drew her legs out from under the dash, and hit the concrete wall nearly head-on at fifty-eight miles per hour.

♪ ♪ ♪ ♪

Chapter 35

JAMES and Jen saw the brake lights as their hot-wired Porsche sped toward the Jaguar doing close to 100 miles per hour. Jen tapped the brakes of the Porsche and jerked the wheel, narrowly missing hitting the back of the XKE as it shot past the front of the car. She nearly lost control, sending the rear into a skid. It took all of her skill to recover.

When they came out of it, Melody was about twenty yards behind them and headed toward the concrete wall, cutting across the lanes of traffic. James watched as cars slammed on brakes and turned wheels hard to avoid hitting the Jaguar as the car plowed head on into the concrete wall. The sound of the impact hit them like artillery. They heard metal ripping like a sheet. It sounded like a hailstorm on a tin roof. The driver's side front wheel flew past them like a meteor before hitting the pavement and skidding to a stop in a shower of tortured sparks more than 90 feet away.

James heard his own anguished cry as he ripped the car door open and ran toward the wrecked car. Headlights blinded him and he heard brakes squealing as oncoming cars came to sudden stops. Something brushed his leg, but he didn't recognize it as the bumper of one car that narrowly avoided hitting him.

When he reached the Jaguar with Jen right at his side, he headed straight for the driver's door. His hands slipped as he tried to open it, until he was finally able to wrench it wide. He had to use quite a bit of force to pry the door open against the crumpled metal of the fender. He knelt down, afraid of what he was going to find, his hands shaking as he pushed the airbag out of the way. He looked up and saw Richard Johnson collapsed against his air bag. The man had hit the windshield and his left arm looked severely broken.

"He's out," Jen said from behind him. "I can't get the door open."

Melody sat leaning back in the seat, her eyes closed and her body limp. He grabbed her wrist and almost cried with relief when he felt a pulse.

Jen yelled to the approaching police to call an ambulance, and knelt down next to James.

"Is she alive?" she asked, the question little more than a hopeful whisper. James nodded, afraid to speak. Jen shook her head sharply and said, "We don't want to move her, Mr. Montgomery."

James nodded. He carefully wiped some blood off Melody's forehead, then picked up her hand and kissed it. Melody moaned and moved her head, then opened her eyes with a start. She saw Rikard and started sobbing.

"Are you hurt?" James demanded, his voice low and urgent. "Is anything broken?"

Melody shook her head. "I don't think so."

James unhooked her seat belt and reached into the car to gingerly wrap his arms around her. In response, Melody threw her arms around his neck. "Oh, baby."

"I didn't know what else to do," she sobbed. "He was going to kill me." Shocky, now, she shook so badly her teeth rattled. "I promised you I wasn't going anywhere," she said with a tremulous laugh, "I had to do something."

Suddenly, she pushed against him, fought his hold until she leaned over and started gagging. Talking past the lump in his throat, holding her hair back out of the way, James said, "It's okay, baby. You did exactly the right thing."

She sat back and took deep breaths. "Get me out of here." She started fighting him again when he tried to hold her still. "Please, get me away from him."

He would have held her down if her voice hadn't hitched at the end, if her eyes weren't glazed with panic. Instead, he carefully pulled her out of the car and stood so that he could hold her in his arms.

"I'm sorry I wrecked your car," she said, her whole body shaking.

He smiled, "You can buy me a new one." She buried her face in his chest and laughed before she started crying.

Jen re-holstered her pistol and pulled her phone out of her pocket. She engaged a call a second before Suarez and Roberts pulled up, driving along the median. They jumped out of the car and flashed badges at the highway patrol who arrived at the scene. Jen walked over to talk with the gathering of law enforcement officials. A uniformed police officer cautiously approached the Jaguar.

"I was so scared," Melody confessed, her breath hitching. She whipped her head around at the sound of a gunshot and screamed when the uniformed police officer by the car dropped behind the rear of the vehicle and drew his pistol.

Melody screamed, "No!" as James spun her, completely shielding her with his body.

Rikard had his gun pointed in their direction as he crawled out of the car through the driver's door. His face had been ripped open by contact with the windshield. Bloody bits of broken glass glistened wetly in his dark hair. His right eye appeared to have been severely traumatized. His left arm, apparently snapped by the impact, twisted up beneath his body at an odd angle as he pulled himself along by his knees and his right elbow. He spit blood from his mouth and wheezed.

"Drop it!" Jen yelled. She had her gun trained on him. Roberts and Suarez did, too, keeping the man in their gun sights as they approached in a crouch. The uniformed officer jumped up with his pistol drawn and leveled it at the man's head.

Rikard glared at Jen as he slowly lowered his arm. Then, his eyes shining, he just smiled. It was a look of total insanity. "The thing about you, Montgomery … that disgusts me so much … is that you always hide behind women. Never fight your own battles. Like a child."

"You don't have to die today," James said, shocking everyone present.

"I'm not afraid to die. I'm taking you and your new wife with me." Rikard spat.

"You can drop the act, Richard. I know you're not insane." James' voice sounded so calm it was as if he were soothing an infant.

"It's Rikard, you American dog." Rikard kept his eyes on Jen as he pulled himself out of the Jaguar. He slowly pulled himself to his feet, wincing as his broken left arm dangled at his side. He never loosened his grip on the pistol he held in his right hand.

"You know why I'm going to kill you?" He asked. "Because you're arrogant. You think you are so smart. I was going to take your first wife from you. Bet you didn't know that, smart guy. Want to hear about how Angela had a little crush on me? You know how easy it was to charm her and steal her research? All those seminars. All those nights she spent alone while you were in London — those long, late nights in the lab. Too bad I had to kill her. She would have been a fun way to pass the time. Want to know how I killed your first wife? Wondering if she put up a fight, too?"

James decided not to engage him on this topic and taint his late wife's memory. "That doesn't matter, now."

Rikard snarled a self-satisfied smile. "Tell me something. Sweet little Melly ever tell you how in love with me she was? Maybe she still is. Yeah? You know that look she gets sometimes when she's with you? That look when her eyes get all soft and she gets that dimple in her cheek? That's when she's wishing she was still with me."

James shook his head. "Your betrayal took it all away, Richard. And, sadly, Melody just hasn't forgiven you yet. She will, though. Why don't you drop the pistol? You can live through this."

"Forgive me? For what? She should thank me. If not for me she would never have left Atlanta."

James shook his head, his eyes never leaving the man's face. "None of that matters. She will forgive you. Just like I forgave you."

Melody felt the hairs on the back of her neck and her arms stand on end at her husband's words. His touch against her as he held her in his arms made her skin feel like pins and needles. In that moment, Melody knew with absolute certainty that she was in the presence of the Holy Spirit.

A look of total incomprehension took over Rikard's damaged face. "You forgive ... me? *You* forgive me? You think I need your forgiveness?"

James nodded. "It doesn't matter whether you do or not. It's just the truth. For a long time I imagined all kinds of scenarios. What would happen if I ever came face to face with Angela's murderer? Honestly, for a long time all I wanted was revenge. It kept me up at night. But the truth is, God even had a purpose for everything you did. In His own good time, He turned it all to good after I let go of my hatred for you. And I assure you, sir, I no longer hate you."

Jen Thorne turned her head to stare at James Montgomery. Though her expression remained largely unreadable, the look broadcast her disbelief that such a conversation could take place given the present circumstances. She calculated whether James might be stalling, trying to get Melody away from the madman with the pistol, but could not reconcile the sincerity in his voice as he spoke.

Rikard propped his back against the Jaguar and laughed. "You're a fool, Montgomery. A weak fool. Any kind of real man would kill me with his bare hands right now."

Melody whispered, "He's an animal."

James gave his wife a reassuring squeeze and shook his head in answer to Rikard's accusation of weakness. "That isn't what defines me. You don't define me. My Father in heaven defines me. The blood of His Son defines me. The Holy Ghost defines me. Killing you now would be as easy as hating you for all those years was. It would be the weak thing to do. It has taken all of my strength to forgive you.

"But imagine this. If I can forgive you, can't you understand that God can forgive you, too? You have a choice to make. You can spend the rest of eternity in hell, unrepentant, or you can accept that gift of forgiveness that Christ offers. You can be forgiven, redeemed, and live forever. The choice is yours. Just make the right choice. Put down the gun."

Rikard smirked at Melody then met James' stare again. "You think I'm going to hell, Montgomery?" Before James could answer, Rikard said, "You go to hell."

Melody stood, frozen, while time came to a stop. In slow motion she saw Rikard scowl at Jen and the detectives, then look back at her with a sick grin as he started to raise his pistol again. As the sound of the first gunshot reached her ears, her eyes slammed shut. She screamed and covered her ears. She heard several gunshots after the first, the sounds coming to her ears as if from a great distance and through a thick fog.

James looked back over his shoulder and Melody slowly turned and saw Rikard lying on his back on the hood of the Jaguar in a pool of his own blood. Suarez kicked the gun that had fallen near the driver's front tire away and kept his own pistol trained on Rikard while he checked the man's pulse. He straightened and his eyes sought James out. Shaking his head, he reholstered his weapon. "We're good," he announced.

Seconds later, Jen stood in front of her. "It's okay, Melody," she said, holstering her weapon. "It's over."

James watched the ambulance pull up, saw the paramedics get a stretcher out of the back and come toward him. When they reached him, they tried to take Melody out of his arms, but she held on tight. "I'll do it," he said, and walked Melody over to the stretcher and convinced her to lie down. She looked panicked for a moment, but he took her hand and squeezed. "I'm right here," he said, brushing her hair off her forehead. "We'll go to the hospital and let them check you out, then we'll go home."

She nodded, and lay down. The paramedic immediately covered her with a blanket. Melody started to close her eyes. "It's over now, right?" she whispered.

"It's over," James said as they secured her on the stretcher. "It's all over." He followed the paramedics as they pushed her to the ambulance.

He climbed into the back with them, staying out of their way. Taking his wife's hand, he put it up to his cheek and closed his eyes, praying to God the most sincere prayer of thanksgiving he'd ever prayed.

♬ ♬ ♬ ♬

THEY sat in a private room in the emergency room and waited for the doctor to come back. Melody had stopped continually shivering, and now just lay still and stared at the wall, a deep shudder passing through her body occasionally. Morgan and Kurt were there as well, but Hal was still with the police. There was a lot to muddle through at this moment.

Morgan opened the bag she'd brought with her, and pulled out some clothes. "Melly, honey, do you want to get dressed now?" Melody didn't respond. Another shudder went through her body.

"Let her lay there right now, Morg. She's still in shock," Kurt said, pulling Morgan back into his lap.

"I feel like I should be doing something," she said quietly, laying her head on her husband's shoulder.

The door opened and the doctor stepped in, followed by Hal. "It's becoming a circus out there," Hal said. "The press is out there in a frenzy. Jen's having a field day trying to keep everyone at bay."

"I've called security, Mr. Coleman. They're sending some people to help." He turned to James. "She's absolutely fine. She could definitely be a spokesperson for the use of seat belts and airbags." He wrote on a pad, and ripped the paper off and handed it to James. "She'll probably wake up really sore tomorrow. This is a prescription for some mild pain killers and some muscle relaxers if she feels she needs them." He pulled a card out of his pocket, and cleared his throat. "This is the office number to my wife's practice. She's a psychiatrist, and the only person I can personally promise you who will offer absolute discretion."

James looked at the card, but didn't take it. "She won't need that," he said. The doctor didn't say anything, just set the card on a table.

"She's free to go. I've signed her release." He started out of the room, but stopped with his hand on the door. "Security will be here any time."

Kurt lifted Morgan off his lap and stood. "We'll go wait outside while you get dressed, Melody." He walked to the door, and Hal and James stood to follow him.

As soon as James stepped out of her line of vision, Melody panicked. "Please don't go!" she said, sitting up.

James went back to the bed. "I'll stay right here," he said. Kurt and Hal left, and James helped Morgan get Melody dressed.

They were putting her shirt on when she brushed their hands away. "I can do it," she said. She got out of the bed, stood there for a moment to get her balance, then slowly got dressed. She sat down in a chair to put on her shoes but ended up laying her head on her knees and crying. James knelt in front of her, but didn't touch her. "He was so evil," she said. "Why am I so upset that he's dead?"

"It's just real fresh right now, Melody," James said. He took her hands. "Will you pray with me about it?"

Melody's lower lip trembled, and she hesitated, but she nodded. Instead of waiting for him to speak, she was the one who did the praying this time. "God, I don't understand these circumstances. But, I'm so thankful they're over. Thank You for bringing me and James through it. If we did something wrong, something sinful, something not noble in the course of the last few weeks, I beg You to forgive us. We did our best to live for You. Amen."

James felt pride flood his chest at her courage in that prayer. He brushed her hair off of her forehead. "Let's put your boots on and get out of here."

She sat up straight and wiped her face. "You know, I promised myself years ago that he would no longer control me." She slipped her boots on and stood, surprisingly steady. "I meant it."

She grabbed the bag from Morgan and looked through it until she found a brush. As she brushed her hair, little particles of glass from the shattered windshield fell out of her hair and clicked into the sink. She grabbed some lipstick out of the bag and applied it to her lips, then turned to James. "Let's go."

James grabbed her to him and hugged her a little harder than he intended. "I love you," he whispered.

She pushed him back and put her hands on either side of his face and kissed his nose, like he'd done to her so many times. "I love you, too. Let's go battle the crowds out there."

♪ ♪ ♪ ♪

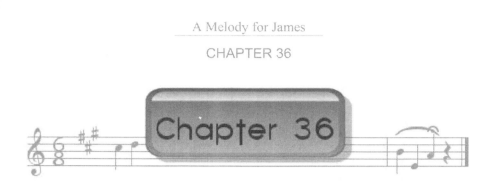

HAL sent the limousine and Jen hurried Melody through the hospital to the waiting car, not stopping to talk to the press. They had agreed that Hal would issue a statement as soon as they got her out of there. He shut the door of the car behind Kurt, the last one in, then pounded on the roof, letting Peter know to go. Then he straightened his tie, and turned to meet the reporters.

Several cars remained parked outside of Morgan's house. Guests at the party waited to hear any news. Morgan and Kurt kissed Melody, then got out of the car to go answer the questions. Then Jen turned the car to take them to their apartment.

They remained quiet on the drive, each lost in his and her own thoughts, but Melody stayed curled up against James, his arm around her. They pulled in front of the apartment building, and the doorman met them to let them in. Melody glanced at the empty sidewalk, abruptly realizing the lateness of the hour. She suddenly felt very tired.

James stopped at the guard's desk and handed the prescription slip over. "See about getting this filled for me, please. I'll need it first thing."

"Yes sir, Mr. Montgomery. I'll take care of it," the guard said.

Jen stood in the lobby. "I'll go to my hotel now. You don't need me anymore."

Melody went to her and, despite Jen trying to take a step back, wrapped her in her arms. "Thank you."

"Please don't thank me, ma'am." Jen Thorne begged, her voice thick with stifled shame. "I failed."

"There's no telling how many times you succeeded," Melody said. "I owe you my life and I appreciate everything you've done for me. Thank you."

Jen stepped back and stiffly nodded. "Thank you for the work."

She shook hands with James and, looking him straight in the eyes, she said, "You're an extremely blessed woman, Mrs. Montgomery. Your husband is one of the strongest men I've ever met. Take good care."

Jen looked like she wanted to say more, say something to him or ask him a question. Instead she stoically pulled her lips into a tight line and turned and left without another word.

James guided Melody to the elevator, and accessed his floor with the key. "How are you feeling?" he asked as the elevator started its ascent.

Melody rolled her neck on her shoulders. "I'm starting to stiffen up. I have a feeling I'm going to have a hard morning."

He leaned down and kissed the top of her head. "Ramming a wall at sixty miles an hour will do it to you every time."

She laughed as the elevator opened. "Remind me of that next time I decide to do something so foolish."

Inside the apartment, James threw his keys on the table, slipped off his suit jacket, and started to loosen his tie. "I'm going to fix you a warm drink. You should get in a hot bath, as hot as you can stand it, to help your muscles relax before they really start tightening up." He turned and walked into the kitchen.

"Okay," She said, staring at his back. His voice sounded a little off, a little formal. She frowned as she went to the bathroom and started the water running, getting it as hot as she could stand. She turned and looked in the mirror, and grimaced at the sight reflected back at her. Her swollen face was already starting to bruise, and her temple was an angry dark purple bruise with bright yellow edges where Richard hit her with the butt of the gun. She knew more bruises would appear by morning and she sighed as she turned from the reflection to start to take off her clothes. Vanity wasn't attractive, she knew, but she couldn't help feeling thankful it wasn't worse.

"James?" She called above the water filling the tub.

"Yeah?" He called back.

"What's your favorite color?"

He didn't answer for what felt like a long time. "I like blue, I guess."

"I'll buy you a blue Jaguar tomorrow."

She eased into the water, and felt the sting of the cuts from broken glass on her hands and fingers. She held them up in front of her face and stared, and considered how much harder that would make playing the piano for at least the next few days. She rubbed her right hand, thinking of the bullet that Rikard had threatened for it, then shook off the dark feelings that started to creep up on her.

Taking a deep breath she let herself slide completely under the water. When she came back up for air, she found James sitting on the side of the tub offering her a cup of herbal tea.

"Thanks," she said, taking the cup from him.

"Want anything else?" he asked her, standing up to leave.

"Wash my back?" she asked with a smile.

"Why don't I go find you something to put on when you get out?" He walked out of the room.

The headache that had lurked in the background suddenly pressed forward, and Melody had to close her eyes against the pain. She ducked back under the water and stayed there until she needed to breathe. She drained her tea, then got out of the tub, too restless to lie in there and soak. She wrapped herself in a big towel and went into the bedroom. James had laid a T-shirt and a pair of shorts on the bed for her, but the man himself was nowhere to be found.

She threw the clothes on, rubbed her hair with the towel until it wasn't dripping anymore, then went into the living room. She wasn't surprised that he wasn't there. He wasn't in the office, either. The only other place he could be was the kitchen, so she pushed open the door and stopped short when she saw him. He was leaning with both hands on the counter, his head bowed, his shoulders stiff. He looked up when she walked in, then turned and straightened.

"Do you have an appetite? I can fix you something to eat," he asked.

"No," she said, putting her hands on her hips, "I want to know what in the world is wrong with you."

He leaned back against the counter and crossed his arms. "What are you talking about?"

"You're acting like you can barely tolerate having me near you."

He uncrossed his arms before dryly observing, "I didn't realize the blow to your head was so severe. Shall I call the doctor back?"

She walked up to him, and stood as close as she could. "Then touch me."

He reached an unsteady hand out to her face, but before he touched her he fisted his hand. "I let him take you," he said hoarsely. "I even handed him my car keys. How can you stand me right now?"

It suddenly dawned on her what was wrong with him. Perhaps he was the one who needed to be held. She framed his face with her hands. "There was nothing else we could do. We had to get him away from all of those people."

He traced the bruise on her temple with a finger, barely touching her. "I stood there while he hit you. I didn't do a single thing when he took the butt of his gun and hit you in the face with it."

"What were you going to do James? Die rescuing me?" She gripped the front of his shirt with both hands. "We didn't have any other choice in the matter. He was in control then." She spoke a little too loudly, a little too desperately, trying to get through the removed look in his eyes.

"I could have tried. I didn't even try," he said, pushing her away.

She ran her hands through her hair in frustration, flinching a little when she hit a bruise. "I never would have gone with him if I hadn't known you'd come after me," she said.

"What do you want me to do, Melody? All I can think of is what he could have done to you," he yelled. He went to the refrigerator and pulled out a bottle of soda, started to open it, but threw it against the wall and watched it shatter.

In a sudden move, he turned back to her and gripped her arms. "You drove the car into the wall. I didn't stop him, so you had to drive a car into a concrete wall. You could have died at any time."

Melody burst into tears. "I'm sorry," she said. "I didn't know what else to do." James let go of her, and she crumbled to the floor, sobbing, her face in her hands. "I couldn't think of anything else," she said through the tears. "James, he was going to kill me, and he was going to enjoy doing it, enjoy knowing you knew that was what he was doing. He probably would have sent you pictures wrapped around roses. I couldn't let him do that to you."

With a sigh, he sat next to her on the floor and pulled her into his lap. She put her arms around his neck. "I couldn't let him. I didn't know what else to do."

James whispered, "He made me doubt."

"What?" Melody sniffed.

His face turned cold and serious. "He made me doubt whether forgiving him was the right thing. Now he's dead and I find that I'm not exactly unhappy about it. In fact, I'm tempted to go spit on his grave. Did I really forgive him?"

She wanted to be strong for her husband. James forgave the man who had viciously murdered his first wife and a number of his friends. That single act of forgiveness was a tremendous witness to her. Melody realized that she would have to find a way to forgive Rikard, too. To her shame, she wasn't ready, yet, to begin that journey.

Maybe somewhere on earth there was a woman strong enough to forgive a man who had beaten her nearly to death then kidnapped her and threatened to kill her a scant few hours before. Melody was not that strong, though she wanted to be. She would have to find a way to ask God to forgive her for all of her hateful thoughts about him. She would have to pray for the strength it would take to forgive him. It would take reading her Bible, praying, and asking James to help her.

That was for tomorrow. Right now, she was ready to help her husband. Through her tears, she said, "James Montgomery, you are the strongest man I have ever known in my entire life. You did absolutely nothing wrong. Don't let that evil man control you from the grave."

He kissed the side of her neck then brushed his lips over her temple. "It's okay, baby. Please quit crying." He rubbed his hands across her back, trying to soothe her. He kissed her neck again, and she turned her head, capturing his mouth with hers. He fought the passion that surged through him, and kept his lips gentle and soothing, keeping his arms loosely on her back.

"I know you loved that car."

"Yeah. But I love you more. And I don't want another Jaguar," he said.

"Okay. I'll buy you a little hybrid. You can brag about your mileage and pack groceries in the trunk."

He didn't laugh.

Melody put her hands on each side of his face and tried to deepen the kiss, but he started to pull away. "No, don't," she whispered, "I don't want gentle." She kissed him again, and he let her deepen the kiss.

♪ ♪ ♪ ♪

JAMES lay in the bed, playing with Melody's hair. "You need to sleep," he told her, looking at the clock. It was almost three.

"You need to sleep," she mimicked him. He shifted and stood. "Where are you going?" she asked as he walked to the door.

"Be right back," he answered. When he returned, he carried two glasses of water. She sat up and took one from him, then leaned over to kiss his shoulder. The movement caught her by surprise with how very sore and stiff her body felt.

"I don't know if I'm going to even be able to perform Sunday night," she said as the realization struck her.

"Can you reschedule?" James asked lightly.

"Not easily, but I guess I could," she answered.

He took a sip of water with the glass in one hand while his other hand drew light patterns against her skin. "Maybe you could postpone a couple of days and we could squeeze in a quick honeymoon."

Melody smiled. "I think that's a great idea." Then her expression clouded.

"What?" He prompted.

She sighed. "There's all kinds of fees. Like if the venue is booked through I'd have to pay all the way through. I'd have to re-contract all the local support people and concessionaires. A certain percentage of ticket holders will want refunds. Insurance would cover most of it but it would be a major hassle. It would be a nightmare, really. But I just don't think I'm going to be able to dance. I'd rather not do a show if I can't do it right."

James pursed his lips and half-closed his eyes. Melody somehow knew he was mentally analyzing the problem with all of the intellectual ability that his genius could bring to bear. When his eyes widened, he spoke again, "Honestly, I think your fans would respect you more for doing the show … gutting it out, you know? They would get the bragging rights to say they attended the first concert you did since the kidnapping. They'll all show hoping you'll reveal something they haven't read in the tabloids."

Melody shook her head, "I just want things to get back to normal."

"I wouldn't worry about that tonight. You need to relax now and get some rest. You've been through a lot in the last few weeks," he said, draining his water and setting it on the night stand. "I think I know how you feel. You feel scattered and anxious instead of focused and at peace. You feel really angry and you're still a little bit afraid. Am I right?"

Melody sat up and took a sip of her water while she examined her feelings. "I guess that's about right."

James smiled, "I felt a lot like that after my wife and three of our employees were murdered by that madman. I was so angry with everybody. And I was scattered to the point that I just couldn't prioritize anything. I'm ashamed to admit it now, but I was also a little bit afraid. I was afraid that whoever could pull off something like that would certainly come after me or Kurt next."

Melody felt herself crossing her arms. "And how did you fix it, darling.

Wait, let me guess. You prayed."

James grinned. "Not exactly. I did a lot of other useless, pointless, and ineffectual things first. Wasted a lot of time. Made the way I was feeling a hundred times worse. Why not wisely benefit from my mistakes and cut to the chase?"

He eyed her with an eyebrow raised in challenge while he took her glass and then helped himself to another sip of water. Melody loved how handsome he looked with his tousled hair and his teasing grin. She uncrossed her arms and said, "I think you're right."

With mock superiority, James announced, "You sound so surprised."

Melody laughed even though it made her muscles twinge. Her husband set her glass of water down on the bedside table next to his. Then he very gently wrapped his strong arms around her and tucked her head under his chin. "Let's pray. We have so much to be thankful for. God is so amazing and so glorious. He has very obviously blessed us with protection and favor. Let's thank Him for revealing and removing this evil from both our lives. Let's ask Him to continue to keep us safe as long as we remain in His will here on earth. And let's do our part to fulfill His will from this day on."

As her husband's rich, baritone voice washed over her, as it vibrated through her skin from his chest and neck, Melody felt herself letting go. She felt her grip loosen and felt herself releasing her fear and her anger. She felt the frustration and the anxiety washing out of her very soul as she and her husband communed with the Creator of the universe. Then she felt such surprise when James prayed for God to heal her and give her strength to perform at her concert despite her recent trauma.

She found herself hearing the beginnings of a song, just a strain of a refrain of an echo of a tune or a chorus, and then it was gone but not forgotten. Clearly, God was speaking to her in a language He knew she would hear and understand and she tucked that snippet of song away for the right time and place. Perhaps a tribute album to raise funds for the orphanage or another ministry, or perhaps her first crossover song into the realm of contemporary Christian music, or maybe even a praise hymn offered license free to modern places of worship in the name of giving glory and honor to her Maker.

In the middle of that prayer she began to pray silently of her own accord, speaking to God from the very depths of her heart. She asked Him to forgive her for so many of her thoughts and actions. She thanked Him for showing her what a terrible person Rikard was before she offered her vows to him all those years ago. She thanked Him for her worldly successes and wealth and promised to better steward her funds for purposes of ministry to those in need. She asked God to help her find the strength to forgive Rikard for all of the evil the man had brought into her life. More than anything, she thanked God for bringing James back into her life.

When her husband said, "Amen," she echoed it wholeheartedly. Then he kissed her very sincerely and said, "Now please get some rest, baby."

♫ ♫ ♫ ♫

Chapter 37

MELODY opened her eyes and slowly stretched a leg, glad to feel no muscles protesting the movement. As she sat up and rolled her neck, she felt only a slight twinge. She had begun to think that she might never feel normal again. Over a week had passed since the kidnapping, and the first few mornings she was barely able to move. James had whisked her away to a little private beach on the Caribbean, and she'd just moved from beach side lounge chair to pool side lounge chair to hammock on the front porch for four glorious and beautiful days. Finally, the last day there, she had started feeling better, and could move without her muscles screaming at her.

Now they were back in Atlanta, and in the last four days, she'd had a crash course in what her new normal would look like. She glanced at the clock and saw that it was five, then looked behind her, not surprised to see the empty bed. She'd learned that James was not a normal human being. During the past few days, he was more and more comfortable about leaving her alone, and she got a picture of what his normal schedule felt like.

After a hot shower that took some of the lingering soreness away, she made her way to the kitchen, knowing a pot of coffee awaited. She was on her second cup and in the bedroom getting dressed when James returned to the apartment, dressed in his normal workout clothes, sweat pants and a sweatshirt with the arms cut off. He didn't say anything to her, just threw his gym bag on the floor of the closet, ripped off the fingerless gloves he wore and tossed them on top of the bag, then pulled his sweatshirt off over his head. Then he started walking toward her with a wicked gleam in his eye.

She held a hand up to stop him. "Don't touch me," she squealed, trying to get around him but being blocked, "you're all sweaty and I just put on this suit."

He grinned and kept advancing. "But if I get you, the advantage is that you would take a shower with me." He whipped his hand out and caught her wrist. She started laughing so hard that she couldn't even fight him. He pulled her toward him, stopping when she could feel his body heat, then leaned forward and gave her a quick kiss before he let go of her wrist. "I'll give you a break, but only because it's Monday. Don't expect this kind of fair play on a Tuesday," he said as he headed toward the bathroom.

She smiled as she finished getting dressed. Grabbing her makeup bag, she moved her hair out of the way and examined the bruise at her temple. It had started to fade, though still a sick looking greenish yellow color. Carefully, she started applying concealer to completely cover it. James came out of the bathroom and saw what she was doing. His eyes met hers in the mirror and flared briefly, but he came up behind her and kissed the bruise.

"What time are you leaving?" he asked while he pulled on a shirt.

"Seven, I think. That was the last time I had, but I didn't talk to Hal yesterday." She leaned back from the mirror and looked. It was still there if you looked close, but not so obvious. She'd have to get a hold of Lisa, see if she knew what else she could do. "He went to Savannah over the weekend."

"I'll wait and ride with you to the airport," he said, coming up behind her and nuzzling her neck.

"James, I don't need a baby-sitter anymore," she grumbled. She felt guilty enough as it was, knowing how much he'd adjusted his schedule during the last two months.

She felt him stiffen and let him turn her around to meet his eyes. She saw understanding replace the quick flash of anger. "If I want to spend as much time as I can with you before we're separated for two weeks, then I will. My first meeting in Tokyo isn't until tomorrow morning," he said as he started to nibble on her lips.

The phone rang before he could deepen the kiss, and he broke away from her mouth to answer it. He hung up the phone and turned to her. "You're leaving at six-thirty," he said, then came back and took her face in his hands, giving her another quick kiss. "I'll drive you and you can meet Hal there. Better finish getting ready."

♫ ♫ ♫ ♫

MELODY spent two days in Nashville working on recording a new album and wrapping up long neglected business, then flew to Los Angeles for a concert on Wednesday night. She woke up Thursday morning and felt a little sore again, but by the time she did her concert on Saturday in San Francisco, her bruises had almost completely faded, and her body felt normal again.

During the day, she sent James little messages with her new phone app, and spoke with him every night, but as the week ended, she began to miss him fiercely. She'd gotten used to having him around all the time, and had a hard time interacting with her crew during their down times.

She had another concert in Portland on Tuesday, and when she got back to the hotel early Wednesday morning, she decided to surprise him. She called Rebecca's assistant Julie and got the number to Rebecca's hotel room, then made the call to Tokyo, where they'd arrived the day before. She looked at her watch and calculated that it was almost eight o'clock in the evening in Tokyo. She hoped that Rebecca was in her room and not having dinner somewhere.

Rebecca answered, and the two of them solidified the plans they needed. Melody could only spend one night, because she had a gig in Seattle on Friday, but she decided that the hours and hours on the plane round trip would be worth it.

She decided to use a commercial airliner to save her pilot from having to do such a long flight. A car met her at the airport in Tokyo Thursday afternoon local time and took her to the hotel. The concierge met her in the lobby and escorted her to James' room. He was breaking hotel policy — but this was Melody Mason. He estimated it was worth the breach in the rules when she smiled at him and took his hand.

She made arrangements with the hotel before coming, and found everything she needed. Rebecca had informed her that James would probably come back to the room by nine that night, so she had a couple of hours to get everything ready. She grabbed the bags that were waiting on her, and began to set up the room.

♫ ♫ ♫ ♫

JAMES' mood did nothing but worsen as the day wore on. He looked at his watch and wished that he could try to call Melody again. He'd tried to reach her off and on all day, but hadn't been able to get through.

He decided he would take a shower and sleep, then try her again in the morning. He could perform long division in his head but the time difference here was going to drive him mad.

He opened the door to his hotel suite and stopped short. Candles of various shapes and sizes flickered all around the room. A small table set for two sat in the corner near a window, and soft music played in the background.

He shut the door behind him and set his briefcase down. He cautiously stepped further into the room and saw Melody rise up from the couch and come toward him. He hoped he wasn't dreaming, and without speaking a word, pulled her into his arms.

♫ ♫ ♫ ♫

"HOW much longer can you stay?" he asked a few hours later. Melody had her head pillowed on his chest, and he lifted her hair just so he could watch the strands fall.

"Just until morning. I have to get back for the Seattle show on Friday." She stretched and nuzzled his chest. "Are you still going to be able to come home on Saturday?"

"I don't know yet. I should have a definite answer tomorrow." He reached over to the night stand and checked the phone that had just vibrated with an incoming text. "How's the West Coast?"

"The fans are terrific. More of a mixed group of people there than in the South, though." She spoke around a yawn. She rolled away from him and sat up, grabbing his shirt as she stood. "If I stay that way, I'm liable to fall asleep. Want some coffee?"

"No. Come back to bed. Sleeping next to you is half the fun," he said as he held his hand out to her. She smiled at him and got back in bed, curling up next to him. She fell asleep within minutes.

♫ ♫ ♫ ♫

MELODY barely made it in time for her concert in Seattle, and took a severe scolding from Hal before she performed. In no shape to fight back, she just sat there shaking while Lisa applied her makeup. Her phobia intensified because of her fatigue.

Hal watched her do the concert, and was surprised when she appeared to have the same energy as usual. Then he had to bite his lip when she fell asleep in her dressing room waiting for security to give the go-ahead for her to leave.

She went straight from the concert to the airport, wanting to get home. She had nearly a week before her next concert, and planned on spending half of that time in Nashville recording. The short distance between the two cities would allow her to commute nearly every day.

James hit a snag in Japan and called to let Melody know he'd return to town on Monday rather than Saturday. She felt a little disappointed, but glad she'd stolen three days to go see him for one night. Melody spent the remainder of the weekend with Morgan.

On Sunday morning, Ginger called and invited them over for dinner after church. Kurt already had plans, so the sisters and Ginger decided to go and make it a girls' night out.

♫ ♫ ♫ ♫

JAMES walked into his apartment and immediately felt disappointed that Melody wasn't there. He remembered all of the time differences and that she and Morgan were at Ginger's having dinner. He called Melody's cell and left a voice mail to let her know he had returned home a day early.

In the kitchen, James pulled a rare soda out of the refrigerator as a treat then paced back into the living room. He was anxious to see Melody and almost called Ginger's house, but hung up the phone before he finished dialing. Then he spotted the box in the corner of the room and decided to take advantage of the time to read through some of Angela's journals while he waited. The research team hadn't made any more progress, and he hoped that perhaps she had written an idea down that she planned to test later, maybe giving the current team something new with which to work.

The spines of the journals each bore a date, surprising organization for his late wife, and he pulled out the three from the last year of her life and settled back on the couch to read. He skimmed through the first few pages of the first book, and then his pulse picked up and he started over again, reading more carefully. He had to reread a paragraph at one point to make sure that he read it right the first time.

He sent me another stupid rose today. Why that man would think I would consider him over James is beyond any rational thought. He seems vain enough to think that I will just swoon and fall for him and give away all of the data we've worked so diligently to assemble over my entire career. If he would spend as much time conducting his own research as he does trying to woo me, he would probably arrive at the answer much sooner than I will.

We are so close, I can almost taste it! Soon, we'll have the algorithm perfected. Compression, encryption, data recovery, and indexing - all of it will be obsolete ...

James kept reading. He found so many similar entries. How had this gone on right under his nose?

I think I spoke well at the conference today. There were, as usual, mostly men in the audience, but once I start speaking they get past the blonde hair and start listening. I was able to bounce several ideas off some of the leading men in the industry, and realized that I've been on the wrong course. Once I realized that, the answer came popping into my head.

We will, hopefully, be marketing them within nine months. Rikard was there, too, and threw out several questions to try to trip me up. Hopefully, I succeeded in making him appear as ignorant as he really is. I finally confronted him about somehow copying my research. He walked away and never addressed my accusations.

I'm so glad I listened to my instincts and removed him from the team. I think I'm going to start looking into his background. If I can bring myself to remember, I'll ask James how to go about doing things like that. If he doesn't know, Kurt might. I think he did something similar when we hired the R&D team at the office.

James read faster and faster, searching for anything to give him a clue as to the last year of his wife's life. He remembered how jumpy she'd been, how much more distracted than normal. His stomach tightened when he realized how different the past and future would be if she'd only come to him with these problems. He knew she hadn't intentionally shut him out or excluded him or omitted telling him about these things. More than likely, knowing the way Angela's mind worked, it just hadn't ever occurred to her to bring it up in conversation.

"WHEN will you get a chance to move into your new house, Melly? I can't wait to see the whole thing completely decorated. Morgan, you should do some before and after pictures, maybe do some sort of book on what you do there," Ginger said as she dished up salad. As far as Melody could tell, the only thing Ginger ate was salad. She spared a wistful thought as to how long it had been since she'd eaten James' red sauce. She decided to ask him to make a big batch she could freeze for the next time he went out of town.

Morgan sorted through what Ginger said. "We'll have it ready in about two months. She'll move in completely then, but her piano is already there. We have strict instructions not to touch the room it's in. I think Melly is afraid that changing the color of the paint will affect the acoustics," she said as she poured dressing on her salad.

"What about the book idea? I'm sure it will sell with it being Melody Mason's house and all," Ginger said. "People will jump at anything they can to have something about their favorite superstar. Look how many awful looking boots people are wearing these days. They might even start painting rooms mint green."

Melody looked up and squinted her eyes, swearing she heard a tinge of viciousness in Ginger's tone, then shook her head. Ginger didn't have a vicious bone in her body. "Some things need to remain private, Ginger, like the color of tile in my master bathroom." Melody took a sip of her tea. "What's this I hear about you and Suarez dating?"

Ginger giggled and put a hand to her chest. "His name's John. When you say Suarez, I have to think about who you're talking about." She put her chin in her hand and sighed. "He's so stiff and proper."

Melody met Morgan's eyes over the rim of her glass and burst out laughing.

♫ ♫ ♫ ♫

KURT ducked under Roberts' arm and took the shot. The basketball hit the backboard and bounced off the rim. Mike got the rebound and made a perfect shot for the game point. The four men walked slowly off the court to their bags, pulling water bottles out, then collapsing on the bench that sat on the sidelines.

Kurt wiped the sweat off his forehead. "I'm getting too old for this," he groaned.

Suarez laughed and lay on the ground, looking up at the darkening sky. "You should try working out with Montgomery. I'm able to pretend until I'm out of his sight. One day, I'm going to disgrace myself and start crying just like a little girl right in front of him," he said. "After that, I can handle this, no problem."

Kurt grinned. "Been there, friend," he said sympathetically.

Roberts put his elbows on his knees and let his hands dangle between his legs. "Is this supposed to be good for us?" he asked.

Mike shook his head in disgust. He felt pretty good, himself. "What would your women say if they saw you like this?"

Roberts didn't even look up. "I don't have a woman so much as I have child support payments that keep my ex-wife and her boyfriend living in the manner to which they have recently become accustomed."

Mike went back to the court and started shooting hoops. He knew the three of them wouldn't be able to stand sitting there admitting defeat if he was out on the floor playing. He looked at his watch. His wife wasn't expecting him for another two hours.

♫ ♫ ♫ ♫

JAMES finished the first journal, then grabbed the next one, making sure the dates on the spine were sequential. So far, he hadn't found anything new, just repeated entries about what Šabalj did on a certain day. He felt such anger that he had a hard time focusing on the words on the page.

Halfway through the second book, he grit his teeth as fresh rage rippled through his system.

> James is in London today. He says he'll be back tomorrow, but I know that he'll call tonight and tell me he'll be back on

Sunday. If he wasn't such an honorable man, if I didn't know how much he really loved me, I'd swear he was having an affair.

I had to go to that party last night at Dr. Epstein's house. Somehow, Rikard Šabalj managed an invitation, and he was there with his girlfriend. I'd been sitting in the corner, writing some notes that had just occurred to me on a way to maximize the space while retaining data integrity. We want to standardize on this with the solid state devices because it should allow us to more than quadruple the compression rate while allowing for ultra precision digitizing. Anyway, I was making my notes when she came over and sat next to me.

It's funny, but during dinner, I could have sworn there wasn't an ounce of intelligence in her head, but in the privacy of those chairs, we had the most interesting conversation about the software being utilized by the film industry. She asked me if I had a hard time getting respect because of my hair color, giving me the impression she did. I answered positively, not wanting to be rude. What was her name? Some sort of spice, I think.

James started flipping through the pages, looking for other references to a spicy 'girlfriend'.

♫ ♫ ♫ ♫

"HEY, I have an idea! Let's go to your new house, Melly. I want to see what's been done so far," Ginger enthused, putting the last dish in the dishwasher.

Melody checked the time. Still early. "Sure, if Morgan doesn't mind."

"Kurt won't be home for another hour. I want to show you the floor we found under the rug in one of the bedrooms, anyway. You may want to keep it and restore it, rather than put down new carpet," Morgan said.

"Ooooooh," Ginger cooed as she dried her hands on a dishtowel, and put it down. "I love old houses. Let's go."

♫ ♫ ♫ ♫

IT was in the last journal that James finally found what he had searched for all along. A piece of yellow paper fell out of it as he turned the page. He opened it up with shaking hands and saw that the front and back were covered in formulas and notations. His quick glance meant nothing to him, and he decided he would give it to the research department to see if they could decipher it. Flipping to the last page, he found the last entry.

> She came over yesterday in tears, saying how Rikard has been cheating on her. She told me it was over between them, and she was no longer going to be working with him on any of his projects. It may be wrong, but I'm glad it happened. Rikard Šabalj is such a jerk. He's still sending me roses all the time, but the cards with them are getting to be a little scary…
>
> …. Ginger called today after I realized how close we were, and I was so excited that I told her. I needed to tell someone, and James was in a meeting. Besides, I should let the team do their thing before telling him. He has more invested in this than being an interested husband…
>
> …. I told Ginger that the team would be testing out my theory next week, and she seemed really interested. Maybe I can convince her to come work with us. Get in on the ground floor. We could use a mind like hers.

He snatched up the house phone and dialed. Still unable to reach Melody's cellphone, James tried to call Ginger's house, but got no answer. Then he called Morgan's cell, but there was no answer there, either. He almost threw the phone against the wall, then tried Melody's cell again, but got her voice mail. The thud the phone made when it hit the wall did nothing to make him feel any better.

He grabbed his keys and, on the elevator ride, pulled his cell phone out of his pocket and sent Melody a quick message, hoping she'd check it tonight.

Driving out of the parking garage he nearly collided with a car coming in. He swerved to miss it and turned in the direction of Kurt's house.

♫ ♫ ♫ ♫

MIKE looked at his watch, and knew he had to leave soon. The game was getting boring, anyway. He had just grabbed his bag to go when James stormed into the gym. He looked surprised at first to see who was there, but recovered quickly.

"Rikard Šabalj had a partner," he said. He sat down, but then stood back up.

"What are you talking about?" Kurt asked.

"Angela kept a journal for years. She must have had twenty of them. I got them from Diane's about a month ago, but hadn't gotten around to reading them until tonight." He sat back down, and told them what he'd just read. He could tell from the expressions on their faces that no one believed him at first.

"Come on, James. Ginger Patterson? She's pretty and rich but, James, she's an air-head," Kurt said, then looked at Suarez. "No offense, man."

Suarez had spent a lot of time with Ginger over the last few weeks, and suspected James was onto something. "No she's not. She hides it well, but if you pay attention and look under the hood, you realize something. She's actually very intelligent and extremely observant as well as being a student of human nature."

Kurt didn't think he could recall Suarez ever assembling so many declarative sentences together in his presence before. Roberts interjected, "Like what you were telling me about the other day?"

Suarez nodded. "She put that together in two minutes. It took us and the FBI task force the better part of six months."

Roberts raised an eyebrow and offered, "She's a trapdoor spider."

James had no idea to what they were referring and assumed it was some private post date conversation the two of them had shared. "Whatever. I tried to call her place and everyone's cell, but I can't get an answer. Where else would they be?"

Kurt started to get worried. "Come on, guys. Ginger's been Morgan's best friend since college."

"I know what I read, Kurt. Now, think. Where might they have gone?" James asked.

♫ ♫ ♫ ♫

MELODY sat in the back-seat of Ginger's car, wishing she'd told them to go on without her. She felt restless and edgy, and didn't feel like oohing and ahhing over wallpaper, paint swatches, and floor tiles. She missed James, and knowing he was due back tomorrow made it worse. She pulled her phone out, and saw that he'd sent her a message.

At home. Call my cell when you get this message.

"Hey Ginger," she said, "Can I use your phone?"

"Sorry, Melly. It's out," Ginger said, then looked at her with the rearview mirror. "What are you doing?"

Melody shrugged. "Playing with an app." She sent James a quick message.

Going to the new house with Ging and Morg. Meet me there if not too late. Miss your voice. No cell service here.

They pulled into the driveway and she tossed her phone back into her purse and tossed her purse onto the back-seat. Then she got ready to pretend to have a great time when all she wanted to do was rush home and see her husband.

They walked through the house, discussing things Melody really couldn't find the energy to care less about. They were now in Morgan's element. As long as the place was big enough for her to entertain, and had room for her piano, Melody was happy. She wandered away from them eventually, and made her way to the music room, where she sat down at her piano and began to play. At first, the songs sounded haunting and dark, sad and melancholy. She realized it and intentionally started to play some more upbeat songs, waiting for Morgan and Ginger to finish looking at some wooden floor.

Her heart skipped a beat when she glanced up and saw David Patterson standing in the doorway to the room. She frowned and stopped playing, wondering what he was doing there. "David. You gave me such a fright! I didn't know you were coming over. What's up?"

"I'm here to talk with you. I've heard some disturbing rumors." David slowly came further into the room, his hands in the pockets of his coat. "I've heard rumors that you're leaving the label, Melly," he said quietly.

She'd known they'd have to have it out eventually, but she'd hoped it would happen later in the year, and at some conference table with Hal sitting next to her rather than somewhere personal like her future home. "I'm considering all my options, David. A man of your business acumen,

I'm sure you wouldn't want me to do anything less than my due diligence."

"The only options you're considering are which other labels will offer you a better deal." His voice no longer came out quietly, and his face started to turn red.

Melody noticed a very unprofessional vein throbbing at the older man's temple. He looked like he was on the edge of rage. She felt her heart skip a beat and tried to think of a way to defuse this. "I'm not prepared to discuss this with you right now, David. It's kind of inappropriate, actually. Let's set up a meeting so that we can all keep this about business."

David shook his head. "Melly, you never realized something that I don't have time or patience to teach you. You have to realize that everything is business all the time."

Ginger and Morgan came into the room. "Hello, Daddy," Ginger said as she kissed her father on the cheek, "Glad you could make it."

♫ ♫ ♫ ♫

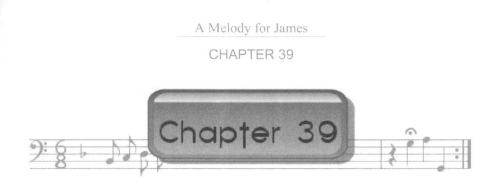

"**WE** can't just sit here and do nothing," Kurt said, pacing the room.

They'd exhausted places where the three women could have gone. "Maybe they just went shopping somewhere," Mike said. "They've been friends for years. There's no reason to think something bad will happen today."

James' phone vibrated. He quickly accessed the message and stood. "They're at our new house," he said, already headed to the door.

They took two cars and sped their way to the other side of the city and out of town. James felt like he was being spurred on. Not that he was being paranoid but that it was important that he get to Melody now. He kept looking at his watch, wishing they could go faster.

♫ ♫ ♫ ♫

"**HELLO**, love," David said to Ginger, "Told you I'd be here."

Ginger reached her hand into her father's coat pocket, "Yeah, well, you're late." She pulled out a .38 caliber pistol and pointed it in the direction of Melody and Morgan. They both stared at it, not fully comprehending what they were seeing.

Melody finally asked, "What's this all about, Ginger?"

"What's this all about? Money, honey. Billions of little dollars," Ginger said. She waved the gun, going between Morgan and Melody. "But, for added spice, revenge, too. Daddy here owes James Montgomery some payback and I owe you."

Melody and Morgan stepped closer together. "If you owe me and he owes my husband, then Morgan has nothing to do with it." Melody said, her confused mind tripping all over the place, trying to find some rationale behind this whole scene. But it didn't make sense.

Ginger put her head back and laughed. "I could let Morgan leave. Except she's part of my little plan. You took someone I loved. I am going to take someone you love while you watch. It's that simple."

Melody was close to a snapping point. Her heart beat furiously and a roaring in her ears almost drowned out Ginger's voice. "What are you talking about?" she whispered.

"Rikard, of course. You killed my Rikard," Ginger said.

Melody put a hand to her head, thoroughly confused. "What does Richard Johnson have to do with anything?"

"Darling, Rikard and I were lovers for years. Long before he even met you. Who do you think you caught him with on your wedding day?"

Melody gasped.

"Oh, come on. If you had continued to be a little traditional Christian prude ... so predictable ... you'd have been none the wiser. Who knew you had some intuition?"

"It was you? That morning, it was you?"

"Oh, don't act so surprised. The whole time you were in England, I worried you'd seen me or you'd figure it out. But you were just as stupid and naive as I always thought you were." Ginger quit waving the gun around and pointed it directly at Melody. "You were nothing more than a means to an end for us. We needed your money. Daddy here was a little spread out at the time, and you had all those billions just sitting in the bank."

Morgan said, "Ginger this is insane. Stop this."

"Oh. Morgan. Right. Let me explain. Shut your mouth or I'll shoot you in the face. Okay?" Gone was any impression of the ditsy Ginger they knew. Her face looked different — intelligent, calculating, and hard.

Melody thought she might be sick. Her head swam and she started praying. *Please God, help me.*

Then she spoke, "I don't understand. He stalked me and threatened me for months. Why was Richard — Rikard — going to kill me?"

"You sure do ask a lot of questions." David finally spoke, crushing Melody's hopes that he might put an end to this insanity. "Ginger and I left you most of those roses. How do you think Rikard could have gotten that close? You really are a little dumb, Mel. Dumb like your dad and self-centered like your mom."

Ginger snickered and David continued. "You wanted to dump Patterson

Records. But if you die under contract, the label gets all the revenue from your dedication album, and you couldn't sell yourself to anyone else. I'd have made a mint in licensed memorial junk. Fans love that kind of thing. Your house in Nashville? Think Graceland east. So we hired Rikard to take care of it. He was motivated after all."

"What does James have to do with any of this?" Melody asked, feeling very strongly that she needed to stall for time, hoping James had checked the message she sent him.

God, I know you brought me and James together, but I can't believe it was to take someone else away from him. Give me wisdom and help me in this situation.

Ginger answered, "James has been on the edge of a revolutionary breakthrough for a couple of years now. Its potential value when it goes IPO makes your father's fortune look like a maid's pittance. Rikard was hired by a former Soviet block country to steal Montgomery's technology and make it to the market before he did. When he came to the States and started establishing a base here, he met me. We fell in love, and he decided to betray his employers. He charmed Angela Montgomery into bringing him on as an intern, but she immediately fired him. Not before he was able to plant bugs and hack the computers. Then he just waited, pulling their daily builds off the backup system and replicating it."

She looked at her father. "Daddy tried to invest in his firm as soon as we realized Rikard couldn't steal the technology from him, but James was too stuck up to sell any private shares. Now he's one of the biggest and brightest minds in the industry, and we're floundering in the background, suffering from a decade of poor investments we've made," Ginger said. She sneered at Morgan. "No thanks to that useless first husband of yours and his so-called investment advice."

Morgan covered her mouth, her eyes wide with shock.

"No more questions. Class dismissed. We're going to reproduce a little scene for James. We don't need to kill him. All we need to do is kill you two. That should send him and his partner over the edge. At the very least, it should make them vulnerable enough to sell their little company," Ginger said. She waved the gun at the door. "Walk downstairs, please."

They didn't move. She said, "We can drag your corpses, but I just had these nails done. You get to live a little longer if you go downstairs on your own. Think of it as a little treat."

Morgan looked at Ginger, starting to get her equilibrium back. "What happened to you, Ginger?"

"Nothing, Morgan sweetheart. I just don't have to act like your brainless lapdog anymore."

"I can't believe you just pretended to be my friend all these years," Morgan said. "We've been too close, shared too much." She fisted her hands and started to step toward her, but Melody grabbed her arm.

"Daddy coached me very well, dear. He knew you'd be useful in the future, as useful as your dad was to him. I was taught early to never show my true nature," Ginger said with a laugh. She stopped laughing and pointed the gun again. "Now move it."

They were directed downstairs where they were instructed to kneel in the middle of the floor of the front room. "The gas is in the trunk of my car, Daddy. Go and get that, and I'll take care of things in here," Ginger said. While David went outside, Ginger walked up to Morgan and put the gun to the back of her head, cocking it. "If you only would have just done what you were told and gone with Rikard without a fight, we wouldn't be here today, Melody. All this is entirely your fault."

Where are you, James? Melody thought to herself.

She bowed her head and closed her eyes, holding Morgan to her. "Father God," she prayed aloud, "I love You. Morgan loves You. God, we ask that You take our husbands into Your loving arms —"

"Oh do shut up," Ginger ordered. "You shut up right now and just watch what I do to your sister. You can thank God I'm killing her first. I'm tempted to just tie her up and burn her to death while you watch," Ginger said. "You have to see what you've done."

Anger mixed with adrenaline suddenly surged through her system, and Melody stood, hoping she'd move the gun away from Morgan. "I haven't done anything," she screamed at Ginger, taking a step toward her. "If your father wouldn't act like some surly, condescending know-it-all losing patience with a disobedient child to absolutely everyone he does business with, then maybe you wouldn't be floundering."

Ginger pointed the gun at Melody. In the corner of her eye, Melody saw the front door behind Ginger's back slowly opening. "Don't you try to put this on, Daddy. He's not the one who's done anything wrong."

Suarez slipped into the room, his gun drawn and pointed at Ginger's back. *Thank you, God. Thank You.* From the other side, Melody saw Roberts slowly coming from one of the rooms in the back. She knew she had to keep Ginger's attention on her. "Of course he is. The only reason we're even here today is because your Daddy doesn't know how to run his own businesses. This isn't some need for vengeance. It's just a way to take out the competition," Melody screamed back.

"Drop the gun, Ginger," Suarez ordered from behind her.

She whipped around and pointed the pistol at Suarez. "What are you doing here, John?"

"Put the gun down slowly and step away from it or I will kill you," he said. "If I don't, I promise you my partner will. I think you know I mean it."

Morgan looked behind Melody, then surged to her feet and ran in that direction. Ginger heard the movement and whipped back around, pointing her gun at Morgan's back. Melody stepped over to block Morgan, and the pistol was suddenly trained on her again.

"Give it up, Ginger." James' voice had an immediate calming effect on Melody. James was here, now. Everything would be okay.

Ginger looked trapped. Her breathing came more rapidly, and the hand that held the gun shook until Melody thought she might accidentally drop it. Eyes wide, glance darting from one police officer to the other, she finally let the gun drop to the floor.

Suarez kept his gun on her as he approached her, then kicked her pistol out of the way.

Ginger stared up at him with eyes full of hate. "I should have made you shoot me. I don't want to live."

Suarez took her by the arm and spun her around, directing her to the wall. While Roberts kept Ginger's face centered in his gun sights, Suarez produced handcuffs from somewhere and cuffed her wrists tight behind her back. Then he unholstered his sidearm again and held it low while keeping his left hand on her cuffs. A gymnast of Ginger's flexibility could jump-rope cuffs to her front with little effort. He watched as Roberts scooped up her weapon from the floor. That accomplished, Suarez very gently brushed her cheek with his fingertips and a sad smile, "Can't die now. You have to live."

Ginger's eyebrows lowered and she stared at him suspiciously. "First, you have to stand trial." Suarez explained. "So does your father. You have to live so that justice can be served. And you have to live for the entirety of what I expect at the very least will be a life sentence behind bars. And baby-cakes, we can continue to discuss it, but I am required to inform you that ... you have the right to remain silent ..."

As detective Suarez continued to inform the suspect of her rights, James turned Melody around and pulled her into his arms. "What took you so long?" she asked him against his chest. James just laughed and hugged her tighter, which was good because her knees were suddenly shaking so hard she didn't think she could stand up on her own. She turned her head and watched as Kurt led Morgan out the door.

"Where's David?" she asked James.

"Roberts detained him outside. He's handcuffed in the trunk of their car. They didn't want him to yell or something and alert Ginger." He framed Melody's face with his hands. "You okay?"

It all suddenly swamped her and she felt her eyes well up with tears. "I'm a little confused, but I'm not hurt."

James kissed her and pulled her back to him. "We'll sort it all out."

♫ ♫ ♫ ♫

ONE MONTH LATER

MELODY finished the phone call with Hal and pushed herself out of the chair by the chess set. She crossed the room and sat down next to James. He sat with his head reclined all the way back against the headrest of the couch staring up at the ceiling. Melody knew by the look on his face that he was lost in thought and she knew that because of the way his brain worked, his way of thinking was radically different than hers. Where she would completely lose herself to emotion and open up the creative side of her mind and let it pour out of her until she felt empty, he would stand in the middle of his orderly library of perfect recollection and go through volume after volume of information, connecting the dots. They'd spent a month coping with everything that had happened, and doing it in their own ways. The only time they came together about it was in prayer, and as they prayed for each other and prayed thanksgiving to God, Melody had some insight to the way her husband's mind worked. But now, she thought maybe it was time to talk about it.

"Penny for your thoughts?" She offered.

"Hmmm? What?" James looked at her then grinned. "Sorry. I'm very distracted." That hadn't been abnormal in the last month. James had given his research and development team a piece of paper he'd found in one of Angela's journals, and they'd made more progress in the data warehousing project in the short time since than they had in the previous four years. James had started splitting his time between Albany and Atlanta almost equally.

Melody was gone for most of the weeks, anyway. The two of them had spent more time in the last three weeks apart than they had together. She felt resigned to that being their life during her tour schedule and was curious about how much that bothered her.

She gently said, "Did you want to talk about something?"

James sighed a little sigh. "Yes, I did. I do. But I don't know if I am ready to talk about it. I'm thinking about how to talk about it with you. That's why I'm distracted."

Melody turned her body toward him. This was obviously something very serious. "James, you're making me a little nervous. Can you just start the conversation maybe?"

James studied her for a heartbeat and then reached out to touch her arm. "Oh, baby. It's nothing bad. At least, I don't think it is."

"What is it? You're killing me, here."

"Well, about the Jaguar …"

"Oh, for Pete's sake, James. I told you I'd buy you a new car one day. You said we had to go car shopping together. Is that what this is about?"

He grinned and somehow it didn't reassure her very much. "Not exactly. See, I don't want you to buy me a new car."

Now she was completely confused. "You're sitting here for most of the morning thinking about how to tell me this?"

"I was thinking I'd rather you bought me a mini-van."

"Why do you want a mini-van?" *What in the world?*

"Well, I don't particularly like mini-vans. They aren't nearly as sporty as my Jag was. But they are a lot more practical when you're starting a family."

"Oh." Melody said. Then, "Oooooooooooooh."

"Yeah, so, I was thinking we should talk about that," he said. "Is this a good time? Would you be willing to pray about it with me?"

"James, with my career, I don't know if I can take the time off right now." A baby. His baby. Her baby. Their baby. A boy or a girl, she didn't care and she suddenly didn't want anything more in the entire world.

"Well, yeah, I know. So I was thinking more along the lines of adopting.

You know, the home where Kurt and I grew up ...” He didn't finish the sentence. It would have been rude to continue speaking while his wife was kissing him so passionately.

THE END

♫ ♫ ♫ ♫

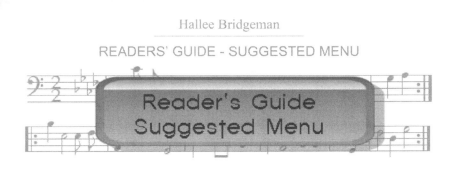

SUGGESTED luncheon menu to enjoy when hosting a group discussion surrounding *A Melody for James*, part 1 of the *Song of Suspense* series.

Those who follow my Hallee the Homemaker website know that one thing I am passionate about in life is selecting, cooking, and savoring good whole real food. A special luncheon just goes hand in hand with hospitality and ministry.

For those planning a discussion group about this book, I offer some humble suggestions to help your special luncheon conversation come off as a success.

For their first date in four years, James cooks Melody a home-cooked meal consisting of salad, bread, pasta with red sauce, and cheesecake. Here you will find recipes to recreate that meal, which is sure to please and certain to enhance your discussion and time of friendship and fellowship.

♩ ♩ ♩ ♩

The Salad:

Crunchy Chopped Salad with Creamy Dijon Vinaigrette Dressing

Melody jokes that salad is one of the only things she can "cook" because it doesn't require applying heat, so therefore she cannot burn it. Here is a super easy salad that perfectly compliments a meal with a red sauce.

INGREDIENTS:

FOR THE SALAD:

5 cups fresh baby spring greens mix
1 large tomato
2 radishes
1 carrot
2 scallions
$^{1}/_{2}$ of a large cucumber

FOR THE DRESSING:

$^{1}/_{2}$ cup extra virgin olive oil
1 TBS red wine vinegar
$^{1}/_{2}$ tsp Dijon mustard
$^{1}/_{4}$ tsp honey
1 tsp salt (Kosher or sea salt is best)
$^{1}/_{4}$ tsp freshly ground black pepper
1 TBS minced shallot

PREPARATION:

Wash the greens.

Dice the tomato.

Slice the radishes, carrots, cucumber, and scallions.

Finely mince the shallot

DIRECTIONS:

Toss the lettuce mix with the tomato, radishes, carrots, cucumber, and scallions.

Wisk all of the ingredients for the dressing together until it thickens. Drizzle over the mixed salad when ready to serve. Toss to coat all of the vegetables.

♫ ♫ ♫ ♫

The Red Sauce:

Turkey Sausage Spaghetti Sauce

Melody misses James' red sauce as much as she misses him when he's gone to Japan. She decides she'll ask him to make a big batch and freeze some the next time he has an extended trip. This is such a tasty pork free sauce! It really goes well with whole grain pasta. It is exactly the right amount of spicy and exactly the right amount of rich and thick.

INGREDIENTS:

about 1 lbs Turkey sausage
2 Tbs olive oil
1 medium onion, chopped
3 cloves garlic, finely diced
2 cans (or 1 large can) organic stewed tomatoes, with the juice and
3 small cans organic tomato sauce

– OR –

about a 16 oz (4-6) garden fresh tomatoes, stewed
$^1/_2$ tablespoon salt, kosher or sea salt is best
1 teaspoon black pepper
2 tablespoons brown sugar or honey
1 tablespoon dried oregano
1 tablespoon dried parsley
2 teaspoons dried basil
1 teaspoon dried sage
1 bay leaf
1 small can organic tomato paste

PREPARATION:

Remove the turkey sausage from its skin.

Chop the onion.

Dice the garlic.

DIRECTIONS:

In a large pot, heat the 2 TBS olive oil over medium-high heat. Add the turkey sausage. When it's brown, add the onion. Cook until tender.

Add the garlic. Cook about 5 minutes longer.

Add 2 cans (or 1 large can) diced tomatoes tomatoes, with the juice.

Add 3 small cans tomato sauce and 1 small can tomato paste. Stir in $\frac{1}{2}$ tablespoon salt, 1 teaspoon black pepper, 2 tablespoons brown sugar or honey, 1 tablespoon dried oregano, 1 tablespoon dried parsley, 2 teaspoons dried basil, 1 teaspoon dried sage, 1 bay leaf.

Bring to a boil, then reduce heat to low, cover, and simmer for at least 1 hour, stirring regularly. The longer it simmers, the more the spices have a chance to infuse the sauce. After about an hour, taste it and see if it needs more sugar, or more salt, or a touch more oregano. Let your tongue guide you. Add a little bit at a time, give it a few minutes to blend in with the flavors, then taste it again. (A good way to taste is to dip a bit of bread in it.)

Serve over whole grain pasta and top with freshly grated Parmesan cheese.

♪ ♪ ♪ ♪

The Bread:

Fresh Garlic French Bread

I *love* garlic bread, and nothing goes better with a "first date in four years red sauce over pasta" than this whole grain bread with fresh garlic and real butter.

INGREDIENTS:

1 packages (2 $^1/_4$ tsp) active dry yeast
1 $^1/_4$ cups warm water (120-130° degrees F)
1 $^1/_2$ tsp salt (Kosher or sea salt is best)
1 $^1/_2$ tsp olive oil
3 $^1/_2$ cups flour (I use fresh ground, hard red wheat)
1 TBS cornmeal
olive oil for bowl
Butter
Peeled garlic

PREPARATION:

Grease one large bowl with a light coating of olive oil

DIRECTIONS:

Fill your bowl with hot water and dump it out. This will warm the bowl. Add 2 $^1/_2$ cups warm water to the bowl. Add the yeast. Let stand for 5 minutes. Add salt, olive oil, and flour. Mix well. (If using a stand mixer, mix for about a minute.)

Kneed for 10 minutes. (If using a stand mixer, kneed for 2 minutes on power level 2.)

Dough will be sticky.

Place the dough in a greased bowl turn to grease top. Cover. Let rise in a warm place for about an hour.

Punch dough down and roll into a 12 x 15 inch rectangle. Roll tightly from longest side and pinch the ends, then tuck the ends under.

Grease baking sheet and sprinkle with cornmeal. Place the rolled dough on baking sheet. Cut small slits diagonally in the top. Cover and let rise for about an hour.

Bake 450° degrees F for 25-35 minutes. The bread is done when you tap it and it sounds hollow.

When it's cool enough to handle, slice it in half the long way, opening it up like you're going to make a sandwich. Spread with butter and place on a pan.

Put it in the oven under the broiler. Broil until the bread toasts and browns. While it's in the oven, peel a piece of garlic and slice it in half.

As soon as it comes out of the oven, rub the garlic, cut side down, against the bread. The garlic will gradually "melt". Rub as much of as you want on the bread.

Slice and serve.

♫ ♫ ♫ ♫

The Dessert:

Mascarpone Cheesecake
with Vanilla Almond Crust

James' late wife, Angela, always chose cheesecake over champagne when celebrating. This cheesecake recipe alone is worth celebrating.

Melody and James were interrupted before he was able to serve her this cheesecake, but if she had a chance to taste it, she would have composed a new song just in honor of this delicious concoction.

INGREDIENTS:

1 cup slivered almonds
²/₃ cup vanilla wafers
3 TBS sugar
1 TBS unsalted butter, melted
2 (8-ounce) packages cream cheese, room temperature
2 (8-ounce) containers mascarpone cheese, room temperature
1 ¼ cups sugar
2 tsp fresh lemon juice
2 vanilla beans
4 eggs, room temperature

PREPARATION:

Preheat the oven to 350° degrees F.

Lightly toast the almonds. Place them in a shallow frying pan and cook, stirring and shifting often, until they start to toast. (This will smell really good – and when you start to smell it, they're just about done.)

Squeeze the lemon.

Seed the vanilla beans. Discard the shells. (I place them in a container with sugar — this makes wonderful vanilla sugar that you can use for all sorts of things from flavoring your morning coffee to boosting up your white cake recipe.)

Wrap a 9-inch springform pan tightly with foil.

DIRECTIONS:

Grind the cookies in a food processor. Measure out $^2/_3$ cup.

Grind the almonds in the food processor. Add the $^2/_3$ cup cookie crumbs. Add the sugar. Add the butter. Mix just until mixed.

Press the crust mixture into the bottom only of the pan.

Bake until the crust is set – 12-15 minutes.

Reduce the oven to 325° degrees F.

In a mixing bowl, beat the cheeses until fluffy. Add the sugar. Add the lemon juice and vanilla bean. Add the eggs one at a time. Mix well.

Pour into the springform pan. Place pan in a large roasting pan. Set the pan in the oven.

Pour hot water into the pan until it comes up halfway up the springform pan.

Bake until the middle is just jiggly – about 1 hour 5 minutes to 1 hour 15 minutes.

Remove from oven, remove from roasting pan, and chill in refrigerator until cold – about 8 hours.

♫ ♫ ♫ ♫

SUGGESTED questions for a discussion group surrounding *A Melody for James*, part 1 of the ***Song of Suspense*** series.

When asking ourselves how important the truth is to our Creator, we can look to the very reason Jesus said he was born. In the book of John 18:37, Jesus explains that for this reason He was born and for this reason He came into the world. The reason?

To testify to the truth.

In bringing those He ministered to into an understanding of the truth, Our Lord used fiction in the form of parables to illustrate very real truths. In the same way, we can minister to one another by the use of fictional characters and situations to help us to reach logical, valid, cogent, and very sound conclusions about our real lives here on earth.

While the characters and situations in the ***Song of Suspense*** series are fictional, I pray that these extended parables can help readers come to a better understanding of truth. Please prayerfully consider the questions that follow, consult scripture, and pray upon your conclusions. May the Lord of the universe richly bless you.

♫ ♫ ♫ ♫

After Angela's death, James sought God, praying to Him and reading the Bible. However, he didn't actually feel God's presence until several months later.

1. Why do you think he didn't feel the presence of the Holy Spirit when he was seeking Him?

2. Have you ever desperately sought God but felt alone?

3. Deuteronomy 31:6 and 31:8 says: *"He [God] will not leave you nor forsake you; do not fear nor be dismayed."* With that promise, do you think that you are ever truly alone?

♫ ♫ ♫ ♫

Two weeks before they met, Melody left her fiancé at the alter. Six months before, James' wife was murdered. Yet, they are both attracted to each other and both of them secretly hope the relationship will continue.

4. Is this really a "good" time to even think of a relationship?

5. Is there ever truly a "bad" time to begin a new relationship?

♫ ♫ ♫ ♫

Melody feels like God turned His back on her when Rikard attacked her.

6. What do you think about that?

7. Do you think it's wrong for her to feel this way?

8. Have you ever felt like God has abandoned you?

♫ ♫ ♫ ♫

Melody and James felt an instant attraction to each other both times they met. They both felt like they fell in love the day they first met.

9. What do you think about the concept of "love at first sight?"

♫ ♫ ♫ ♫

Melody and James get married very quickly after meeting the second time.

10. What do you think about their chances of having a successful marriage?

11. What do you think will make their marriage stronger?

♫ ♫ ♫ ♫

Melody rediscovers her relationship with God after four years; yet she continues performing and writing contemporary secular music.

12. What do you think of the idea that God grants talent which is often misused in worldly pursuits?

13. Do you think she should have started focusing on a career in Christian music?

14. What do you think of professed Christians with careers in the entertainment industry who do not make offerings of their time or talent to bring blessings to Christian entertainment?

♫ ♫ ♫ ♫

Melody suffers from crippling stage fright.

15. How much of the stage fright was directly related to Rikard never being apprehended by the police?

16. How do you think her renewed walk with Christ will affect her phobia?

♬ ♬ ♬ ♬

James tells Rikard that he forgives him for killing Angela and her team and also for terrorizing Melody. He then opens the door to lead Rikard to Christ.

17. What did you think of that conversation?

18. What is most difficult for you about forgiving those who hurt us?

♬ ♬ ♬ ♬

PLEASE enjoy this special excerpt from the upcoming full length Christian suspense novel, *An Aria for Nicholas.*, part two in the *Song of Suspense* series.

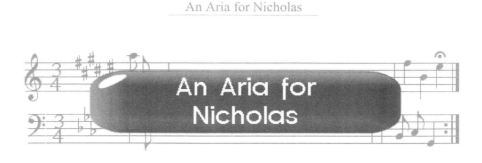

An Aria for Nicholas

ARIA Suarez stood on the corner of Fifth and Madison observing the man wearing the dark blue shirt occupying the corner table of the outdoor café. Sunlight glinted on his brown hair, revealing highlighted streaks that nearly glowed, lending his visage a halo-like appearance. He'd flirted with the waitress each time she'd come by, and had even grinned at a small child making a mess at a nearby table. He looked harmless enough, though she couldn't completely make out his face behind the sunglasses he wore and the newspaper he continuously ducked behind.

She clenched the envelope in her hand a little tighter. She kept a sharp eye toward the crowd, scanning faces for anyone who looked familiar or out of place. Finally, she mustered the courage to step forward.

Aria hesitantly began her approach, unsure of how this might work and trying very hard not to reveal even a hint of uncertainty. Then she remembered that she also didn't want to attract any undue attention to herself by appearing uncomfortable or out of place in any way, and she smoothed her stride.

When she reached his table, she stood still and waited for him to look up from his newspaper. When he failed to do so, she cleared her throat. When that didn't work, she said, "Excuse me."

He shifted the newspaper downward enough to peer over the top of it in her direction, staring at her through the dark lenses of his sunglasses, but she still couldn't see his eyes. All she could see was her own reflection in the tinted lenses. "Are you waiting for me?"

The man very purposefully and very carefully folded the newspaper and set it on the table at right angles to his silverware directly next to his cup. That accomplished, he gestured with his left hand in the direction of the chair across from him, silently inviting her to join him. As she perched herself on the wrought iron chair, she thought to herself that this man looked somewhat familiar.

All those weeks when she had felt such apprehension, glancing over her shoulder in foreboding. She had checked all the shadows and every corner, certain someone was following her. Had her trepidation been well-founded after all? Had this man been following her? Had she seen him somewhere before? Or was her nervousness and disquiet simply getting the best of her? Did this man just have one of those faces that you felt sure you recognized?

Aria started to feel some very deep, very real anxiety and did her best to quell it. She waited for him to speak, assuming if everything was on the up-and-up that he had done this kind of thing before, and would take the lead to get them to the next level, whatever that was.

The waitress came back to the table and Aria ordered a cup of decaf with cream, no sugar, then folded her hands and waited. The man across from her sat up a bit straighter then took a deep breath and finally spoke.

"Hello, Aria." His voice flowed over her like a warm baritone blanket. It was deep and comforting and frighteningly familiar. He removed his sunglasses. Azure blue eyes calmly met her glance. Already tense muscles contracted in her stomach. She felt a constriction around her heart, stealing the breath from her body, sending a surge of adrenaline that made her palms sweat even though her fingers felt ice cold. Her throat let out a startled gasp as recognition dawned.

It can't be! her mind screamed. *It's not possible!*

"How've you been?" he asked. "You look even more beautiful than I remember, if that's imaginable."

Aria didn't know what to say, literally shocked speechless. After all, she had never spoken to a ghost. Her mouth felt so dry that the air coursing in and out of her lungs scorched her throat. Finally, she made an attempt. "What? ... How? ..."

Nicholas "Nick" Williams leaned forward and spoke very quietly but with great urgency, his low voice pitched for her ears alone. "It's okay, Aria. It's fine. It's a long story. I'll be happy to share it with you. But I have to call my superiors in less than twenty minutes, so right now, just show me what you have. We can stroll down memory lane just a little later on. Okay?"

Aria gripped the wrought iron chair handles beneath her fingers and leveraged her weight with her palms, preparing to rise to her feet. She finally felt able to speak. "Nice try, but you aren't Nick Williams," she announced as she stood. "I buried Nick fifteen years ago."

♫ ♫ ♫ ♫

Heavenly Heroines

The Virtues and Valor series
The battle begins in 2013 ...

SEVEN women from different backgrounds and social classes come together on the common ground of a shared faith during the second World War. Each will earn a code name of a heavenly virtue. Each will risk discovery and persevere in the face of terrible odds. One will be called upon to make the ultimate sacrifice.

INSPIRED by real events, these are stories of Virtue and Valor.

THE JEWEL SERIES

More Great Christian Fiction…

The Jewel Anthology

by Hallee Bridgeman

Hallee Bridgeman's critically acclaimed best selling award winning Christian anthology, together in one book. The complete novel *Sapphire Ice*. Inspired by *The Jewel Series*, the all new novella *Greater Than Rubies*. The second full length novel *Emerald Fire*, and the final novel *Topaz Heat*. All works complete, uncut, and unabridged.

Sapphire Ice

Robin's heart is as cold as her deep blue eyes. After a terrifying childhood, she trusts neither God nor men. With kindness and faith, Tony prays for the opportunity to shatter the wall of ice around her heart.

Greater Than Rubies

Robin plans a dream-come-true wedding. Anxiety arises when she starts to realize the magnitude of change marriage will involve. Forgotten nightmares resurface reminding Robin of the horrors of her past. She gives in to her insecurities and cancels Boston's "Royal Wedding." With God's guidance, will her bridegroom convince her of her true worth?

Emerald Fire

Inspirational Novel of the Year RONE Award Finalist: Green eyed Maxine fights daily to extinguish the embers of her fiery youth. Barry's faith in God is deeply shaken when he is suddenly widowed. Just as they begin to live the "happily ever after" love story that neither of them ever dreamed could come true, a sudden catastrophe could wreck everything. Will her husband find peace and strength enough to carry them through the flames?

Topaz Heat

Inspirational Novel of the Year RONE Award Nominee: Honey eyed Sarah remembers absolutely nothing from her bloodcurdling younger years. Derrick fled a young life of crime to become a billionaire's successful protégé. After years of ignoring the heat between them they surrender to love, but must truly live their faith to see them through.

Available in eBook or Paperback wherever fine books are sold.

The *Song of Suspense* Series...

A MELODY FOR JAMES

PART ONE in the *Song of Suspense* series, will soon be followed by:

♫ ♫ ♫ ♫

AN ARIA FOR NICHOLAS

ARIA remembers her first real kiss and the blue eyed boy who passionately delivered it before heading off to combat, but the news of his death is just a footnote in a long war until Aria learns she was his beneficiary. His parting gift allows her to pursue a lifelong dream to become a world class pianist.

Years later, Aria inadvertently uncovers a sinister plot that threatens the very foundations of a nation. Now, stalked by assassins and on the run, her only hope of survival is in trusting her very life to a man who has been dead for years.

♫ ♫ ♫ ♫

A CAROL FOR KENT

BOBBY Kent's name is synonymous with modern Country Music and he is no stranger to running from overzealous fans and paparazzo. But he has no idea how to protect his daughter and Carol, the mother of his only child, from a viscous and ruthless serial killer bent on their destruction.

♫ ♫ ♫ ♫

A HARMONY FOR STEVEN

CONTEMPORARY Christian singing sensation, Harmony, seeks solitude after winning her umpteenth award. She finds herself in the midst of the kind of spiritual crisis that only prayer and fasting can cure. Steven, the world renown satanic acid rock icon who has a reputation for trashing women as well as hotel rooms, stumbles into her private retreat on the very edge of death.

In ministering to Steven, Harmony finds that the Holy Spirit is ministering to her aching soul. The two leave the wilderness sharing a special bond and their hearts are changed forever.

They expect rejection back in their professional worlds. What neither of them could foresee is the chain of ominous events that threaten their very lives.

♫ ♫ ♫ ♫

About the Author

HALLEE BRIDGEMAN lives with her husband and their three children in small town Kentucky. When she's not writing Christian romance novels, she blogs about all things cooking and homemaking at Hallee the Homemaker.

Hallee started writing when her oldest child and only daughter was a baby, but a busy professional career and being the wife of a deployed soldier had her shelve her books for another time. Two more children, a cross country move, and God's perfect timing brought the books off of the shelf to be dusted off and presented to you now.

Hallee loves coffee, campy action movies, and regular date nights with her husband. Above all else, she loves God with all of her heart, soul, mind, and strength; has been redeemed by the blood of Jesus Christ; and relies on the presence of the Holy Spirit.

♫ ♫ ♫ ♫

Hallee the Homemaker blog
www.halleethehomemaker.com/

Hallee Bridgeman, Novelist blog
www.bridgemanfamily.com/hallee/

Hallee News Letter
http://tinyurl.com/HalleeNews/

Never miss updates about upcoming releases, book signings, appearances, or other events. Sign up for Hallee's monthly newsletter.

♫ ♫ ♫ ♫